Developing Minds

An American Ghost Story

Jonathan LaPoma

ALMENDRO
ARTS

San Diego, California

Originally published by Laughing Fire Press

ISBN: 978-0-9988403-6-9
Library of Congress Control Number: 2019937723

Cover design by theBookDesigners
Cover images © Shutterstock
Interior design by Polgarus Studio
Author photograph by Emilio Azevedo

For more information, contact info@almendroarts.com.
www.almendroarts.com
www.jonlapoma.com

Praise for *Developing Minds*

"Inspired by his own travels, screenwriter and author LaPoma's narrative is raw and edgy, effectively anchored by two protagonists whose brio and 'same sense of adventure' keep the story alive . . . Entertaining and authentic look at the troubled American educational system, courtesy of two men propelled by perseverance and adventuresome spirits."

—*Kirkus Reviews*, Recommended Review

"Should be required reading for anyone who is considering or has ever considered teaching as a career . . . most highly recommended."

—Jack Magnus, *Readers' Favorite*

"Not a read for prudes, but for those with an open heart, mind and admiration of satire. Jonathan LaPoma has adeptly captured the darker sides of teaching in Miami public schools and also experiencing the high (in all senses of that word) life in local bars and beaches. His raw, honest and rhythmic voice kept me going to the very end. I taught in inner city schools for over twenty years and I'm sorry to say that I know many of the stories he tells are not entirely fiction."

—Jill G. Hall, author of *The Black Velvet Coat* and *The Silver Shoes*

"Incredibly artistic . . . The vast majority of college grads will relate with themes of alienation, addiction, and misguided hopes . . . Filled with drama and drugs, this novel is raw and endearing. It teeters on the edge of obscene, but really stays true to the life of an early 20-year old, amidst the drama and guise of self-discovery. Instead of idealizing public schools or idolizing functional drug addicts, it just lays out the truth."

—*San Francisco Book Review*

"Not for the faint of heart, *Developing Minds* will either have you furiously flipping the pages or fearfully enrolling your kids in home school."

—*Will's Weekend Wrap-Up, NoiseTrade*

"Poignant, engaging . . . a frighteningly accurate depiction of inner-city schools . . . a full-bodied work of fiction that will ring true with both students and teachers and provide a point of hope in an industry that has become increasingly profit-minded and complex."

—*Red City Review*

"*Developing Minds* is a raunchy, yet captivating story of two best friends, one gay, one not, who decide to spend a year teaching in the dysfunctional Miami school district . . . Jonathan LaPoma is an extraordinary writer."

—*Stargazer Literary Prizes* (Winner: Visionary & Metaphysical Fiction)

"In many ways, the novel was spiritual, as well as coming-of-age . . . plenty of action and adventure, as well as some poignant soul searching . . . Anyone who enjoys realistic fiction, with a gritty edge will enjoy this novel. The characters are extremely well written and believable, and the dialogue is perfect. Despite the serious matter, the book is also very humorous, visual and vibrant to read."

—Chantelle Atkins, *Underground Book Reviews*

"Sometimes the meat of a title lies not in fire and flames, but in simmering passion. Such is the nature of the coming-of-age experience depicted in *Developing Minds*, which offers a multi-faceted exploration of growth, maturity, and eventual transformation on the parts of all involved."

—D. Donovan, Senior Reviewer, *Midwest Book Review*

"This book is incredibly raw . . . about as far removed from 'Dead Poets Society' as you can get."

—Gem L Thompson, *The Book Eaters*

"There are at least two competing ways of sizing up Jonathan LaPoma's very entertaining novel *Developing Minds: An American Ghost Story*, and both have merit.
(1) It is a scathing comic novel about the failures of American urban education, sort of a M*A*S*H for Miami schoolteachers.
(2) It is a Bildungsroman about the personal growth of a young man who happens to be a Miami schoolteacher for a year."

—Patrick Murtha, *Book 'em, Danno*

"Readers will be gripped by the many dimensions the plot has to offer . . . The story is honest, authentic, entertaining and poignant, and the contrasting images of a young man trying to grow in his personal life and the failures of the Miami school system have been woven together well without sounding forced."

—Mamata Madhaven, *Readers' Favorite*

"I found myself laughing out loud . . . As a young adult myself, I find Luke's personal life so relatable and realist. We learn how to get out of toxic relationships, to be able to move on and to recognize true friends or, simply, the friends that are not good for you anymore. The author puts it in a subtle and smart way . . . The character development was rightfully done . . . don't miss it!"

—Trang Tran, *Bookidote*

Chapter 1

It began as a competition—albeit one in which I didn't know I was a contestant.

"I think the only reason that bitch hired me is 'cause she's in the first throes of a midlife crisis. You see the way she kept winking at me? These Cubanos see nothing but sex. You know . . ."

Billy was the first to speak after we exited the East Miami Senior High Library and stepped onto the parking lot. Billy and I had driven together from New York to the American Tropics on a whim. I'd spent the previous five months living in a small Mexican town and had only been back in the country for a few weeks before I was at it again. Within a week of hearing about a three-day teacher recruitment event in Miami, I had my reservation and the car packed. I'd planned to go alone, but a few days before leaving, Billy gave me a call. He was teaching at one of the roughest schools in the New York Public Schools District, PS 490 in Jamaica, Queens, and had no plans to leave. But these were the times . . .

"Miami, you say?"

"Yeah, why don't you come with me?"

"I already have a job."

"Some fun in the sun?"

"Well, Diego *is* driving me crazy . . ."

1

For the past year, Billy called me every other day with another story of some terrible thing his students did to him, or other teachers, or each other—or some terrible thing he'd done to himself in retaliation. But that's just the way it was surviving in America's public schools. Every day was a struggle. Every day was psychological warfare, and if you didn't stay sharp, the system would grind you into human pencil shavings.

I'd spent most of the previous year in various Buffalo public schools, either as a student teacher or long-term sub, temporarily replacing a man who'd taken a few months off to nurse a worsening stomach ulcer. I hated the job, but felt chained to it. I didn't know why. I didn't want to teach. After finishing the long-term subbing gig, I was offered a full-time social studies position at the same school, but the day before I was supposed to go in and sign the contract, I bought a one-way ticket to Mexico. I'd only recently gotten back. The darkness had been settling into my life, but something in that small Mexican town, Mariposa, helped me see through it. It was in that light I'd realized I wanted to be a writer.

I'd started a novel almost immediately after my return from Mexico, jumping out of my bed in the middle of one humid Buffalo summer night and upchucking memories and quotes and themes on anything I could grab hold of: tissues, blank pages in books, the front cover of *the White Album* . . . Once I started, I couldn't stop. It felt like an addiction, but of a new sort—one that didn't eat into me as I ate into it. I started writing every day, for hours. It was my obsession, but in giving into it, the pain eased. I'd found my calling. But there was something else calling me . . .

"Don't forget," Barbara Sutters, the woman running the recruitment fair, walked outside and bellowed to all us dejected souls wandering to our cars, "tomorrow's session will be at Sojourner Truth Middle in Homestead. We hope to see you all come back!"

God, I fucking hated teaching. I wasn't sure what I was even doing at that fair. I was a little more than halfway through my book and knew it'd be shelved the moment I got a job. But I went left after right toward one anyway with a determination equal to that put into my writing.

"So, what's the name of your school again?" I unlocked the doors and got behind the wheel.

"Little Havana Elementary." Billy opened his door and sat in the passenger seat. He fanned himself with a copy of the school contract he'd just signed and turned up the A/C before I'd even put the keys in the ignition. "I don't know what that bitch was thinking hiring me. They got me teaching Spanish and the school's almost a hundred percent Cuban. And, I don't know what the fuck I was thinking taking it. But it's an A school, so it can't be all that bad."

"Naw, it'll be cake."

I started the car and pulled out into the perplexing Southeast quadrant streets. I took a wrong turn and quickly got lost in the byway of east/west streets and north/south avenues, but I knew where the ocean was, and drove toward it.

"Hey, we should get some work done on our screenplay tonight," I said. "I can't wait to finish that thing. Miami is like LA Junior. We need to head out West to the big leagues."

The day was stifling. Summer heat in Miami could draw sweat from a stone. I dripped into my dark polyester suit. I followed my instincts and made it back to Miami Beach; though our motel was north, I drove south, almost reaching the end of the island. I then began the slow journey north through South Beach.

"Shit, this place is like a gigantic pussy waiting to be fucked," I said, while driving under the shade of row after row of towering hotels and condo complexes. "We gotta start again on that screenplay soon. My head's swelling."

"Yeah . . . hey, would you get a load of all these boys? So tanned, so pretty. This is like a homo's paradise. After all, you know what a gay man's favorite food is, right?"

"I dunno, corn dogs?"

"No, papi-cock!" Billy giggled. He seemed pretty pleased with himself.

We passed more pastel colored, pleasure-ship-inspired Art Deco buildings and eventually arrived at the appropriately named Seaside Motel. We went up to our room, changed, and went for a dip in the ocean.

"I really need to step it up tomorrow. Can you imagine living here? This place is paradise. Every weekend is like spring break." I dipped my head underwater—so warm, so blue—and popped back up.

"Yeah, I can't believe it's a part of the US. This city's like no place else in the country. But I don't know what the fuck I'm doing here—I mean, I'm still employed at the NYPSD. PS Four Ninety is expecting my gracious return at the start of the fall term. I signed a two-year contract with Educate America and can incur some pretty stiff penalties for reneging on my contractual obligations."

"Fuck PS Four Ninety. You hate that place."

"There's no place better than Four Ninety, honey-pie. I can't imagine what my principal would say if she saw me standing in those lines today. D'nisha Xavier. That bitch is the devil herself, don't kid yourself otherwise. She's this emaciated, angry, spite-filled, agro nutcase. The kids used to give her such hell 'cause she was half-Israeli. They called her 'Halfrican.'" He started laughing. "And we used to call her Xavier the Savior."

"I don't know how you put up with her."

"Whenever shit would get bad, I just made a joke of it—I mean, what else can you do? She used to go on the PA and call me down to her office all the time. 'Will Mr. Lalina please report to ma' office.' Then she'd chew me out for whatever the hell popped into her head, and she always finish the beatdown with, 'You need a pa'fessional development in basic social skills and manners. Now get outta my sight!'"

"Fuck that."

"Yeah, she was the worst, but I'm convinced it's because of the weight coming down on her from the top. All these schools live and die by their ratings. And PS Four Ninety was an F minus. These principals only got so much time to flip their schools before they're out on their asses, and the Savior was on the precipice of her tenure with the NYPSD. She used to hold these meetings with the staff to contrive school spirit, but it would always just end up with her cussing us out while we ripped into her boney ass. The black chicks there were tough as shit, but they loved me. I think they knew I was gay, so they took me in on their side. Whenever the Savior'd be giving a speech, we'd just sit there and heckle her. 'That ain't in my contract, girlfriend.'"

I laughed. "I can picture you doing that, too."

"Oh my god, one time she was going crazy on the chalkboard writing some crap about how chalk-n-talk was dead—with chalk, mind you—and she dropped a piece. Then when she bent down to pick it up, I made this loud fart noise and everybody erupted in laughter. D'nisha went crazy and started screaming that she was gonna fire everybody if they didn't learn them some respect." Billy started laughing. "She was the Savior of American Public Education."

"Well, Miami is a chance for you to start over. I mean, look left then look right. White sand as far as the eye can see. This is gonna be the place, man. This is gonna be paradise. I just need to find a job first, and you need to show up to yours."

"Oh my god, what am I doing? I came down here for a vacation, and I walk into a job. I guess I'm just too lovable for my own good."

"Well maybe you could lend me some of that charm, or you're gonna be lovable all by yourself."

"Oh god, I fucking hate teaching." Billy dunked his head underwater and stayed down for a while.

Billy and I had been friends since college. We lived across the hall from each other in the McKinley University dorms. He began as a philosophy major and I as an architect. Together we were going to design America's revolution. It only took one semester before we'd both changed majors and only another after that before I'd transferred to a different school. But Billy and I continued to wax revolution despite these trivial changes in our lives. We were kindred spirits. We shared the same sense of adventure, the same sense of wonder, the same general curiosity and marvel of life. But we also shared the same detachment, the same exhaustion, and the same lack of tools to survive life in society. Even so, nobody was keeping us down.

Our most recent struggles had brought us to Miami—and the trip seemed cursed from the start. I was living in Buffalo and he in New York. He called me the day before the Fourth of July to tell me about a spontaneous recent trip to visit a "friend" down in Puerto Rico. "Oh my god, I just had to get the fuck outta New York . . ."

Things had been getting tense between him and his boyfriend, Diego, so Billy hopped on Perdido Air and hopped off onto the warm sands of PR. He had a Dominican boy in the City and a Puerto Rican boy in the tropics, so when I said the magic word, "Miami," he responded, "Whoa, Miami is literally between the two. I could take flights to either place every few weekends. It'd be great!" Though this would take him out of direct contact with either boy toy, it was also the logic of a man who once bought a sixty dollar Greyhound ticket from Buffalo to O'Hare Airport just so he could save fifty bucks on his flight. Perhaps he'd never heard the phrase, "A boy toy in the bed is worth two on the beach?"

Either way, Billy told me to pick him up in New York so we could drive down to the American Tropics together. He'd left his aging Honda in Buffalo when he moved to the City after college and didn't have another car with him. I agreed, drove straight through the hilly guts of New York, and met him under an L train in the Bronx. Billy was living in a Dominican neighborhood and sharing an apartment with a Dominican family. The dude was one hundred percent Irish-

American, born and raised on the streets of Buffalo, but he was an Hispanic at heart. I hadn't seen him in ages. He'd only recently come out. And when I saw my once-slouchy and ever-lethargic friend standing under that train tall and proud, I almost didn't recognize him.

"Hey, just park somewhere over there." He pointed to a spot down the street.

"You sure it's okay? I hear New York meter maids get a hard on for writing tickets."

"Oh, don't be such a bitch."

I parked, grabbed all my stuff, made sure to lock the doors, and followed him up to his apartment. We went out for a few drinks that night, then popped into a bodega for some malt liquor forties, finished those off in an alley, and smoked some of the stuff he'd swiped from the old Dominican lady he lived with. "She won't mind. Her son supplies the whole block and he leaves dear old mom a green gift each week. She usually just gives it to me anyways."

We woke late the next morning. We'd planned on hitting the road by nine, but that didn't happen. Our goal was to drive halfway, sleep at a rest area somewhere in the Carolinas, then continue down the I-95 to its near end and spend the afternoon at the beach, relaxing before the big show started early Tuesday morning. We walked to the street around noon and encountered a challenge.

"You sure you parked it there?" Billy said.

"Yes, I'm sure! Look, there's the spray-painted picture of a dick on the sidewalk."

I called the cops and they directed me to the traffic enforcement squad. The surly woman who picked up told me my car had been towed for being parked in a restricted site and that I wouldn't be able to retrieve it until the next day. I took down the name and address of the lot where I could pick it up, hung up, and cussed Billy out for his stupidity.

"Eh, whatever," Billy said. "So we just leave tomorrow instead of today."

"The teaching fair starts on Tuesday! We'll never make it on time."

"We will if we drive through the night."

Billy's boyfriend, Diego, stopped over that night and threw a fucking fit after hearing of his lover's spontaneous plan.

"So you planned on just leaving me like that? Just like that? Just like I am nothing? And who is this asshole you are going with? Does he think he can just replace me?"

Sometime around 2 am, I gave up on trying to convince him that I had no intentions of courting Billy, nor any other guys for that matter, but he just kept coming with it. "What, you think maybe 'cause you are a teacher and you have some money, you can take my man, well you got another thing coming, *culero* . . ." I left the apartment and walked the streets until about three, and when I came back Diego was cuddled up next to Billy in his bed.

The next morning, I called the lot where my car had been towed to be sure it was there. It was. I gave Billy the address and asked him if he knew anyone who could drive us. He said no, so we took a cab. I'd cashed in my savings bonds before leaving Buffalo and had about five hundred bucks on me—my total worth. Fifty-five went to the Turkish fellow who brought us to the lot. I walked into the trailer at the impound yard and handed over another $365 to the ill-tempered bitch behind the counter, who felt the need to give me a lesson before giving me my car. "Don't you know not to park in a restricted zone? Is you stupid or somethin'?"

I didn't respond.

She opened the gate, and Billy and I were off. We hit the I-95 just before 11 am. The teacher recruitment event was scheduled to start at 9 am the next day. We pulled into the East Miami High parking lot that morning at 9:07. People were still shuffling into the school. Billy and I got dressed in the car.

"Yo, man, you got a stick of gum or something?"

Though rushed, I felt fine until we walked through those double doors into the crowded library. I didn't know if it was the size of the crowd or the speech that Barbara Sutters was giving, but something about that scene got inside of me. The walls started vibrating, the books started whispering to me their secrets, the manic stories of all those desperate job seekers swirled in the mix. I started sweating.

Ms. Sutters spoke throughout.

"I want to congratulate all of you for coming down here and seeking employment with the Miami Public Schools District. There are thousands of kids in this city who need good people such as yourselves to help guide them through this crazy adventure called life. We are looking for the leaders among you. The role models. Those who came here not only for a job, but to start along the path to inspire young minds, as well as your own."

"Man, we shouldn't have smoked that shit last night. I feel like I'm gonna puke." Billy wandered out into the hall in search of a bathroom.

Ms. Sutters continued, "We have representatives from over fifty schools, elementary through senior high, set up at tables in the library." She pointed out the tables; all heads turned. A low murmur rumbled throughout the crowd. I felt their energy, heard their hushed words, "Today is my day, today is my day!" I wanted to wish them all well, but they were my competition.

"The representatives are all ready and waiting for you. In one moment I'm going to ask you to calmly approach them in an orderly way."

I could see the springs ready to uncoil beneath their feet and asses. People hung at the edge of their seats like those greedy, rabid shoppers waiting behind closed department store doors in the pitch-dark, pepper-spray Black Friday morning, ready to stampede anyone who'd gotten between them and this year's vibrating sweat-shop sensation. Billy wandered in just as Ms. Sutters gave the signal. Few paid any respect to her pleas for "calm" and "order." Even the little old ladies were clawing at their fellow man to be the first to those tables. It made me sick to know I was a part of it all.

"What the hell's going on here?" Billy wiped his mouth with his sleeve.

"It's on . . ."

I had no idea what I was doing. The insanity bum-rushed my good sense. I could feel my stomach turn and sweat pour into my cheap suit.

"I guess we should join humanity, huh?" I said.

"Eh, whatever . . ." Billy shrugged his shoulders and we chose two separate tables at random. The scene was a goddamned circus. "I was in line here first!" "No you wasn't, you was behind me, fool." A great way to make a great first impression. There were about ten people in line at each table. I wasn't sure if this was a first-come-first-to-get-the-job type of event, but I didn't want to invite that kind of dread into my already fragile subconscious, so I assumed it wasn't. I decided to play the whole thing cool. I struck up a conversation with the guy in front of me, an awkward, overweight and balding man with little, dark hairs curling through what looked like his body's every unclogged and still-functioning pore.

"So what subject do you teach?" I said.

"Middle school history," he snickered into his fat hands with what seemed like sick undertones of unconscious sexual depravity. "I specialize in the Age of Exploration and did my dissertation on the Franco-Prussian War . . ."

"Gotta love those Prussians—"

". . . But my real area of expertise is in my graphic organizers. Those are my true passion. Just as a blacksmith would marvel at a great sword he's crafted, I too marvel at my organizers. I've had several patented by the US Copyright Office . . ."

"Can you patent a graphic organizer?"

". . . Let me finish." The guy was practically frothing at the mouth now. "Well, no, they said no, but I wanted to be certain anyway. Look," he dug into his pocket and pulled out a business card, "anytime you're in the market for a good organizer, you call me. I'll get you what you need. Venn Diagrams, flowcharts, t-graphs—I've got 'em all."

"I'll be sure to file that away." I grabbed the card by its corner with my thumb and pointer, not knowing what hideous things may have been smeared on it.

The lunatic turned away from me smiling as if all that nonsense about t-charts and graphs were the culmination of some weird fantasy he'd pulled me into. I set the card down on a nearby table.

The line I was in was moving much faster than most of the others. I wasn't sure if this was a good sign or not. The graphic organizer guy only got a few sentences into his spiel before the crotchety bitch behind the table sent him away. He walked to another table, mumbling something to himself about her "lack of organization." The woman motioned for me to sit. I obliged and shook her hand.

"So." She folded her hands and set them on the table. Excellent form. "Tell me why you'd like to be a teacher at the Horatio Alger Academy for the Gifted and Talented?"

"Well, uh, I've done some extensive research into your, uh, program and am excited to be part of what you've got going on there . . ." My eyes felt as if they were turning blood red.

"Hmm, yes, of course. So, tell me your experience with data tracking for the F2ST."

"Uh, well, I think it's extremely important to track all your data so you always know exactly where it is. And, uh . . ."

"Do you know what the F2ST is?"

"Well, it's the, uh, Florida . . . Two . . .?"

"Hmm, no, no it's not. The F2ST is the Florida State Standardized Test, the most important assessment in the state. Each student in the Sunshine State is tested in English, science, and math

11

and the schools are assigned a letter grade based off the results. You see, Mr. En—"

"—telechy."

"Yes. You see, Mr. Entelechy, we at the Horatio Alger Academy are an A school, and have been for the past ten years. We only recruit the best and the brightest to educate our young minds." She pulled down her glasses with her index finger and gave me a look.

"Yeah, loud and clear, ma'am, but I don't think that my ignorance of the state's jargon should preclude my application—I mean, what are they doing tossing a random two in there anyways? It's a test, not a boy band. Wouldn't it be easier if they just called it the FSST? And I am familiar with state testing, just—"

"We'll be in touch with you, Mr., uh—thank you." She held out her hand.

"Wait, did I tell you about my graphic organizers?"

She shook my hand and motioned for the next poor sap to sit. I scanned the room. The place was a battleground of human will. Each time another one of those rejected souls walked away from a table, it looked as if they'd just been told they'd contracted a terminal illness. Conversely, every so often someone would leap up from their seat, clap their hands, and shout something like, "Oh, thank jesus!" then rush over to the team behind the circulation desk, whose members were handing out the employment paperwork and manning the fingerprinting machine. The lucky applicants would then continue their celebration as they exited the double doors.

I scanned the room for Billy. He was in an interview with a cheery middle-aged woman from an elementary school. The interview must have been going well because both she and Billy were cracking up. They soon shook hands, and Billy got up from the table. I walked over to him.

"That looked like it went well," I said.

"Eh, she said all their Spanish jobs were filled, so they'd have no place for me."

"Then what the hell were you talking about?"

"Remember when me, you, and Dana Samson drove out to Maine that one night just because we wanted to see what a real lighthouse looked like?"

"You told her about that?"

"Eh, no, but I did tell her what it was like skinny dipping in the Atlantic Ocean in the crest of New England spring."

"And she didn't give you a job?" I smiled.

"You don't get it, man. What do you think these tired, old bitches want? Sex. You gotta give 'em sex, and they'll give up their own jobs for you. All these dried up, lonely old biddies were once moist little girls with heads full of big, wet dreams. You give them reason to moisten up again, and they'll give you anything."

"You're forgetting something."

"What's that?"

"That you're not exactly the guy to be manning the hose."

"Hell, for all they know I boned ten Cubanas in a South Beach bungalow last night. Just give it a try. Most of the figureheads whoring out their schools here are old hens. And besides, Miami is the City of Sex."

"Eh, what the hell . . ."

I scanned the room for the frumpiest-looking sweetheart and got in her line. Soon, I was sitting before her.

"So, what brings you to our booth at West Miami High?"

"Well, uh, your big, beautiful eyes, and, uh . . ."

"Uh, excuse me, I don't know what kind of school you think is West Miami, but we don't tolerate comments about my eyes. I think you'll be better suited someplace else. Good day."

I got up and gave Billy a thumbs down. He smiled. As the afternoon continued, the tension grew. A few brief shouting matches had broken out between candidates, once when a woman took the last croissant from the refreshment table while another claimed to have been "already reaching for it, bitch," and another time when an older woman confronted a young male for snickering at something she said while she was participating in an interview. Also as the time passed, the candidates' celebrations were more glorious and their defeats more dispiriting. After being offered a job at a middle school, an older woman threw her arms in the air and said, "Oh praise you, jesus. Praise your wonderful name." But rather than leap out of her chair during this exchange with her Great Spirit, she stretched out her arms on the table, folded them together, rested her head in them and wept—her shoulders and back heaving up and down under the pressure of tremendous breaths. It looked as if she hadn't slept in a lifetime. She continued to praise jesus, now with her face pointed at his mortal enemy.

Billy approached me after striking out at Coral Gables Middle.

"Christ, Billy, what the hell are we doing? We're poaching jobs from the locals. These people need the work."

"And we don't? It's a fuckin' jungle out there, man." Billy smiled at some thirty-something Latina admin giving him the eye from behind one of the booths. "And I see a tiger that could use some meat."

He walked over and sat in front of her. Time was running out, so I started skipping lines and asking representatives if they had any social studies positions. If not, I didn't even bother waiting. Some people standing in line didn't like this, but fuck 'em. About ten minutes had passed, and Billy was still there chatting it up with the Latina admin. The people standing behind him in line were growing impatient. One woman kept checking her watch and a man was tapping his foot. Time was of the essence—the double doors would soon be closed—but those two just engaged in what seemed like leisurely, flirtatious conversation. She smiled, then he smiled; she ran her fingers through her hair, he did the same. He eventually got up and smiled at me, then walked behind the circulation desk, signed some papers, and got his fingerprints taken.

This sent me into a frenzy. I started dashing for lines with fewer people, but that usually meant the school had fewer availabilities. I looked over at Billy. He was smiling and talking with some guy behind the counter. Fuck! I don't even belong here! Soon, the representatives started closing up their booths.

Billy and I walked into the parking lot.

"I'm never gonna get a job," I said.

"Eh, whatever. I think the only reason that bitch hired me is 'cause she's in the first throes of a midlife crisis. You see the way she kept winking at me? These Cubanos see nothing but sex. You know," Billy ran his hands through his hair and smiled, "despite my problems with Diego and The Savior, the real reason I said yes to coming down here was to prove I could get a job before you—I win!"

Chapter 2

Billy and I went out that night and celebrated. I was running dangerously low on funds and had to dip into credit to cover my bar tab. I woke early the next morning to be sure I'd make it on time for the start of day two of the recruitment fair.

I drove to Sojourner Truth Middle, parked, and walked through the school and into the library. Only about a third of the people from the day before showed up that morning—but these people looked even fiercer. There was none of that nervous small talk, none of that group-interview horseshit where people smiled and tried to act friendly in hopes that one of the suits with the hiring pen would be looking on from behind a one-way mirror and dig their charm and sign them up on personality and effort alone. No, none of that shit today.

I continued my previous day's tactic of cutting in lines to see who had vacancies for social studies positions, but nobody had any good news. There was one vacancy at an F high school in Opa Locka, but it filled before I could interview. The joy on the faces of these people who got hired into these shithole schools fascinated me. I guess everybody just wants to be accepted, and into where does not seem to matter—at least, initially. These fools would certainly be marched to their deaths come the start of fall.

I called Billy.

"You might be here on your own, man. This ain't lookin' too good," I said.

"Well if worse comes to worst, you can always get a job at McDonald's."

"You gonna pay my student loans, Mr. A school?"

"We'll figure something out."

Soon, that out got figured on its own. Just as I was about to leave and trash my dream of educating Miami's best and brightest, a hurricane of a woman blew through the double doors and over to an empty table. She dumped what little she was carrying onto the table, grabbed a marker, wrote something on a piece of cardboard, and put it on display. George Washington Middle School. The woman was just as disorganized as I was, and I got caught in her gravity. I wandered over, and she called to me before it could be clear that her table was my intended destination.

"You look like a man who's got something to say," she said, as she rummaged through her purse.

"Yeah, you got any availabilities in social studies?"

"We just so happen to have one." She pulled out a can of deodorant and shot the ol' girls a few sprays. "You got any experience?"

"Yeah, I did my student teaching in an eighth grade US History class and also did some long-term subbing in a sixth grade reading class. They were analyzing *Ulysses* by the time I was done with them."

She laughed. "And probably doing a better job of it than I ever could." She put the can of deodorant back in her purse and tossed a stick of gum in her mouth. "We just so happen to have an opening for an eighth grade US History teacher. I consider myself a good judge of character and think you're just the man for the job." She offered me a stick.

I took the gum and smiled, remembering the stellar business advice Jenna Becker gave me as we sunned ourselves on the McKinley

U campus green one unusually warm Western New York spring day. "Whenever you're trying to make a sale, if the customer offers you a cup of coffee, you take it."

". . . But I've got to warn you," she said, "these kids are going to be a serious challenge. We're not an A school, if you know what I mean."

"Well, I'm not an A teacher, so I guess we're a good match." Careful, buddy. "Folksy" has its limits.

She laughed. Thank Jebus! Or perhaps not . . .

I laughed nervously. "Well, I'm looking for a challenge."

"Great. Why don't you go see Debbie over there and fill out the papers. Stop by the school tomorrow morning around nine. The principal, Mr. Rodriguez, would like to meet you."

"Excellent. And you are?"

"Karen Dawson, vice principal." She held out her hand. I met it, and we shook.

"Pleasure to meet you, Ms. Dawson. I'm Luke Entelechy."

"Pleasure to meet you as well, Mr. Entelechy."

We smiled. I was a pretty good judge of character as well, and could sense some warmth about her. Even if the school was hell, it's always a comfort being around strong leadership. I walked over to Debbie, flirted while signing papers, gave up my prints, and walked through the double doors. I drove back to the motel, enjoying every bright green palm and tropical blue body of water I passed.

Billy wasn't there when I got back. I walked down to the beach in my suit and saw him sunning himself near the water.

"Guess who finally got a job?" I shouted to him.

"Jonathan Taylor Thomas?"

I laughed. "Round one is done, man. I met this great lady named Karen Dawson—seems like a real winner. The school's a bottom feeder though. Been an F since they started giving out ratings."

"Can't be any worse than PS Four Ninety. Not even Michelle

Pfeiffer could keep those little shits in line."

"We gotta celebrate tonight!"

"We should start with some dinner. I'm itchin' to try la comida Cubana."

That night, we went to the Cuban place behind the motel and had a three-course meal. I got some ropa vieja, and Billy, arroz con pollo. We got drinks and desert, and when the bill came, we paid on credit and left. We wandered the South Beach strip in search of a place selling beers for cheaper than five buck, and eventually found our spot when some sketchy slimebag passing out cards for a trashy club ushered us through its door. We paid a relatively cheap cover charge, which included all-you-can-drink beer and rum, and got our money's worth of Dominican brew. We sat at a couch in the back.

"This place is great," Billy said, "but it's no New York. That city's the be-all and end-all. There's no better in the world. And I just up and left it. I didn't even tell my roommates I was leaving. I should probably give Senora Ramirez a call."

"Yeah, but look at what you've got here. The beach, the boys, the A school. You got it made."

"Eh, whatever."

A guy and a girl were making out on a couch next to us.

"Oh my god, I haven't been in a straight club in so long," Billy said. "This feels like such a regression. Just don't expect me to be coming to anymore of these bars with you. I'm done with this shit."

"Yeah, that's fine—just as long as we get some writing done."

A pretty mami walked by. Her skin was stretched tightly across her bones like a canvas on a wooden frame. Billy saw me staring at her.

"These girls will probably love you down here," he said. "A guy with a professional job has got to be plus with any of these chicas."

"Yeah, well teaching doesn't exactly make you a millionaire."

"Yeah, but it makes you less of a fuck-up."

"Or at least look like less of a fuck-up. Besides, I kinda have a girlfriend in Mexico."

"Well, you'd make a bad faggot. We fuck everybody, ain't no matta'."

"I guess I'll drink to not being a good faggot."

"Just don't expect me to be coming to any more of these bars with you."

We did a "Cheers" and kept the party going until late night. Miami never stopped if you knew where to go. We asked the right questions and found the right spots, and stayed in them into the sun started to come up. We took a cab back to the motel, and I got a few hours sleep before the alarm went crazy at eight.

I got up, put my sweat-stained suit back on, and drove off into the tropical blue and green morning—salsa and meringue on nearly every radio station. What joy! The heat was brutal and humidity unbearable. It reminded me of the weather in Mariposa. It was so bad there I couldn't take more than a few steps in the afternoon without what felt like my daily water intake draining from my every pore. Even so, there was something about the extreme heat that I loved. But I think there was just something about extremes in general that I loved.

I cruised the causeway, then the mainland boulevards before taking the I-95 north and the Palmetto Expressway west, and getting off in Opa Locka, the very spot my uncle, who grew up in Boca Raton, told me to "avoid like herpes" when he heard I was moving to Miami. I made a few turns, and there it was; the place had the feel of an abandoned trailer park. The building was two stories and spread thin across a parched brown field. I pulled into a fenced-off parking lot and hesitated to leave my car. The sign out front read G orge Was ington. Fuck this place already.

I walked inside and some custodian babbling to himself in a language I didn't understand pointed out the main office with his mop handle when I approached him. I walked into the office and a kind secretary, whose desk and every inch of personal space was filled with Neil Diamond memorabilia, called the principal and led me into his office. The principal, Mr. Rodriguez, was a tall and thin man who exuded grace and charm. He walked out from behind his desk, shook my hand, and asked me to sit. I was nervous, and still incredibly drunk, and almost missed the chair as I lowered myself.

"Whoa, did that just move?" I said.

"Careful, Mr. En—"

"—telechy."

"Mr. Entelechy." Rodriguez smiled and followed the perimeter of his desk back to his seat behind it. Karen Dawson joined us and sat on the couch near my chair. She also smiled at me. We made some small talk about the heat and competition for jobs but soon came a stinger.

"So, tell me, Mr. En," Rodriguez said, "why should we hire you at George Washington Middle?"

"Oh, well, uh, I thought I already had the job . . ."

"We just want to be extra sure that you're the correct fit. This isn't an easy place to work. We're not trying to scare you off but just want to know that you know exactly what you're getting into."

"Well, like I told Ms. Dawson, I love a challenge." I started sweating . . . bad. The A/C unit in the office was broken, and the whole place stunk of rotting, old books and mildew.

"Well, that's what you're going to get." The interview went on like that for another ten minutes before I officially got the job. I think they were just testing my hull for leaks. Regardless of how badly I didn't want to work there, or any other school for that matter, I just kept smiling and nodding and reassuring them that I had no fear indeed to teach the children of the damned. They gave me a tour, and I felt ill. The place looked like an old juvenile detention hall—bars on the windows, heavy-duty doors, security cameras . . . When they released me from the facility, I raced back to the Seaside and told Billy all about it.

"Welcome to ghetto teaching, my friend," he said. "I went through a year of that hell, and now it's your turn."

We had a few weeks before school started, so Billy and I decided to return to the Empire State to pack, say good-byes, and return to Florida for some fun in the sun before the crushing weight of professional work would destroy our wills to live. But before we left Miami, we looked for an apartment.

We drove to Tropical Rentals, a seedy agency located between a Laundromat and a doughnut shop in a shitty plaza. Before we got entirely through the door, some overly tanned, thirty-something male dressed like a teenager jumped at us. His fake gold chain almost popped me in the eye.

"Hey, fellas, the name's Greg. You in the market for a place to live? 'Cause you came to the right spot. Or maybe you just came to hit on these fine ladies." He pointed at the women in back, busy talking on phones or dealing with customers. None even looked up.

Greg didn't look Latin, but rather, an Italian-American transplant, whose New Yawk accent was faded but still recognizable.

"Yeah, we're looking for a two bedroom," I said.

"Well I got just the place for ya'. Come on, follow me!"

The guy led us out to the parking lot. "See that car over there?" He pointed to a shiny BMW. "That's me. I bet you guys like that, huh? A couple good-lookin' guys like yourselves would do well with the ladies in a thing like that. I'd take you out for a spin, but ya' know, work and all." He started laughing then slapped Billy on the back; Billy almost fell over. "So where are your wheels?"

I pointed to my discolored Chevy four door.

"Hey, a man's car is his chariot, am I right?" Greg said.

I didn't know what that meant.

He continued, "We should take your car 'cause mine's all full of boxes and taxes, and stuff you guys don't really care about. Coupla' young studs like you two. Bet the ladies love you!"

We piled in, and Greg got in the back. He sat in the middle and leaned forward, putting his elbows on the backs of the front seats. He had this big, goofy, eager smile like a weird kid on his way to the circus.

"So, what are the funds like? We talkin' J. Lo, or J. *Low*, if you know what I'm sayin'?"

"Just a regular place."

He took us to a few spots, and we settled on the cheapest, a two bedroom roach trap right off the A1A, with on-street parking, no laundry room, and some crazy-ass neighbors. We went back to the office and signed on the dotted line, but not before ol' Gregor really laid it down.

"Say, fellas, I know you guys are teachers and all, and a coupla' guys like you, I don't gotta worry about. But my boss tells me I gotta let everybody know—you guys miss one payment and you're out on your asses, you hear me? I hate to say it, but ya' know, I could lose my job. But I like you guys, you know that?"

"Eh, whatever . . ." Billy said. "And what if we break the lease? I don't know how I feel signing the next ten months of my life away."

Greg got solemn as if someone had just insulted Frank Sinatra.

"Well, fellas, you both seem like smart guys. I don't know if I'd have to spell out what would happen in court. Let's just say it won't be a good thing for either of you or your credit scores. Or maybe, we don't even tell the courts." He put his hands on our shoulders and leaned in between our heads. "And we wouldn't want that. I like you boys."

"Yeah, sure," I said.

He patted our shoulders and backed up. "Just be sure to slip that rent check under the door at the start of each month." He smiled, big and wide. "Here are the keys. Welcome to Paradise, fellas!"

We checked out of the Seaside and into Paradise, the two-story dumper nestled in the valley between two rows of towering hotels and condo complexes lining the edges of the thin slice of land right in the heart of the northern section of Miami Beach. The one redeeming feature of the place, other than that it was pretty big, was the view. For whatever reason, developers didn't build up one parcel of prime real estate between our apartment and Biscayne Bay, giving us a clear shot across the gorgeous blue and the sun setting behind it each night. We could see it all from our front porch.

For dinner, we went to the Winn Dixie down the block and bought a bottle of wine and a few bags of chips, then came back and had a feast while sitting cross-legged in the center of the white tile living room floor. After dinner, we bought a few more bottles of wine, got good and drunk, and passed out on the tile. We woke the next morning, packed up the car, and headed north.

"What the fuck did we just do?"

Chapter 3

I was the first back to Miami from New York. I left Buffalo early one Sunday morning after packing nearly every square inch of my car with crap I didn't really need. I drove through the night—less in bravado and more out of the fear of getting my stuff raided from my car while it was parked in a motel lot overnight.

When I finally arrived in Florida, I was exhausted to the point of near collapse. I wanted to get to my new place at the tip of America's wang as quickly as possible, so I took it as a sign from the gods when a car full of wild teens blazed by me doing about a hundred. I sped behind them, figuring any cop with a radar gun would be too dumbfounded after the first car passed to shoot the rapidly slowing sedan behind it. I followed those cats for over two hours, all the way through the sunny shaft to the start of the swampy mushroom tip, but lost them to an off-ramp somewhere near Port St. Lucie. I roared into Miami in a little under four hours after crossing the state line— that must have been close to some kind of record. Fear can be a hell of a motivator.

I pulled up to the apartment, parallel parked between a rusted-out pickup and an old Ford Escort with a trash bag for a window, and immediately started hauling shit up the stairs, starting with the most valuable. The downstairs neighbors were outside and greeted me on the front steps. They were both middle-aged women, one a Bahamian with an enormous smile, and the other a burned-out Cuban who took every opportunity to curse out Castro. "That bastard! When I was a little girl, they took my father away. The communists, they stole my family. Castro, you dirty dog!"

They both offered to help me move, but I wasn't letting any hands other than my own touch my stuff. This wasn't because I distrusted them in particular—I distrusted everybody. The Bahamian lived in a two bedroom with her, what seemed like, ten fucking kids, who never shut the hell up or stopped playing violent and loud games. "Fuck you, Ula, it's my turn to throw the rock at Gary!" I turned on the A/C unit in my apartment and that dull rattle drowned out their voices. Because I was there first, I chose the bigger bedroom. The place had two bathrooms and I claimed the larger of those as well. I didn't necessarily care about its size but that it provided a wonderful view of the bay from a window in the shower.

I put my things in my room and went to a department store to buy cleaning supplies and household necessities. When I got back, I started scrubbing the kitchen. There were little animal hairs everywhere, including the inside of the fridge. It was fucking disgusting. I bleached the lot of it and hosed it down with the sink sprayer. I spent the afternoon unpacking my stuff, then drove to the mainland to get some furniture. I bought a queen-size bed from some guy named Bob who operated out of a storage facility in Opa Locka. "Hey, follow me. Lemme show ya' tha works. See this here mattress, this is the one I personally own. Sleep on it every night with my wife. We never miss a wink—top quality, this one." He gave me a good price, and because I felt it wasn't my place to ask where he got his inventory, I just said yes when he tacked on free delivery.

By nightfall, I was set up. The place was moderately clean, my stuff was safely locked inside, and I had a bed with sheets. I'd been making great progress on my book before this little detour in Miami and was eager to start writing again. I turned on my computer, but just wasn't feeling it, so I shut it off and went to sleep.

I called Billy from the beach the next day. He was going to fly down that afternoon but ended up cancelling his flight.

"Eh, whatever, I'll just come down in a few days. I wanted to spend some more time with Diego. I don't know what the fuck I'm doing. I never should have signed that lease."

"Well you did, so deal with it. The apartment isn't bad. I mean, I do get the vibe there may have once been a murder/suicide here, but it's not bad. The beach is a five-minute walk away. It's sunny . . . A school, man."

"Yeah, yeah, well, I gotta go. Diego is calling me. See you soon."

Billy arrived a few days later. I picked him up at the airport in Fort Lauderdale. He was the last off the plane. I was glad to see him.

"I didn't think you were gonna show," I said.

"Oh, uh, yeah." He had this shifty, vacant, and dreadful look in his eye, as if he'd just committed involuntarily manslaughter, and I was the first person he'd spoken with since.

"So where are your bags?" I said.

"I, uh, just brought this one. I mailed the rest of my stuff."

"What do you mean, you mailed it?"

"Like, I put it all in four big boxes, brought them down to the post office, wrote our address on them, and mailed it."

"Jesus, and what if the boxes get lost?"

"Eh, I'll figure something out."

The days passed, and sure enough, one did get lost—the one with most of his clothes, his computer, and most importantly, the legal documents he needed to win his recent lawsuit against the NYPSD, which had apparently withheld five grand from his pay because of some bullshit technicality he was now fighting. But not without his papers.

"Fuck, how could I be so stupid as to trust the US Mail?" he said.

"Forget it, man, let's just go to the beach."

We went to the beach and lay out on the sand.

"I'm so fucking stupid," Billy said. "I can't believe I came down here. I had a good thing going in New York. I was making good money, had a great boyfriend. And I was starting to get known in the gay scene." Before I could respond, he threw his hands in my direction. "Don't laugh, you don't know what I mean. The right people were starting to know me. I was getting VIP treatment, getting in secret entrances. That doesn't just happen to everybody. They all thought I was hilarious—said that I was a star. But I'm just a fucking idiot."

"Well if you were nearly famous in New York, you can easily do the same here. You just need a better tan."

"Eh, I guess."

The days passed, and we spent our time at the beach or our apartment with Dominican beers, cheap bottles of wine, and tense conversation. Finally, the day came for new teacher orientation. All rookie teachers were to meet at a hotel by the airport for a solid day of pep talk and professional development. As usual, Billy and I showed up ten minutes late after getting lost trying to find the right causeway. We walked through the main entrance and stopped at a table with about twenty nametags on it. Billy picked up one in particular.

"Margo Liberty—sounds like the name of a Euro football club."

I laughed. "You see mine?"

He nodded and passed it over, then grabbed his own.

We put on our nametags and braved our way through the hordes of vendors at the entrance pitching worthless crap. One jumped right in front of us.

"Boom! You're dead."

"How's that?" I said.

"That's how it happens, gentlemen, just like that." He snapped his fingers and grinned like an asshole. "You need to be sure you cover all your bases—don't want to leave all those funeral expenses to your family, now do you? Heck, nobody should be so selfish. Now if you'll just step this way—"

"Sorry to cut you off, charlie," I said, "but we gotta join those legions of poor young saps who just signed up for a lifetime of hell. Besides, should I go prematurely, I'm just gonna have ol' Billy here stuff me in a box and ship me home via the US Postal Service. We know they always deliver."

We started toward the group but were stopped by a beautiful representative from the MPSD teachers union.

"You've both just gotten yourselves written up and are in big trouble," she said.

"Fuck, I told you we should have left earlier," I said to Billy.

"According to our statistics, one of you is likely to hear that very phrase within your first ninety days on the job. As you know, you can be dismissed very easily within that trial period, which is why you need protection from UMPS."

I leaned into Billy's ear. "I wish she'd give me a *different* reason to need protection."

Billy chuckled, then stared vacantly into the distance. I didn't know if there was too much or too little on his mind. The woman soon wandered away.

We joined the herd and sat somewhere in back. Some far-too-energetic young woman, who probably had a horrible childhood she never left, was hopping around onstage trying to contrive spirit as some '80s pop crap blasted from speakers behind her. She was nearly out of breath, punctuating her performance with "Yeah"s and "Super"s. The music soon stopped, and she stepped to the mic. "Congratulations to all of you for being where you are. You now join the wonderful family that is the MPSD."

"Yeah, the dysfunctional family," said the brunette sitting beside Billy.

"And we're their bastard children," Billy said.

"I really hope that woman isn't the mother," I said. "She fucking scares me."

The bitch onstage was smiling like a goddamned idiot.

The brunette held out her hand. "The name's Abbi. I just got sentenced to West Miami High."

"Hey, my school's the feeder to yours!" I said, with far too much enthusiasm. I hung my head.

"Yeah, and my school's the feeder to Dade County Corrections," she said.

Billy let out a loud snort. Several people turned around to see where it came from. I started chuckling.

Some crazy, old woman stumbled onto the stage, and the cheerleader passed her the mic. The woman spared no time in upping the day's level of insanity. "Hello, my name is Sandy Frankles, and I'm the Deputy Superintendent of the Miami Public Schools District, and I want to say that I'm appalled by the likes of your filthy people slandering our dear Superintendent's name. Dana Canterbury never misappropriated any funds and to suggest that her recent purchase of a yacht in any way hurt our children makes you a damned fool—" The cheerleader came back out and yanked the mic away from Ms. Frankles. Her words were amplified through the speakers. "Sandy . . . SANDY, this is the *new teacher orientation*, not a press conference. Get it together!"

Ms. Frankles, who may have been drunk, took back the mic. "I'm sorry, I mistook you all for something you weren't. Fear not, for I have the ability to change gears quickly, and I will deliver you a wonderful introduction. That is, after all, what they're paying me for—"

"Yeah, too much!" yelled a heckler.

Ms. Frankles pointed indiscriminately into the crowd. "I wouldn't take a red cent that wasn't mine! Show yourself, you coward!"

The cheerleader grabbed the mic away from Ms. Frankles and

started ushering her from the stage. "Okay, okay, Sandy, I think we've got enough from you today."

But Sandy wasn't going quietly. She kept pumping her fists and threatening she'd show us all!

"What the hell was that about?" I said.

"I don't know, but it can't be good for business," Billy said.

I scanned the crowd, but no one seemed fazed by what had just happened. People were texting, sleeping, reading books, and one woman was even crocheting a blanket. Perhaps this was just another day in Paradise . . .

Soon, the cheerleader came back onstage and addressed the crowd with a big smile as if the previous act were just a part of the show. "Okay, ladies and gentleman, that was great, wasn't it? Now, we're now going to break out into groups based on our school locations. Please follow the color on your nametag to the appropriate table in the cafeteria. We'll meet back here in an hour."

"This should be fun," Abbi said.

We all got up and followed the masses to the cafeteria. An overeager girl shot over to Billy.

"Hey, you're blue, just like me!" she said.

"What?" Billy said.

"The color on your name tag is blue. See, me too." She pointed to her stupid nametag. We introduced ourselves, Abbi included, and continued toward the cafeteria. The girl's name was Christy, and she was about to start at Little Havana with Billy. She thought this an adequate icebreaker, and soon she was flapping away as if Billy were her very bestest friend.

"I really can't wait to get started, can you?" Christy said.

"I absolutely can," Billy said.

"I mean, there're so many great things we can do with the kids. But I don't want to be like everybody else, just be all mean and authoritative and stuff. That's the key to changing lives. I mean, we're literally saving lives, if you really think about it."

"Eh, whatever . . ." Billy turned away from her.

"Yeah, you're a regular EMT there, Christy," Abbi said.

Billy and I chuckled.

We scattered when we got to the cafeteria. Abbi and I ended up in the same group because we'd be teaching in the same region, the green region. We played one of those ridiculous scavenger hunt games, where we had to ask each other for odd items in an effort to break the ice. It was during this activity that I first met the other tyros of George Washington Middle. There were six in total. All but one were white kids from white neighborhoods, educated at white public universities. And while she fit the same description, one was impossible to miss. She lunged for me long before I even thought to do the same for her.

"The name's Liberty, Margo Liberty. It looks as though we're going to be colleagues."

I stuck out my hand to shake, but she passed that by, pulled me close, and planted a friendly kiss on my right cheek. I was used to that kind of greeting in Mexico, but never in the States.

"Uh, nice to meet you Margo. I'm Luke."

"Charmed, dear. So we're the ones leading the revolution then, huh?"

"What revolution?"

"The revolution in American education. This system is broken and needs some serious repairwomen, and men, to patch it up. I came ready to get my hands dirty."

"And where are you coming from?"

"Newark, New Jersey, born and raised, but I'm basically from the City."

"You mean, the city of Newark?"

"No, *the* City—New York. You obviously need to get out more, dear."

"Gotcha . . ."

Margo was a pretty, rail-thin brunette who carried herself with the grace of a Golden Age Hollywood starlet but one who'd already been run through the gears of the fame machine. Everything about her screamed deception. She had huge fake tits, swollen botoxed lips, and a nose too perfect for it not to have been shaped by a surgeon— but it all somehow looked natural on her. She called everyone "dear" or "darling" and was "charmed" with everything. People were always nervous at these get-to-know-you events, but this seemed to be her default character—a highly functioning psychopath. I observed her as she told stories to the other newbies.

"Yes, darling, I spent the year before last waiting tables on a pleasure cruise that made trips between Northern Australia and several islands in the South Pacific, but my manager was a brute and a bore, so I prefer to just ignore that era of my life. I told him I was better suited onstage, tap dancing or perhaps even singing, but he kept me on tables. The brutish bastard. I've been in Miami since returning State-wide and couldn't be happier."

Ms. Liberty was an aspiring novelist and had recently found an independent publisher in New York she said was "just *dying*" to put her in print. She was also the highlight of our scavenger hunt activity, pulling from her purse such random items as a real Hawaiian lei and authentic Japanese chop sticks.

Of the others, I spoke the most with two: Ben Fallon, a chain-smoking twenty-five-year-old booze hound from Wilkes Barre, and Rachel Golden, a twenty-two-year-old nervous daddy's princess from Madison, Wisconsin.

"So, it can't be as bad as everyone's saying, right?" Rachel asked me, then quickly turned to whoever might possibly answer her first.

I, however, bit before the others. "I sure as hell hope not. I mean, they can't exactly kill us, can they?"

We met back in the main room shortly thereafter. The cheerleader was back onstage trying to pump us up by throwing UMPS hats and T-shirts into the crowd, but nobody seemed to care. In fact, several of the hats and shirts fell to the ground where they remained. Soon, Ms. Frankles wandered back onto the stage and grabbed the mic away from the cheerleader.

"Excuse me, excuse me everyone, I seem to have misplaced my car keys. If everyone could just check the floor around them, I'd be ever so gracious. Attached to the key ring is a bullfrog made out of beads, if that helps. Be aware though, not all of the beads are green. My niece made it for me, and she's colorblind . . ."

"Yo, this is a fucking circus. Let's get the hell outta here," Billy said to me.

"Do you think we can just leave?" I said.

"We signed in, right?" Billy stood up and walked away.

I followed.

"Don't you boys know never to leave a lady behind?" Abbi got up and followed us out the door and onto the parking lot. "So drinks, fellas?" She smiled. "I know a great pub on Collins."

"Eh, I really should look for a car today." Billy turned to me. "Would you mind taking me to a dealership?"

"Shit, I didn't even think about that. How'd you plan to get around without one?"

"I checked the bus lines. There's one that runs right into Little Havana. Fuck, I mean, I've been taking the train to work every day for the past year in NYC."

"Yeah, well that's NYC."

He shrugged his shoulders.

"Yeah, I got some stuff to do today," I said, "but I can take you to check out cars."

"Okay, well I guess this is where I leave you guys." Abbi pulled out a pen and a piece of paper. She wrote something down and handed it to me. "Here's my number. You guys should call me up sometime.

Maybe we can talk about lesson planning . . ." She smiled at me with an intent only Billy picked up on. He later told me, "Dude, she wants you. How could you miss that?"

We piled in my car, blasted the A/C and salsa music, and pulled into the first dealership we found.

"What kind of car you want?" I pulled into a parking space and turned off the engine.

"Eh, I don't really care. Cheap."

The lot was a GM dealership, so we were in the right spot. It only took a moment after getting out of my car before some clown was trailing us. Billy told him straight away, "I just want your cheapest car."

The guy's smile went limp-dick, and he escorted Billy to an Escort. Soon, Billy was again signing on the dotted line while letting out a tremendous sigh.

"You should be happy, buddy," the prick behind the counter said. "I just gave you a great deal on that car!"

"Eh, whatever . . ."

We walked out of there and back to my car. It was going to take a few days for everything to clear before Billy could drive his new wheels off the lot, but he didn't seem to care.

"What the fuck am I doing?" he said. "I own a car in Buffalo."

"Why didn't you just bring it down?"

"Because my parents won't let me. They've been holding it hostage in my garage back home. My dad says he won't let me have it until I get my head out of my ass, move back to Buffalo, and take a job waiting tables at the family restaurant."

"Do your parents know you're a grown man?"

"Eh, I think they're still a little bitter that lil' Billy grew up diggin' willies."

"They can't legally do that, you know?"

"Tell that to mi padre."

We stopped at a Cuban restaurant for some more authentic comida. I was hooked already. That shit was incredible. Our waitress was a gorgeous young thing from Argentina. I really dug how Miami was a magnet for people from the entire Latin world. So sexy.

"Yo, that Christy bitch was driving me insane today," Billy said.

"Which one was Christy?"

"That little god-head, 'we're-gonna-save-the-children' wack-job."

"She seemed okay." I shoveled some more ropa vieja in my mouth. Fucking incredible.

"I just can't stand all these overeager morons who really think they can change this system," Billy said. "The train's fucking derailed and no amount of struggle is going to get it back up and running again."

"Maybe you're right, but I certainly hope not."

"Believe me, I've seen it firsthand. You know how much learning was going on in PS Four Ninety? Little Sandra Jones once lost her mind when I told her to sit down and stop dancing during class. She said, and I quote, 'Fuck you, you stupid, white bitch,' then she ran outside, grabbed a fire extinguisher, and came back in the room and started hosing the place down. It took security ten minutes to get there after I hit the panic button, and all they did was laugh as lil' Sandy was riding that empty can on the classroom floor like a hot papi."

I laughed.

"These schools are nothing more than state-funded babysitting rings," Billy said. "You think you can teach lil' Sandy Jones, then be my guest, 'cause there are hundreds of thousands of little shits out there just like her. Schools are a fucking joke, don't kid yourself. I've been there. I know what goes on in those classrooms."

"I've been there too, man—"

"Not like you're about to see. I hope you're ready . . ."

I shoveled in another bite of shredded beef. The train was boarding in two days, and I knew the ride would be shitty.

"Just make sure you don't go crazy on that panic button," Billy said. "They keep a record of that stuff. Hit it too many times and they start wondering why you can't control your class. Sometimes it's just better to suffer in silence, you know what I mean?"

We went back to the apartment. Billy started setting up his room and I paced in my own. Soon I was out the door and into the tropical night. I wandered around the block and stopped at the Tide Pool, which was exactly as it sounded, a dive littered with sundried locals looking for cheap drinks and a less-than-casual atmosphere. The bar itself was an oasis in the middle of the place. Drunks of all ages, races, and social classes sat around its fringes, sucking at that intoxicating teat. I sat at the least crowded section at the bar. The barmaid, a tall and pretty Latina with thick curves, came over.

"What can I get for you?" Her accent sounded Brazilian.

"A bottle of your cheapest beer."

She went for it and was soon back. What a figure . . . "Four bucks."

I handed over the loot. She took it, but didn't walk away.

"Are you alone?" She leaned in and gently touched the top of my hand.

I shook my head. "You're never alone so long as you got Jebus."

"Aww, poor thing. Well, you're in the right place." She took her hand off my own and gestured to the other patrons: bikers and withered old drunks and young going-nowhere hot shots playing billiards and throwing darts. The maid and I exchanged names. Hers was Paola, and Paola stayed with me long enough after that beer sale to imply at least one of life's many forms of attraction. She was pretty and became more beautiful each time she walked away from me. All the men called to her as she passed by them. They smiled and told her jokes, and said things like, "Don't work too hard now, sweetie," in a desperate bid to stay relevant forever. And each time after doing her rounds, she came back to me, even if I was still half full. I told her where I was from and that I was a teacher, and she told me she was from São Paulo and that she had supreme respect for teachers. I almost felt guilty when she smiled at me after saying that.

Just as I finished beer number two, Paola set down another before me.

"From him." She pointed at a middle-aged Hispanic man sitting alone at a booth in the corner. He smiled and waved.

I did the same.

Soon, he walked over. "Hello, my name is DJ Tango." He handed me his card—it was shaped like a turntable. "I play all that dance music that everybody loves."

"Nice to meet you." I shook his hand. "My name is DJ S.O. Terric, and I play all that arcane minutiae nobody's ever heard of."

"Huh?"

I pointed my finger in his face. "Exactly."

"Would you like another beer?"

"No, I'm good with this one. Thanks."

The DJ tried engaging me in conversation, but I was more interested in sitting in silence. He didn't take the first several hints but finally caught on when I pulled out my phone and faked a conversation. I had a few more beers and caught the attention of an older gentleman, also sitting alone, on the other side of the bar—although he seemed to have different motives than the DJ. He soon came over and sat next to me. He took a long look around.

"Go slowly, you horses of night," he said to no one in particular. His eyes carried great sadness.

"Excuse me?" I said.

"Christopher Marlowe." He gestured to Paola, and she brought him another tumbler of whiskey. "You know, I got a grandson about your age." He brought the glass to his lips. His hand was trembling, but he got that liquid down smooth. "So what's a guy like you doing all alone?"

"I, uh, don't think I'm really alone. I mean—" I motioned to Paola and the DJ.

"Sorry, didn't mean to pester you with questions. I hate that myself."

"No, it's okay, I don't mind."

He pulled off his glasses and wiped them with his dirty T-shirt. "I overheard you telling Paola here that you were a writer. That a fact?"

"I mean, I write . . . I don't know if that makes me a writer."

"So long as those words come from you, and no one else, then you're a writer."

We had a few drinks, which he insisted be on his tab. The man's name was Sam, and he was born and raised on a small farm near Omaha. He'd left the family fields as a teenager and tramped around the country, living off wages from migrant farm work and day labor, and wrote poetry and prose in his every free moment. He lived this way well into his fifties, until he'd moved to Florida under promise of managing a citrus farm, which he did for a few years—but the farm soon went under, and he made his way south, eventually settling in the Tide Pool, where he'd lived since. We talked about poetry and our favorite authors. He was big into the Romantics, Wordsworth topping his list. Sam said he loved originators. After three or four more whiskeys, he went silent. He stared upwards, and his eyes welled with tears.

"This is something I wrote when I was a little older than you. I call it, 'So That's my Job':

> It takes two to tango.
> It takes two to love.
> So why are we made
> Ourselves of only one?

When I was seventeen I was stronger,
Stronger than I ever was—
So strong, I put that needle to my vein
And let it do what it does.
And I've never been strong enough since
To go back and retry,
So I sit here upon a bar stool
And drink myself dry.
Time allows for many things,
Loss and lines, regrets,
But in this generous allowance of commodities
It won't allow one to forget—
So that's my job."

He held up his glass and smiled. "Nobody was born to be a citrus farmer."

We touched glasses and finished the last of our drinks. Soon Sam was up and sitting at the opposite side of the bar, all alone again. I had a few more drinks and was awakened by Paola's wonderful voice. "Honey, you can't sleep here."

I pulled my head off the bar and staggered back to my apartment, wondering the entire way how ol' Sammy still had such strength in him.

Chapter 4

Billy and I woke early the next morning—the last before the start of classes—and went to our respective schools for a mandatory prep day. Billy planned to take the bus, but got a late start after searching his room for his wallet for thirty unsuccessful minutes, and I ended up giving him a ride.

I dropped Billy in front of his gorgeous, well-manicured A school, whose parking lot was full of the cheapest model of BMWs available, driven in from the stamped-concrete driveways of mansions all across Coral Gables, Coconut Grove, and Pinecrest. I honked as Billy walked away, and shouted, "Have fun on your first day of school!"

Billy turned and smiled and waved like a dumb, little kid. I made for the I-95. Though there were no students coming that day, I still felt this horrible wrenching in my gut.

When I got there, I signed in with Ms. Laurel, who was busy singing along to "Cracklin' Rosie" blasting from her computer speakers. She waited until the end of the first chorus, then called Ms. Dawson. Ms. Dawson met me outside of her office. She was talking on her cell phone and speaking with a custodian out back at the same time.

"Uh, miss," the custodian said.

Ms. Dawson held up an index finger to him. "Can you hold on for one sec, Dave?" She put the phone down and smiled at me. "Hello, Luke, welcome to your first official day at GW! How do you feel?"

"Tip-top and ready to go."

"Here are your keys." She dug into her pocket and pulled out a ring with two keys on it. "Just gimme one sec, and I'll take you down."

"Miss," the custodian said. "Miss, I think one of your new teachers just threw up all over the bathroom."

"Okay, okay, I'll take care of it . . ." Ms. Dawson now held up an index finger in my direction. ". . . one sec."

Just then, a large and poorly maintained woman waddled her big, bad self into the office. "God, another year of this crap." She meant it.

"Hello, Ms. Rotter." Ms. Laurel's voice had none of the usual charm in it when she said that.

Rotter paid her no attention and said, to no one in particular, "So I heard we're switching rooms around this year. I already told my union rep I'll be damned if they stick me in another classroom with a filthy A/C unit. No siree, not for me. I spent a week straight at the clinic this summer with an infection in my lungs. I think it gave me the black lung of death . . ."

Ms. Dawson hung up the phone. "Don't worry, Darla, your A/C unit will be working just fine."

"Who's this?" Rotter pointed her chubby finger at me, almost poking my chest.

"This is Mr. Entelechy. He's taking over for Ms. Henderson."

"That poor woman's never gonna be the same," Rotter said. "They ran her outta here on a rail."

"Who's Ms. Henderson?" I said.

Rotter snorted with laughter.

Ms. Dawson's phone rang again, and she answered.

"Hello, yes, just gimme one sec, okay?" Dawson put her hand over the phone receiver. "Darla, uh, would you, uh, mind taking Luke here to Ms. Henderson's old room?"

Darla rolled her eyes. "Sure, I guess I could manage that, I mean, it *is* on the way."

Dawson leaned in to Rotter, but I could hear her hushed words. "And for the love of god, tone down the crap, please! He's new, have a heart."

Rotter led me into the hall as two teachers were passing by.

"Hello." I smiled at them.

They both kept walking, but one turned her head. "I hope you brought your flak jacket." She and her buddy liked that one; they both chuckled their way down the hall. Rotter and I continued in the opposite direction.

"So who's Ms. Henderson?" I said.

"You don't wanna know. But it looks like you're gonna be in her room this year, and it's cursed. Nobody who's been in that room has lasted the full year for the past five straight. They've gone through twelve different teachers. You're lucky number thirteen."

We walked down a barren, bleak hall that stunk of mildew and arrived at a door just before the last. Rotter stuck in the keys.

"You better hope they changed that air filter." She opened the door, but hesitated to walk inside the room; we stood in the hall. "These A/C units are the black lung of death. They're as old as the school, and they never change them. I called my union rep every day this summer and told him I would *not* be teaching a single class if they hadn't changed my filter. They found a dead mouse in there last year . . ."

A large custodian walked by pushing a broom. I said hello, and he responded in a language that sounded like a combination of English, Spanish, and French. Had I been unable to understand a single word he said, I would have been less confused, but as it was, I thought I was seriously cracking up. He continued pushing the broom down the hall and a tall, hip, greaser-type gentleman approached us. He had thick, slicked-back black hair and wore a tight white T-shirt over some faded black jeans.

"Are you still bitching about the fucking A/C units, Darla?" he asked her.

"I told you I think they gave me the black lung of—"

"Alright, why don't you just take it outside then if you're so worried about the air?"

She decided that was a good idea and waddled out the door.

"Good god, that bitch pisses me off," the man said.

"She always like that?" I said.

"All-fucking-ways."

I grabbed the key out of the door and walked into the room. It was dark and stunk of moist, rotting life. A thick layer of black dust covered everything: cabinets, desks, chairs . . . The place was run-down and in bad need of repair. Security bars lined the windows in such close intervals that they blocked out a good portion of the sun.

"So, they gave you Henderson's room, huh?" the man said.

"Yeah, did she go crazy or something?"

He laughed. "Something like that." He followed me inside. "The name's Eric Wolenowitz, but everyone calls me 'Wolo.' I teach social studies, too."

"Luke Entelechy." We shook. I liked Wolo right away. I could tell he didn't hold anything back. He sat in one of the student chairs and threw his legs up on a desk. I started dusting some tables.

"I know what you must be thinking right now," he said. "I'm rounding my fifth year here, but I remember my first with graphic detail. Don't worry. It's not as bad as everyone says. You'll be fine just as long as you stay in control. That's the key—just be cool, be yourself."

The custodian popped his head in my room and said something I didn't understand.

Wolo responded. "Naw, why don't you come back later and sweep, D-man?"

"No prob, Woller." D-man started to leave.

"So, the Canes gonna break five hundred this season?" Wolo said.

"Oh don't even get me started on those unranked muthafuckas . . ." D-man laughed and walked away muttering something about their offensive line.

"Is that Spanish?" I said.

"Creole. Lotta Haitians in Miami." Wolo took a bite out of a green apple.

A pretty, young woman stuck her head inside my room.

"Wolo, what'd I tell you about kickin' your feet up on the desks?" she said.

"That it helps cover the graffiti?"

She laughed. "How was your summer?"

"Fantastic. Me and Amanda went down to the Peruvian Amazon for a few weeks. Unbelievable. You?"

"Just livin', you know how I do . . ." They both laughed. "And who's this fine young man?"

"This here is Luke Entelechy, Lisa Henderson's replacement," Wolo said.

"Oh, well I wish you better luck than she had," she said.

"Should I be worried or something?" I said. "I'm not going to be killed, right?"

They laughed again.

"No, sweetie, you will not be killed," she said. "These kids look tough, but they're really just angry and confused little pussycats. If you can learn to see them like that, they ain't so bad."

I smiled.

"Hey, we should all go out for some drinks after we get done preppin' today," she said. "I'm gonna need some margaritas after throwin' up my Word Wall."

"Throwin' up is right, Yolanda," Wolo said. "I can't take all this arts and crafts bullshit."

Yolanda smiled and left the classroom, but stuck her head back in.

"Hey, Entelechy—you're gonna do great, I can already tell." She smiled and walked down the hall.

"She seems nice."

"That's Yolanda Royce. Remember that name—that right there is the best teacher in the school. It might not look like it, but she's tough as nails. She's probably the only person here who can keep a classroom in line, and she's led the school in F2ST math scores for the seven years she's been here. That woman is the Queen of George Washington Middle."

I started dusting off my new desk and another new face popped in.

"Hey, Santoro, good to see you, man! How you been?" Wolo got up to shake his hand.

"Pretty good . . ." Though average height, Santoro walked ten feet tall, chest expanded, eyes piercing and proud. He was an unnaturally handsome Puerto Rican man born on the Island, but he and his family immigrated to Miami when he was just a kid. He married a Cuban woman he met while studying history at the University of Miami, and inherited some of her struggle. ". . . But I'd be better if somebody finally put a bullet in that bastard Castro. Carm and I tried to visit her cousin in Havana in July, and it all got fucked up again . . . Porqueria!"

He gave me a good look. "This the new Henderson?"

"Yeah, his name's Luke," Wolo said.

Santoro stuck out his hand, and I met it. He had a great handshake.

"Welcome to the team. Listen to this guy," Santoro tapped

Wolo's shoulder, "he knows what he's talking about."

"And this guy is the best department head in the school." Wolo put his arm around Santoro's shoulders. "Just be glad you're on his team, 'cause other heads ain't worth a head of lettuce."

"I am glad, real glad. So what exactly happened with Ms. Henderson?"

Santoro laughed. "About halfway through the year, she just went crazy, man. Ran outside during the middle of class and started doing snow angels under the GW sign in the front lawn. Guess she just couldn't take it anymore."

"Goddamn, man, that's horrible. Poor woman . . ." I said.

"Hey," Santoro said, "you guys should follow me. D-man gave me the key to one of the annexes in back. We should raid it for supplies before anybody else gets to it."

I dropped my dust rag and followed the guys to one of the several trailer-classrooms out back. We passed two different teachers. I said hello again as I passed, but they didn't so much as look at me. They did, however, smile and say hello to Wolo.

"There like a racial thing going on at this school?" I said.

"It may look like it," Wolo said, "but they did the same to me when I first started. This school sees so many new teachers come and go, the older ones don't waste their energy getting to know the new ones. If you make it past the first year, you'll see those pearly whites."

When we arrived at the trailer, Santoro took a good look around to be sure no one was watching before sticking the key in the door. We walked inside and wandered around, gathering any supplies we thought we might use. I grabbed a globe, overhead projector, and a few maps, Wolo a podium and some educational posters, and Santoro a new student desk and some whiteboard markers. We walked around to the side entrance and snuck our stuff back inside the school. We passed Margo's classroom on the way. Several of the new teachers were inside having a pump-up session for the start of the year. Margo was, of course, holding court.

"No, don't be silly, Rachel, these kids will not eat you alive." She put her hands on Rachel's shoulders as would an older sister comforting her younger. "At least, not if I have anything to say about it. You just need to be cool with them—show them you're like them. You'll be okay."

"Uh . . . well . . . I'm not so sure," Rachel said.

Wolo, Santoro, and I tried to pass discretely but were spotted.

"And just where did you boys get all those educational toys?" Margo came to the door.

"They fell off a truck," Wolo said.

"Now, we're all colleagues here, gentlemen. I don't want to find out you boys are hiding secrets from the rest of us."

"Don't worry, you won't find out," Wolo said. We kept going and dumped our supplies in our rooms. Wolo came back to mine.

"Damn, that bitch is fierce—cute, but fierce. She don't back down."

"I think she's here to revolutionize teaching," I said.

"Well, good luck to her." He laughed. "Man, some of those others looked spooked. I'm gonna go back there and help ease them in. You let me know if you need anything."

"Thanks! Take it easy, man."

Wolo left, and I got back to dusting.

Mr. Rodriguez came on the PA later that morning and announced a mandatory staff meeting that afternoon. When the time came, we all walked to the library. I sat with the History Department: Wolo, Santoro, Rotter, and Beverly Windsong. Mr. Rodriguez took the floor.

"Welcome back to George Washington Middle. We're all looking forward to a wonderful start of this new school year. As you all know, this is my third year here at GW, and I want to thank everyone for their support so far. George Washington has been an F school now for the past ten years, and it is my goal to bring us up to a C. I know the district, backed by 'Every Student Must Succeed,' has demanded all schools be an A by next year, but I think that may too big a jump for us to realistically make. I know we have some fine educators in our school and I believe achieving a C is a definite possibility. I'm asking for your cooperation and support."

I looked around the room. It was the same as the new teacher orientation: side conversations, people on cell phones, blank stares off into space . . . Occasionally someone would yell out, "That's not in my contract!" or some variation, and their buddies would chuckle. I wanted to at least give this thing a try.

"I've appointed Karen Dawson this year's F2ST supervisor . . ." he continued.

Ms. Dawson gave Mr. Rodriguez a wide-eyed look, as if this was the first she'd heard about the position. A few teachers shook their heads and started whispering to each other.

". . . If you have any questions about the F2ST or F2ST preparation, please go to her for answers."

"That poor girl," Santoro said.

"What?" I said.

"He's gonna chew her up just like he did to Mancini last year," Wolo said.

"What's that mean?" I said.

Wolo leaned in close to me. "When the state comes calling after the F2ST results are announced this year, it'll be awful easy for Rodriguez to just pass off the phone to his 'F2ST supervisor' to have her explain our inevitable failure."

"Shit," I said.

"That position means nothing other than impending doom." He glanced at Dawson. She was smiling. "And she doesn't even know."

"It's better that way," Santoro said.

I picked up Billy from Little Havana later that afternoon, and we went down to an Argentine restaurant around the corner from our junker apartment. Billy and I ordered a single steak. Our waitress was a gorgeous Brazilian with a smile like the sunshine. Soon, she brought our dinner.

"You should talk to her," he said.

"You know I have a girlfriend." I cut the steak and presented the halves to Billy. He chose the smaller piece.

"And tell me, when do you talk with this girlfriend?" Billy said.

"Usually the same times you're talking to Diego."

"Eh, whatever." He poked his piece of steak with a fork and pushed it around his plate. "You know, honestly, I think I prefer the ghetto. These bitches are serious in Little Havana. At least in the hood people knew this was a game, but somebody failed to tell these chicas. That school is overrun with Cubana trophy wives taking a break from watching their stories in their mansions each day to come down and play with the little kiditos." He cut the steak but put no pieces in his mouth.

"Well, whatever spirit there was at GW died a long time ago. Or maybe it was killed . . ."

"Oh god, and everybody—I'm talking, every-fucking-body—speaks fluent Spanish there. The school is like one hundred percent Cubano, aparte de mi and Christy. They speak it in the office, the lounge. I feel bad for Christy. I'm at least fluent. I don't even know why they hired her—she doesn't speak a lick. I mean, they won't even change to English to include her in the conversation. It's like a fucking little ninita's club—and I'm the fucking Spanish teacher!"

The waitress came by and smiled again. There was something about her warmth that made me recoil when I felt it.

"Hey, we should put in some work on our screenplay tonight. I really want to get into that thing," I said.

"Yeah, we really should."

On the walk home, we passed three homeless people nestled in the alcove of a dentist's office. One was an old Hispanic man named

Carlos and the other two were sun-reddened, middle-aged female twins. Billy offered them his completely uneaten half of the steak. They took it, but didn't offer any thanks. It was as if the transaction were somehow implied. Billy and I continued walking back to the apartment.

We both went to our rooms shortly after our return. I turned on my computer to do some work on my book but turned it off almost immediately afterward. I hit the sheets around nine but didn't fall asleep until sometime around four. I kept going through any possible scenarios the next day may bring, over and over, until my mind collapsed on itself and allowed me rest.

Chapter 5

I woke early the next morning, ate, and got ready. Just as I was about to leave, Billy came storming out of his room.

"Holy fucking shit! I overslept. How can I be so fucking stupid? I'm such a goddamned idiot!"

"Damn, I thought you left already."

"You gotta drive me. You gotta take me, please!"

"But then I'm gonna be late, too."

"Not as late as me."

"Take a cab."

"Please, just this once."

"Fuck it. Hurry up and get ready. We really gotta get moving."

On the drive to Little Havana, Billy told me why he overslept. "Oh my god, I could not fall asleep until like five in the morning. My head is fucking killing me."

I pulled up to Little Havana Elementary and dropped the idiot by the lot full of Beamers. He waved and raced into the school.

It was a half-hour trip to GW, but I floored it and got there in twenty, pulling into the parking lot just as the last buses were dumping their loads. They were everywhere, kids dressed in red or white shirts and khaki pants. But those uniforms did little to provide any structure. I opened the car door and was hit with the energy.

"Fuck you, you just a git" was the first distinctive phrase I heard among the cacophony of terrible sounds. They wrestled and threw fake punches and chased each other around like idiots.

I got out of my car, locked it, checked the handles of the front and rear doors, checked both again, and walked past the mass of adolescence for my cursed room. About twelve or thirteen students were huddled around the door when I got there. I heard one of the girls say, "He prolly ain't gonna show up. The kids here are terrible." To which a tall male responded, "Yeah, not as terrible as yo' breath." He started fanning his nose, and she punched him in the shoulder. The others got into it, "Ohhh, he rankin' on you!"

"Hey, let's take it easy there," I said.

They stopped and turned to me.

"You gotta be Mr. En—"

"—telechy. You all have a good summer?"

"Hell yeah," said the tall boy, "I set the all-time record for touchdowns at Manfield Park."

"That's only 'cause he smells so bad, nobody wanted to tackle him," said another boy.

"Yeah, well yo' sister doesn't think I smell so bad. She set an all-time record this summer too, I just ain't sayin' in what."

I opened the door, and they filtered inside.

"Okay, please find the card with your name on it and take a seat at that desk. We'll wait until everybody gets here then do a little get-to-know-you activity."

I set my leather satchel behind my desk where it couldn't be seen and started writing my name on the board. I could hear their comments:

"He looks alright."

"Alright? He looks cute, that's what he looks like."

I guess that was better than the first comment I'd ever heard from a student. On my first day of student teaching in Buffalo, the first moment I'd turned to write something on the board, I heard a girl in the back of the room say, "This guy is a fucking idiot."

Students kept coming in long after the late bell. There were thirty-two in total; they filled every seat. Despite my expectations, these kids weren't bad—a little rough around the edges, but so was I.

"My name is Mr. Entelechy. I'm from Buffalo—"

"Man, the Bills suck ass."

"Well, I guess I can't argue with you there, but, uh, I can, uh, disagree with your choice of language."

"Oh yeah, ma' bad."

I walked behind the protective cover of my podium and leaned on it.

"Anyway, I'm from Buffalo, and I've been teaching for roughly a year, but you are the very first class of my own." I felt somewhat sentimental in saying it. "I'm really looking forward to working with you all this year. You seem like a good group."

"You're right about that, mister," a girl said with a big smile.

"Yeah, we the best in the school. You gonna love us," said another.

"Uh, yeah . . . Well, I'll let you know right now that I can be pretty easy-going but that's only if we can respect each other. That's number one to me, respect."

I got a few smiles, so I walked from behind the podium and started moving through the aisles.

"My goal isn't to fill your heads with a bunch of stuffy facts but rather show you how to learn and think for yourselves." I picked up a textbook off of the tall boy's desk and flipped through it. "History can be confusing, and even downright disturbing, but if we can find the humanity somewhere inside of it—why these people did what they did—we can start to make some sense of it. Then it isn't so overwhelming anymore. I think the best way to do that is by relating it to your own lives. What would we have done? What would we do now? What *can* we do now? We've got Leonardo da Vinci's and Joan of Arc's and Harriet Tubman's in this classroom. I'm hoping that the study of history can help you to find more meaning in your own lives and ultimately help you to create a better world around you."

I kept going like that, giving classroom rules, and telling stories about my travels in Mexico, until eye lids started closing, a few heads started hitting desks, and a murmur spread throughout the room.

"Okay, why don't we hear something from you. We'll go around the room. Everyone should give their name, something they're passionate about, and one thing they want to learn this year. We'll start in the front with this gentleman here." I pointed at the tall kid.

"Well," he gave a shit-eating smile, "my name is Janjak Bouregard, but you can call me JJ." He turned and pointed at a pretty girl sitting nearby. "And you can call me 'daddy.'"

The kids got into it. "Ohh, damn! He rankin'."

"Shut up, Jan-Jack-Off," the pretty girl said. "Nobody likes yo' dumb ass."

"Hey, remember what I said about respect. Let's leave the cursing out of the classroom."

They both apologized.

JJ continued, "I love football. Canes, baby! They gonna top the ACC this year—you just watch."

Most of the boys started cheering and most the girls rolled their eyes. One of the boys said, "You know, his brother is Dante Bouregard."

"Who's that?" I said.

They laughed as if I'd asked who George Washington was.

"The leading rusher at the U of Miami last season. Don't you have a television?"

JJ stood up and took a bow.

"Sit ya' ass down," the pretty girl said.

I let that one slide, then said to JJ, "And what would you like to learn?"

"I don't know . . . maybe how to make that green, know what I'm sayin'?"

"Well, I hope you're talking about money and not something else," I said.

That went over most of their heads, but a guy in the back of the room liked that one. "Damn, this guy's alright."

I continued introductions with other students. Most just gave one or two word answers, but a few gave more. The guy in the back who said I was alright was one of these few.

"My name is Arman. I love football too, but my real passion is music. I'm like Lil' Wayne, baby, just writing day and night. I put down those alien lines. Man, I ain't from around here. I'm from another planet. Jus' don't know which one that is."

One of the boys in the front of the class turned around. "Man, you from planet crackin'-up, that's where you from."

Arman laughed. "Man, you wish you were like me, ya' broke, dumb ass."

"Hey, language, man," I said.

"Oh, sorry."

Another was the pretty girl JJ had gotten into it with.

"My name is Carmen Perez, and I'm from Puerto Rico."

"Love me that Boricua booty." Arman licked his lips and blew her a kiss.

I chuckled at that one—mostly because I loved me the same—but knew I had to play the teacher so I gave him a disapproving look.

Carmen continued, "My favorite thing to do is draw. See." She held up her binder, which had several pictures of anime characters. I was no judge of such artwork, but they looked damned good to me.

"You got some real talent there, Carmen," I said.

"Man, she a wannabe Chinese with all them dookie drawings," some boy said.

"Yeah, well I'd rather have dookie drawings than your dookie face," she said.

"Hey, what did I say about respect? Apologize, please."

They did. That get-to-know-you activity took the rest of our time. Soon the bell rang, and it was over. I didn't want it to be. Despite a few setbacks, those kids were pretty cool. But they were also an honors class, which meant they were just a hair of the GW student body. Soon, I was to meet its torso . . .

I put name cards on each of the desks again and stood at the door, greeting students and instructing them where to sit. I looked down the hall. Margo was really giving some boy hell. "How dare you say something like that to a lady!" The kid gave her the finger and ran away. She lunged, as if she might run after him, but stopped herself. I'd imagined she realized that chase would only bring defeat.

The crowds surged in the hall. Kids were everywhere, slapping each other, screaming, throwing shit around. A storming sea of activity. But there was one section that was tranquil.

A kid with tremendous size strolled through the rapids, which calmed and parted several feet before he met them, allowing him to pass unmolested. The kid said nothing and looked at no one. He just kept moving down the hall—but he slowed when he got to me. He looked me directly in the eyes, gave me a onceover, smiled, and said "I got you."

"I got you, too." I didn't hesitate—I didn't know what the fuck I was doing, but I didn't hesitate.

He kept going.

The bell rang, and I was again faced with thirty-plus students stuffed in that dungeon classroom.

"Hello, welcome to class. My name is Mr.—"

"Cracka'."

"Excuse me?" I didn't hear who said it, so I addressed the whole group. "Does somebody have something to say?"

"Look at him, actin' like any of us give a damn," said some snarling bitch.

"Now, uh, you don't have to use language like that—" I walked back behind the podium.

"Now, uh, now, uh . . ." said some boy from the back corner of the room.

"What's your name?" I said to the boy.

"Fuck Ya', that's my name."

"What'd you just say to me?"

"He said, 'Fuck You.'" The bitch rolled her eyes and settled her stupid ass into a comfortable position in her seat. "Man, this guy is dumb."

"Who do you think you are?" I walked to the side of the room where she sat but didn't venture into the aisle.

She snorted. "Who do I think *I* am? I know who *I* am. Somebody better tell this man who *I* am."

"Yeah, why don't they." I turned to the class.

"Oh, leave him alone, Chante, you always gotta act like such a bitch," some girl said. I didn't care if she swore—she was my hero, even if she was just using me to pick a fight.

"Excuse me, you better know who you're talkin' to, skank!" Chante slammed her fists on her desk.

"Girls, please—" With the heat off of me, I could again pretend as if I had some authority. Now I was just a responsible teacher trying to break up a fight between two students, rather than a broken man-child desperately trying to maintain what little dignity I'd been able to sneak through my own youth—a dignity that withered a bit more each passing moment I allowed this little girl to stand up for me. But maybe we'll drag this out just a little longer . . .

Okay, time to be a teacher again. "Girls!"

"Cracka'!"

"Hey—" I said, but turned my attention to Chante when she got out of her seat and towered over the other girl.

"Don't nobody be rankin' on me." Chante looked down on her.

"Cracka', Cracka', CRACK-UH!"

I got between Chante and my hero, who was also now standing,

"Girls, stop! Do I have to call security?"

"Fuck this little skank bitch," Chante said, before sitting down again.

"Cracka'."

I now knew who was saying that: Frantz, the boy in the back of the room.

"Do you even know what that word means?" With the other crisis averted, I could focus entirely on this issue. I walked over to his desk.

"It means you a stupid cracka'-ass, cracka'," Frantz said.

"Yeah, well for anybody that doesn't know, this little punk is basically calling me the white version of the n-word, and I don't appreciate it." I walked over to Chante and pointed at a picture of Martin Luther King, Jr. on the wall. I know it was a fucking cliché, but I was against the wall myself, so I said it anyway. "You see that man up there? You know *his* name? Who is that?"

Chante crossed her arms and rolled her eyes, but a girl in the front answered.

"That's Martin Luther King, Jr."

"That's right. Do you know what he fought against?"

"White people," another boy said.

"He didn't fight 'White People,' he fought against racism—the very same racism you allow to continue each time you use a horrible word like 'Cracka'." I turned to Chante. "Now you're right, I don't know you. I don't know any of you. But none of you know me either. I'd like to know you, and I'd like to understand where you're all coming from, but that just can't happen until we learn to respect each other and listen to what we have to say to each other." Maybe I didn't need little girls to protect my dignity?

While nobody broke out into a slow clap, they at least ceased their attack. I felt tremendous success in hanging in there, but this was no way to live a life. We started the get-to-know-you activity but only got about a quarter of the way through it before the bell rang and the next class shuffled in. I again walked out of the classroom and saw one of the new teachers screaming at some kid in the hall. My new class came in, and it was almost as bad as the previous.

Lunch finally came. I shut the door and got into my turkey sandwich, but someone soon knocked. It was Wolo.

"Congratulations, you've already made it further than some people." He walked in and sat at a desk in the front row.

"What do you mean?" I returned to my desk and got back into my sandwich.

"I mean, one of the new teachers didn't make it through first period, and Ms. Windsong called an early retirement. She just walked down to the office, turned in her keys, and said she was too old for this." He pulled out a glass food storage container and dug a fork into some beans and rice.

"Christ! These kids are horrible."

"Well I hope you enjoy this week. The first few days are usually the easiest. The kids come back and they're adjusting to new friends and teachers and schedules, so they aren't as likely to fight back." He shoveled another fork load in his mouth.

"Well, I'd hate to see what it's like next week, because it's already been war today." I took a long look at my sandwich and decided to wrap it up and stuff it back in my bag.

"You can't argue with these kids. They're pros at roping people in. They're going to test you in every way possible, and you just gotta show them you won't take their shit."

"People keep saying that, but I'm not sure I know what it means—to not take their shit."

"You'll figure it out." He took another bite. "You gotta try this. My wife's such an amazing cook—all vegan. Good shit."

Lunch soon ended, and the second half of the day resumed. There were three more periods after lunch, but I only had to teach two. Fourth was my free period, and I spent it sitting in my chair and staring at the wall. Fifth and sixth were pretty much the same as the second, and soon the day was over. My voice was shot, and I barely had enough energy to walk to my car, which I was happy to see still was still there when I exited the school.

I walked toward the parking lot, struggling through the crowds of kids who were fighting and screaming and running around out front. It was the job of the school security staff to maintain order, but they were nowhere to be seen, except for the head security guard, Ms. Robespierre, who was great. Though in her late fifties, Ms. Robespierre had the strength and vitality to keep up with the quickest and toughest of these kids—and if it came to blows, I'd probably take her over any of them. She was tough as shit, but also one of the kindest people I'd met at GW, and she and Ms. Dawson did the work of ten people. They spread themselves out, broke up fights, ushered students onto their buses, made sure kids got into the correct cars . . . In my trip to the parking lot, I saw Dawson pull at least two or three girls out of cars full of adult gentlemen, while saying things like, "She's thirteen! How old are you?"

When I finally got to my car, I was just about to unlock the door when I saw one of my male students rip the weave off a little girl's head. She started crying, and he ran away. I walked over and shouted his name. "Curtis! Curtis, get back here!"

Curtis kept running, but the big kid—the one the other kids parted for in the halls earlier that afternoon—filled in for him.

"Who you talkin' to?" He was with a group of four or five other large males; they slowly started approaching me. "My name ain't Curtis, it's Percy, bitch."

"Well I wasn't talking to you, Percy." My body sent mixed signals; my blood warmed as my extremities turned to ice.

They got closer. The other students had gone silent. They began grabbing those who weren't looking, tugging on their sleeves and saying things like, "Yo', it's goin' down!" Dawson and Robespierre were on the far side of the lawn. No other teachers in sight . . .

"Who you callin' Curtis when my name is Percy?"

"I wasn't talking to you, Percy, I was talking to the punk who ripped that poor girl's hair off. Did you rip that girl's hair off? 'Cause I didn't see you do it."

Percy walked within an arm's reach of me. The kid had me by three inches and at least twenty pounds. He stared down into my eyes. I didn't blink.

"It's Percy," he said.

"Yeah, Percy, fine."

He held the gaze just long enough to be sure I knew he was granting me reprieve and not suffering a breakdown in resolve, then strolled away with his crew the same as they'd come—all five with red bandanas hanging out of their back pockets. I stood my ground just long enough afterward to prove to all those students watching that my clothes showed no signs of dampness.

I walked back to my car, unlocked it, got in, backed out, and headed for the exit. Margo had driven off a few seconds before I had. I followed behind her but stopped when I saw the masses swarm on her. The kids ran in front of her car. She slammed on the brakes and one of her students, K'deysha Jackson, jumped on her hood. Margo revved her engine and jerked the car forward, but stopped. She stuck her head out the window.

"GET THE FUCK OFF MY CAR!"

The kids blocking her way ran—but K'deysha stayed. Margo revved again; K'deysha steadied herself. She stood up and spread out her legs for balance, as if she were surfing. Margo took off, and K'deysha went with her. She made it for a half a block before Margo slammed on the brakes and shot out of the car. K'deysha jumped off the hood and took off down the street with Ms. Liberty trailing behind. In her haste for justice, Margo had left the door open and the car running. Some kid hopped inside and took it down the street, but stalled out as he rounded the corner. Margo came running over and the kid shot out of the car and took off. This time Margo protected her possessions before her pride. She started up the car again and drove off, cursing out the GW "DELINQUENTS!"

I waited for a moment after Margo was out of sight before I tried for my exit. The kids swarmed my car too, but none hopped on. I could hear their comments as I passed.

"There go Tom Brady."

"Fuck that white man."

I rolled down my window and stuck out my favorite finger, and left it out there to dry until long after GW had disappeared from my rearview. A hundred and eighty more fucking days of this . . .

I drove south to Little Havana to pick up Billy. He was waiting for me at the edge of the road when I pulled up.

"Fuck," he said, before even getting fully into the car, "take me back to the ghetto."

He got in, and I drove off. "I'm sure your day couldn't have been any worse than mine."

"These bitches are already on me, combing through my lesson plans and observing my classes," he said. "My principal said I was going to have to work on keeping my lines straighter when walking the kids down to lunch. Can you believe that shit?"

"Yeah, well the kids at GW did their best to run me out of town today, but I held on."

"Uh huh . . . oh and Ms. Perez, that salacious old cooze who hired me, I swear she wants my nuts. She called me into her office today and just kept winking at me and smiling. I know, I just know, she's gonna find out I'm gay, then she's gonna can me. I know why I got this job, and if I don't perform, I'm toast. I mean, why else in a school full of Cubans would they give one of the only Spanish teaching jobs to a white guy? Just send me back to the ghetto."

"Well, I'd be happy to switch positions."

"You know, Little Ricardo Bunuel corrected me today when I conjugated the past tense of 'saber' wrong. They're gonna run me outta there, man. Send me back to the ghetto, please."

Chapter 6

The rest of the week was pretty much the same. School was horrible, and Billy and I did nothing but bitch about it. Billy's car was ready that Friday, so I drove him to the dealership after school, and we took our separate cars back home. Margo called me around five and invited me to a restaurant/bar near her house, called Manolo's, for some drinks. The place was, as she called it, "The most authentic Cuban bar you'll find in the city." I asked Billy if he was interested, but he just said, "I already told you, you wouldn't be getting me to any straight bars. Besides, I look disgusting. I've been eating like a pig, and my hair's a mess. I just can't be seen like this." I called Abbi, and she was in.

I took a bus south, got off near 40th Street, found Manolo's, and walked in. The place was a dive; it stunk of rum and rotting wood, and despite its "authenticity," was filled with dopey, white tourists. There was a group of five teachers scattered at the bar, dancing and celebrating an end to the week. Abbi came in shortly after Margo introduced me to the rest of the group. They were all teachers at various schools who'd met through the Educate America program, and they were already hammered.

"Of course there were some challenges here and there, but I handled it well. Show no fear, that's what I always say, darling." Margo finished her speech then took a shot of tequila with two of her friends.

"What about that kid I saw in the hall giving you the finger?" I asked her before she finished her shot.

"Oh, that was nothing," she said after sucking on a lime. "We were just playing around. The kids really love me, I can just tell."

Margo offered me a shot, but I refused.

"C'mon, darling, don't be a child," she said. "I should hope you don't think you're above us."

"Naw, I'm just not feeling it." I walked to the bar and ordered a water. I wandered into a conversation Abbi was having with a bearded male.

"I'm telling you," he said to her, "I finally got 'em today. For the first four days straight they wouldn't even let me get a word in, but today I finally found a way to relate it to them. Most of my kids want to be rappers, so I told them, 'Do you think Jay-Z has a poor vocabulary? Do you know how smart Tupac was? If you want to rap, English is the most important subject you're gonna take. If you wanna be the best, you're gonna have to know as many words as you can.'"

"Yeah, well I haven't had that 'breakthrough' moment yet with my kids. They fucking hate me," Abbi said.

"Just hang in there, it'll come. I mean, look at me!" He started dancing around like an idiot.

I couldn't take any more of those conversations. I finished my water and decided to call it an early night. I skipped the bus and walked back along the shore. Even at night, the city was sweltering. I welcomed the A/C when I opened my apartment door. I could hear Billy in his room talking to someone on the phone. "Yes, so I'm sorry. I made a mistake in coming here, but what would you like me to do about it?"

I walked into my room, shut the door, and turned up the A/C. I fell asleep quickly that night.

When I exited my room the next morning, Billy was in the living room lying on our recently purchased futon.

"Morning," I said.

"Oh my god, I did *not* even sleep last night. Not at all."

"Not me, man. I was a log."

He ran his hands through his hair. "Do you see this? My hair is literally falling out."

"Anybody's hair would fall out if they pulled on it like that. Just leave it alone." I walked to the kitchen for some cereal, opened the cupboard, and saw the box was covered in new hairs.

"Hey, you weren't shaking your head in the kitchen this morning, were you?" I wiped off the box, poured a bowl of cereal, and walked back to the living room.

"No, why?"

"There're hairs everywhere."

"Uh, I think there's something living in the wall. I could hear noises all night last night. Maybe we have rats?"

"Sounds about right."

"Yeah, well I'll call Greg at Tropical Rentals on Monday and see if he can take care of it." He walked to the kitchen, grabbed a banana and peeled it, but didn't take a bite. "Oh my god, you know I forgot to even call the NYPSD to quit my job in New York? They called me yesterday asking why I missed the first day of classes." He started laughing.

"And you wonder why the Savior gave you an unsatisfactory rating."

"Oh, fuck you, you don't even know what you're talking about." He took one bite from the banana and threw it out. "I miss my friend Julian. There's no way he'd let me eat as much as I have been. He'd just slap the food out of my hand and say, 'What are you doing, you fat pig! Put that down.'"

"You know they got a name for that, right?"

"Awesomeness?"

"No, but it does start with an A."

I looked out the window and saw a small crowd of people huddled around something at the end of our block.

"What's that?" Billy walked to the window.

"I don't know. Let's go check it out."

We walked outside and up the block. As we got closer, we saw what everyone was looking at. There, smashed up so hard that it was now on the sidewalk, was Billy's brand new Ford Escort.

"Holy shit! My car . . ." He pushed by a few people and assessed the damage. "Oh my god, oh my god!"

The whole rear had been destroyed—back wheel raised off the ground, bumper lying on the street, trunk wide open. It was a total loss. Billy called the cops, and they told him some drunk asshole had smashed into three other cars just up the road that night—only Billy's car got it the worst.

On top of his lawsuit in New York, now Billy had to go through all the paperwork to deal with this. The cops arrested the drunk driver, but he was an illegal immigrant with no insurance, so Billy had to eat the costs. I took him out to dinner that night to take his mind off it.

"Of course . . . of course *my* car was destroyed worse than all the others." He sucked down a hearty gulp of Dominican beer.

"Hey, at least you didn't have enough time to get attached to it."

Billy started laughing, and I joined in.

"Fuck, only *I* could have my car totaled within twenty-four hours of buying it." He started cracking up with deep, gut-heaving convulsions.

"How many miles did you have on it?" I sipped my water.

"Twelve." More laughter. "Just call me 'Total-Loss Lalina.'"

On Monday, two new teachers filled in for those who'd made a run for it the previous week. One was an English teacher, a Haitian immigrant named Mr. Marcel. Marcel was all smiles and eager to get started. He moved into the classroom next to Wolo's, just down from mine and across from Margo's. The other teacher moved into the classroom right next to mine at the end of the hall. Her name was Norma Jean Carver, and she was no rookie. In fact, Ms. Carver had already put in twenty-five years at Ulysses S. Grant Middle, a school that might have been the only in Miami that could rival GW in poor academic performance and delinquent student behavior. She said that she hoped GW would be an improvement. I guess we all needed hope . . .

Norma Jean was a sweet woman, born and raised in Liberty City. She now resided a few blocks from GW and had been trying to transfer there for years. And with Ms. Windsong making a run for it that previous Wednesday afternoon, Ms. Carver now had her chance.

Ms. Carver was put in the History Department with Wolo, Santoro, Rotter, and me. We met in Santoro's room before school every Monday, and that Monday was no different. We were sitting in student desks and eating our breakfast when she walked in.

"Five more years, just five more 'til I retire, thank the heavens!" she said, shortly after introducing herself.

"Welcome onboard, Ms. Carver," Santoro said.

Frank Lumet, the computer tech guy, popped in.

"Oh, Norma Jean, I've been trying to track you down," Frank said. "We hooked up all the computers in the History Department to print to your classroom. Ms. Windsong was good about regulating the amount of ink people were using. I think we're going to switch that responsibility to Mr. Santoro, because he's been here the longest."

"No, don't worry about that, Frank." Santoro stood up, walked over to Frank, and put his hand on his shoulder. "We'll keep it hooked up in Norma Jean's room."

"You sure?" He took a look at Ms. Carver and leaned in toward Santoro's ear. "It's a big responsibility."

"Sure, Norma Jean's part of the team."

"Suit yourselves." He took off.

Frank Lumet had been the proud owner of a computer shop in Jacksonville, and had a wife and kids and house and the whole spread. But one day, a group of about a dozen or so punks ran into the shop, raided as much as shit as they could, and took off in a flash. They wore masks and gloves, and Frank couldn't identify a single one. Frank counted his losses and rebuilt his inventory, but soon it happened again. After that, he made sure he was ready for the bastards. When they came back a third time, Frank grabbed a baseball bat from behind the counter, picked out one of the kids at random, and beat the shit out of his knees. The cops found a switchblade on the now-handicapped kid, and he was the wrong color, so they called it self-defense. But the community wasn't so quick to let it go. Soon, Frank started getting death threats. He decided to move the family down to Miami and took a job as GWs computer tech guy. Frank was a middle-aged, short, lumpy, balding, discount-department-store-clothes-wearing bastard. Even though he was an awkward and nonathletic fuck, he had some strength to him. He looked like a guy who'd been pushed around his whole life but never went down without a fight—who knew how to absorb a beating so he could tire out his opponent and administer a far more severe beating of his own. I liked most people, but something about Frank irritated me from day one.

"God, that guy can be a prick." Santoro sat down again.

"Yeah, he simply refuses to change my A/C filters—" Rotter said.

"Will you stop with the damned A/C filters?" Wolo folded his hands together and shook them at her.

"I'm sorry to cause a stir here. Y'all can print whatever you'd like and come get it whenever," Ms. Carver said. "Well, I think I'm gonna take my coffee in my classroom. It was nice meeting y'all."

"No, no, please sit, Norma Jean, you're part of our team." Santoro pulled out a seat for her.

"No, it's fine. I have lots to do." She smiled and took off.

Frank walked by the classroom and Rotter went running after him, shouting something about her filters.

The bell rang, and soon I was in front of my first period class. I'd been making good use of the overhead projector I'd swiped from the annex and started each class with a bellwork activity I'd written on a transparency. After that, I'd usually give a ten- to fifteen-minute lecture on whatever chapter and unit we were currently studying. We just so happened to be on the conquest of the Americas by the Spanish, and I'd placed a specific emphasis on Mexico.

"And soon after discovering silver in the hills of Guanajuato, the Spanish built a beautiful town, with colonial architecture—"

"Man, enough of this Spanish crap." JJ dropped his head on his desk and covered it with his arms. "I'm tired hearing about Mexico and how great it is."

"Yes, this is a *US* History class, isn't it mister?" Arman said.

"Yes, it is US History," I said, "but we're discussing the Age of Exploration. The American colonies won't exist for about another century."

"Man, we about a century from anything interesting."

"Well, what would you like to learn about then?" I walked to the front row of desks.

"How to make beats like Lil' Wayne's," Arman said.

"Man, I wanna learn how to throw down like Kimbo Slice," JJ said.

"Yo, he garbage. Georges St. Pierre would knock his ass out," a guy from the back said.

"They're in two totally different weight classes," I said, "with two totally different styles of fighting. You can't compare them."

"Hey, can you boys please stop talking about fighting?" Carmen rolled her eyes.

"Oh, yeah, sorry . . ." I said. The bell rang and the kids shuffled out the door. "Please remember to answer questions one through five on page forty for homework tonight!" I walked into the hall and saw Wolo speaking with a small group of kids outside of his door. I assumed he was telling a joke because they were all watching him eagerly then suddenly erupted with laughter when he said what looked to have been a punch line.

My second period class shuffled in. I put up the same transparency for bellwork but only a few students sat and did it. Frantz came running into the classroom, screaming in a high-pitched tone.

"Frantz, do I need to call security?" I said.

"He tried to kiss me! That faggot over there be tryin' to put his nasty lips all over me." He pointed at a kid in the hall who looked ready to beat some ass.

"I wouldn't be pointing at him like that if I were you," I said to Frantz.

The kid in the hall walked to my door and said, to no one in particular, "You tell that little bitch I'll see him after school."

Frantz walked over to Chante and sat in her lap. He curled around her, and she held him as a mother would a small child.

"Come on, Frantz, you know you gotta stop playin' around with those guys. They finna kill you," Chante said.

"But he tried to kiss me!"

"You an' I both know if he tried to kiss you, you'd stick ya' tongue right down his throat," Chante said.

Frantz smiled. "Yeah, I know. He *is* cute, isn't he?"

I walked over to Chante's desk. "Frantz, will you please get off her lap and get to work?"

"What, you got a problem with gays? You got a problem with my sweet, sexy little ass?" He got up and tried to rub it on me.

"Goddamn, man, will you please just sit down!" I backed away from him.

The class got into that one. "OHHH, you said a swear word! You always tell us not to swear!"

Frantz continued to try and rub his ass on me, and I continued moving backwards, almost reaching the front wall.

"Frantz, I swear I'm gonna call security!"

He finally stopped just as I ran out of space to back into, danced in place for a few seconds, and returned to his seat. I started into my lecture but hardly got ten seconds in before Chante was hitting herself in the head with the palm of her hand.

"Chante, please stop that," I said. "History's not *that* boring."

She and the rest of the class started laughing.

"Do you even know what she's doin'?" some girl said.

I shook my head, and they giggled.

I tried to start up the lecture again, but the room was nearly always filled with conversation. I spent most of my time trying to stop their talking. The bell finally rang and not a goddamned thing was taught. The next period was roughly the same: students arguing, sleeping, threatening to kick each other's asses, starting shit with me . . . But at least nobody was calling me a cracker anymore. At least nobody was swearing directly at me—in my presence, yes, but not at me. I went to Wolo's for lunch.

"Goddamn, man," I sat in a student desk, "these kids are impossible to teach. They never shut the fuck up."

"Hey, look on the bright side. At least they haven't ridden you out of here like they have with some other people. That must mean they like you." Wolo lit a stick of incense and opened a window in the back. "God, do you smell that? This whole place stinks."

"Yeah . . . hey how do you do it? I hear the kids saying what a great teacher you are. I see how they flock to you."

"No big secret, really. Just gotta be yourself. I've been doing this for five years now, so I've learned a few tricks. These kids aren't going to listen to you lecture or read from a book—they're not going to respond to someone giving them orders. You need to find ways to relate to them. Well over half these kids can barely read and write. Instead of spending your time fighting with them, you should just find what drives them and milk it. And if that doesn't work out, you just need to separate the ones who will learn from those that won't. There will always be those who won't stop talking. You could pay 'em a hundred bucks to shut the fuck up, but even that only works for a short time. Just group those kids together and stick 'em in the back of the room. I don't even pay attention to them. I just focus on teaching those who want to learn."

"Yeah, well even my honors classes don't seem interested in much, other than fighting and football."

"You'd be surprised, man. Just listen to what they tell you and use that as a way in. Most of them do want to learn, despite what you, and everyone else, might think. Some of the other teachers have just given up on them. They pass out worksheets or have them work out of the book for fifty minutes. But if you can get their attention, you can get something out of them." Wolo lit a second stick of incense. "God, this place is terrible. I can't take it. C'mon."

I followed him past Ms. Carver's classroom and out the side door. We sat on a bench just under an awning.

Wolo took a deep breath. "Ahh . . . you know, if you close your eyes, the expressway sounds just like the ocean."

I closed them. He was right.

"When times get real bad, and they will, you just gotta do one thing. Think of your paycheck. That's what always gets me through." Wolo took a bite from his banana.

Ben Fallon, one of the other new teachers, walked outside. Wolo and I said hello to him, but he just kept walking. He crossed the street, pulled out a cigarette, and lit up.

"Has that guy even spoken to you?" Wolo said.

"Nope."

"Me neither. I guess everybody's got their own way of dealin' with the shit."

Wolo finished the banana and tossed the peel next to a small bush that was surrounded by several larger bushes.

"That's my buddy, there. He's just a runt, so I try to feed him whenever I can."

A bus pulled up, and a teacher named Jean Toussaint helped the driver wheel off the dozen students in wheelchairs inside. They did this every day around this time.

Mr. Toussaint smiled and waved at us as he pushed a student toward the school. The man was always smiling and saying hello. Wonderful guy. Those kids were lucky to have him. The kid he was pushing reached out his hand, and Mr. Toussaint shook it.

"You know," Wolo said to me, "in ten years, none of these kids are gonna remember what you taught them, all they're gonna remember is how you made them feel."

The kid started smiling as widely as Mr. T.

"Hey, life could always be a lot worse, right?" Wolo said.

Chapter 7

A few weeks passed and it was just more of the same, tension at work and at home. Billy's insomnia was getting pretty bad. According to him, he hadn't slept more than a few hours total since moving to Miami. I, however, was having the opposite problem, falling asleep nearly every moment I had away from the classroom.

Billy had been taking the bus to Little Havana every day and it was starting to wear on him, so he took a flight up to Buffalo at the start of a long weekend, literally got down on his knees and begged his parents to release his Honda—which they did, under certain conditions: "You need to call at least three times a week, send your grandmother a card on her birthday, and for godsakes, do something about that hair . . ." He drove it down before classes started on Monday.

I had a few different routes to GW, but after about two weeks, I finally settled on one, which took me along the eastern edge of Liberty City. I enjoyed the ride, but the drivers in Miami were some of the worst I'd ever seen. The I-95 was a goddamned free-for-all. It was common to be cut off or passed even while doing ninety; nobody signaled, and the second it rained, some idiot always spun out and slammed into a wall or another car. Everyone in every town everywhere always bitches about their drivers, but Miami really is the worst, hands down—at least, in this country.

But the highway was a day at the beach compared to what awaited me in Opa Locka. I'd taken Wolo's advice to cut out the lectures, and I started doing lots of projects and group work instead. This cut down on some of the discipline issues, but nothing would ever get rid of them all. In fact, one group got considerably worse about a month into the school year. I'd somehow gotten on the bad side of a clique of about eight of the queen bee, pretty girls in my once-favorite first period class. Anytime I told one to stop talking, the others would jump to her aid. If I asked one to sit, three more would stand. If I reprimanded one for telling me to "get outta my face," the rest would jump in. "You tell him who's who, Destiny!" I'd rather have Percy and his red bandana crew step to me every day than have to deal with those bitches even once a week. Few things are worse for a teacher than having to deal with a cluster of sad, angry, insecure little girls who've banded together for the sole purpose of making ol' Teach the target of their considerable, and likely justifiable, angst. This was psychological warfare, and I wasn't going down without a fight. I called them the Asshole Eight, and they'd terrorize me the rest of the year.

Sometime in early October, I'd broken my first period class into groups to work on a Revolutionary War project. No matter how I grouped them, at least two of the Assholes would always be together.

"Destiny . . . excuse me, Destiny." I walked over to her. "Can you please stop talking and get to work?"

"Ahem, she don't gotta listen to you, mister," said the other Asshole in her group.

"Yeah, she doin' her work, why don't you jus' leave her alone?" said another from across the room.

"Why don't you just worry about yourself, Tatiana?" I said. "I'm not talking to you."

"Eww, why you gotta be so rude, mister?"

"I have a name, you know!" I said. "We're at least a month into the school year. It's not that hard to pronounce."

The bell rang, saving me from throwing a desk against a wall.

I went to Wolo's classroom for lunch.

"Yo, I'm gonna fuckin' kill somebody," I said.

Wolo lit a stick of incense and took a deep breath. "Calm down, man, you can't let these kids get to you."

"They're ganging up on me, man. This is the absolute worst!"

"Just do your best to ignore it. But if it gets real bad, I can let you in on me and Santoro's exchange program. If a kid is acting up, just send them to one of our classrooms. We'll keep 'em for the rest of the period. When a kid is being an asshole, the best thing to do is just get rid of 'em."

"Yeah, well what if you've gotta get rid of eight of 'em?"

"Well, there're other tricks, too. You can call their parents. Once while I was teaching, a kid wouldn't shut the fuck up, so I called his mother during class. The kid was so loud the mom couldn't hear me, so she asks, 'Who is that yelling?' and I answered, 'Well, that's your son. Would you like to talk to him?' I gave the phone over, and his mother chewed his ass out. He was good for about two weeks after that, but started up again. Some of these kids are just animals. You just gotta get rid of 'em sometimes."

"Yeah, I guess."

He reached into his lunch bag and pulled out a note from his wife that was shaped like a bean. "Beans, beans, the magical fruit, the more you eat, the more I love you." Wolo smiled and put the note back in the bag. "Man, Amanda is the greatest. I love that girl so much, but her fuckin' parents are visiting this week from Alabama."

"You're from there, right?"

"Yeah, we're from Montgomery. She's incredible, but her family is just straight white trash. Her dad will not stop talkin' 'nigger' this and 'nigger' that. That's part of why we moved down here. My family's the same, man. Got some ties to the Klan. I just wanna get away from all that, live as peacefully as I can." He took another deep breath. "Man, this school stinks ta' shit. These kids can navigate a fucking inner tube here from Haiti, but not a single one can figure out how to use deodorant." He got up and motioned for me to follow.

We walked down the hall to the side door and passed Ms. Carver on the way. Though lunch had started ten minutes earlier, she was still grilling the shit out of her kids to make a line "straighter than an arrow, or you ain't gonna git no lunch."

"C'mon, miss, it's pizza bagel day!"

Wolo continued his speech as we walked outside and sat on the bench. "That's the kind of shit we need to be teaching in schools like this. Life skills. How to survive in this world. Hell, why are we teaching kids who can't speak English about George Washington? They need intensive round-the-clock reading and writing, and on topics that interest them. They'd benefit most from learning a trade. Auto mechanics, plumbing, electrical. Those are good jobs right there."

Wolo finished up his apple and threw the core under the small bush. Ben Fallon walked by us, crossed the road, and lit up a cig just as Mr. Toussaint was wheeling his kids off the bus. A guy with a tie-dyed Grateful Dead T-shirt and a ponytail helped Mr. T with the kids. Once they were all inside, the guy came back out and started up a conversation with Wolo.

"So what's the good word, Professor K?" Wolo asked him.

"Just doin' my thang, man," he said. "Hey, I don't mean to ruin your lunch, but I gotta tell you what happened with Ms. Baxter in the library today."

"Oh, that bitch is the worst!" Wolo said.

"Yeah, so two weeks ago I signed out the computers in the library for third period today. But when I bring my class down there, the doors are locked. I walked around to the side and had Chad Jamison lift me up on his shoulders so I could peer in her office window, and there she was, playing Yahtzee or bridge, or whatever the hell, with the secretary, Whitney Laurel, and her library assistant, Rhonda. So I started slamming on the window, and she pretended not to see me. Just walked over and shut the blinds."

"That fucking cow," Wolo said.

"Who's Ms. Baxter?" I said.

"She's the worst librarian in the Miami Public Schools system," Wolo said. "She's two years from retirement and does not give a single fuck about anything."

"Except rigidly enforcing the school's no-gum policy," the Professor said.

Wolo started cracking up. "Oh man, two kids could literally be beating each other to death with bricks, but she'd walk right by them to stop a kid who was chewing gum."

"Mmmhmm," the Professor said, "I know you ain't chewin' gum in *my* library. Spit that out, now!"

"You know," I said, "the first time I went to the library, there was this crazy woman chasing a kid around a bookshelf with a garbage can in her hand, yelling for him to spit out his gum."

"Welcome to GW. You're Luke, right?" the Professor said.

"Yes, sir."

"Ahh, I've heard some good things about you. These kids talk, and it seems they've really taken a liking to you."

"Well, you obviously haven't met the terrible bitches from my first period. I swear, those girls want nothing other than to saw off my head and parade it around school on a spike."

"You know," the Professor said, "with kids like that, you just gotta fall back into the Great River, my friend. Let the spirits guide you to the correct answer. Never fails."

Just then, Percy stormed out of the side door, stomped over to one of the annexes, and kicked the sheet-metal wall.

"Hey—" I got up, but the Professor put out his hand. "The River is flowing."

He walked over and said, "Hey, why don't you pick on someone your own size—like the Empire State Building?" Despite Percy's brilliant rage, the kid let out a smile. The Professor reached out and shook his hand, and almost immediately the situation was neutralized.

"If you wanna know how to control these kids," Wolo said to me, "look no further than the Professor. That man's a fuckin' genius, and he's funnier than hell."

"What'd he mean with all that 'Great Spirit' shit?" I said.

"That man's big time into Buddhism. He uses a lot of meditation techniques to deal with these kids, and of all the white people in the school, he's got the best control of his classes. We're at a disadvantage here. Who do you think's raising these kids? It certainly ain't daddy, and it certainly ain't a white mommy. The sistas got a distinct advantage over any male, especially a white male, when it comes to discipline. But the Professor's almost at that level."

"Why you call him the Professor?"

"He moonlights teaching a philosophy class at South Miami Community College. The dude's a fucking genius. Ask him anything and he'll know the answer."

Just then, Percy and the Professor dipped back inside the school, arms over each other's shoulders like a coupla' good ol' buddies. I heard some of what he told Percy. "I know you get mad sometimes, but you gotta learn where it's coming from if you want to control it. You're a good kid. I don't want to see you become a statistic like so many of the other idiots around here . . ." The door shut behind them, and that was the last of the conversation I heard.

Since the start of the school year, I'd been cutting down on my drinking and smoking, but it wasn't until about the end of September and early October that I'd taken an almost militant stance against both—at least, on weekdays. I'd been smoking weed on a fairly consistent basis for years but quit it almost entirely at this time. I'm not sure exactly what aspect of that lifestyle I wished to cut out, but I think it mostly had to do with the places my mind wandered to while high. I had a love/hate relationship with my thoughts, and weed only intensified whatever mood I was feeling. But school interrupted these elongated trails of thought, which, before signing my contract, I could ride out for days, taking me to places both good and evil, both soothing and terrifying. And the fact that I couldn't indulge in these extremes constipated my creativity. But it also brought me some strange new comfort.

While I continued my drinking on the weekends, I completely cut out any consumption on the weekdays. I wouldn't even have a glass of wine with dinner or go out for a beer with friends after work. And while I was able to find the willpower to do this almost immediately, these unsatisfied compulsions started manifesting themselves in other areas of my life. I'd also stopped writing, taking an almost fervent stance against it. It was as if I'd begin one sentence, I'd somehow slide right off the face of the earth. It wasn't that I didn't have words to say. It wasn't that I was without desire. It was that I just couldn't risk it—and the words were building up inside of me, magma, pressure, steam . . . This went for songwriting, and poetry, and ornate correspondence with friends as well. I'd even gone so far as to cut out listening to music. Those tunes could take me far away and I needed to be right here, ready to show up to school the next morning. The only musical style I allowed myself to enjoy was salsa, and, I believe, that was not only because I couldn't understand a fucking word, despite my abilities with Spanish, but also because I had no history with such a style. It was as fresh and new as this teaching job. Billy and I hadn't written a single word on our screenplay, which was a large reason why we'd moved in together in the first place, other than ass-brained competition. We'd saved our work on a disk that, for some idiotic reason, I'd actually allowed Billy to care for. Well, that disk was in the box that never showed up in Paradise, courtesy of the negligence of the US Postal Service. I wanted to chew Billy out, but I didn't. The kid's hair really was falling out, and he was putting on weight and spoke incessantly about what a mistake it was to leave New York.

I'd been doing research on a trip to Key West since moving to Miami, and after discovering a ten-day annual Halloween festival called "Fantasy Fest," I figured that'd be the best time to go. Billy was in. I drove to Little Havana on the Friday of the start of the festival to get him from work. I parked on a side street and strolled into his classroom, an annex in back. Billy was frantically switching the configuration of desks in the room. He didn't see me come in.

"Hey, Billy . . . Billy!" I said.

"Oh, hey . . . oh my god, you wouldn't believe it. Ms. Perez, my AP, came in to observe my class today, and oh man, she was *not* happy. Little Edwardo Colon threw a crayon at Emilia Diaz, and all the kids started cheering for her to hit him. I tried to calm them down, but they wouldn't shut the fuck up."

"What'd Ms. Perez say?"

"She didn't say anything. But I could just tell she's judging me with her eyes. I'm telling you, man, if I don't hand over the sausage, she's gonna toss me out the door." He moved another chair. "I gotta keep these little kiddos as far away from each other as I can. Fuck, sometimes I think these kids are just as bad as the little demons terrorizing Queens."

"I'm sure you're not going to get fired over that. These APs know how bad the kids are."

"Puh-leeze, I've seen people get fired for so much less in NYC. It's all a big scam. These admins terrorize one or two horrible years of your life before finding some random reason to can you. It's a hell of a lot cheaper to pay thousands of rookie teachers with zero years on the pay scale than it is thousands of old hens with twenty plus, and don't kid yourself otherwise. Christ, I mean they axed Valerie Stevenson, seriously, because she didn't replace her Word Wall one week. These APs and principals get on these power trips, man, you just don't know."

"I dunno. Ms. Dawson seems alright . . ."

"Pfff, don't say I didn't warn you."

I helped Billy rearrange his room. We spread the desks as far apart as space would allow then walked to the car.

"Oh my god," he said, "I totally forgot to bring my bag with me."

"What the fuck, man? Going home and back is gonna delay us at least an hour. Traffic's supposed to be bad for this festival."

"Eh, whatever. I'll just buy a toothbrush and some extra underwear when we get there."

We started driving around six. The day was still sunny and beautiful. Something about getting back on those highways made me feel at ease. We cruised south through housing developments and past the High-Rise City whose skyline was littered with construction towers, and kept going until we reached the edge of the mainland and started on those gorgeous bridges. For anyone unfamiliar with this ride, I implore you to take it sometime. It will help you shake off the filth of whatever job currently dragging you across the ground. The countryside was gorgeous. The trip was peaceful until we hit traffic around Marathon. Cars weren't moving, so we stopped at a bar next to a row of mangrove trees, and had a few drinks. Some guy in a Hawaiian shirt was playing Jimmy Buffet tunes on his acoustic. Soon, cars started moving again, so we hopped back in mine and kept pushing until we hit the final inhabited island in the archipelago.

It was dark and the sky pouring rain when we'd arrived. We pulled into the Seaweed Motel—aka the cheapest we could find—unloaded our stuff, and wandered into the soaking night. We wasted no time finding cheap drinks at a bar off of Duval Street, then hit the strip. We bounced in and out of bars, doing shots and pounding beers. The party was as wild as promised. There were people everywhere dressed in costumes and singing and dancing and slamming down drinks. At any time, I expected the masses to conduct some ritual sacrifice of a calf or a drunk, disoriented tourist, ripping them to pieces, and burning their limbs to ashes in the streets. This was hedonism if I'd ever seen it. But I just couldn't feel it.

We popped into Sloppy Joe's and got to work. We grabbed a couple of seats at the bar, despite the large crowd. Soon the pressure was building, so I headed for the men's room. On the way back, I stopped at an ATM. I barely punched in my code before a well-endowed woman wearing nothing but rain-streaked body paint pushed me up against the wall, leading with those gorgeous tits. She started rubbing them on my arm. I reached around and grabbed a big handful of ass, but nothing. I tried to imagine something—anything—but still no. I pushed past her, grabbed my cash from the machine and headed to the bar. I sat beside Billy, whose head was drooping, but each time it dropped just low enough, he forced it back up in some jerky defensive against time. At one point, it dipped so low he made contact with the bar. In an instant, he jumped out of his seat, slapped me playfully across the face, and said, "Yo, I told you I wasn't coming to anymore straight bars with you. I'm gonna go find some papis."

Billy wandered out into the night. I stayed. I bought another beer and looked up at a picture of Hemingway on the wall. He'd likely once sat in the very spot I was in. He'd often come here after fishing the tropical blue Gulf waters. But even if he came alone, he'd speak to people. He'd strike up conversations with bartenders or other bar patrons. He knew people—how to write people. But I could barely keep my head off of the bar. People came and went. The crowds surged. Women danced and sang and shook their exposed soft parts. I hardly noticed.

Soon, I staggered out into the street and wandered south down Duval. I looked for the rainbow flags and started popping inside places in search of Billy. I'd walked inside two or three before I found him sitting at a table in back of some dive beside a young Hispanic male. I started toward them, but stopped when Billy leaned in and gently kissed the man's cheek. It was so tender and sincere. Something changed in me. I'd known Billy while he was still "straight." We used to pick up girls together all the time. But he always jumped on the undesirable one without question. "A moustache? Eh, whatever . . ." I'd heard many stories of his exploits and sexual prowess in NYC, but it wasn't until then I'd seen him as such with another man. The way he touched him, the way he caressed his cheek. It was so soft and natural. Billy's face carried none of the tension I'd been so accustomed to seeing. I'd planned to pry him away and drag him to another bar with me, but I backed out of there, unannounced, and wandered into the street. I got swept up in a crowd of Bahamians who stuck what I thought to be a small cigar in my mouth.

"No, you need to inhale it, mon."

"You don't inhale a cigar," I said.

"That's not a cigar."

Fuck . . .

I woke up late the next morning and felt strangely refreshed. I stretched my arms and took a deep breath, then looked over and saw the door wide open. I looked at Billy's bed. Empty. I thought maybe he'd gone out for breakfast or something and forgot to close the door. Then I remembered I had the room's only key and left the door open for him the night before. My phone started vibrating. I checked it— one new voice message. I played it. "Hi, Luke, this is Officer Jenny of the Key West Police Department. We found your friend Billy here, sleeping in a street just off of Duval. We woke him up and tried to help him get back to his hotel, but he told us he couldn't remember where he was staying. If you could, please call me back at—"

I hung up, and just as I started to call the police, I got a call from Billy.

"Oh my god, you're not even going to believe what happened to me last night," he said.

"I think I may have some kind of an idea. Where are you?"

"I don't even know. Some pier near an old restaurant—"

"Just hold on. I'll find you."

I checked a few spots and found him sitting on a stone bench facing the ocean.

"So Officer Jenny sounded like a nice lady," I said.

"Oh, hey—yeah she was really nice. Fuck, I can't believe what an idiot I am. Do you even know what happened last night?"

"I saw you talking with a guy at some bar. How'd that turn out?"

He started laughing. "Don't even get me started. Yeah, I met a really cute Rican, and things were going really well 'til he stepped out to make a phone call. Some hideous, old Cubano came over and told me he had some really good blow, so I followed him back to his apartment. Oh my god, he was so disgusting! He had hair all over his back, and his breath smelled like rotting tuna. We did a few lines then we went to his bed. I told him I wasn't going to fuck him, but he just wouldn't stop. I mean, I kept almost falling asleep, and each time, he'd just start rubbing it in my asscrack, and try to stick it in."

"That's hideous. Did he succeed?"

"Eh, not really . . . I mean, he did get it in there for about a minute before I realized he wasn't wearing a condom—but that's not too bad, right? Fuck, I'm so stupid. I grabbed my clothes and took off, but I left my phone there and forgot where our motel was, so I just laid down on the sidewalk and fell asleep. I went back this morning for my phone, and he answered the door naked. That guy is so disgusting!"

"Yeah, Officer Jenny said she found you in the street."

"Oh, and I never even found out what happened to that cute

Rican I was with. All I know is that his name is Pedro and that he lives in Hialeah."

"There can't be too many Pedro's in Hialeah. We'll find him."

"I'm so fucking stupid."

"C'mon, Total-Loss, I'll buy you breakfast . . ."

"No, I'm just gonna go back to the motel, wash that guy's stank tuna off me, and take a nap."

I handed over the room key, showed him how to get back, and joined the celebration already going wild in the streets. I stayed on the island's fringes, hitting all the tourist hot spots: the Southernmost point landmark, the "One Human Family" emblem in the sidewalk, Key West Key Lime Pie. But my favorite spot of all was the Hemingway house. I paid and took the tour. The guide was a bearded fellow dressed like Papa. He did a great job, telling a number of stories about Hemingway and his indiscretions with his wives and mistresses, as we walked through the house and its grounds. We saw the cats, and urinal fountain, and writing room—each with its own rich history.

Of all the guide's stories, my favorite came when he showed us the wine cellar. Hemingway invited a few friends over while his soon-to-be-ex-wife was away for a few days, and the group proceeded to suck down the marital couple's vast prized wine collection in what could possibly be one of the finest "fuck you" send offs to a torrent affair in the history of love jaded. But of all the stories, the one that most haunted me was Hemingway's descent into madness—the worst part being his inability to write after electroshock treatment—to lose memory, even of those things most painful. How do you write the wrongs when you can't remember? I suppose if it were me, I wouldn't have been so haunted by this treatment if I hadn't gone along with it—maybe if I were simply strapped to a bed, kicking and screaming, and hooked up to wires, I'd be able to cope. I spent the majority of that morning strolling casually around the grounds, but each sight, rather than liberate my mind, only further confounded it.

I left sometime past noon and wandered deeper into the heart of the island, finding a Caribbean-themed festival on some side streets. I got some jerked pork, rice, and beans, and sat on the sidewalk and ate it with my hands. I then wandered onto Duval for a few cocktails.

The rain started sometime around four and continued to intensify all night. Billy met me for dinner at a diner off the main strip then we went in search of some entertainment. On our way to the heaviest concentration of bars, we passed a psychic's booth.

"Yo, I wanna give this a try," Billy said. "I've never had my fortune told before. This guy seems kinda legit."

The psychic sat cross-legged and wore a turban and the whole nine yards. Billy walked over and paid the fee. I sipped a beer while waiting for him. He wandered back about ten minutes later with this dreadful look on his face.

"So, are you going to have some struggles, but learn from them, and live happily ever after?" I had a natural skepticism of psychics.

"I don't even want to talk about it. Let's just get some drinks."

We popped into a straight bar and ordered some shots. Billy started eyeing a pack of guys but focused on one in particular. "That cute white boy in the *Yankees* hat."

"Hey, Billy, man, they don't look to be cruising for salchicha."

"You never know until you try . . ."

Billy cut through a thick crowd of party people too busy dancing and imbibing to ever really know what the hell was going on, and walked straight up to the guy in the hat. Everything around me—all the noise and commotion—ceased. Billy smiled, started flapping, and put his hand on the guy's shoulder. The guy smiled. But his friends seemed to catch on long before he did. They started whispering and pointing—their curious laughter soon soured.

Once the boy in the hat saw the disgusted expressions on his friends' faces, his followed suit. It was as if he suddenly realized the subconscious horror that had been so insidiously set upon him and the impending public humiliation he'd soon have to endure for having, even momentarily, dropped his defenses against the unknown, and he knew he *had* to do something about it—but just what, he did not know. So, in the confusion, he simply grabbed Billy by his shirt and shoved him, just as one of his friends spit in Billy's face. I stormed over. Billy tried to hold me back, but I pushed past him, grabbed the asshole with the hat, and shoved him into a wall. The bouncer came over and grabbed me by the back of my shirt, but I pulled away and it ripped down the center. I was able to get just far enough away from him to grab that stupid hat off the asshole's head. The bouncer grabbed me by the shoulders and threw me out into the street, and Billy followed behind. I stood up and threw the hat into the crowd while cursing into the night. In my rush to be human, I'd forgotten how terrible most were.

"Eh, whatever . . ." Billy shrugged his shoulders and we made our way north. We'd been told the day before that we just *had* to see the Key West sunset. "One of the best in the world!" We stopped at Mallory Square, the supposed best spot to see it—but not that night. We'd assumed the sunset would have delivered as promised if not for the thick, dark clouds blocking our view. Only in one small spot, just above the horizon, was the cloud cover thin enough to permit a glimpse of the dying light. It was enough for me.

We wandered back down Duval and again split ways, but not before I took back the motel key. I dipped back into Sloppy Joe's and again found a spot at the bar. A pretty girl sat next to me and kept trying to hold my tattered shirt together, but I paid her little attention. I got kicked out sometime around one for passing out on the bar. I wasn't quite sure why resting was considered wrong while a guy wearing nothing but a flesh-colored G-string was free to do shots across the bar from me—probably because sleeping people can't buy drinks—but I put up little fight. I wandered back to the motel, left the door open, and again fell into a deep sleep. Billy was there in his bed when I opened my eyes the next morning.

"Let's get the fuck outta here."

We stopped at a small stretch of beach for a bit then hit the bridges—everything blue and gold. "So, what exactly did that swami tell you?"

"Eh, well he just said that I was going to achieve something brilliant in my life—something incredible and rare—but that it was going to ruin me. He said after that, I was going to start growing further and further detached from reality, until I end up losing it all, and dying prematurely, spending my final years as a poor and obsessive-compulsive hermit." He gazed into the ocean and ran his hand through his hair. Several strands fell into his lap. "Oh god, I'm fucking doomed."

Chapter 8

Despite a few misfortunes, I felt pretty refreshed after our weekend in Key West. I got up at 8:10 Monday morning, threw on some clothes, ate a quick breakfast, brushed, and was out the door. I had to be in school by 8:45. It was a twenty-minute drive, so I only had about fifteen minutes to get ready. I'd been getting up around 8:10 fairly consistently, so I was used to cramming my morning routine into such a short period of time. I'd even buzzed my hair the first week of school to streamline the process.

I always parked on the left side of our street, which was a one-way, three-lane highway heading south, and I usually had from twenty to fifty yards, depending on where I'd parked, to get over all three lanes to make my turn onto a street going north. Despite the odds against me, I made it all the way over every day—even if I usually did get a horn or ten laid on me.

I loved the ride to GW. I cruised over small islands and bridges spanning narrow waterways. I found just as much delight traveling through Little Haiti and Liberty City, as I did over those tropical bumps and plains. There was life here just as there was anywhere else. I passed a homeless man who begged for change at the same traffic light in Liberty City each morning. He'd wait for the light to turn red then walk out among the cars with his palm upward. The man was a corpse. Whatever life was once in him looked to have been eaten away by some disease or addiction. That light was only a few blocks from another just before a bridge. Under the bridge was a bustling burg of its own. Walking zombies pushed limbless neighbors in wheelchairs to the road's edge, where they all stuck out their hands and begged for whatever could be afforded by passing motorists. I passed them a buck or two every so often, but didn't want to make it a habit—not so much because I thought I was enabling them, but more so to protect myself from being taken advantage of. I'd then turn onto the I-95 and join the absolute insanity that it was. It either flowed like piss or was backed up like over-dried shit. I'd cruise onto the Palmetto, get off in Opa Locka, and my stomach would start wrenching the moment I saw that G orge Was ington sign. Even if it was early, those kids were already up fighting, cursing each other out, and ripping out each other's weaves. I'd park, check the handles of each door twice, give the trunk a test tug, and walk into school.

I never knew what I was going to walk into. Some days it was, "Yo, Mr. En, look what I drew last night!" or "There go Mr. En. Man, he the best teacher in the school!" but others it was, "Yo, there go that bitch-ass white man." The words, however, weren't as bad as the laughter. When I passed a group of kids who were cussing me out, I at least knew where I stood. I at least knew to fight back. But the ones who'd just start giggling—those were the ones who really knew how to play games.

"Excuse me, what are you laughing at?"

"Damn, mister, you always gotta be actin' all paranoid."

"Yeah, nobody's even lookin' at you."

When we all knew for damn sure they were laughing at me. I did my best to ignore it. I'd just open the door, walk to the office, sign in, check my mailbox, and walk to my classroom. Ms. Carver would usually just be arriving at this time each day. I'd look through those hideous prison windows and see her pull her enormous boat with no disabled parking placard into the handicapped lot next to our classrooms, then open the door, hop out, and stride to class on her two good legs. I usually stood at my door and greeted the students as they came in, and always did the same with her.

"Good morning, Ms. Carver. You're looking lovely today!" I always meant it. The woman had some serious style. Every day she came in decked out in one solid color from head to toe. That day, she was purple: purple dress, purple Sunday bonnet, purple shoes . . . I fucking loved it. And it was Margo who'd first pointed it out. "Check out her bag next time you see her. I swear to god, she just paints it a different color every day to match her outfit." After observing for a week, I realized Ms. Liberty was right.

"Good morning to you, too, Mr. Entelechy." She always said my entire name, and she said it correctly. Then she'd unlock her room and walk in muttering, "Five more years, just five more years 'til I retire, praise be the lord . . ."

Some of Mr. Toussaint's students would arrive around this time each day as well. Despite their anger and downright terrible attitudes, any kid I'd ask to help Mr. Toussaint would jump out of their seat and wheel those kids in with a smile, no questions asked. Even the Asshole Eight would head out into the hall without protest.

"Destiny, would you mind helping Mr. Toussaint this morning?"

"No problem, mister."

It was often the only time we spoke to one another in a civil manner.

The first period bell rang, and I got right into a lecture on the Columbian Exchange.

"This stuff is sooo boring." Arman dropped his head on his desk.

"Well, what would you like to talk about?" I walked through the aisles.

"Anything but this," Carmen said.

"You said you're Puerto Rican, right Carmen?" I said.

"Yeah."

"You know what the Europeans did in Puerto Rico?"

She shook her head.

"After killing nearly all of the natives through either disease, forced labor, or outright murder, the Spanish brought in slaves from Africa to work in their place. Same thing happened on other Caribbean islands like the Bahamas and Hispaniola, which is the present day Dominican Republic and Haiti."

"Really?" JJ said.

"Yeah. How many Haitians do we have in this room?" I continued to walk among them.

A lot of hands went up.

"The odds are very likely that your ancestors were unfortunate and unwilling participants in this Columbian Exchange."

"I didn't know that . . ."

"What do you all know about Christopher Columbus?" I said.

"That he sailed the ocean blue in 1492," somebody in back said.

Arman turned it into a song. "Columbus sailed the ocean blue, in 1492, YEAH/Columbus sailed the ocean blue, in 1492, UH . . ."

"Maybe you should stick with history, Arman," I said.

"OHHH, he rankin' on you, Arman!" They liked that one.

Arman smiled. "Yeah, well I bet your lyrics are about as beat as ya' shoes."

"OHHHH, damn!"

I laughed. For some reason, insulting someone's shoes was one of the ultimate put-downs among GW kids.

"Yeah, well right now my lyrics are about Christopher Columbus," I said. "Does anybody know what he's famous for?"

"Because he started America, right?" JJ said.

"Close. He didn't start America, but he certainly was one of the first Europeans to discover the Americas, which includes South America and Central America." I pointed to a map—one of the maps

I'd taken from the annex at the beginning of the year—and showed them a picture of the area I was referring to.

"Who can tell me where Puerto Rico is?" I said.

Carmen got up, walked to the map, squinted while looking in the general area for a few seconds, then pointed it out. "There it go."

"Is she right, ladies and gentlemen?" I said.

"I don't know if she's right, but she sho' is fine," Arman said.

Carmen crossed her arms, gave him a nasty look, and sat down.

"She is right," I said. "What about the Bahamas?"

A girl from the back of the room walked up to the map and pointed the islands out.

"Very good. Now imagine this trip Columbus must have taken across the ocean. He convinced the King of Spain to fund the journey, then set off into this great blue void that, at the time, was widely accepted to be the edge of the entire world."

Eyes were opening. Heads were coming off of desks.

"Some people tried telling him he'd fall off the face of the earth or that he and his crew would be eaten by sea monsters. But he continued anyway. Soon, he landed on San Salvador, an island in the present-day Bahamas. How many Bahamians we got in here right now?"

A few put up their hands.

"Unfortunately, Columbus had no respect for the native people living there, called the Taino. Eventually, he and his men enslaved the Taino and forced them to mine for gold. Solders killed people for sport, chopping off heads or limbs just for the fun of it. But disease was the biggest killer. Because the native people weren't immune to the Europeans' diseases, those diseases wiped out nearly the entire population of people living on the island. How many people here have ever had the flu?"

Most raised their hands.

"Well, the flu is a disease. Do you know how a disease works?"

"Uh, yeah, it attacks yo' ammune system, or somethin' like that," a boy said.

"Good job. Diseases attack your body, and your immune system works to fight them off. If your immune system has experienced this type of disease before, it will know how to fight it off the next time it attacks. But if the body has never experienced a particular disease before, the immune system won't know how to fight it. Even a disease that might seem mild to us might be able to kill someone who's never experienced it before. That's what happened to the Taino. African slaves were only brought in afterwards because they were more resistant to the European diseases than were the Taino. Thus began the slave trade, and thus began an extremely important event in, possibly, most of your own histories."

"Wow, I didn't know all that . . ."

After that, I had them break into groups and draw a picture of the flag from whatever nation they or their ancestors came from, then write or draw pictures of as many facts about that culture as they could. When the bell rang, I received about twenty completed flags.

The second period soon shuffled in. I felt them out, waiting for an opening, and when I found one, I started into a similar speech with them. But halfway through, Chante got into it with Frantz. "Man, if you keep lookin' at me, I'm finna walk over there and slap yo' stupid ass," she said to him.

"Fuck yo' big ass, bitch!" Frantz said.

Chante got up and stormed over to him, pushing desks aside on her way. She threw a punch, and Frantz dodged it, then he grabbed a handful of her hair and wouldn't let go. I ran out to the hall and looked for the security guards. I saw them standing at the end of the hall, crowded around one of the more well-endowed and attractive eighth grade girls. They were smiling like a group of old perverts.

"Hey, fellas, I got a fight going on here!" I shouted to them. But they didn't move. "Hey, fellas! They're killin' each other in here." Still nothing. Despite Billy's warning about suffering in silence, I grabbed my phone and called Ms. Dawson.

"Okay, I'm coming down."

She showed up with Ms. Robespierre about a minute later. They shot into the room and separated the two, still fighting. The adults led the children outside to the hall. Ms. Dawson spoke first.

"Someone tell me what's going on here. You know you're not allowed to be fighting in school."

They both leaned against the wall, staring away from her eyes—either at the ground or down the hall.

Ms. Robespierre got into it. "One of you had better answer the lady, now." Though firm, her words weren't harsh. There was a warmth to them, inviting the kids to speak. This was a trick I needed to learn.

Chante went first. "I don't know. He be lookin' at me all the time."

"Well, lookin' doesn't give you the right to throw punches, does it?" Ms. Dawson said.

"You don't get it, miss, he—"

"Yes, I do get it," Ms. Dawson said. "He hurt your feelings. How does that make you feel, Frantz?"

Frantz smiled widely and looked down the hall. "I don't care. She a big, nasty beast."

"Fuck you!" Chante said.

"Sorry, big an' nasty ain't my type," Frantz said.

"Don't talk that way about her," I said. "Just last week I saw her stop some boy from stomping you in the hall."

He looked me up and down, as if sizing me up, and snickered.

"Now, you don't have to go and treat each other like this," Ms. Robespierre said. "This world is hard enough out there without you two adding more garbage to it."

"Well," Chante said, "he just been sayin' nasty things to me since he found out he's finna be movin' to his auntie's in Orlando."

"So, Frantz, would you say you're maybe feeling scared about moving away from your friend?" Ms. Dawson said.

"Man, she ain't ma' friend, this big, ol' beast," Frantz said.

"Alright, come with me, Frantz." Ms. Dawson grabbed him by the hand and started leading him away.

One of the young, male security guards finally wandered over.

"Ms. Robespierre," Ms. Dawson turned around, "could you please escort Chante to my office in a minute?"

"Sure thing, Ms. Dawson."

I heard part of the young security guard's conversation with Chante. "Damn, I woulda knocked his teeth out if he called me any of that . . ."

Ms. Robespierre escorted Chante away a few minutes later, and the twenty-something-year-old security guard went back to talking with the thirteen- or fourteen-year-old eighth grade girl down the hall.

The kids were going wild when I walked back into the classroom. A couple of boys were throwing paper at each other, two of the girls were having loud conversations on their phones, and a boy was drawing on his desk with markers. I tried to control the situation but was stopped by a knock at the door. When I opened it, there were four kids standing there holding crumbled pieces of paper from the counselor's office. I said something to them, but they didn't respond. One of my students, a chubby kid named Pierre, walked past me and said, rather comically, "Don't you worry, Mr. En, I'll handle this." (Humor wasn't his intent—I just found it hilarious.)

He started speaking with them in Creole and their faces lit up. They seemed like sweet kids. Pierre asked me where I'd like for them to sit. I thought about the question, then said, "Why don't you have them sit in the back. But sit with them and translate what I'm saying." I knew this would present an obstacle to Pierre's learning, but what the hell else could I do?

The bell soon rang, and third period started. It was just more of the same.

I went to Santoro's for lunch that day. We normally had meetings on Monday mornings, but he was running late that day and decided to reschedule for lunch. Rotter and Wolo were already there when I arrived. Rotter was saying something about how she refused to use the F2ST workbooks, and Wolo was burying his head with his hands, saying, "I don't care, I don't care, I DON'T CARE!"

I sat at a desk and started on my turkey sandwich.

"Man, you guys shoulda seen the fight in my room during second period," I said. "I thought this kid was gonna rip a girl's head off."

"Is that what that noise was?" Santoro said.

"And you shoulda heard what this security guard said to the girl—"

Ms. Carver walked in.

"Hello, Norma Jean, please take a seat." Santoro got up and pulled out a chair from one of the student desks for her to sit on.

"Oh, well I prefer to stand." She walked to the front corner of the room, away from the rest of us. Wolo got into a story about something funny his wife said, and we all started laughing. Ms. Carver forced a smile and walked over when the small talk ended and the meeting began.

"Okay," Santoro said, "we're getting closer to F2ST prep season, so expect the hammer to start coming down from above. That's pretty much all I have for you guys, except to limit use of the printer. I know we buy our own paper, but the school will only give us so many printer cartridges a year, so we need to conserve. That's pretty much it."

We spoke about the F2ST for a few minutes before concluding the meeting and getting back to our lunches. Ms. Carver filled a brief moment of silence with a story.

"Is that turkey, Mr. Entelechy?" She returned to the corner, where she stood, leaning toward the door. "You know, I had the best turkey this weekend. I went down to Hialeah with my cousin, and we crashed a funeral. They always got the best buffets, you know? I'm sure y'all have done it before. Anyway, they had this man there carvin' turkey. It was so good."

None of us knew what to say.

Santoro, always the politician, spoke first. "I'm sure it was great. I love a good turkey roast . . ."

Frank Lumet eventually popped his head in the door, smirking like an asshole.

"Can you believe José Torres actually called me up to his room to help him put the ball back in his mouse? What's wrong with these people? And I've told them all a million times, before asking of my services, you need to write an electronic ticket so I can keep track of my jobs."

He eventually left, and I went back to my classroom. I usually spent fourth period staring at the wall and decompressing, but that day I brought a notebook to do some writing. Almost immediately after I opened the notebook, some kid ran by and slammed on my door. By the time I got out to the hall, he was already around the corner. I sat back at my desk and glanced at my notebook, then at the wall. The wall won. I stuffed the notebook back in my bag, hid it behind my desk, and continued to stare.

My afternoon classes were atrocious. By sixth period, I'd skipped all discussion about Columbus and just had the kids color a picture of "The flag of whatever country you're from—or, better yet, just draw a picture of anything."

Mr. Rodriguez called a faculty meeting that afternoon. We met in the library. The librarian, Ms. Baxter, waddled her fat ass out the door just before it started. I sat with Santoro, Wolo, Professor K, and Rotter. Mr. Rodriguez took the mic and started his spiel.

"Good afternoon, and thank you for meeting here today. I know you're all tired so I'll keep it quick . . ."

Several people gave a hearty "Amen" to that.

". . . I wanted to congratulate you for the start to a wonderful year—"

Several people snickered when he said that. But Rodriguez continued without addressing them. "I called you here today to remind you of the importance of F2ST preparation. Remember, our goal is to get to C status at the very least. We're going to begin rigorous instruction in math, science, and English classes. All lessons must now be centered on the F2ST. We're going to ask teachers of subjects not tested to please step it up and incorporate some of the F2ST instruction in your curriculum as well. There are prep workbooks in each subject that teach general F2ST skills, and I ask that you use these as a supplement to your teaching. That's all I have for you about the F2ST. We're going to have a few other presenters today, starting with Yolanda Royce from the Math Department."

Yolanda stepped up front and center, and Rodriguez passed her the mic.

"Hello, GW teachers, it's a pleasure to speak before such a fine faculty. As Mr. Rodriguez just mentioned, we are beginning our wonderful adventure into F2ST preparation. I want to remind you that the best way to train students for the test is to motivate them. As you know, these tests mean nothing for the students themselves—it's just an indicator of the school's performance—which means, most of these students don't take it very seriously. We need to give them an incentive to learn. I encourage each of the departments to come up with strategies to motivate independent learning, which will not only boost test scores, but also encourage overall academic achievement. That's about all. Thank you, and continue to be the best and most beautiful selves you can be."

Ms. Royce sat, and Mr. Rodriguez called up Frank Lumet. He yanked the mic out of Rodriguez's hands before he even offered it.

"Yeah, hi guys, now uh, listen, I've told you all several times now that if you want me to perform any repairs on your computers or other technological equipment that you're gonna have to fill out a ticket first—"

"I think you need ticket—ta' fat camp," said a woman from the back.

"Excuse me now, Debbie, was that necessary?" he said.

"Is it necessary for you to talk to us like we're one of your idiot kids?"

"What do my kids have to do with your incompetence? Really, just how hard is it to keep your own browser updated? I mean, christ—"

"Ladies, and gentleman, please!" Mr. Rodriguez said.

Wolo rolled his eyes. "Yo, I'm ducking out of here. I'll see you guys tomorrow." Wolo crawled behind a few bookcases, commando style, and snuck out the back door, guiding it closed with his foot so that it wouldn't slam shut. Santoro, the Professor, and I laughed.

When I got home, I started up *The Good, the Bad, and the Ugly*. Billy came in about an hour later. He pulled up a chair and sat almost directly between me and Blondie.

"Oh my god, I am in *trouble*. I swear, our gym teacher, Mr. Sanchez, knows I'm gay. He looked at me today, and I saw it in his eyes—he just knows. He's sooo hot. I'm pretty sure he's gay, too. I mean, he's got a wife and two kids, but how many faggots pull that charade? Do you think I should fuck him if I get the opportunity?"

"I don't know, man. Can you just back up a little? I'm trying to watch a movie here."

"I'm so sick of all these gay guys who have wives and kids. I mean, how hard is it to be honest with yourself? It's such a slap in the face to the rest of us—like somehow we're the wrong ones. Oh my god, and he's best friends with Ms. Perez, my AP. Once she finds out, I'm gonna totally get fired. Then who's gonna hire me?"

It went on like that, so I got up and walked to the kitchen for some water. There were new hairs around the sink. We'd called Tropical Realtors about the rat problem a few weeks back, but all they did was hand us a pack of poison pellets without so much as a "Good Luck" or a smile. I checked the floor where I'd put down a pellet the night before, and it was gone. Those fuckers had already chewed through about ten big pellets as if they were cheese balls. Either the pellets were defective or there was a goddamned army of those beasts living rent free in our walls. Every time I opened a cabinet, I expected one to jump out at me. They'd gotten into Billy's low-calorie popcorn—the only shit I ever saw him eat, by the way— but had yet to raid any of my food. I was just waiting for one of us to come down with the hantavirus.

With Billy babbling in the living room, and certain rat attack in the kitchen, I decided it best to burrow away in my room. I sat at my desk and checked my email. There was one from Lila—the first one I'd received from her in weeks. All it said was something like, "I miss you, baby! I went down to such-and-such, and here's a photo."

It was a shot of her, eating dinner at a nice restaurant with another white guy. If that wasn't a message, I don't know what is. I started pacing in my room then went back out to the living room where Billy was playing with his hair.

"Goddammit, man. She's playing games with me!" I said.

"What are you talking about?"

"My girl. She just sent me a picture of herself smiling with another guy—fucking scumbag moving in on my girl."

"Well, if my memory serves me correctly, didn't you break up with her? Didn't you move away?"

"Yeah, but I didn't *really* break up with her. Just needed some separation. I don't fucking know."

I started pacing again. "Son of a bitch! What was I thinking? Why'd I move back here? I should have stayed in Mexico. These kids are terrible! This job is terrible! I have no idea what I'm doing—"

"You're having a fucking meltdown, that's what you're doing. Just calm down, man. If you can't learn to relax, you're gonna literally drive yourself crazy."

"Oh yeah, and you should fucking talk, huh? Mr. Gonna-Be-A-Hermit-Someday. And what are you gonna invent? A hairless toupee?"

"Eh, whatever, I'll be all right."

"Oh yeah, and what makes you so sure?"

"'Cause," he smiled, as if it were irrefutable truth, "I'm the King."

I paced back to my room and picked up my guitar. I started strumming a few chords, despite how horrible it made me feel. It was as if those few chords would be the ones to finally break me down. I was making it at least to the end of that school year—at least to the end of our apartment lease. I didn't know what lay beyond it, but I was going to be damned if this city or those kids got the best of me. Which meant no music, or writing, or booze, or love . . .

Despite the odds against me, I caught a wave of inspiration. I grabbed a notebook and spurted down a few lines of a song replaying through my head.

> Walking down the back roads
> And feeling strong, so strong
> For so long.
> Round the corner onto Main Street
> Watch my wet lips lose their song—
> It's all gone.
> And even if you had it
> Now you know you always had it wrong.
>
> We fall like all Kings do.
> We break like our own rules.

I got the first verse down, but felt the wolves coming. I shut the notebook before they could sink their teeth in, then walked down to the street. I wandered the road along the ocean up to about 95th Street, then walked back a part of the way on the sand. Miami Beach was alive at night, creatures lurking in the shadows and frolicking down the beach before the light would threaten to rise and force them off to the depths of the ocean again. I walked back onto the street, passing an Argentine neighborhood. There must have been a big soccer match on; the bars were filled and everyone was watching television and shouting. I got a call from Margo.

"Hey, I'm up in your hood," she said. "Would you care to meet for a cocktail?"

"Well, I'm not going to drink, but I'll meet you anyway."

I walked to the Tide Pool and saw Margo at the far end, getting into it with a large biker.

"Oh, please, darling, I could burn you on my Vespa any day," she told him.

He laughed. "More shots, baby?"

"Only if you're paying, dear."

I walked over. Margo introduced me to the biker. I'd seen him before on some other hazy night. The Tide Pool had become my local spot. It was open until four, so I'd head there after whatever else had fizzled away, and stay until either the lights came on, or they kicked me out—usually for sleeping on the bar.

"Make that another shot for my colleague here, too," Margo said to the bartender.

"Oh, no thanks, I don't drink on the weekdays," I said.

The bartender finished pouring the shots.

"Nonsense, darling." Margo stuck a shot of tequila in my hand. I reluctantly accepted and took one down with her and her biker boy. Big Bike soon wandered onto some lumpy, withered hag in a darkened corner. Margo ordered a mojito and got me a beer.

"Oh, no thanks . . ." I pushed it away, and she set it back in front of me.

"I figured I'd give you a call since I was in your neighborhood. You live near here, correct?"

"Yeah, just around the corner."

"Ekk, you should be careful. This part of the beach isn't very safe."

"Then what's a lady like you doing here?"

"Please, I dare any thief, rapist, or crook to take this on." She made a muscle and urged me to touch it. Solid. Then she pointed to a sizeable switchblade buried in her purse. "If all else fails, ya' know?" Apparently a can of mace was too ladylike.

"So how's everything been going with you at school?" I said.

"Simply wonderful. Those kids are really learning a great deal. I've had so much experience with writing, I think it just naturally rubs off of me."

"You haven't been having any discipline problems?"

"Well, I wouldn't exactly call them 'discipline problems.' Kids are kids, am I right? I sure gave my teachers just as much hell as these kids give us, but it was all good-natured."

"So you cursed your teachers out and showered them with racial epithets?"

"Oh, you need to just lighten up with all this. They're just kids. Besides, I think it's funny when they call me a cracker. Sorta makes up for all the damage we've done."

"We?"

"Oh, don't be such a bore. You gotta just let these kids run wild at times."

"That'd be fine with me if I wasn't getting paid to do otherwise."

"So, anyways, tell me about yourself. Do you have a girlfriend?"

"That's a complicated question."

Paola came out of the back room. She saw me and waved, then

came over. "Luke, I'm surprised to see you here on a Monday night. I usually don't have to wake you up until the weekend."

"I don't really feel like being at home right now."

Margo pulled on my arm. "Oh, tell me, darling, what's going on at home?"

"It's complicated."

"Everything's 'complicated' with you, isn't it dear?" Margo said.

I shrugged my shoulders.

"Oh, poor baby," Paola said. "Do you need a hug?" She came out from around the bar and threw her arms around me. My face was at breast level. That was wonderful.

Margo started rubbing my thigh. "Say, would I be able to grab something to eat at your place? I'm starved."

"Uh, well, we don't really have much except low-calorie popcorn, and that's all hairy—"

"It's no matter. I'd just like a mouthful of something." She smiled at me.

I'd been holding out for far too long. Maybe it was those Brazilian tits rubbing in my face, but I could no longer ignore the desires of my little estranged friend. I chugged my beer, grabbed Margo by the hand, and led her through the back alley to my place.

We walked into the living room, and she sat on the futon. I offered her a glass of water and she accepted. Billy walked out of his room as I handed her the glass.

"Oh my god, Little Diegosito just broke up with me," he said. "Oh, uh, sorry. I didn't know you had company."

"Oh you poor thing," Margo said, despite her ignorance of the situation, "what happened?"

"Eh, he just said he couldn't deal with my insanity anymore. I'm so stupid. I followed this guy here from New York on a whim, and here I am." He pulled up a chair and sat with us. I could feel it shriveling.

"It's okay. I broke up with my boyfriend too before I moved down here. I know how difficult it can be." The two hit it off from there. After that, it was a half hour of story time—mostly about boys, but plenty on shopping, and the delights and superiority of foreign cultures. Then they started on school.

"So, she seriously paints her bag a different color every day?" Billy cackled with laughter.

"Every day!" Margo said.

"Yo, I gotta meet this Ms. Carver. She sounds like my kind of people."

Margo stood up. "Hey, you know what we need? Cervecitas!"

Billy started laughing. "How'd you know? Well, Little Margsita, where do you suggest we get these cervecitas?"

"I know the perfect spot, Little Billsito. It's called Manolo's. It's an authentic Cuban bar that only locals know about, and it's right by my apartment."

"I just need to change my shirt. I look disgusting in this."

"Yeah, you really can't be seen like that . . ."

"No, no I can't!" Billy smiled widely and ran for his room.

And so it was. The fantastic car wreck. Everything was Little Margsita this, and Little Billsito that. I was gonna kill one of them, I swear. Billy got ready and took off after Margo out our front door. Neither even thought to ask me to join. At least I didn't have to live with the next morning regret with that thing. Billy didn't come back until about 3:30. He woke me up. It was a school night.

"Oh my god, that girl is insane! We're going to start a tap dancing act!" he said.

"Shut the fuck up and go to sleep!"

He wandered into his room and started singing and stomping the floor. From then on, he and Margo were joined at the dumb ass.

Chapter 9

A few days passed before a midmorning email sent GW into a goddamned frenzy. I first noticed the chaos when I saw Ms. Carver power-walking down the hall during the middle of a period, mumbling to herself, "They cannot do this to me! They cannot do this to me! I only have five more years . . ." I hadn't yet read the email, so took this as the regular GW day-to-day and shut the door. But when I sat down during my free period and read the email from Ms. Dawson marked "Urgent," I realized this was no normal day.

Dear Teachers,

As some of you may know, Gretchen Yangston retired unexpectedly last week. This left an opening for an English teaching position, but due to some financial issues, we won't be able to hire a new teacher. Instead, Darla Rotter has volunteered to transfer at the start of next week. If you're reading this it means that your schedule will be affected by the change. Many of you were told in the beginning of the year that your schedules could change, and unfortunately, that's just what's going to happen. I've included all changes listed in the document attached to this email. I know this is sudden, but please bear with us as professionally as possible as we try to deal with the changes."

Thank you,

Karen Dawson

Just then, I got a call from Margo.

"God, are you reading this email?" she said. "They can't do this. They absolutely cannot do this! I'm organizing a meeting. Come to my room. We need to fight this!"

Margo's schedule was the only in the English Department that was changing. Somehow in the shakeup, the school counselor discovered that Margo had been given an extra free period. She was now losing both.

I walked down the hall and knocked on her door. I smelled smoke. She opened the door and exhaled a plume of grey air.

"Hurry, come in, come in." She motioned for me to enter. I walked in, and she closed the door behind me. She was alone. She took another big puff of her cigarette, then wandered to the window and exhaled. "Have you seen the hack job they've done to our schedules? This is unacceptable. I mean, we're professionals. I *need* that time to plan and find my balance. I was changing lives—"

"Yeah, but they did give us a warning. The situation ain't exactly peaches for them either."

"Oh my god, are you on *their* side? You are, aren't you?" She took another nervous puff and exhaled in the middle of the classroom. "I knew from the moment I met you, you were just one of *them*."

"That's not true. I'm just saying that they probably didn't want to lose Ms. Yangston either. I guess, you know, we're a team and all—"

She snorted, "Well, a team always does have an overachiever, doesn't it now, darling?" She pierced into my eyes with her terrifyingly vacant gaze.

"Listen, I'm hungry. I'm gonna go." I walked to the door and opened it.

She followed behind and shouted, "One of them!"

I walked through the door backwards; something told me not to turn my back to her. I kept imagining that the moment I did, she'd put out her cigarette on some part of my exposed flesh. I walked to my room, grabbed my turkey sandwich, and headed to Wolo's. I could hear someone inside laughing. I knocked, and Santoro answered. He scanned the hallway both ways before saying, "Come in, come in." He opened the door just wide enough for me to squeeze inside and shut it quickly after. Wolo was lighting a stick of incense on his desk.

"God, I can still smell her. Nothing's gonna get that stink out," Wolo said.

"Yeah, well you can thank Gretchen Y for giving her this opportunity." Santoro stood by the door and periodically checked through the window.

"I don't even care that my class sizes are going to get bigger," Wolo said, "we should give Ms. Y a medal. Thank god no more meetings with that wildebeest. If I heard one more thing about her fucking filters—"

"So what the hell's going on here?" I walked to a student desk and remained standing beside it.

"Chernobyl, my friend," Wolo said. "I'd advise you to stay in your classroom and lock the doors. These bitches have all lost their minds." He pointed at Santoro. "Did you *see* Norma Jean Carver, man?"

Santoro started laughing. "I got eyes, don't I?"

"What happened with Ms. Carver?" I said.

"She had a meltdown in Dawson's office," Wolo said. "I don't know if you saw the new schedule or not, but a bunch of our classes are gonna change. They're trying to pack another class in her free period and switch her second period with yours."

"Holy shit! You mean, no more Chante Brown?" I said.

"No more Chante Brown, or Jamar Jack-Off, or Shawniqua Shit-Stain—none of them," Wolo said.

"Oh man . . . holy shit . . . that's great news . . ." My body was overtaken by gravity. I felt for the chair with my hands and plopped my ass down when I found it.

My second period was my worst—sixth might have actually been more difficult, but it was the last period of the day, so I gave several less fucks.

"It's rough out there. I'd suggest laying low for a bit," Santoro said.

I didn't respond. I was too busy picturing life without Chante—and smiling.

I ate and went back to my room. Someone knocked on my door. I hesitated to answer, but did regardless. It was Ms. Carver.

"Oh, they can't do this! You heard the news, right? They just *can't*!" She walked inside and started pacing.

"Hey, I'm sorry. Is it even legal to make you teach six classes a day?" I said.

"Heck no it ain't! I'm marchin' right over to my union rep now. I swear I'm gonna quit if they do this to me. I just got five more years. Just five more." She wandered off and up the back stairwell. Her words echoed in my mind.

I picked up the phone and dialed. "Hi, Ms. Dawson, would you, uh, mind if I came down there to speak with you?"

"Well, I'm a little busy, but I can make some time," she said.

I walked down and saw her in Mr. Rodriguez's office, standing between Rodriguez and Margo.

"If you do this, then this school stands for nothing," Margo said. "It's just a joke, and—"

Dawson started gently ushering Margo out the door, while saying, "Okay, Margo, please, just please come with me. Please, just please come with me."

Dawson was able to move the immovable Margo out into the secretary's office. Though she whispered, I could hear her words, "Look, Margo, you're a fantastic teacher, and we hear great things from your students, but please just be easy with this one. Mr. Rodriguez cares about you and this school and wouldn't do anything to intentionally hurt you."

"I know you're okay, Karen, but my union rep is going to be hearing about this." Margo stormed off like a child. Dawson got a gander of me and invited me into her office. I accepted. She shut the door behind us.

"Hey, I'm sorry you have to deal with all this," I said. "You really don't deserve it—"

"No, it's okay, Mr. Entelechy. It's all in a day's work. Now what can I do for you?"

"You know, I've been thinking about this new schedule, and I may have found a way to make it all a little more fair—at least for the History Department."

She gave me a look, urging me to proceed.

"What if I took a class during my free period so Ms. Carver could keep her free period? It only seems fair. It is my first year and all—"

"You're right. It is your first year. But she's a veteran. She should be able to handle this."

"I know, I know. But she's a nice lady—she's put in her time. Would you at least let me take a crack at it? The schedules, that is?"

She reached out from behind her desk, put her hand on my shoulder, and said, "Swing for the fences, Lukie." She smiled, and I took off.

I went back to my room and came up with something I thought everyone could live with. Santoro and Wolo were already going to lose their free periods as well, but Santoro was overloaded with asshole classes, so I split the tough kids between the two of them, then sorted things out between Carver and myself. I figured if I was going to lose my only free period, I should at least be given a good group, so I asked for Carver's one honors class—her favorite—to fill the spot, and I also asked for us to switch our second period classes. I ran this by all parties before taking it to Dawson. Carver didn't like it but gave me her blessing. I brought it down to Dawson's office before the end of lunch. She took one look at it and said, "Are you sure?"

I nodded and smiled.

She smiled, too. I left. No more Chante Brown! It was a win all around—and it came with a slight pay raise. All I lost was a free period.

If only I'd known what I'd done . . .

I told Billy all about it later on when I got home.

"So, she was actually smoking?"

"Like an Irish dock wench between blow jobs."

"During school hours?"

"Nobody tells that bitch what to do."

Billy started laughing. "Eh, whatever. I know people who've done a lot worse. Hell, I've done a lot worse. At PS Four Ninety, we used to head down to the bathroom for a little pick-me-up between classes. Sometimes that Colombian Caffeine was the only way to get through the day. You'd be surprised how many teachers do that shit."

"Surprisingly, I don't think I would."

Billy kept laughing. "So, she had two free periods?"

"Two fucking periods! And she tried to justify it by saying that those two periods helped her to better prepare for the class that followed them."

"Shit, I don't even know how that could happen. We're lucky to even get one."

"They probably threw the schedules together last minute at the start of the year and didn't realize their mistake."

"Margo is out of her damned mind. We went shopping last weekend and she spent seven hundred bucks."

"On what?"

"Whatever she put her hands on. Designer sun glasses, a new bag, a fur shawl. You know she pays fourteen hundred a month for an apartment in South Beach? The bitch is making no more than you or I, but is pissing away half her pay each month on an apartment. If it wasn't for credit, she'd be going toe-to-toe with the repo guys. When the cards run dry, I wouldn't want to be around to see that."

"Yes you would."

"Guilty." Billy laughed. "You know, it was really great what you did for Ms. Carver. She sounds like a nice lady. Why'd you do it?"

"I don't know—other than the pay raise, she's one of the only people there who's nice to me. I guess I just want her to make it to retirement on her own terms." I told Billy the story about her funeral crashing. He couldn't stop laughing.

"Oh my god, I need to meet this woman!" he said.

I started laughing too.

"You know," he said, "she probably just brought all that funeral stuff up because she was uncomfortable. I mean, she's an older black woman surrounded by young white guys. She probably just wanted to make conversation. I wouldn't be surprised if she made it all up." He laughed again. "But still, it's pretty damn funny."

I went into school the next day, but the fever hadn't subsided. I walked by Margo's classroom on the way to my own, and it was dark inside. By the start of first period, Ms. Carver still hadn't pulled into her VIP parking space. She never showed that day. Neither did Margo. I met my new fourth period class that afternoon. They were an honors group, like my first period, and they, like any, had their good, bad, and ugly. In the good column was Zara Bailey, the Jamaican wonder child who'd given the F2ST a smackdown in her seventh grade year.

She had one of the highest scores in the state in math, and was right up there in science and English. The girl wanted to be a lawyer—she had the temperament for it. She was rational and inquisitive and had a strong sense of right versus wrong. There were a few others like her in there, too. Overall, it was my most academically gifted group. But it also had one of my biggest challenges, Teonnie Hawkins, who only one-upped Chante in evilness because she was craftier. Both were bitches, but Teonnie was smart, and she knew it. She came straight from the depths of hell. But it was Teonnie who rushed to defend Ms. Carver once we'd started introductions that day.

"Thank god we're out of that woman's class," Zara said. "You know she actually told us, with a straight face, mind you, that all people who are tall or fat are larger than normal because they're filled with the devil. She tried to do an exorcism for Tim a few weeks ago during class." She pointed at a chubby kid in the back of the room.

"Man, Tim needs *exercise* not an exorcism," some boy said.

"Yeah, I think someone stuffin' his voodoo doll with marshmallows," a girl said.

"Fuck you," Tim said. "I'll put a curse on both of you."

"That woman is insane," Zara said.

"Shut your bitch ass mouth up, Zara!" Teonnie said. "That woman was always nice to us, you shouldn't talk about her behind her back."

"Please, we could be having this conversation in her room right now," Zara said. "She's probably asleep." Zara looked at me. "You know, all she does is pass out papers, write some stuff on the board, then fall asleep at her desk?"

"Eh, well—" I wanted to defend Ms. Carver, but didn't know how.

"Just last week she gave us a list of one hundred theater terms to memorize," Zara said.

"Yeah, that lady's crackin' up," some kid said.

"Shut yo' ugly mouth, Rudy!" Teonnie got up and walked over to Rudy. He covered his head, preparing for a blow, but it never came.

"Alright, alright, take it easy, Teo—" I walked over.

"It's Teonnie!" she said.

"Well, you gotta give me a chance to finish. I was gonna say that." I stood between her and Rudy.

"Oh, and every Friday she used to give us cotton candy. She's got a machine in her room. She called it 'Candy Fridays,'" Zara said.

"Alright, well, let's all just calm down," I said. "I agree with you, Teonnie, Ms. Carver is a nice woman. And, Zara, if you feel she's wronged you in any way, fear not, because you are no longer with her. I'm looking forward to getting to know you all and hope we can make up for lost time. My other honors class has just started studying the Constitution. Were you around the same?"

"Man, we was trapped backstage," Rudy said.

"Well, it looks like someone was studying his theater terms," Zara said.

Rudy smiled.

"Okay," I walked to the front of the room and stood before the class, "well we're just going to have to power through the Age of Exploration, early Colonial America, and the Revolutionary War. If we work together, we can make this happen."

Teonnie rolled her eyes at me.

"And what was that for?" I said.

"I don't wanna be doin' all this stupid shit. You like this so much, you do it."

"Excuse me, but I don't care for your tone right now."

"Yeah, well I don't care for your tone." She rolled her eyes again, and crossed her arms.

"Stop being a bitch, Teonnie," Zara said. "You always wanna hold us back."

"No, I just don't like this man here, that's all," Teonnie said.

"Well, this man here is gonna call security if you don't stop with the disrespect," I said.

A few of her friends got into it. That was always the worst. If it was just one student, you could single them out—kick them out of the room—stick 'em in the back of the class. But you can't send out four.

"She ain't trying to disrespect you, she just being honest and you giving her all that shit," said one annoying bitch.

"Yeah, and you're talking about making up all this time, but you're wasting it right now," said another.

"Excuse me, who do you think you are?" I walked over to her.

"I know who I am, who do you think you are?" said the annoying bitch.

I thought about calling security to escort these girls to the office, but Billy's words echoed in my head. "You better not make it a habit to hit that panic button. Soon, they're gonna think that's all that's going on in your room." And I'd already hit it several times throughout the year.

"Look, uh, it's not okay for you to talk to me like that." I walked over to Teonnie. "Please separate yourself from these other girls and sit in the back of the room."

She rolled her eyes and huffed her stupid breath and shuffled her damned feet, but she did it. And that's where I kept her the rest of the year—separated from humanity by at least three desks. I had Zara switch with one of the annoying bitches to keep them spread throughout the room. I tossed some worksheets at them and waited out the bell. When it finally rang, I realized the folly in playing god with the schedules.

Chapter 10

Billy had lost his car keys again, so I had to drive him to school that morning. I picked him up after I got off of work. He was standing there at the edge of the sidewalk hanging his head and crossing his arms like a timid, little eight-year-old, but he perked up when he saw me.

"Eh, it's official—Mr. Sanchez knows I'm gay." He got in the car. "The jig is up. T minus a few hours 'til they can my ass."

"You pop a boner in the men's room or something?" I drove away.

"No, I was walking by him in the hall today, and he just looked at me. I don't know how to describe it, but I know he knows I'm gay. It's all over!"

We drove over the I-395. That bridge view was almost worth going the thirty minutes out of my way to pick up Billy.

"Yo, was Marge in school today?" he said. "I tried calling her again, but she's not answering her phone."

"No, she's been out for two days now."

"That's weird. She usually can't go a half hour without texting me some sordid or salacious bit of gossip. I'm missing Hurricane Margo. I need my fix."

"No, what you need to do is fix your room so you stop losing your damned keys, and wallet, and shoes, and every other goddamned thing."

"Oh puh-leeze, like you got it all together. Just because you wear a tie to work doesn't mean you're better than me." He pointed his finger right in my face. "And you'd better not kid yourself otherwise."

"Yo, I'll drop you off right here." I slowed and veered to the right side of the bridge.

"Oh, relax . . ."

I pulled back into the lane and picked up speed.

". . . But you'd seriously better not think you're better than me."

Friday soon came. I made it through the day without much incident—I caught a kid drawing a picture of a hard wiener on one of the back desks, but that was about the worst of it.

Sometime around the end of October, I'd gotten myself into a little routine. On Friday afternoons after work, I'd drive down the I-95, passing my normal exit in Liberty City, and take the 395 East into South Beach. I'd then pop in *Let's Dance*, and replay Bowie's version of "China Girl" as I cruised up the coast. For some reason, this was the one window of time I'd allow myself to feel life, and that Friday was no exception. There was something about being young and owning a car and being able to take it anywhere I pleased that I drove to the prettiest place I could think of and just let my imagination run wild with the scenery—if only for an afternoon.

It was clear to me by now that this city had no intention of treating me as did Mexico. The women here had seen their fill of white boys, and I was having difficulty maintaining conversations with any on those rare occasions when I actually tried. Billy frequently mentioned that Miami was "The City of Sex," but that certainly wasn't true for either of us. It'd been a long time since I'd dipped into that well, and I feared it would forever dry up . . .

When I got home, I laid down on the futon. Soon, Billy walked through the door.

"Guess who finally called me today?" he said.

"The Hurricane?"

"Yep-o! Get this, the bitch has been in NYC for the past week. Just took a random trip up to the City because—wait for it—she says her friend's uncle *thought* he had a heart attack. Who does that? She said she didn't even call into work. 'Oh, they'll understand,' she said. 'It was a matter of life and death.' Talk about your nervous breakdown. Believe me, I know what they look like. I had several friends in the NYPSD take that very trip themselves at some point in the year—hell, I took a four-day paid vacation down to Santo during a school week after Little Tina Sanderson threw a pair of scissors at me. Shit's serious."

"Holy crap! So she didn't even tell anybody?"

"No. She said she has this 'relationship' with Ms. Dawson, that you nor I would ever understand. That Dawson 'just gets' her."

"Yeah, well she should be 'just getting' her a pink slip. That was a five-day unearned vacation."

"I'm telling you, man. This is one unhealthy profession. It drives people fucking insane. All the cards are stacked against you. If you correct a student the wrong way, you could get sued or fired. If you say the wrong thing, you could get sued or fired. If you do nothing, you could get sued or fired. Teachers have absolutely no authority in these classrooms and everybody, students especially, knows it. You kick these kids out for swearing at you and threatening your life, and they're back the next day, and then you got the state and feds bearing down on you, making sure the little hell demonios are scoring As on every damned assessment, or it's your ass. Something horrible is gonna happen in this country in the next few years, don't kid yourself otherwise. Nobody talks about it, but the whole fucking system is rotting out from the inside. And everybody just keeps pushing the teachers more and more, expecting them to somehow pump out these unbelievable test scores even as the kids get worse and worse. This whole country's going down, man. Maybe Margo is right—just taking off. She may be the only sane one out of all of us."

Billy and I rode the bus south and met Margo at Manolo's for a few drinks that night. She was all makeup and fake pearls, and her hair was now bleached blonde. She was sitting at the bar and chatting merrily with some young, bearded bartender. She gave a contrived laugh—laughing with her throat, not her gut. I could tell she was hurting.

"Darlings! How I've missed you boys! Come, sit, have a drink." She patted the chairs next to her.

"Ben," she said, "fix these boys up with my patented Pink-Manito cocktail."

She'd spent so much time there, they'd actually made a drink in her honor. The bearded one dumped long shots of several different liquors into a cocktail shaker, added some fruit juices, shook, poured into glasses, added parasols, and handed the drinks over.

"I'm good with a beer." I pulled out the parasol and gave it a twist as I threw it in the air.

"Oh, darling, now's not the time to act superior. Just drink it."

I pushed the glass aside and ordered a beer.

"How's your friend's uncle?" Billy said.

"Oh, he's okay. It was a false alarm anyhow. He just had a serious case of gas—and she's not really a friend, just an old college roommate I keep in touch with. But, I think, once you've spent any amount of time with anyone, you categorically owe it to them, yourself, and humanity to be there for them when they need you, no matter the circumstance. I was just defending the honor of our silly, little human race." Margo ordered some tequila shots. "Put 'em on my tab, too, Little Bensito."

We did the shots, and she started getting to the center of it. "They just can't do something like that. Don't they have any class? I was helping those kids—inspiring them—and then they just ripped it all away as if our work meant nothing. It really is one of the greatest tragedies this city has ever experienced—I do believe that to be true." She did another shot and continued, now lowering her voice, "You know, I had my kids writing ledes for fake magazine articles. I wouldn't expect *you* to know how nuanced and essential a process that is, but I tell you it is not easy . . ." She said that to both of us, but was looking right at me when she said "you."

I felt like arguing with her, but she had a point.

She continued, ". . . And, if you can write a good lede, you can lead a good life—that's what I always say."

Her friend, Tika, showed up a little later. Tika was a gorgeous Indonesian woman who worked on the same cruise as Margo in the South Pacific a few years back. They both quit and moved to Miami together with dreams of making it big. Tika pulled out ahead early on; she'd been a fairly successful bikini model for a local designer, but quit when he started pushing her toward "adult" modeling. She got another job serving drinks on a cruise, which was currently docked in Miami.

"Hey," Tika said, "I just went to see Miguel." She smiled.

Margo's face lit up like a slot machine spittin' nickels.

"Excuse us, gentlemen." Margo and Tika made off for the bathroom, but Margo came back and grabbed Billy by the arm. "I'm gonna borrow him for a second, okay, darling? Don't wait up!"

"Oh, don't worry about that," I said.

The three plowed into the ladies' room and didn't come out for at least as long as it took me to ask Ben the bartender for the number for a cab, make the call, and walk out front to wait for it. While sitting on a planter box out front, I heard a commotion in the back alley. I wandered over just as Margo was hurling a beer bottle into the bar's brick wall.

"Hey, Nolan Ryan," I said, "why don't you take it easy there?"

"What, do you think you're better than me?" she said.

"Not a class act like you, no dear."

"I don't think I like your tone. I think you're judging me."

Tika and Billy just snickered like idiots.

"Alright, well, if you wanna vandalize the place you love so dearly, go right ahead. I'm gonna go wait for my cab out front. Have a fun night."

As I walked away, I heard them making plans to head farther down into South Beach. Margo promised they could all fit on her Vespa. That was the last I heard from them that night.

I sat back down on the planter box and waited for the cab. Twenty minutes passed and none stopped, so I just thumbed down the first I saw. It pulled over and I got in. The large Russian driving turned his head toward me but kept his eyes on the road. "This crazy, fooking place. I wish I was back in Saint Petersburg. People here are assholes. Assholes, I tell you."

Normally I would have said something to either antagonize him or fuel his rant, but this guy was straight loony tunes, I could just tell, so I left it alone. "This guy calls me for cab. He tells me his name and says, 'Viktor, yes, I will be waiting for you outside place called Manolo's. But when I get there, there is nobody waiting. I drive by once and honk, then I drive around block, and come back twice, and nothing. I know what these people need." He reached under his seat and grabbed what looked like a sawed-off wooden baseball bat with some dirty grip tape wrapped around the handle; it showed signs of heavy wear. "They need some of this." He held it up and started pumping it in the air. "So, what is your name?"

"Uh, Esteban . . ."

I had the psycho drop me off a block before my place. I paid him, left a decent enough tip to temporarily distract him from his urges to kill, and walked up the block. The Cuban woman was on our porch, babbling and pumping her fists in what I'd assumed she assumed to be the direction of Castro's palace. "That filthy rat!"

I couldn't handle that conversation, so I kept walking and stopped for a drink at the Tide Pool. I sat at the bar and Paola handed me a

Dominican brew. Sam was there again and talking with some other poor sap. Though I could have used some company, I was glad he didn't get up and sit next to me. That night I had no patience for Romance, good or bad. One beer turned to several. I woke up sometime around three to Paola tapping me on the shoulder. "It's time to go, hon."

I got up, and she grabbed my arm. "You know, I get off in an hour. It'd be nice to wake you up someplace other than this shitty bar . . ."

I hesitated, but gave the married woman my number, then wandered home. On the way, I saw the Hispanic homeless man kneeling in the middle of the sidewalk and staring up at the bright half moon.

"Hey, Carlos," I said.

He nodded and motioned for me to come over. I squatted next to him and asked if he knew what he was doing. I think he immediately understood what I was really asking him, because he responded, "I spent five years in the army in Puerto Rico. Too many rules. My brother has lots of money and has offered some to me, but I prefer to live like this. I do what I want, when I want." He pointed at the empty streets. "These people are all crazy. Want everything they can't have. I have nothing and am very happy. I have the moon. I am very happy." His face looked peaceful. I left him to continue staring at his celestial possession.

I got home a few minutes later. I pulled off my shoes and lay in my bed. When I woke up the next morning, I had three missed calls, one from Paola, and two from the idiots. I checked my voice messages and got an earful of the tap dancing act. "Hey Lukie, you'll never believe—ow, that hurts! You're stomping on my foot, Margo . . . MARGO—" Then the message cut off. I had no idea where they were, but by the sound of the crowds and traffic in the background, I'd place them somewhere on the streets of South Beach.

I went back to sleep, but woke a short time later to Liberty and Billy singing "Under the Boardwalk" and stomping around in the kitchen.

I reluctantly walked out to the living room.

"Oh, Little Lukesito's up." Margo was mixing something in a plastic bowl.

"Finally," Billy said. "Damn, you sleep forever, man." His dark brown hair was now bleached blond.

I yawned.

The idiots had made a fucking smorgasbord for breakfast: french toast, scrambled eggs, biscuits and gravy . . . But it didn't look as if they'd eaten any of it.

"Have a plate, darling!" Margo served me; she wore fake pearls and an apron. She went back to the kitchen and started up the blender. "Would you like a Bloody Mary? Billy and I have already gotten started."

Billy held up his glass and smiled.

"Oh, no thanks," I said. "My head's killing me and—"

"Oh, darling, I should hope you don't think you're better than us."

"Huh?"

"You're not judging us, are you?" she said.

"No, I'm just—"

"Little Lukesito, always judging everyone . . ." She turned it into a damned song. "Oh, Little Lukesito, he holds his nose so high, he misses the flowers down at his feet, and cries and cries and cries." Billy got into it too. I left my plate of cold Americana morning feast, brushed my teeth, threw on some clothes, and was out the door.

"Little Lukesito, he holds his head so high—"

I slammed the door behind me, walked down to my car, and pulled out my phone. "Hey, Wolo, what are you up to?"

"Party at the beach. Come on up!"

I headed north into Hallandale and pulled into Wolo's condo complex. I walked inside his place, a small and charming two-story unit overlooking a nearby park, and he offered me a drink. His wife,

Amanda, said hello from the bedroom. She was sitting at a desk with her head down beside stacks of books. Wolo and I each sucked down a beer, then headed out the door. Amanda stayed, saying she had too much homework to go. I drove down to the beach, parked, and we hit the boardwalk. There was a festival going on: food, games, live music—a grand celebration.

"I woulda slapped them both," Wolo said, as we walked along the boardwalk.

"Yeah, they wouldn't stop accusing me of being better than they are."

"I got no problem with the gays, but guys like that are just straight fags."

"Well, you don't know him—"

"I would have slapped him straight across the face the second he gave me any shit like that. You can't let people push you around. That bitch Margo is off her rocker too. She's cute, but crazy. You just gotta get away from them, man. They're toxic. I don't even know why you hang out with them."

"Well, I don't really care for Liberty, but Billy—you don't know him. You might not realize it looking at him, but that kid is one of the smartest motherfuckers I've ever known. You know he's got an IQ of one forty-seven—one-motherfucking-forty-seven! And Margo won't shut the fuck up about rejecting Mensa . . ."

"That's just a number."

"And he's a brilliant writer—I don't know. We used to be best friends. We took road trips, hit on girls . . . we even started a screenplay. I mean, it's rough, but it's got its moments—"

"Yeah, but was that before or after he came out?" Wolo's eyes followed the backside of a gorgeous dark-haired beauty walking by in a thong.

"Before."

"People change, man. You can't force relationships that just aren't working." He followed her ass until it disappeared into a crowd.

"He's pretty funny, too."

"Yeah, but still, I woulda slapped him."

I didn't respond.

"You just need to move out. Get your own place, get a girl. Fuck Miami—too many immigrants. You should move up north here. Look," Wolo pointed inside a bar at a towering man surrounded by young blondes in bikinis, "even the Worm loves it."

"Holy shit, is that really Rodman?" I said.

"The one and only."

And there he was, the man Phil Jackson himself once said was, pound-for-pound, the best athlete he'd ever coached. He was one of my all-time favorite basketball players and was now within three-point range. I thought about wandering over, but imagined the horrible crap I'd end up saying. "Wow! Dennis Rodman, is that really you? Holy cow, sorry about Carmen Electra . . ."

We popped inside a beach bar and sat at the counter. A pretty girl took our orders. After she set the drinks down, Wolo reached out and grabbed her wrist, gently turned her palm upward, and placed a fiver inside. She blushed, smiled, and walked away. The man had the gift.

We had several drinks then wandered to a back room where a group of rowdy thirty-something women were celebrating some female rite of passage—someone in the crew was getting married, or divorced, or lobotomized, or getting a new exotic bamboo cutting board or some other dumb thing to distract them from the chaos perpetually erupting from both without and within—and Wolo's quick words got us a seat at their table. The girls were cute. I don't care so much about a woman's age, just the lass behind the lines. One of those lasses took a liking to me, and was soon on my lap, grinding her love parts into my own. Wolo gave me a thumbs up from across the table. We had a few drinks, and soon I started hearing a thumping sound. I looked at Wolo; he had his head back and this ecstatic look on his face. I looked at the girl beside him. She was busy jerking his cock under the table. I pulled my legs onto the bench where I was sitting and put the girl on my lap's legs on top of mine as a shield. I'm not sure if the floor or any legs were ever made sticky, but Wolo was sure walking funny when we left. I dropped him back at his place.

"Hey, it was nothing. I love my wife. I was just getting my rocks off, you know? It's different . . ."

I drove back to my apartment, parked, and walked down the sidewalk. As I neared the building, I could hear glass breaking. When I got to the front, I looked up and saw Margo and Billy throwing beer bottles off our balcony and giggling like morons. There was something about the destruction caused by these two idiot savants that was loaded with subtext. Both had genius-level IQs, but were cackling like inbred children each time one of those bottles missed the bush they looked to have been aiming for and smashed on the sidewalk instead. If they were two regular, everyday run-of-the-mill morons, there'd be nothing noteworthy about this performance. It'd be like viewing a snapshot of a cattle ranch taken by your Aunt Gladys on her first trip out to the Wild Wild West. Any conversation about it would begin and end with the image— it'd be history, it could be interpreted as art, but likely not in and of itself. It would need interpretation by an outside influence to ever gain motion. But these two characters *were* motion, and were interpreting life with each bottle that flew off course and slammed into that concrete sidewalk. The warped ambition, the inexplicable anger, the aborted sexuality. Aunt Gladys would never be able to capture these two—not what they were really doing. They weren't still, but rather streaks of paint, speckles, droplets, on a canvas—a living, breathing abstract expression. But a theme wasn't necessary. Their movements weren't real, but merely interpretations of the reality they'd likely thought they were currently avoiding—the reality we all knew they so desperately wanted to be a part of. And with each bottle broken, they were both a little closer to and a little further away from this reality that they, whether they liked it—or even knew it—or not, were already an absolute part of. I didn't know if they were chronic underachievers desperately avoiding the path of responsibility, or if they were chronic overachievers desperately doing whatever they could to escape the darkness and exhaustion that had claimed so many others like them. While they may have been desperate either way, at least they were something. Because they were in Miami. Because they were bleached blonde. Because they were teachers—professionals. They were artists.

I left the performance piece and slipped off to the Tide Pool. Paola wasn't there that night. Her replacement was some pock-faced Puerto Rican from North Miami. He filled me up with tall boys of some eight-percent superbrew. I awoke to his aggressive poking of my shoulder sometime around two. "Hey, meng, what you think this is, the Howard Johnson? Yeah, you go now . . ."

When I got back to the apartment, the sidewalk studio was unoccupied, but the paints were still splattered everywhere. Glass in the bushes and walkway . . .

I went upstairs, got in my bed, and closed my eyes. I swear I heard Billy sobbing in his room.

Chapter 11

When I left my room the next morning, Billy was on the futon, running his hands through his hair.

"Oh my god, Hurricane Margo struck again last night. You won't believe what she and her friend Tika did. We drove around Lemon Grove for an hour looking for their dealer. We stop at this apartment complex, go inside, then they then suck and fuck this hideous middle-aged Rican for a freebie. They had the cash and everything. I just sat there watching. I love Liberty and all, but that bitch is fucking trouble. Don't get me wrong, I think a little blow every now and then is good for the heart and soul, but the blows for coke should stop with the nose, if you know what I'm sayin'. I need to just stay away from her. I was getting too deep into that shit in New York. I had to get away. But you know what they say? No matter where you go, there it is . . ."

"Yeah, well there's a lotta glass outside. You should get your little hairdresser to come back and help you clean it up."

"Yo, she fucking fried my hair. I told her no, but . . ."

I spent the rest of the weekend at the beach or locked away in my room, and soon it was over.

Mr. Rodriguez organized a pep rally to get the kids excited for the beginning of their F2ST preparation. It started after lunch that

Monday and lasted the rest of the day. I had my fourth period line up in the hall and took them down to the auditorium. It was a madhouse in there. Those kids were already buck-wild and needed no extra "pep." My kids were horrible. Once I got them seated, they kept throwing paper at each other, and swearing, and doing the regular bullshit that gave adults who tried to control them ulcers. I looked over and saw the Professor's group sitting quietly with their backs against the chairs. I observed him. One of his kids stuck a piece of gum in his mouth and threw the wrapper on the floor. The Professor just strolled over, squatted down next to the perpetrator, and said loudly, "Excuse me, kids, would everyone please turn around and point at the litterbug."

They all got into it, turning, and pointing, and smiling. The kid who threw the wrapper shouted a few swear words and showed a few people his middle finger, but soon, he picked up the wrapper and walked it over to a garbage can. Across the aud, Margo was having as much of a hell of a time as I was trying to control her kids. She looked as if she was starting to lose it.

"K'deysha, I've told you three times now to sit. NOW I MEAN SIT!"

K'deysha just shook her ass at Liberty and continued talking. Liberty called Ms. Dawson over, and Dawson got the little demon to sit.

When the rally started, most of the kids stopped talking. Mr. Rodriguez walked onstage and gave some speech about them being the wave of the future, and how he believed in them, and all that crap, and soon the lights dimmed and the music started. The curtains opened and three eighth grade boys walked to the mic. They took turns rapping, but not about the F2ST. Lyrics I heard included, "That bitch drop to her knees," and "I make the ladies go crazy." Perhaps I didn't hear them correctly, because even the other teachers were cheering them on. The rap act was followed by the cheerleaders. Again the music started, but the girls broke out into what could have only been inspired by the movements of strippers. They shook their asses and tits, and at one point dropped into a squat and put on a slow spread that their miniskirts were helpless to conceal. I got a shot of jailbait muff and had to turn away. I again looked to the crowd for someone to shut this down, but even Dawson and Rodriguez were pumping their fists and whooping it up with the other teachers.

A few, however, weren't. Rachel Golden looked horrified, Margo turned her back to the stage, and Ben Fallon just stood there laughing and recording the whole thing on his phone. I kept my eyes averted until the music ended and the girls hopped off stage. I felt both perverted and violated all at once. It was a confusing and shaming combination.

The next day, I got into an inspired discussion with my new honors group about whether or not there should be censorship in schools. Zara led the discussion. "The First Amendment protects our right to express ourselves. I don't see why anybody should try to limit that."

"Are there any topics you deem inappropriate for school?" I said.

"I can't think of any. I mean, we're here to learn, right? Why not be honest?" Zara said.

"Yeah," Rudy said, "and it's not like we haven't heard all that shit before."

"I think you just made your point," I said.

"Oh, sorry," Rudy said.

"You're such a dumbass, Rudy," Teonnie said from the back of the room.

"Easy," I said.

"Well," Teonnie said, "you just said it was okay to express ourselves and to be honest. I'm just bein' real. You a dumbass, Rudy, and that's a fact."

"Yeah, and you're a real bit—" Rudy looked at me and stopped.

"What's wrong with that? It's not like it ain't true," Teonnie said.

"There's a fine line between honesty and abuse," I said.

"And where would that be?" Zara said.

"I, uh . . . I'm not really sure. Just lay off the swearing, alright?" I said.

The conversation continued like that for the rest of class. I didn't know why, but every so often I could engage the students in wonderful and passionate discussions like this. This usually only happened once every few weeks. Experience would later prove that I couldn't force these things; they just happened naturally. Sometimes I think these conversations were inspired by current events in the news, other times by current, or repressed, events in the kids' personal lives. But either way, it was good to talk it through.

A knock at the door interrupted Jenni Pierce as she laid into a diatribe on why it was necessary at times to censor speech, otherwise "All hell breaks loose."

All hell was about to . . .

I opened the door, and on the other side was Lorraine Jessup, the she-beast at the helm of the English Department. She stood there and observed the class for a moment before addressing me.

"Mr. Ent . . . uh?"

The kids laughed.

"Entelechy," I said.

"Yes, well sir, I just came down to see how instruction was going for the F2ST."

"Oh, uh, well, we, uh, were having a discussion—" I said.

"Well, Mr. Ent . . . uh—whatever, you were at the faculty meeting the other day, weren't you?"

"Yeah, I was—"

"Can I have a word with you outside?"

"Uh . . . sure?"

"OHHHH, you in trouble Mr. Entelechy!"

"No, I'm not!"

Ms. Jessup held the door, and I walked outside. I stood against the wall and put my hands in my pockets. She towered over me, pointing her damned finger in my face.

"Now, Mr. En, Mr. Rodriguez was very explicit that all the departments work together for F2ST preparation, was he not?"

"Well, yeah—"

"Well, I don't think I need to tell you how important these tests are for the school. Now, we can't all be so lucky as to be in the History Department or whatever other department that doesn't have to worry about their students' scores. But we in the English Department need you all to come together to assist us in preparation for these tests. You received your F2ST workbooks, did you not?"

"Uh, yeah I've got a stack of them, but the students hate them. I think our time could be better used for—"

"*Your* time? Unfortunately we are not working on *your* time, Mr. En, are we? You're working on the school's time. And if the school says to study, you say, 'How long.' Got it?"

"Well, uh—"

"Excuse me, I didn't hear you."

"Yeah, sure."

"Good. Now have a nice day!"

She power-walked to the next classroom on her route of terror. I saw Santoro's door slam shut before she could reach it. I walked back in my room.

"Oh, you in trouble, Mr. En."

"Yeah, yeah . . . okay guys, let's get out our F2ST books," I said.

"Oh, I hate those. They're boring and you don't learn anything."

"I SAID GET OUT YOUR DAMNED BOOKS!"

They shut right up and got to work. Not another word was said until the bell rang. Even Teonnie was quiet.

I stayed late that afternoon. I'd been staying until about 5:00 or 5:30 on most days since the start of the year to honor a pledge I'd made with myself to never bring work home. That pledge was broken a few weeks into the year, but I still did my best to separate GW from Paradise. I finished grading some essays, put the grades in the computer, shut it down, and headed down the hall. I passed Santoro's room on the way. The light was still on. I knocked.

He waved from inside. "Come in, come in."

I walked in. "Working late again, huh?" I said. The man was there long after everyone else left almost every day.

"I was just working on a proposal for a field trip. I think it'd be great to take the kids down to the Everglades for an airboat tour. I've been trying to put something like this together for years, but it always gets rejected. The administration seems to think the kids can't handle it."

"That'd be great. Do you need any help with it?"

"No, I can take care of it." He walked over, right up to me. "You know, I saw your little conversation with Ms. Jessup today."

"Oh, uh, you did?" My head dropped to my chest.

"I'm gonna tell you something important—something you should never forget. Never, and I mean never, take shit from anybody . . . Porqueria!" He pumped his fist to his chest.

"Yeah, but she was just doing her job and—"

"Is it her job to humiliate you, especially in front of your students?"

"Well, I guess not."

"Hell no."

"I've heard other people telling me I shouldn't take shit, but I don't think I know what that means."

"It's much simpler than it seems. Just listen to that voice inside of you. If you feel like someone is violating it, then you speak up."

"I don't know. I mean, I guess it doesn't bother me all that much. I think it might just be better to suffer through in silence."

"It's never better to suffer through anything in silence." He pointed to a picture of the Civil Rights March on Washington on his wall. "It's by remaining quiet that we lose our power. It's by suffering alone that we suffer together. If you don't learn how to stand up for yourself, then how can you stand up for anyone else?" My head perked back to default. I nodded a few times, said good-bye, and headed out the door.

Chapter 12

I checked my computer when I got home that night. Lila still hadn't responded to my email. Amira Kadiri, however, had. Amira was my sixth grade art teacher at St. Anthony's Elementary in North Buffalo. Amira only taught for a year before quitting and opening up a flower shop across the street from my house—but that year was one of the most significant of my childhood. The woman was a half-Lebanese, half-Spanish vixen born in Beirut. And she was lethal any time she went out in public. I couldn't count the number of times I'd seen cars swerve as they passed her walking down the street. Every so often you'd hear, "Hey, baby, why don't you shake that thing my way?" or some variation, and I knew she'd just left her shop—which is probably why she avoided the public as much as she could. She'd arrived in my life near the beginning of my adventure through puberty, and those images I had of her leaning over a table and sculpting clay or rubbing the paint off of brushes were just enough to bring me through many a session locked away in my upstairs bathroom. She'd come over to my house and invite me to her shop sometimes when the screaming was so loud she could hear it across the street. She'd give me some paints and paper and say, "Trust the art." Sometimes I'd paint, even though I hated it, but other times I'd pretend I was and watch her move throughout the shop, smelling flowers and humming tunes. At forty, she was still as gorgeous as ever. And for some reason, maybe because we both knew I was moving away forever, she actually gave me her number and email address when I asked for them the day before I left for Miami.

And it was her email I read that night. "Hey, Little Lukie, it's so nice to hear from you. I can't believe you're all grown up and teaching now. I'm sure all the girls can't concentrate with such a cute teacher! I love Miami and am so jealous of you. I have some friends that still live there, and I was thinking of visiting them sometime in December. Maybe we could get together for some drinks?"

Oh my god! Suddenly, all of those fantasies rushed through me. I decided to give them a proper exit, which I did . . . twice! I wrote her back something innocuous, then I ate a late dinner and went to sleep.

Wolo and I went kayaking after school the next day. Around that time, I'd started darting out of school earlier than usual once or twice a week and heading with him to Hedman State Park to kayak or hit the bike trails. Hedman was a gorgeous spread of land and mangrove open to the public for a small fee, and was a great spot to, as Wolo put it, "Wash the stank of GW from our hair." I didn't have a bike, nor a kayak, so I'd rent whichever I needed when we went. Wolo had one of each and always told me, "It'd be cheaper in the long haul to buy one. I mean, we'll probably be doing this for years to come, right?"

But I always rented.

That day, we pushed the kayaks into a small clearing in the mangrove, and took off through the narrow, canopied waterways, which ran like aquatic highways around the perimeter of the park. The place would have been flawless if not for one thing. "Are you sure there are no gators here?" I'd always ask, and "Yeah, stop being a pussy," he'd always answer.

"I can't believe that beast Jessup actually came into your room." He paddled beside me. "Some of these grownups are just as bad as the kids."

Some people glided by quickly, but Wolo and I always paddled slowly, taking in the sights.

"Yeah, they are," I said. "Santoro was telling me I should stand up to her."

"Hell yeah, you should. If she comes back, just tell her to fuck off. I'm serious. Say 'Fuck off you dumb, dry cunt.' She has no authority to be monitoring your classes anyways."

"Yeah."

"I'm so glad we got Santoro as a department head. He's the fucking man."

"Yeah, he is."

"He's not exactly the greatest teacher. All he does really are arts and crafts, and coloring projects, and shit like that. The kids don't learn much, but at least they're not tearing the place apart. He's more of a politician than a teacher. He really has a way of dealing with people."

"Sure does."

"But enough of that hell hole. Let's make a rule to never speak about that stank pit ever again while we're out here in the bosom of Mother Nature."

"Fine by me . . . speaking of Mother Nature, should we happen to see a gator, what should—"

"Will you stop with that shit? Man, I fear for my life more at GW than I do here with the gators."

"Hey, you said we weren't going to mention school, Wolinski."

"Yeah, fuck you." He splashed me with some water using his oar.

We glided to the edge of the highway where it met Biscayne Bay. "C'mon, man." Wolo paddled ahead of me. "You see that island over there?"

"That one way out there?"

"Yeah, let's head over."

And so it was. The water looked deep here—indistinguishable from when travelling over the middle of the ocean.

"Hey, Wolo, sharks don't come into the bay, do they?"

"No, they all get eaten by the gators."

I paddled ahead, never erasing from my imagination the horrifying image of a twenty-foot great white suddenly emerging from the dark blue void, mouth opened wide, barreling upward upon my thin, plastic kayak.

The waters got a little choppier the farther out we traveled, and every so often, we'd get tossed around as the wake from a speedboat or yacht passed through. We eventually made it to the island. We dragged our kayaks onto the sand, and Wolo reached into a small cooler and pulled out a six-pack. He tossed me a brew then wandered into the water, submerged his lower half, and took a shit.

"How are you gonna wipe?" I said.

"I'm in the world's largest bathtub," he said with a smile.

He finished, bobbed up and down a few times, and we drank some beers while lying in the sand.

"Man, we really gotta get you laid," he said. "What do you think about that Margo chick? I mean, she is half plastic, but there's something about her that I'd really love to fuck. And god, them titties . . ."

"Well, I kinda got a girlfriend in Mexico."

"Yeah, and when was the last time you saw her?"

"About five months ago."

"Five months, huh? And when was the last time you spoke with her?"

"Well, she sent me an email a few weeks ago . . ."

"I said, spoke with, not email with."

"I don't even know. Probably four months."

"I hate to break the news, but that girl isn't your girlfriend."

"Well, it's complicated."

"Only 'cause you're making it complicated. Even if it was love, one of you is going to have to make a commitment. Either she'll have to move here, or you'll have to go there. Fuck it! I mean, look around you, man. This city is literally filled with gorgeous women just waiting for a young stud like you to defile them. You're young. You shouldn't be worried about commitments."

"Well, how old do you have to be before you start worrying about commitments?"

"Hey, if you're talking about that little tug job a few weeks ago, that was a mistake. I was drunk. I love my wife."

"Yeah, well how many mistakes do you need to make before you see it as a lifestyle?"

"New rule. Why don't we leave the wives and girlfriends out of Mother Nature as well, okay?"

"We might as well leave ourselves out of it then, too."

"Let's just keep going, alright." He got up and walked to his kayak. "Hey, I heard a funny joke the other day. How does an Alabaman mother know her daughter just had her first period?"

"I don't know. How?"

"Her son's dick tastes a little funny."

"I didn't know you had a sister."

"Fuck you, man."

We got back in the kayaks and did a lap around the island, then headed back for the small opening in the mangrove leading inside the park. We paddled to the spot where we first launched, and I left my kayak with the other rentals and helped Wolo carry his to his car. We strapped it to the roof and headed to a nearby bar for some drinks and dinner. I didn't get home until about ten. When I walked through the door, I heard Billy in his room, arguing with someone on the phone.

"I told you already, I had no case. I lost the paperwork, remember? Yeah, well you aren't exactly the brightest person either . . ."

I shut my door and flipped on the A/C. That dull rattle cooed me right to sleep.

I woke early the next morning. I went to the kitchen and started into a bowl of cereal. Billy came to the kitchen soon after and got a glass of water.

"Oh my god, I didn't sleep at all again last night. This is getting serious," he said.

"Shit, man, when was the last time you got any sleep?"

"I don't even want to talk about it. I've maybe slept the whole night through once or twice since moving here. These bags under my eyes are gonna be permanent."

"Maybe you should go see a doctor?"

"Yeah, and what are they gonna do? They'll take a two-second look, throw some sleeping pills at me, and send me on my way so they can take care of the next five hundred people they're trying to cram in that day. Fuck it. You just gotta learn to take care of yourself 'cause nobody out there's gonna do it for you."

"Well, I don't know if that's true."

"Don't kid yourself, Mr. En. You're no different than anyone else." Billy grabbed a banana from his side of the cupboard. It was covered in rat hairs.

"I never said I was. I just don't think that life is merely a game of survival. There are plenty of people in this world who care about you."

"Typical Lukesito, always living in a fantasy." Billy wiped the hairs off his banana with a towel and unpeeled it.

"Hey, I've experienced it. I know what real love feels like. You telling me that's not real?"

"Puh-leeze, love is bullshit. You think any of these guys I'm seeing wouldn't go tip-first into another sphincter the second it opened for them?"

"Yeah, well, I feel sorry for you." I slurped down the milk and put my bowl in the sink.

"Of course you do." Billy took one bite of his banana and threw it out. He wandered back to his room, tossed some things around, and came back outside. "Oh my god, I can't find my keys. Would you drive me to school today?"

"No." I went to the bathroom to brush my teeth.

"I'm gonna be late . . ."

"Well, that's your fucking problem. You lose something else every fucking day."

"I'll never make it on time! You gotta help!"

"No, I don't. I'm tired of bailing you out."

"Fuck you! Margo's right about you, you know! You really do think you're better than us. Don't you think for a second just because you wear a tie to work, and you're bigger than me, that it means you're better. I could take you in a fight if I had to!" Billy walked to the bathroom.

"What the hell are you talking about?" I spat out the toothpaste and started rinsing my mouth.

"I may look small, but I'll never let anybody take me down! I'll bite your jugular if I have to!"

"Yo, I really think you may be going crazy. You should seriously see a doctor." I dried my mouth with a towel and walked to the door, but Billy blocked my exit.

"You're the crazy one! When was the last time you got laid? Do you even like women anymore?"

I pushed past him and continued into the living room.

"Fuck this," I said. "I don't need this crap. Look, I'm leaving. I'll leave the house key under the mat so you can get in after work. Have fun on your precious bus!"

I shut the door, walked to my car, and took off for school. I made it over the three lanes for my turn in probably the shortest distance I ever had—maybe about ten yards. The causeway I normally took was under repair that day, so I had to take a new route. I was late, and driving like a Miamian, and in my haste, did something stupid. I was on a busy road and noticed that the right lane was moving faster than the left one I was in. I kept my eye on the side mirror, watching the van coming down behind me in the right lane. I had to wait for the tractor-trailer on my right to pass before I could cut in front of that van, which was quickly closing in. I focused on the van, watching the trailer with my peripherals. I saw the rear trailer wheel pass and turned my car, not realizing there was a second wheel to the rig—which I turned directly into. The crunch I heard was nowhere near as bad as the shame that came with it. "God-fucking damn it! I'm so fucking stupid . . ."

I continued to GW and assessed the damage in the parking lot. A group of kids gathered around.

"Man, somebody fucked up yo' car!"

"You don't own nobody money, do you?"

"Get the hell outta here!"

The front right headlight was busted and the right side, from passenger door to front bumper, was dented in. I kicked the car and walked to class. I could hear their words. "There go that white man!"

First period was particularly bad that day. I asked Destiny Taylor to sit and the Assholes got into it with me.

"She don't gotta listen to you, mister."

"Yeah, it's a free country."

"I'm going to count to three, and if you're not sitting by then, then you're outta here. One . . . Two . . ." I counted with my fingers.

She continued to stand, crossing her arms, and bobbing her stupid head around like an asshole.

"Three!"

Still standing.

"Okay, tough guy," I said, "please head down to Mr. Wolenowitz's classroom."

"You can't make me."

"No, I can't, but security can."

I looked out into the hall and was delighted to see Ms. Robespierre walking by.

"Excuse me, Ms. Robespierre, would you please escort Destiny Taylor here to Mr. Wolenowitz's classroom?"

"Why, I certainly can." She popped inside my room and started motioning for Destiny to follow. "C'mon, child."

Destiny grabbed her books and stormed out, stomping her feet like a dickhead.

"Does anybody else want to join her?" I stood in front of the class and spread my arms wide.

Huffs and puffs and eye rolls, but no verbal challenge.

I ate lunch at Wolo's that afternoon.

"I'm cracking up, man." I paced the floor in his room.

"You really need to get away from that guy. I know he's your friend, but he's just as toxic as these kids."

"He's not that bad."

"Tell me again how great your morning was?"

I stopped pacing. "Alright, it's bad." I walked to a desk and sat.

A knock at the door. Wolo answered it and on the other side was one of his eighth graders.

"Mr. Wolo, can I eat lunch in here today? Some girls are after me."

"I'm sorry, Dina, I really can't let you eat here. You're supposed to be in the cafeteria. I could get into a lot of trouble—" Wolo stood between her and the classroom.

"Please! Every day they pick on me and take my food and—" she said.

"Alright, you know what, just take a seat." Wolo swung the door open and got out of her way.

"Thanks, Mr. Wolo! You're the best!"

She sat somewhere in the back of the room. Wolo sat back down behind his desk.

"Man, my wife is great. Look what she made me. Vegan chili. She's busy as hell with studying for exams, and she took the time to make me dinner last night."

"That smells good," I said.

"Hey, Dina, what you got in that bag there?" Wolo said.

"Oh, just some chips and a hot sausage."

"Put that crap away." He reached into his lunch bag and pulled out a banana and a yogurt, and brought them over to her. "Here, eat these instead. If you wanna be big and strong enough to fight off those other girls, then you need to start feeding your body right."

She smiled, said thank you, and started on the banana. I got a text message from Billy.

"Hey, he just sent me a message," I said. I read it. "'I'm sorry for blowing up at you this morning. I'd like to talk when you get home.' See, he's not that bad."

"He sounds like your girlfriend."

Dina laughed at that one.

I got home earlier than usual that day. I took a shower and was able to make dinner before Billy got back. He started into it almost immediately. "Yo, I'm sorry for getting so upset this morning . . ."

"It's okay, man. I know you've been stressed—"

". . . But you really need to stop acting so superior to everyone. Do you really think you could take me in a fight? I'm a lot tougher than I look . . ."

I took my dinner into my room and locked the door.

Friday came slowly. I took my weekly cruise up the beach while listening to "China Girl" and came back to the apartment. Billy was just finishing a phone conversation as I walked inside the living room. He hung up and put his phone in his pocket.

"Oh god, that was my friend, Giovanni. He works on Wall

Street. The guy's pulling in about a half a mil a year. He used to buy me things all the time. I mean, he's actually pretty hideous, and he's a huge asshole, but he knows how to treat a fella."

"Sounds like a catch."

"Oh shut up. I told him about my lawsuit. He said I should try to take the NYPSD for as much cash as possible and store it away. He said the word on Wall Street is that this country is headed for an economic disaster—'cataclysmic' he called it. Something about a house bubble. He said there's never been one like this before—that it could seriously send the US back to pre-World War II status. Those guys are all hush hush about it, but it's supposedly gonna happen soon. This whole fucking country is going down, and I'll be damned if I go down with the ship. I'm just gonna save what I can, then move to the DR, marry a rich papi, and spend the rest of my days by the beach."

"Shit, man, I really gotta get back to Mexico."

"Eww, Mexicans are gross. Caribbean papis are the best. They're just so much sexier."

"That's what I was thinking."

"God, and that kid does enough yip each weekend to power a small city. He ain't gonna last much longer. You know what he told me?"

"You should get checked for the booty-clap?"

"Eww, no! He said, and get this, 'I already know I'm gonna OD, but that's the life. I'm going up hard and coming down the same way.'"

"The man knows his physics . . ."

"I think he seriously wants to die. He said he doesn't care to see thirty."

"Thirty ain't no guarantee."

"Kid makes half a mil a year, but is somehow living in debt. He spends it faster than he makes it . . . You know, the worst part of all this is that he's not even that smart. He was always right there in the middle of the grazing herds in school. I graduated second in my class of over four hundred. And yet, you look at us now, and he's making well over ten times what I am."

"Yeah, and spending it twenty times as fast."

"Yeah . . . I don't know. Sometimes I think about this stuff. Like maybe I could have been something better. But then I think about this kid, who's so willing to go down with the ship and I ask myself, 'What's the point?' Why even take that first step?"

"Yeah, but not all success ends up like that. Hell, I wouldn't even call that a success. That guy's mistakes aren't yours, ya' dig?"

"Yeah, I guess so. I don't know. I just think about these things, and I can't stop." He got up and walked to his room.

I thought about those things too.

I walked to my room and locked the door. I checked my emails. Amira wrote back!

"Hey there, Lukie! I want to come down to Miami sometime before Christmas, but my friend is going to be out of town. Do you know a place I could stay?"

Oh, this was too good.

"I sure do, dear. There's plenty of room at my apartment . . ."

I couldn't walk anywhere the rest of that night without pointing out my destination with my wiener.

Margo came over later on and tossed a baggie of white on the coffee table. This seemed to be a declaration of some sort; she'd at least been discreet about it before.

"Don't worry, Little Lukesito, we'll cut you a few lines," she said.

"No, you can take it all," I said. "I don't roll with snow." I got up and walked to the kitchen. I grabbed a beer, but stopped myself from opening it when Margo got into her usual shit. "Lukesito the Judgmental strikes again!"

They broke into a song and dance, so I put the beer back in the fridge and walked out the front door. I started down the stairs but was stopped by a curious male about my age whose eyes were twitching at irregular beats.

"Oh, oh, oh, don't you worry about me. I'm a—a good boy. I stay with my mom." He was a big guy. His ass blocked my passage down the stairs.

"Uh, okay?" I didn't try to pass him—something about this guy told me not to push. It was clear he was either drug deranged or suffering some psychotic disorder. The Cuban woman's door opened as far as the chain would allow. She stuck her snout through the gap and said to me, "Oh, he don't bother you, he don't bother you. Paco, come inside, now!" She shut the door, slid off the chain, and opened it.

"I'm a, I'm a, I'm a good boy . . ."

Paco got up, walked inside, and the door slammed behind him. I could hear the chain being slid shut and a lot of yelling. I wandered to the Tide Pool, but stopped myself from going in. Paola was there, and looking luscious, and was chatting with some handsome, bearded gentleman in the back. Both were laughing. I kept going. I popped in a bodega and bought a sixer of tall boys, and walked to the beach. The place was different at night. The creatures came out of the shadows and reveled in the darkness. Some of their faces were now familiar to me. One guy would run up and down the beach, pumping his arms and twirling, dancing to the music in his head. Another guy would stand at the water's edge and just stare into the darkness for as long as I'd be there. Fishermen would sometimes stand at that water's edge too, casting their lines into the unknown. They were the only normalcy in the scene.

I sat there that night, drinking brew after brew as the dark thoughts I'd so repressed came pounding into my consciousness. It'd been four months since I'd first come to Miami, and I hadn't written more than a sentence or two of my book. I feared it would never be finished—and that fear wasn't so much that I'd never find fortune or fame, but more that I'd soon disappear into those dark waters without ever having so much as said properly my own name.

School was claiming my absolute best. Every day was a struggle to stop the panic from taking over. Every day was a fight to stay at the head of that classroom without the kids realizing the utter terror I felt facing them day in and day out. When they finally did realize this terror, I knew they'd run me the hell out of there straight into oblivion. Who the fuck was I to tell them what to do? Who was I to guide their lives? If they'd only known how many times they almost had me—how many times I was only one more "Fuck this," or one extra "White man," from throwing my podium through a window, hopping through, and running off into the paved horizon, never looking back. If there was a way to write and teach I hadn't yet found it. If there was a way to hold a full-time job and maintain myself, it was lost on me. I was this job and this job was me. I wanted to quit more than I'd ever wanted to quit anything. But I made a commitment, and I signed a contract and an apartment lease. I put myself into this situation, and I knew if I ran from this, it'd set a pretty bad precedent for future endeavors. I wasn't a teacher, but I also wasn't a writer. A writer writes. A writer lives. I saw stories everywhere around me, but had no patience or energy to develop them. There were so many Americans who'd fight to the death to try to convince me that what I was doing was honorable. That working full time at the expense of my identity was the only way. That sacrificing everything good in me for the tax beast was my duty as an American. But this seemed as large a load of bullshit as Margo's self-medication regimen. I agreed with convention that it was wrong to just piss it all away. But it was just as bad to go left after right into a horrifically shitty job every day without ever questioning why. Without ever questioning whether it could be better—whether we could improve things, put health and humanity at the center, not needless sacrifice, which manifested itself in these hideous ratings we gave things. I had a theory that we needed these ratings—"evidence" of something's worth—because we had no idea how to gauge value for ourselves. We needed to know The Eternal Committee deemed this school an F or this restaurant a C or this daughter a "lesbian" or this kid a "thug" because we had absolutely no fucking idea what the hell was ever going on, and these ratings just gave us some semblance of security. These people who can't decide a single thing for themselves. These people who hold so strongly onto their tired beliefs and jobs because otherwise life would just be one big, inescapable nervous breakdown, where we'd be faced with nothing other than the hideous demons and repressed, echoing, vicious voices in our heads, forever wailing and tormenting, born of a life plagued by trauma and shame. Where it'd be entirely up to us to craft life and experience with our own inadequate fingertips and clumsy labor. Where we'd never have to touch a single thing but eventually the bottom of a grave—and even then, a poor quality of sleep. Restless, time wasted, potential missed—haunted for all eternity.

Miami had already chewed up Abbi. She'd applied at NYU Law and was there in *the* City, eagerly awaiting the start of her new career. But it wasn't getting me. Every day I went into school, I walked into that place thinking, 'Today is going to be the day. Today, they're finally going to run me out of here." Part of me felt at place on that dark beach. But another part was undeniably drawn to the GW challenge.

When I returned home that night, Billy wasn't there. I figured he'd gone out with Margo. I went to sleep.

When I woke up the next morning, Billy still wasn't there. I made breakfast and ate it while watching some banda music videos on the Mexican cable station. Billy wandered in during a wavering grito. He looked and smelled like shit.

"Yo, you'll never believe what happened to me last night," he said.

"Damn, you look like you spent the night in a dumpster."

"Close. Oh my god, Margo is seriously psycho. That bitch blew enough yip last night to help Freud discover a new level of consciousness. I kept telling her I didn't want anymore, but she didn't listen. She just kept cutting me lines and forcing me to take them. This is not good! We went down to South Beach, but got into an argument on the bus, so I just ended up hopping off and walking back up north. I realized I lost my keys again, so I just ended up sleeping with Carlos and the twins in the alley behind the Tide Pool. I woke up this morning literally laying on an empty bottle of wine."

"Holy shit!"

"Yeah, that bitch is trouble. I need to stay away from her. This is the same shit Julian was getting me into in NYC. I just need to get away from these people. They suck me up into their crazy whirlwinds and I have no idea what happens."

"I told you that bitch was crazy. Just stop answering her calls."

"Eh, whatever. She's not that bad. Oh my god, teaching and blow just do not go together. I mean, I know all teachers are alcoholics, but a coke hangover and a regular hangover are just no comparison. Seriously, it takes me days to get over a night of snow blowing. I don't know how she does it. I don't know where she even gets the money for all that. You see the glacier she was carrying around last night?"

"It looked like the third act of *Scarface*."

"I'm gonna try and get some sleep."

"Yeah, well take a shower first. You smell like Carlos's boxer shorts."

I finished breakfast and went to my room. I flipped on the computer and checked my emails. There was one from Lila. "Hola Luke! I have missed you. I have been thinking about us. I'd prefer for to talk to you about all this, not write it. Cuidate amorsini! Besos . . ."

I wrote her back, then immediately started looking for flights. Everything over winter break was too expensive. I thought about pulling a Margo, and just taking a week off of school, but remembered

I had a four-day vacation in January. I checked prices, and they were more reasonable, so I called the airline to book a flight.

"Well, sir, it will cost eight hundred for a flight to Mariposa International, but only four hundred to Guadalajara. You could always take a bus from Guadalajara into Mari—"

"Direct to Mariposa!"

And like that, Mr. Entelechy was going back to Mexico.

Wolo and I went biking at Hedman that afternoon. We hit one of the expert trails, which had a spot that opened up to a gorgeous view of Biscayne Bay. We stopped and sat on a picnic table. Wolo pulled out his one-hitter and took a rip. He passed it my way. "Take a hit. This is great shit—it'll mellow you right out."

"Naw, I'll pass." I waved it away.

He took another hit. "So you're going to Mexico, huh?"

"Yeah, the second week in January."

"You better not disappear. I'll send Rotter down to capture you and bring you back in one of the folds in her ass."

"Oh, no thank you, sir. I'll come back of my own accord."

"So, you really dig this girl?"

"She's everything, man. I don't know what I was thinking leaving her. I mean, she's perfect. Gorgeous, kind, intelligent, classy. I don't know."

"Yeah, but didn't you say you also felt miserable while you were there?"

"Yeah, but this time it'll be different."

"What makes you think that?"

"I don't know. I'm just different is all, I guess?"

"Well, like I've said, if you're gonna be together, either she'll have to come here or you'll have to go there. You got a good job here, man. I mean, I know GW is shit, but you know how many people out there would love to have full-time employment and benefits? You gotta think about your paycheck sometimes and not all the crap you can be spending it on, know what I'm sayin'?"

"Yeah—oh shit, you know, I just remembered this friend from back home is coming to visit next week. I totally forgot about that!"

"What, is he like an asshole or something?"

"No, *she* is like a fucking Arabian goddess. She played some seductress role in a telenovela when she was like twenty. She used to live here. The woman is unbelievable. She's a fucking belly dancer, too."

"So, what's the problem?"

"The problem is that I'm trying to patch things up with Lila and now this little visit's in the way. What am I gonna do?"

"So, you got a bikini model waiting for you in Mexico and a Lebanese belly dancer coming to see you in Miami? Sounds to me like you're gonna have one helluva time!"

"Shit, this is horrible! I never think anything through."

"Seems to me you have the exact opposite problem. Look, man, you're what, twenty-four?"

I nodded.

"Why don't you just allow yourself to have a little fun before you start having a midlife crisis, alright?"

"I don't know. I don't know how. Let's just hit the trail, alright?

He nodded and soon we were at it.

Wolo had a date with his wife that night, so I went back to the Beach. When I returned to the apartment, Billy was in his room getting ready for the evening.

"Yo, Margo called. You wanna head down to Manolo's?" he said.

"Uh, yeah sure." Anything to get out of my head.

We took a bus south and got off on 40th Street. Margo was at the bar and already a one-woman party. "Hey, Ben, another shot of Jaeger!"

Billy and I walked over and sat next to her.

"Why hello, darlings! I've got some good news. I've decided to start my own publishing company."

"I thought you had a publish—" I said.

"What could they possibly know that I don't? Gentlemen, this is where the real money is at. By this time next year, I should be well on my way to high society. It's time to celebrate."

We did some shots. Margo tried to stick another one of her pink, fruity cocktails under my snout, but I again refused.

"Oh, dear, there he goes again!" she said.

Sometime during the conversation, my problem rose to the surface.

"Oh, that is just delicious!" Margo said. "You know, this is just like a sequence from a great novel, *The Sun Also Rises*, or *The Great Gatsby*. Darling, you need to realize the poetry of this situation. You have the sexy childhood fuck fantasy coming to life and your true love waiting for you on an exotic beach in some tropical country. You get to fuck the past and the future. Just scrumptious!"

"Christ, well my future's fucked if it finds out about my past."

"Are you even together?" Billy said.

"I guess, technically, no we're not."

"Then what's the problem? I went to Puerto Rico while I was still with Diego, and I got down with plenty of papis there. I don't see what the problem is."

"Well, maybe that's the problem," I said.

"Darling, just take life as it comes," Margo said. "You need to just imbibe it as if it were a wonderful, barrel-aged wine. We only get so much time here. You just need to drink it up!"

She held up her glass and we did a "Cheers." I was partially glad that I was three for three in receiving friends' blessings for what I already knew I was going to do, but partially devastated by the ease in which I rationalized this approval. We drank heavily and returned to Liberty's place when the bar closed.

"Who wants hot toddys?" she said as we stumbled through her front door. Her building was a gorgeous, pink Art Deco wonder settled across the street from an opening between two high rises, giving her a perfect view of the ocean. Opposite of the beauty of the exterior was the interior. The kitchen sink was littered with dishes that looked to have been sitting there for weeks. Roaches scurried all over the floor, claiming some of the many small, crusted treasures scattered across it and hauling them back to the safety of the holes in the walls. A large aquarium sat against a wall in the living room and inside was a small Burmese python; the whole place stunk of snake shit. Her computer desk was piled high with self-help books and novels that were all published before the 1950s. Sylvia Plath, Jane Austen, and F. Scott Fitzgerald seemed to be her favorites.

She walked to her bedroom, which was a disaster—clothes everywhere, dirty dishes on the bed, overfilled ashtrays—and changed into something more comfortable, but she didn't shut the door. She was wearing peach panties and a black bra that night. But the most curious of the oddities of that apartment was the sound coming from the bathroom.

"Uh, Margo, did you forget to turn off your shower before you left your house today?"

"Oh, no." She slipped a cotton shirt over her head and met us in the living room. "My neighbors can be quite noisome and inconsiderate. I run the shower to drown out the noise."

"Even when you're not home?"

"Well, I don't use *hot* water, if that's what you're implying."

Liberty went to the kitchen and whipped up the toddys. Mine tasted like a steaming cup of spiced kitchen cleaning products. I set it down on the coffee table beside a book. I checked out the binding: *Everything's an Affair*, by Margo Liberty. I nudged Billy. He picked it up.

"So this is the infamous book, huh, Margo?" He flipped through the pages.

"Yes it is, darling—but that's about the only copy which exists.

Those brutes down at Albatross wouldn't know a good book if it came in the title. They said, and I quote, 'It's fabulous, but we just don't know how to market it.'" She got up and walked to the kitchen. "Which, in publishing talk, simply means that it's ahead of its time." She came back to the living room with a teaspoon of allspice berries; without asking, she dumped more berries in each of our drinks. "The world needs about ten solid years to catch up. I'm just going to enjoy myself until then. Teaching is so innocuous—I can do that in my sleep. Just a way to pass the time, really . . ."

"What about your publishing company?" I said.

She laughed. "What kind of etiquette would it be to publish my own novel?"

"Etiquette?" Billy said. He set his cup on an end table.

"Yes." Margo picked up Billy's cup, set a coaster beneath it, and put it back down. "Which is something you obviously still need to learn."

"How did you go about getting published?" I said, still ignoring my cooling toddy. "What's the process?"

She started laughing so hard she spilled half of her drink on the carpet and didn't seem to care. "Oh my goodness, *you're* not thinking of getting published, are you? How cute!" She walked over and patted me on top of my head. "That's a real *novel* idea, isn't it, Billsito?"

Billy started laughing as well.

"Fuck you both." I got up and walked to the door.

"Oh, darling, I should hope you won't judge us if we continue to drink without your perfect self."

"Don't worry, I won't be judging you for *that*." I took off. I decided to walk the twenty blocks back to clear my head. The sun was already starting to rise over the Atlantic. The horizon was amber and blood red and quivering, and the warm tropical water filled my lungs. This was such a gorgeous place; the people living here were no match.

Chapter 13

The next week in school was more of the same shit. New kids came, old kids left, swear words were upchucked, fights were threatened. But none of that chaos compared to what I'd put myself through preparing for Amira's visit. On Wednesday, Lila and I spoke via video chat. We discussed how we'd missed each other. We blew each other kisses, smiled while making comments with sexual connotations, and said we loved each other. Then I hung up and took my bed sheets to the Laundromat.

On Friday afternoon, I skipped out on "China Girl" and my usual trip up the coast and headed inland to Miami International Airport. I parked and walked through one of the country's ugliest airports, and soon met up with one of the country's most beautiful women.

"Hello, uh, Ms. Kadiri. How was the flight?" I walked over to her. I wanted to hug her, but I hesitated, waiting for her to open to me. But she didn't.

"The flight was nice—and don't you call me Ms. Kadiri, call me Amira." She smiled, but it quickly vanished. "I, uh—we should get my bag."

"Okay, Amira . . ." I gave her a hug anyway. Once she accepted it, it lasted far longer than I would have anticipated.

We walked to the baggage terminal, got her enormous suitcase, I rolled it to my car, and we took off.

"So, how do you like Miami? It's nice, right?" She rolled down the passenger window and took a deep breath.

"Oh yeah, it's great here. I love the beach and the sunshine." I had nothing to add to the conversation.

"And the teaching?"

"Oh, the teaching is good . . ." I reached for her hand, trying to make some sense of her visit. I touched the top of it, and she opened her fingers and gently closed them on my fingertips. Bingo. I reached for her thigh and started rubbing it.

"It's nice to see you again," I said.

She blushed. I was in.

Billy was sitting on the futon when we got back to the apartment. I introduced them, and she knew right away. "Does he have a boyfriend? He seems nice."

She took a shower then went to my room to change, and when she came out—skyrockets! The woman was a treasure. The curves, the smile, the warmth.

"Whoa, you really clean up nice," Billy said. He leaned into me, "Damn, she's fucking sexy. She deserves better than the Tide Pool, alright?"

I nodded. We walked down to my car, got in, and headed south. I parked in a multi-level garage, and we strolled north on Ocean Drive. All of the clubs that were once closed to me were bending obsequiously before us—or her. The men out front with earpieces kept trying to show her inside, but she'd just smile and keep going. We eventually wandered to Lincoln Boulevard, and Amira picked a quiet spot that had something of a Mediterranean meets Arabian nights theme going on. It was perfect. We sat at the bar. The bartender shot over and rattled off his drink list. Amira picked something fruity, and I a beer, and soon we were talking. I saw the guys around us looking.

Every so often, they'd take a "casual" look around the room and settle on her for a moment, only to repeat the cycle a few minutes later.

"I'm so glad you came down. Where does your friend live?" I said.

"Well," she smiled, "I have a confession to make. I don't really have a friend down here anymore. She moved away years ago. I just wanted to see you."

My blood level started to rise. "That's surprising. You've never seemed to want to 'see' me before."

"Hmm, well maybe I did, but could never tell you. I've known you since you were little. What would your parents think?"

"You honestly wanna know what my dad would think?"

She laughed. "All those summers I saw you running by my store with no shirt on, I just wanted to chase right after you."

"Well, you caught me!" I held up my drink, and we did a "Cheers."

We had a few drinks and she went to the bathroom. When she came back out, nearly every guy in the place watched her ass return to the cover of her seat.

"You have quite the effect on men, you know that?" I said.

"Oh, I don't want to think about that."

"Why not? I mean, you got this wonderful gift—this talent to attract men. You should use it."

"Yes, that's what my girlfriends always tell me, but anytime a guy approaches me, I just yell out, 'No!' before he can even say a word. I don't even know why."

"Hey, well we're not exactly all scumbags, you know."

"Yes, I know. I just haven't really dated much since I left my husband."

"Wasn't that before you moved to Buffalo?"

She looked sad. "Yeah . . ."

"Look, I'm sorry if it's a sore subject—"

"No, it's okay."

"So, if you don't talk much with guys, what are you doing here with me?"

"I don't know. It's different with you. It's just . . ."

"Just what?"

"I don't know . . . I can't say."

"*Can't* or *won't?*"

"Shouldn't."

I put my hand on hers and looked into her eyes. "That was a long time ago."

She turned her hand over and interlocked her fingers with my own. "I can see that."

"So . . .?"

"So . . . There was always something special about you—something warm and powerful. I've wanted to say that for a long time, but I couldn't."

"I could say the same about you. You gave me a safe place to hide out so many times."

"And now you return the favor." She leaned in and kissed me. Ms. Kadiri kissed me! If only I'd had a brush, I could have given the world something to rival the Mona Lisa.

We continued our celebration of life. Many more drinks came, and soon the bartender presented us with the enormous tab. I then remembered one of the many other reasons why I'd avoided South Beach for the previous four months. We headed down the street in search of a new place. We walked along the main strip, then along the beach.

Amira told me about her divorce. She met the guy when she was nineteen. She'd left Beirut only a few years earlier to escape the war and had only been in Miami for about a year before he saw her on television and just had to have her. He was rich, and fifteen years older, and quickly brought her out on yachts and luxury getaways. The first year was a fairy tale, as it so often is, then his true self emerged.

It began one day when he wouldn't let her go to the beach with her friends. He demanded she never wear a bikini in public again. Then he stopped allowing her to wear shorts or skirts that showed off her legs—then she had to cover up her shoulders, then her arms, until she had to cover almost her entire body before stepping into the light of day. He wouldn't let her go to school, or hang out with her girlfriends, and heaven forbid she ever speak to a boy, even if he was a waiter or a cashier at a store. Then the disease spread to the bedroom. He wouldn't let her wear sexy lingerie or go entirely naked during sex. He quickly got her pregnant, but she miscarried on two separate occasions. He thought her somehow cursed and soon avoided her touch altogether. It took her five years to work up the courage to leave him, but by then the damage was done. She'd moved to Buffalo because she had a friend there who let her live rent free at her house while Amira got on her feet. At twenty-five, she thought she was too old for modeling and television, and even though she was stunning, she felt too hideous to ever be seen like that again. She was beautiful, truly beautiful, and I was honored she'd chosen to spend a moment of her life with me.

We went to a club on Ocean Drive, one where women in lingerie were dancing on tables. Amira took me by the hand and led me onto the dance floor. She pulled me close, and put her hands on my hips, and showed me how to move along with her. Her body felt wonderful against mine. At one point, she leaned in and whispered, "I feel safe with you." I kissed her. I could feel her pain running through her lips, but it was met at that frontier by that of my own. We stood like man and woman on opposite sides of a wall built by the hatred of those warring men who'd long ago died, but whose legacy of terror still reigned. I wanted nothing more than to feel whom she really was, to feel the little girl inside of her who never got to grow old and enjoy the fruits of maturation and adult life. I wanted to give her more time. But even so, time had already been generous with her, giving her this unique gift, this ageless frame that seemed, no matter how old she'd gotten, to keep her youthful and vibrant, despite the heavy despair in her eyes, and exhaustion in her smile.

We danced at the club and continued the dance in my bedroom. I shut and locked the door, and she slowly took off her clothes, dropping down to nothing but a black thong and bra. I grabbed a bottle of wine from my desk and took a hearty gulp, like a medieval king at feast. She took off her bra and started belly dancing for my eyes only. The dance began cold, but I brought the bottle to her, and she took a gulp and started flowing like the liquid passing through her. I took off my clothes, having patience no more, and pulled her to me. I absolutely ripped off her underwear, tossed her on the bed, and licked every square inch of her womanhood. She moaned as if she hadn't been touched in centuries. When I couldn't take it anymore, I got up, and though there was a condom within arm's reach on my nightstand, I had no time to grab it. I slid inside and gave her everything I had. She sighed and clawed my back and shouted something in French or Tok Pisin or some other language I didn't understand. I continued like that until I felt explosion working through me. I pulled out, ripped back her thick, jet-black hair, and released all over her face. She moaned and rubbed it into her skin. I went back down for seconds on her gushing lady, licking everything in tongue's reach. I ate her forever, enjoying her taste and texture, then I flipped her around, stuck it back in, and fucked her like a dog until the sun began to rise. I wanted to do everything with her, and absolutely would have if only there were enough darkness in the night.

I was the first to wake the next morning. I looked around the room— wine stains on the carpet and walls. I looked at Amira, sleeping peacefully by my side. Her eyes opened.

"I can't tell you how badly I needed that last night." She pulled herself up and kissed my cheek. "You're an animal."

I started clawing at my hair—some came out in my hand. "What the fuck have I done?"

"It's okay, Luke. I haven't been with a guy in years. And I've been tested—"

"No, it's not that—I've been trying to get back together with my girlfriend for like the past six months, and finally, just last week, she tells me she wants to be with me again. I feel like such a scumbag."

"Oh, I'm sorry if my trip caused any problems—"

"No, no, I'm glad you're here. I'm sorry if I'm causing you any problems. I know you've got a lot to deal with, too. It's just, I feel like everything I always do is wrong."

"Does it feel wrong having me in your bed?"

"No, and that's the problem! It should, shouldn't it?"

"It shouldn't be anything. There's no use in worrying about it. God, if anyone should be worried, it should be me. But what have I always taught you?"

"Feel the art. Trust the art."

I pulled the covers off her and gave her naked body a once over. I was ready again.

I got on top of her, rubbed it outside of her until she was ready, and went in again. Hell, there was no point in using a condom now. I gave it to her until I could take no more, then straddled her chest, held together her breasts, and finished myself off between them. I went back for seconds and even thirds, licking every square inch of that woman's body. There was no place my tongue didn't go. Somehow, I think we'd fucked each other out of a dream.

She got out of bed sometime around two and took a shower, washing all my fluids from her skin. I wanted to hop in with her, but she was adamant to get some girl-time to freshen up. Billy was on the futon watching television.

"Yo, I think you might have set some kind of record last night.

That was some serious screaming I heard."

"I don't know if I've ever fucked anyone like that before. Stress can have some wonderful effects from time to time."

"Well you'd better appreciate that, 'cause women like her don't come knocking on dudes' doors all that often . . . Oh, and I love her skin. I need to ask her what products she uses . . ."

"I can give you some of the product she was usin' last night." I grabbed my crotch.

"Eww, gross."

Amira emerged from the bathroom. She put on a bikini, and we walked down to the beach. We'd only lain out on the sand for about fifteen minutes before we couldn't take it anymore. We practically ran back to my room and ravaged each other some more. I couldn't get enough of that woman and would have extended any of those sessions for an entire lifetime if possible.

Monday came, and I drove her to the airport before school started. I dropped her out front, and got out and gave her a long kiss.

"I'd like to see you again," she said. "I haven't felt this way in a long time."

"I'm sorry, Amira, but I love Lila."

She nodded and wiped away a tear. She walked to the door, but turned back.

"Don't tell your parents."

I smiled. "Never."

I got in the car and drove to school. I'd felt like a King all weekend, but that distinction was robbed from me the second I pulled into the GW parking lot.

"Look at Mr. En's tired-ass car. Shit's lookin' beat as (fill in the blank here with the latest woman celebrity who'd gotten her ass beat by her dipshit boyfriend—a dipshit who'd still go on to sell ten million records or win the Teen Choice Awards . . .)."

I was no longer an animal; I was now an educator. But there was a lightness in my step that day—hell, I'd probably lost about a pound of sex fluids alone.

"Yeah, well it's not as beat as yo' shoes." I yelled back.

"OHHHHH, damn!"

School was horrible that day, but it was horrible every day. Sometime during third period, there was an enormous commotion coming from the hall. My kids could pick up on a fight between two hummingbirds ten blocks away, but it wouldn't have taken well-honed senses to know what was going on in the hall that morning. I opened the door and peeked outside just in time to see a seventh grade student screaming inside Mr. Marcel's classroom. "Fuck you, you broke ass nigga'! You couldn't teach a sick dog ta' shit!"

Mr. Marcel came tearing out of the classroom. The kid took off down the hall and Marcel sprinted after him. The kid made a grab for the door leading outside, but it was too late. Marcel already had his hands around the kid's neck. He looked to be clamping down with all his might. The security d-bags finally did something to earn their pay when they pulled Marcel off the twelve-year-old he very well may have killed otherwise.

"NO RESPECT!" Marcel screamed, as security ushered him away. "I WILL LEARN YOU ALL RESPECT!" He shouted that into the hall, so I'd assumed he meant that as a threat to the teachers as well.

Marcel disappeared for the rest of the day. My fifth period filled me in on what happened.

"Mr. Marcel lost his mind. He started insulting Haiti, saying any person who'd stay on the island was stupid, so Charlie stood up and said, 'Don't you talk about my country like that.' So Mr. Marcel kicked him out of the room. Then Charlie just started yelling at him outside, and Mr. Marcel chased him down and tried to kill him."

I guess it was all in a day's work, right? Marcel was back the very next day, smiling and waving as if he hadn't attempted student slaughter the previous. I'd say GW was the worst school in the world, but it probably wasn't even the worst in a two-mile radius.

Chapter 14

Margo came over for dinner that Friday night decked out like a flapper. She was wearing a short dress with a plunging neckline under a fake-fur shawl, and she had a big floppy hat covering her now jet-black hair. She set a place for herself at the table and carved up a powdery dessert for the three of us before we'd begun to eat.

"Luke, due to your conquest over your silly fear and pride by taking care of that woman who came to visit you last week, you simply must come to blows with us tonight." She dove nose first for the phonebook.

"Eh, no thanks." I went to the kitchen for the spaghetti.

"Please, darling, Little Billsito told me all about how you, for once, just manned up and met the Call of the Wild." She went back down for seconds.

"Well, that's between me and the lady." I piled some wet noodles on my plate.

"Who I also heard was too hot for you," she said, with a wink and a smile.

"Aren't you charming! I think that may be my cue." I passed my plate to Billy and went to my room, grabbed my hat and shoes, and started for the door. Margo turned her offensive on her gay ally.

"Oh c'mon, Billy, you know you're such a bore without it." She pushed his plate of spaghetti aside, put her hand behind his head, and guided his nose to the phonebook.

"Look, Liberty, I told you last week I wanted to take it easy with this stuff." Billy pulled back, but was quickly under her spell again.

"You said yourself it was good for the heart and soul,"she said.

"Yeah, in moderation. What you're talking about is cardiac arrest," Billy said.

I opened the door and started to leave, but came back inside. "Why don't you lighten up, Liberty? He said no."

"I can tell he's been spending far too much time with you," she said. "C'mon, Billy, if you do your share, I'll go with you to Shout. And we can try out our new dance act on Lincoln! It'll be perfect."

"Eh, whatever." Billy hit the phonebook nose first.

"Fuck this. Have a nice night!" I slammed the door and walked to the street. I wandered by the Tide Pool but decided to ride the bus to South Beach instead. But when I got there, I stayed on the bus and took it back up north. Liberty's car wasn't there when I returned to the apartment, so I just went upstairs and went to sleep.

When I woke up the next day, I saw I had a message from Wolo. "Kayaking?"

I gave him a call and soon we were launching into the mangrove. We hardly got a few strokes in before I was at it. "I fucked up, Wolo."

"Don't worry, I brought plenty of beer for the both of us."

"No, I can't stop thinking about how I cheated on Lila. I'm done. Mexico's done for me."

"Man, you need to lighten up. That's all you've been talking about all week. You did say, and don't get me wrong, that you enjoyed Amara or whatever her name is, coming down, right?"

"Amira, and yeah, I think so."

"That's your fucking problem, man. You think too much. I got a cure for that. Follow me." He paddled down an unoccupied stretch of water and stopped under thick cover of trees. He pulled out his one-hitter, packed it, and passed it.

"You just need to relax," he said.

"Yeah, yeah I know. Fuck it." I grabbed the pipe, lit it, and took a big rip. It hit me almost instantly.

"Good stuff, right?" he said.

"Whoa—" It started with intense euphoria. I couldn't fight it any longer: I allowed my mind to wander. After all, I deserved a break, no matter how brief, from my tired existence, right? But it was a big motherfucking mistake.

I dove into a few thoughts, riding the waves, allowing myself to briefly relive my childhood, but this time done right. My body quickly went numb and the mangrove grew silent. Wolo spoke to me, but I didn't understand his words. The repressed thoughts, which had been coiled into dark, little springs by necessity and the hand of time, were—because of this one brief lapse of vigilance—now flinging through me, making it impossible to concentrate on a single one. I grew confused, and distant, and the fear crept in. We'd been paddling for about a half hour before I'd realized the seriousness of my condition. In still nature, I had no benchmarks to check myself; however, when we passed a father and his young son on their kayaks and they waved hello, I realized just how far out I'd gone. I watched Wolo say hi and smile. I tried to do the same, but when I smiled, I couldn't stop. Then with the giggling. I tried to wave, but instead I put both hands over my mouth to hide what lay beyond. The smiling hurt my face. I finally got some semblance of control and put up my right hand to say hi, but by that time they were long gone. I wanted to shout to them, but the words were too weak in my chest—my voice was distant, even from myself. Wolo and I entered a larger waterway filled with those casually enjoying the calm waters: couples in canoes, people in kayaks . . . I couldn't look at them. Their smiles paralyzed me; their casual conversations sent me further away. Wolo said hi to a few, but I was gone. My spirit started leaving my body. I felt as if I were hovering a few feet above myself—detached from my psyche. I was working on a heavy delay—something high school and college kids might have mistaken to be humorous if they'd seen me—but there was nothing funny about this. I felt as if I'd lost complete control of my mind. I couldn't stop the giggling. I didn't feel playful, or sinister, but rather, further from humanity than I'd ever been before.

"Hey, Wolo, let's get out of here," I said.

"C'mon, I want to head down to the island."

"Fuck that, man. I really need to get out of here."

"You okay?"

"I don't even know how to answer that question. I just need to get away from their smiles."

"Okay, we can paddle back to shore."

"Just don't say hi to anyone else, please? I've never asked for very much in my life. Just please don't even look at them."

We got back to shore. Wolo dragged his kayak to his car. "Gimme a hand, man."

"No, uh, I gotta, uh, do something . . ." I looked around and, though I had no desire for food, walked to the snack stand. I grabbed the first thing I could find—a bag of salted almonds (I hated almonds)—and tossed them on the counter.

"Three bucks." But the cashier wasn't looking at me; he was staring at some guy launching in the wrong spot. "I told him not in the mangrove! Goddamn it!"

"So, it's three bucks?" I opened my wallet and counted my money.

"Yeah, three bucks." He stuck out his hand, and I tossed in three singles. He put them in the register, but I continued to stand there. "You need something else?" he said.

"Oh, uh, my change?" I realized my error as soon as I'd said it.

"What change?"

A line started to form behind me. I started sweating. The guy at the counter motioned to the woman standing behind me.

"Uh, this is gonna sound weird, but, uh, can I give you a five instead?" I went through my wallet again.

"This some kind of joke?" the guy behind the counter said.

"Uh . . . err—Please, can I just pay with a five?"

The guy ignored me and rang up the woman behind me. I walked out of there, cursing myself for a multitude of reasons. I walked back to the parking lot and saw Wolo ripping the one-hitter in his car. A middle-aged man walked by with his son.

"Oh, uh, nice weather, huh?" I said.

The man just nodded and kept going, staring me down as he passed as if I were rabid. Wolo called for me, but I just wandered to my car. I started it up and turned on some AM talk station, but all the voices seemed so far away. "Fill her heart with the Gift of Diamonds." "That's just what's wrong with this country now, Bob . . ." I finally found a station that seemed less distant and blasted the volume. I backed out and took off, hoping the reality of driving would shock me back into my body. But it didn't.

I got halfway down the block before I had to pull into a fast-food restaurant. A homeless guy was begging for change out front. I knew *he* would talk to me, but I also knew that I might not ever come back from that conversation. I couldn't take anymore of that toothless smile. I sucked it up, got on the A1A, and took it directly home. Not the fright of crash, or the fear of arrest, or the fresh air on my face could do it. I'd had similar experiences with drugs before where I'd gone way out there, to the point where return seemed hopeless—that the more I tried to come back, the farther out the tide sucked me. I knew from those experiences to just ride it out, that life would snap back in sooner or later, that no matter how bad it seemed, I'd someday look in the mirror and see myself again. But it didn't happen on that drive home, nor did it happen as I paced my empty bedroom that night, or on Sunday morning, or Sunday afternoon while I shopped for groceries. None of those people in the aisles could help me. None of this was enough. I couldn't sleep Sunday night. There was no way I could go into battle in this state. Perhaps I should go to the hospital? Perhaps I should call the police? But I knew what the voices of those people sounded like—cold, authoritarian. "Now what did you go and do to yourself? Don't you realize this number is for emergencies only! Call back if you're bleeding!" But when did it become an emergency? When did humanity recognize my need for healing? Perhaps if I were saner, I would have checked myself into a mental institution. But I'd been dealing with the detachment my entire life—just never this bad. This was bad. This was the worst it had ever been. I only had one out I could see . . .

I drove to work earlier than usual the next morning. I wanted to get to school before the masses of kids pooled out front and succeeded in what they did best. I power-walked to my classroom, skipping all chitchat with colleagues, and locked myself in my room. When the first bell rang, I could hear them gathering outside.

"Yo, maybe he ain't here today?"

"Naw, I saw his beat-ass car in the parking lot."

They started pounding the hell out of the door. The sound echoed like big tympanic drums banging in my head. I was sweating all over—the walls were pulsating and dripping condensation; I took big, heaping gasps of air. I'd had a few minor panic attacks over the past few months on those GW mornings, but this was the big one. The knocks intensified. I could hear Frank Lumet in the hall playing with his keys. "Well if he doesn't get here soon, I'll let you guys in and security can watch you 'til he gets here." I heard a key slide in the door. I took a long look at the window by my desk, then made a break for the door. I wiped the sweat off my face, took a deep breath, and opened it. They came flooding in.

"Man, we didn't think you was here."

"Yeah, what you do, fall asleep or something?"

"Oh, I, uh, I'm not feeling well." I rubbed my eyes.

"Damn, you really don't look too good."

"Yeah, you gonna hurl or something?"

"No, I'm, I'm fine. Just sit down."

I hoped they bought that I was sick. I hoped they couldn't see the panic in my eyes. I hoped they didn't realize that even the slightest of resistance would have sent me screaming through the door and doing snow angels under the GW sign out front. I hoped they'd for once just be kind to me. Why was that so difficult? Compassion. And as that bell rang, my wish had been answered. For whatever reason that day, there were no "She can do whatever she wants"s or "This is stupid"s. They opened their books and got to work. I remembered a phone conversation I'd had with Billy a year back while he was still teaching in NYC. "Yo, these kids can be absolutely terrible, but sometimes, when you really need them the most, they'll pull through for you—but only if they really care about you. If you tell them you're sick, they'll take it easy on you, or if you tell them you're having a bad day, they'll lay off. If you only give it to them once in awhile, and they know you're serious, they actually do listen sometimes."

Life seemed to have a way of evening out the score. It seemed to know just when you were at your limit; if you'd been good and played by the rules, it just might bend for you and give you just enough of what you need to keep you sane and on that good path. Maybe those kids could see it in my eyes that morning and just left me alone? Maybe they really didn't get any enjoyment out of pushing people until their brains snapped? Maybe they really did care? And by the time the first period bell rang, it seemed the scale had begun to tip— that the reality that had once left my body was now slowly being restored. I don't know why it was this place that had done it, but I couldn't imagine another I could have gone to for healing. Maybe these kids just needed a hell of a lot more from me than any cashier at a snack stand? How this job played tricks on my psyche! How this place both pushed my sanity to its limit, but also somehow kept it from going over! I was starting to understand why I needed this place so badly. Underneath the chaos and terror here was a humanity as powerful and pure as any I could find in any other place on this earth. And I needed it, and it needed me. But it wouldn't reveal itself without a fight. And it was precisely that fight that I needed to keep me from slipping off into the eternal darkness.

When lunch came, I was still feeling fragile, but also tremendously proud for standing my ground. I reluctantly headed over to Wolo's—not so much for company, but to bring my out-of-body experience full circle. I explained to him what happened, but he didn't seem to understand the extent that it terrorized me.

"Look, you're here, you're fine—it's not like I laced the pipe with PCP," he said. He lit a stick of incense on his desk.

"Yeah, but that's not really the point. I don't know how to explain it—I mean, I left my body, then found it again in this hell hole."

"Yeah, well you think you had a crazy experience, I got pulled over by some asshole cop on the way home. A real short-side-burned, grilled-meat-eating bastard. There's some real money at the southern edge of Broward County and the cops keep the place on lockdown. Stopped me because I was doing thirty-six in a thirty-five. Can you believe that? I was high as fuck! I think he knew because he kept asking me the same questions over and over. 'So where you comin' from?' 'Oh, yeah, and what were you doin' there?' But I didn't let him shake me. I answered all his damn questions like a pro, and he let me off with a warning."

"Shit, I don't know how you did that. If a cop stopped me that day, I'd have been strapped to a bed in Jackson Memorial."

"You're just being dramatic. Hey, we should go see Blues Traveler up in Boca Raton in a few weeks. I'm gonna get some more of that herb—that was good stuff, wasn't it?"

"Yeah, sure . . . blew my fucking mind . . ." I couldn't handle anymore of that conversation. I grabbed my lunch, took it back to my room, and ate it in silence. In a strange way, I was looking forward to the chaos of the next period.

That experience with the one-hitter while kayaking changed my future with the greenery I'd ever so loved. While I still continued to smoke every so often, that moment marked the end of my casual-to-heavy use. From past experience, I knew the shutting of one door to a compulsion could certainly open the door to another. I was prepared for the challenge to spin that compulsion into something positive.

Chapter 15

Billy came home late that night. He'd spent two hours after school grading papers and calling parents, and now he was back on our futon telling me how hard it was to do with a coke hangover.

"You don't even know, man. You think alcohol is bad, try teaching after blowing a fucking blizzard up your nose. Anytime Hurricane Marge hits, I'm down for the count for at least three days. I don't know how she keeps up with that. Bitch is drunk or high every fucking night. I'm gonna get fired, I know it."

"You just need to stay away from her. She's using you. If she could carry you in her purse, you know she would."

"Yeah, I've decided I'm done with her. No more. My nose and sanity can't take her. You know she got into a fight Saturday night with some poor woman on South Beach?"

"No, what happened?"

"This crazy, old woman was playing a boom box and dancing for quarters on Lincoln, and Liberty just walks up and shoves her out of the way, and starts breaking it down—oh my god, she's got the worst moves too! All elbows and knees, no rhythm." We both started laughing. "So anyway, the old, crazy bitch gets up—I mean, Liberty *really* shoved her—and she punches Margo right in the gut.

But Margo wouldn't stop dancing. The lady started ripping her hair and pulling on her shirt, but Margo wouldn't stop. There's something seriously wrong with her."

"She's living on the other side, man."

Billy started laughing harder. "And people actually thought it was part of the act, too! They started tossing her bills. Margo came out of it with forty bucks, but took it straight down to papi-town for another brick of snow. That bitch is either gonna die soon or marry some rich guy and outlive us all. Oh and get this, she says she wants to have a kid—that a kid is the answer to all her problems. She thinks it'll sober her life right up."

"Sounds like a great idea."

"And she wants me to be the father."

"Just tell her to shave her head and get a tan. You could make it happen."

Monday morning was one for breakdowns. All of the academic departments were holding parent/teacher conferences during their weekly meetings that day, and they were a disaster. The administrators extended these meetings well into homeroom, even though only a few parents showed. This was nothing new. We'd had a similar conference earlier in the year and only about fifty or so parents showed, even though there were over a thousand kids in the school. Wolo told me even that was a pretty good turnout. The mother of one of my little hell-raisers from third period was one of the few there that morning, and she dragged her son along with her. She was this gorgeous Dominican woman, all tits in front, and all ass from behind. She didn't speak any English, so I finally got a chance to work out my Spanish.

"Hello Ms. Diaz. Thank you for coming down."

She smiled at me in that special way. I started with a compliment about her son, as was advised by Santoro, then gave her the real deal. "I wanted to let you know that while Osner shows up to class on time every day, he constantly talks and says rude things to other students. I'm afraid he isn't learning much at all."

She scolded him in Spanish, but she spoke so quickly that I couldn't understand much. I picked up a few words here and there, but nothing noteworthy. She again smiled at me. "Well, profi, I thank you so much for your time. I tell Osner to do his work and listen to you. If he is a problem at all, you can call me." She reached into her purse, pulled out a pen and paper, and starting writing something. "Or if he's doing better you can call me, too. This is my cell phone and this is my number at work. You just call me anytime." She smiled again and rubbed my thigh. I'd normally stand and shake the parent's hand after such a meeting, but I continued sitting.

I only had one other parent show up and that meeting was another bust. The kid only came to class once or twice a week, and when he was there, he wouldn't stop insulting everyone around him. Mom gave me the story. "Oh, I want him to be in school more, but he gotta watch his little brothers and sisters. He's the oldest of nine, so you know how that is."

Turns out, the kid's father was in prison and mommy wouldn't let him visit daddy, calling him a liar and a thief. Kiddo just sat there as mom gave him the same tired lines I'd heard a million times before. "Now you start doing your work and listening to your teacher, okay?" The kid would always nod his or her head, then a few hours later they'd be back in my classroom lighting some kid's shoelaces on fire.

It was a relatively easy morning for the history folks. Santoro's meetings went well, as usual (that guy could charm even the most disgruntled of parents), and Norma Jean didn't get any visitors. Wolo only got one parent and that meeting served to be the most entertaining. Wolo never backed down from anyone—I think that's why the students loved him so much.

"Well, my daughter says she's doing her work, but now you're tellin' me she isn't," the mother said. "So, which one of you is lying to me?"

"Ma'am, do you sit down with her at home and make sure she's actually doing it? Do you help her with any questions she has?"

The woman laughed. "And who's got time for that? I got things to do."

"I understand you're busy, ma'am, but your daughter needs some support at home. I'm afraid she's falling behind in class—"

"Well, that ain't my problem now, is it? What happens in your class is your problem and what happens in my house is my problem, okay?"

"Tell me, ma'am, what's your daughter's favorite movie?"

"I don't gotta answer any of your dumb questions." She got up and left.

Wolo shouted at her as she walked down the hall. "What about her favorite book? And what are her best friends' names?"

Wolo approached Santoro and me.

"These people drive me fucking insane," Wolo said. "I'll give each of you a thousand dollars right now if what she meant by, 'things to do,' didn't have anything to do with getting her nails or hair done. You see the claws on that bitch?"

"It's sad, really, how few people show to these things," I said.

Santoro laughed as he recalled a memory, then shared it with us. "Well this was nothing. Last year, I had this woman come to my classroom—she was either coming from or going to work. Mesh dress with her titties mashed together, black thong, four-inch clear heels. Just walks right into my classroom and sits down. I swear, I almost popped right through my pants. The woman turned out to be the older sister of one of my students. She'd come down to tell me her brother was in the hospital and that she wanted to bring him some school work to keep him busy. I would have liked to have given her something to keep her busy . . . Porqueria!"

Just then, shouting from the hall. "YEAH, WELL FUCK YOU, TOO!" We ran outside just in time to see Darla Rotter giving the finger to someone inside the classroom where the English meeting was being held. She stormed down the hall, tearing posters off the walls and cursing out anyone between her and the exit, parents and students included. But before leaving, she walked into the mailroom, tipped over the shelves filled with staff mail, spit on the floor, and stormed out to the parking lot—it was a magnificent display.

A parent and student stood yelling at each other in the hall outside of the classroom Rotter just left, and Ms. Jessup was guiding them toward the exit. Wolo, Santoro, and I walked over.

Margo came out.

"What the hell was that?" I said.

"Oh nothing," Margo said. "Ms. Rotter just called that parent and child the n-word and preceded it with a 'dirty' and a 'fucking.' You know, all that standard stuff."

"Holy shit! That's it. That woman is gone," I said.

"She's gone alright," Wolo said. "Gone fucking insane."

"What happened?" I said.

"Well, apparently the kid called Rotter a 'fat, disgusting bitch' in class the other day and the mother just laughed when Rotter told her about it. Rotter started to flip out, so the mother forced an apology out of the kid, but when the kid apologized, he mooed like a cow. Rotter lost her damned mind and let the epithets fly. It's really too bad—she's a pretty good teacher. Her kids were improving with their F2ST practice scores. She was actually tops in our department."

"Yeah, well now she's at the bottom of the unemployment line. Good riddance," Wolo said.

Darla Rotter wasn't in the next day, but she showed up bright and early the following. No word of her egregious outburst seemed to follow her. But that was just a day in the life of GW. The Professor once said, "You could do anything short of whipping it out and saying 'Suck it,' and still keep your job here."

Although it came with a slight pay raise, picking up a sixth class wasn't worth it. I needed that free time to decompress between periods, but now had students coming at me in wave after wave of endless terror. I had about 180 kids in total, but that number changed on a regular basis. There were always kids disappearing off to "auntie's house in Orlando," or "grandma's in Atlanta," while every few days I'd get a knock at the door and some kid would be standing on the other side holding up a crumpled paper from the counselor. "They sent me here." "Okay, just find a spot somewhere in back." There weren't enough chairs for my larger classes, so the kids would sit on the side bookshelf, which ran the length of the classroom, or stand in the back. I could rarely get through a single class without raising my voice at least several times. Wolo recommended I blow a whistle instead of shouting, and I started wearing one around my neck for the rest of the year. This cut back on the number of sore throats I suffered on a near-daily basis. In a fifty-minute period, I probably spent about thirty of those just getting kids to stop talking, or getting out of their seats, or hitting themselves or each other. Most of the time I wasn't even a teacher, but rather, a poorly paid babysitter. Of those twenty minutes that I wasn't correcting behavior, there was still always a murmur I could never quite silence. I did what Wolo suggested, to separate the kids who wanted to learn from those who didn't. I'd group the idiots together and let them fuck around in the back of the room while I taught the other sixty percent lessons on whatever seemed to get through to them. I'd begun the school year by preparing rigorous and differentiated lessons, but sometime in mid-December, I'd just started winging it. I'd throw a few topics out there, see which excited the kids, then just get into it. I figured if I could at least give them the very basics—general geographical knowledge, victors of major wars the US fought in, significance of important documents and key historical figures—they'd have something to take away from my class.

Most kids knew how to read, albeit at an extremely low level, but few could write a coherent sentence. I'd started the year by giving them tips on writing essays, then brought that down to tips for writing paragraphs, then for sentences, and finally all the way down to some of the basics of language. "You need to capitalize the first letter of a sentence." This was extremely frustrating, but I didn't know if that was because I was projecting my own values onto them. My seventh grade teacher grilled us on grammar. We diagrammed compound-complex sentences and the like on the regular, but these kids didn't know where to put a period. I didn't know whether or not this was happening in all low-socioeconomic schools, but I gathered from anecdotal evidence and general teacher misery that it was—but it didn't stop there. Many teachers I knew in the pretty suburban joints were saying the same. I'd stopped assigning homework in October, after only a few kids since the start of the year did it. I didn't know if I was the reason for their poor performance or if they were, but either way we had a tacit agreement—they wouldn't let me down if I stopped expecting them to produce.

Though I'd made it to December, the other teachers in the school were still looking the other way as I passed them in the hall. No smiles, no hellos—no humanity. The only ones who talked to me were those in my department, the administrators, the other new teachers, and a handful of veterans who didn't give a shit about wasted energy. Yolanda Royce always gave me a smile and a warm hello, and even invited me out for drinks after work a few times. Dawson was still busting her ass every day, chasing kids around the school and reminding the teachers how much she appreciated them. It was nice hearing her yell at kids to get to class or stop throwing stones at the annex. I didn't know what role I was playing in all this. I didn't quite believe in Billy's "education is impossible" horseshit, but the fairy tale that all kids can learn was almost irreparably tainted for me. Maybe other teachers could get through to the kids I couldn't? Maybe I was getting through to those they weren't? Maybe I just sucked at what I was doing? I'd thought nonstop about quitting, but I hung in there—perhaps to the detriment of every party involved.

Chapter 16

On the days I wasn't at Hedman with Wolo, I was still staying in school until around 5:00 or 5:30, well into December. But one day I took off right after the bell, and that changed it all. On the ride home, I thought about all the wonderful ways I'd spend the extra time: writing, playing music, taking an extra-long shower while staring at Biscayne Bay. But when I walked through the front door, I didn't make it past the futon. I fell asleep in my button-down shirt (no tie—I'd given up at that point) and woke up about an hour later to a peculiar sound coming from the kitchen. I'm not sure how, but I immediately knew what was going on in there. I got up and started toward the kitchen—then I could see it. There, in the corner, was a ten-inch rat, snout-to-tail, chowin' down on a hearty, green poison pellet. I was still half asleep, but something in me knew the score. I grabbed a steel rod from one of the kitchen chairs we never assembled and approached the beast. It didn't react to me—it just kept chewing away. I'm not sure if it was this failure to react that caused such a stir in me, but all the sudden, I was hit with a flash of light: if I'm going to be responsible for an animal's death, why not take a more active role in the process? I poked the beast with the rod—it barely moved. I, however, did move. Without hesitation, I brought the steel rod down on the furry little guy's head. Blood shot from its neck like a geyser, covering the wall and tile floor in juicy red. The rat convulsed a few times, then stopped kicking. I scooped it up in a plastic bag and tossed it in the dumpster out back. I returned to the kitchen and wiped up the blood.

Billy came in shortly after I'd finished cleaning most of the wall and floor. He took a deep breath and dropped his bag the moment he passed through the door.

"Oh my god, my parents are coming to visit. They called and asked about my lawsuit with the NYPSD. When I told them about how I lost the paperwork, they flipped the fuck out. They said they're flying down this weekend to talk some sense into me. I don't know what that means, but it can't be good."

"No, it can't."

"Don't worry," he said as he walked to his room, "they won't be staying here."

I took one last swipe at the wall with a paper towel. "That's probably for the best."

The week passed quickly and soon the parents were here. Billy drove up to Fort Lauderdale after school on Friday to pick them up from the airport, and soon they were in our living room. After being away for so long I'd somehow forgotten where I was from, but Buffalo in all its glory was again invading my personal space. The three came through the door like a bad sitcom.

"I already told you, it's okay, Dad! These are trainers, not sneakers. And even if they were, they don't care if you wear sneakers to work here."

"It's not professional."

I inched backward as the 'rents approached me. "Hello, Mr. and Mrs. Lalina."

His mother smiled and said hi ("Luke, right?"), but his father hardly paid me a glance.

"Just get ready, I'm starving," his father said.

Billy stumbled into the coffee table and nearly fell over.

"Watch where you're going. What the hell's wrong with you?" his father said.

Billy got up. "Oh, it's just, I haven't really slept in months." He continued toward his room, and his mother followed. "I think there may be something wrong with me."

"I'll say," his mother said, after Billy opened his bedroom door. "Look at how you keep your room! Who could sleep in that mess? You're gonna clean this tomorrow, and that's that, mister. Henry, take a look at this mess."

Billy stood between his parents and the opened room. He spread his arms against the doorframe and braced himself. "No, you don't get it—I think there may be something seriously wrong with me. Do you think I should see a doctor?"

"I think you should see an Army recruiter. You need some structure," his father said.

"I don't know—I think I should talk to somebody. I mean, Uncle Steve had that brain tumor and—"

"Look at that mess!" his father said. "You can hardly see the floor. No wonder why you lose everything. I can't believe how you live!" He took a long, evil look at me. "I can't believe you do this to yourself. You really are hopeless, you know that? You and your brother." He pointed at his wife. "He takes after you, Dolores . . ."

Billy surrendered. He lowered his arms, walked into his room, and started tossing the mess from his floor onto his dresser.

"I can see why you're having so many problems at work," his father said. "Fucking useless . . . You're moving back to Buffalo at the end of this year, and you're gonna get a job at the restaurant just like everyone else in the family. I don't know who you think you are, moving all over god-knows-where all the time. You better not think you're better than us . . ."

"Oh, Billy, you're doing it all wrong!" his mother said. "Just . . .

just let me do it." She grabbed a pile of clothes from his hands and started folding them. "Just go get ready."

Billy walked to his bathroom and started up the shower.

"I don't need to help wash you, too, now do I, Billy?" his mother said.

It was painful. I locked myself in my room and started up the A/C.

Billy came home later that night. His parents weren't with him.

"Oh my god, I forgot how insane those two both are. We went down to some Cuban restaurant in South Beach and my father started correcting our waiter's English—fuck, and they're gonna be here another two days."

"You really don't have to take their shit, you know? You're a grown man, you pay your bills, you work . . ."

"Yeah, but you don't know them. They mean well. Besides," he walked to his room, dropped to his knees, and started picking up more clothes, "I owe them. I mean, they're right. I did abandon them."

"Yeah, like a lamb abandons a lion's den."

"You don't get it, man. I'm just a selfish asshole."

"Well, that would make two of us then, papisito."

I walked inside Billy's room, got down on my knees, and helped him fold clothes. We cleaned his entire room, but it returned to its fine form again a few days after his parents left.

We got a week and a half off for winter break. Billy drove back to Buffalo. I'd thought about going with him, but I stayed in Miami Beach. My goal was to write as much as possible, but it just wasn't happening. When the break ended, I'd written only a few wine-stained pages, and it took all my energy just to get that. I did, however, get drunk for several days in a row. On Christmas Day, I took a few bottles of wine to the beach, got sleepy drunk, and passed out. It was dark when I woke up. I got some steak at an Argentine restaurant, then bought a few more bottles of wine and went back to my place. I woke up the next morning on the futon, lying beside my guitar. The more I tried to write, the more that dark void sucked at my good sense and happiness. The more I tried to play, the more despair I felt. My only saving grace was in my only out. Vacation would soon be over. GW to the rescue!

This was no way to live . . .

Billy got home a day before break ended. "Fuck, I'm never going back there again. They didn't even get me a single present. They said now that I have a job, I'm completely on my own."

"Well, them leaving you alone is probably the best present they could ever give you."

Things at school were starting to get tense. Wolo had warned me early on, "Just wait until after Christmas. The school starts going crazy worrying about the F2ST. That's all you're gonna hear about until the test in March."

It was true. Mr. Rodriguez held a staff meeting the Monday morning after break. We met in the library before school. He again told us about the importance of test prep. A few teachers went up to the podium and gave speeches, Ms. Jessup included. Soon, the day started.

I had my first period class work on an essay, with the prompt, "'We hold these truths to be self-evident, that all men are created equal.' A quote by Thomas Jefferson—a man who owned slaves. Was Jefferson a revolutionary or a hypocrite—or both?" I had to explain the question, but once I did, they got right to work, even the Assholes.

A knock at the door halfway through class. It was Ms. Jessup. I opened the door just wide enough for her to stick her lumpy head inside.

"Mr. Ent . . . uh, whatever, it doesn't look to me like your students are working from their F2ST books."

"Well, your eyes don't deceive you, Lorraine."

She tried to push her way inside the room, but I put my foot against the door.

"Were you at Mr. Rodriguez's meeting this morning?" she said.

"Yes, and I don't care—"

She gave the door a good shove, but I held firm.

"Mr. En, what do you think you're doing? Now I'm finna give you to the count of three to let me in here."

"Get away from *my* classroom before I call security."

"Oh, that's it—" She gave the door another good shove, but I held it tightly. I ripped her hand from the edge of the door, pushed her hand outside, and slammed the door shut. I could hear her cursing outside. The classroom was silent. I looked at the students, hoping they weren't watching. I was wrong.

"Damn, Mr. En, you a gangster."

"Yeah, way to show her who's boss."

"Damn, that lady scares me."

I started smiling and couldn't stop. JJ slapped me up while Arman was pumping his arm and cheering in the back of the room. Even the Assholes got into it.

"Wow, Mr. En," Destiny said, "I didn't know you had it in you."

"Hey guys," I swaggered to the front of the room, "I just wanna let you know that you should never, and I mean never, take shit from anybody."

A standing ovation. The bell rang. I was liberated.

I went to Wolo's for lunch. He and Santoro gave me the slow clap as I walked inside.

"Atta boy!" Wolo said.

"I told you this guy was a killer," Santoro said.

"Christ, you think I'm gonna get in trouble? I mean, I literally pushed the bitch out of my room and slammed the door," I said.

"Mr. Marcel put a kid in a headlock during class yesterday, and he's still here." Wolo smiled. "Sit down, take a load off, and *stop worrying*. In this place, normal rules and etiquette don't apply."

"It's all just survival of the fittest. You can't bring worry to the jungle. You just gotta react," Santoro said.

I smiled and sat. Dina and three other girls came in. They sat in the back of the room and played five-card stud. Wolo brought in enough food for the four of them, and gave me some too. Beans, and pasta, and vegetables—delicious.

No one ever reprimanded me about Ms. Jessup—in fact, no one even brought it up. And that bitch never came back to my classroom. Respect.

After school that day, I explained to Billy how I'd killed the rat in the very kitchen I was now stirring spaghetti sauce in.

"That's so disgusting!" He shoved a handful of low-calorie popcorn in his mouth. "I think there's like a whole colony of them living in the walls. I still hear them every night, scratching and squeaking. I even saw some little shit pellets in my bathroom. They're everywhere."

"Well, they've certainly eaten enough of that poison."

"Maybe it's expired or something?"

"Maybe it's actually nourishing them . . . Hell, it did come from Tropical Reality, right?"

Billy laughed. His phone started ringing. He checked the ID screen. "Oh, it's Margo. She wanted to get drinks tonight."

"It's a Monday. Does that bitch ever stop?"

"Category Five, baby!" He started laughing.

"Don't answer."

"I have to."

"No, you don't."

"It's rude." He hit a button and started to put the phone to his ear, but I grabbed it away and hung up.

"Hey!" he said.

"Fuck her, man. You gotta learn to start saying no."

She called back. Billy looked at me. I gave him the phone. He hovered his finger over the keypad but didn't press any buttons.

"Fight it," I said.

The phone rang a few more times then went silent.

"She's gonna be soooo mad," Billy said.

"Like I said, fuck her."

"Oh my god, what am I gonna do now? That bitch was one of my only friends here. She's gonna be so pissed."

"Look, I'll make you a deal. I'll start going to some gay bars with you, if you start coming to some straight ones with me."

"You know I'm done with that shit," he said.

"Yeah, well gay bars ain't exactly my cup of chamomile, but I'm willing to compromise."

"Okay, fine. Let's go down to Shout on Friday. So many hot papis."

"Fine, but Saturday, let's get some writing done on our screenplay."

We made a deal. I was determined to stick to it.

That Friday, we took the bus down into South Beach. We got off at Lincoln, walked the strip, and popped into a bar full of toned and stylish men. Billy quickly got absorbed into the crowd. I sat at the bar and drank. Somewhat to my dismay, none of the guys hit on me. I felt a peculiar feeling of rejection in that. I sucked down a Dominican brew and watched Billy go to work at a table surrounded by Latin men. They were all laughing with Sir William at the center holding court. I couldn't hear him, but knew by his face he was in character. The kid had a gift. Despite the neurotic tension, Billy was a funny motherfucker. In college, we used to push him to give stand-up a try. He wasn't a joke teller, but he told funny stories well. He'd get into character, create an accent, and nail the essence of the humor of the story he was telling. He knew how to get deep down in there and see situations for what they were—absurd, dark, ironic . . . But at the same time, people were really laughing at him because they very well knew he lived the highs and lows of each of story he told.

Billy said he was becoming famous in the underground gay

scene in NYC. I wouldn't doubt it, if such a thing even existed. In his element, Billy was a king, but in any other context he could barely zip up his pants without getting his dick caught. Some people only thrive in one area, or at one job, and can't make it anyplace else. That fear kept me moving left after right into GW every day.

Billy and I left Shout around one that night.

"Oh my god, so many cute papis. I got like three or four numbers," he said.

"Well, congratulations. Not a single guy hit on me. I feel strangely inadequate."

"Honey, your hair is a mess. These are the *gays*, not the *guys*."

We popped into a bar on Collins, had a few drinks, hit on a few girls, and rode the bus north back home. When we got there, there was a blond wig on our Welcome Mat.

"That's too bad," I said.

"What?"

"Your mail order drag queen costume arrived about five hours too late. You coulda' killed tonight!"

"Yeah, yeah, fuck you."

I unlocked the door, and we stepped over the wig, entered the apartment, and went to our rooms. When I woke the next morning and exited my room, I saw Billy standing at the front door and rubbing his head. "Yo, you gotta check this out."

"What?" I walked over.

He pointed at the door with his thumb. "Just go look outside."

I did.

"Check out the wig," Billy said.

I looked at it. The side of it was covered in blood.

"Holy shit!" I said. "How'd we miss that last night?"

"I don't fucking know." He pointed at the windowsill at the top of the stairs. "Check that out too."

More blood.

"What should we do?" Billy said.

"Should we call the cops?" I said.

"I dunno—I mean, we saw the wig last night and didn't say anything. What if they think we did it?" Billy said.

"I don't know, but this is creeping me out. What if there's a body stashed away in one of these apartments?" I said.

"Don't even say that. Yo, if we snitch on our neighbors we could be next."

We shut the door and debated the issue for another hour or so, giving a comprehensive, and neurotic, analysis of the situation, dissecting its every angle, and we decided against calling the police. It may have been survival of the fittest at school, but it was the same shit outside of it as well.

Chapter 17

When Monday morning came, the wig was gone and blood was cleaned. I got in my car, but I tried to pull into traffic too quickly and ended up scraping the driver side door on the rear bumper of the old truck parked in front of me. I drove to work and, despite having further fucked up my car, I was having a pretty decent day until fifth period. It started when Johanne Burel refused to sit.

"Am I going to have to call security?" I said.

"You can do what you want, but I ain't sittin'."

"Look, I really don't want to bother Ms. Robespierre over something so stupid. Just sit down so we can get to work."

"OHHH, Johanne, you in trouble!" a boy sitting near the windows said.

Still, Johanne remained steadfast. I didn't want to make a big deal out of this, but she was leaving me no choice. If I backed down after having already asked her to sit, it would have made me look weak, inviting other attempts from the crowd.

"Alright, Johanne, I'm going to give you one last chance . . ." I said.

"Mister, just leave it alone," her friend Claudia said.

Johanne didn't move. I called security, specifically requesting

Ms. Robespierre. She showed up a few minutes later and brought Johanne over to Wolo's room.

"You didn't need to do that!" Claudia stood up and pointed at me.

"Don't get involved, Claudia, this has nothing to do with you."

"Well, you wanna know why she wasn't sittin'?"

"Why's that?"

"Because her momma whipped her ass last night with an extension cord. She *can't* sit."

"Oh shit . . ." I mumbled.

"And that stupid-ass moron Mr. Marcel told her, 'If you gettin' hit, that's your own fault. That's just how your momma disciplines.'"

"Yeah, he an idiot," someone else said.

"Oh, well I—" I didn't know what to say.

Claudia started to cry. "All you teachers tell us that you care about us and want to help us, but then when we askin' for help, you just turn the other way. This whole school's a fuckin' joke."

"I'm, uh, sorry, Claudia, I, I, really didn't know . . ."

Claudia got up and stormed out of the classroom. I shouted to Ms. Robespierre, who was still in the hall. Ms. Robespierre saw Claudia run into the girls' room. I gave Ms. Robespierre a look, and she smiled. "It'd be no problem, Mr. Entelechy." Ms. Robespierre walked into the bathroom and Claudia returned to class about fifteen minutes later. Ms. Robespierre later told me that Claudia had confessed to her that she'd been getting it too, just with a belt, not a wire.

When I got back to my apartment that night, the Cuban woman was out front power-puffing a cigarette and mumbling to herself. "They won't do this to me, they won't do this again . . ."

"Everything okay?"

She practically jumped on me, grabbing my shoulders and

pulling me toward her. "They want my boy committed. They want to lock him away. But I know what goes on there. I know better. They will never take my boy."

Something crashed in her kitchen. She dashed into the house and locked the door behind her. "Paco, I said stay out of the kitchen!"

I walked upstairs and locked the door behind me.

I ate dinner at Manolo's that Friday with Billy and Margo. She and Billy were talking again. "Oh, Margo's okay," he told me before leaving. "I was just getting a little dramatic. She hasn't even touched the stuff in a week. She wants to clean out her system so she can have her baby. She's been eating nothing but passion fruit for two weeks . . ."

We rode the bus south, and Margo was drunk when we walked in. We got some drinks, did some shots, and ate. Somewhere along the way, Johanne Burel came up in conversation.

"I don't know. You think I should call CPS?" I said.

"Puh-leeze," Billy said, "you call it on that girl and you'll be calling it on half of America. You know how many shitty parents are out there?"

"I think it's just as bad if teachers turn their backs away," I said.

"Well, all parents have different styles of disciplining their kids," Margo said. "Who are we to interfere?"

"I don't know—I mean, I used to get my ass beat all the time, but looking back now, it just seems wrong is all," I said.

"Oh my god, it's all coming back to me." Billy started laughing. "My dad was a serious rage-aholic. One summer when I was like seven, he took me fishing while we were up at our place on Silver Lake. We were catching bass or walleye, or whatever. For the first four hours or so, neither of us caught shit. Then, all the sudden, I felt this tremendous jerking on my pole. I gripped it as hard as I could, but then my dad shouted, 'Yer gonna lose him!' and I just. . . let go.

I don't know why. He started screaming at me about how much the pole cost, then—get this—the bastard slaps me out of the boat and straight into the water." He started laughing. "That motherfucker broke my nose—and he wouldn't even help me back on the boat. I was clawing at the side and calling to him for help, but all he did was lean down and say, 'You're gonna work until you pay me back every last penny for that pole, you fucking little faggot.' Then he dunked my head underwater." Billy started laughing so hard, he was gasping for breath. "I guess he already knew."

"Your father sounds like a common brute," Margo said. "My father never lifted a finger to me or my mother. I was very lucky. My parents took a hands-off approach to child rearing. They never disciplined me, only told me when they thought I was making poor decisions, and gave me suggestions to alter my course. It was a wonderful experience—very organic. They believed in nurturing creativity, not forcing me to blindly follow authority. I lived a very happy childhood until my father ran off to some artists' colony in Oregon when I was a senior in high school."

"That's insane," Billy said.

Margo gave him a disgusted look. "And who are you to judge, Mr. Judgey-Pants? Anyway, so he left my mother and me and just moved into the woods. He changed his name and everything. He'd been an engineer for twenty-two years, but couldn't take it anymore. See, I always knew my father was a genius, but no one ever supported his gift. He's a wonderful artist. He hasn't spoken to either my mother or me since leaving, but I don't blame him. He has the right to choose whatever path he wants in life. In a way, I think that leaving us was the greatest love he could have ever given to us."

"Kind of like an emotional paradox, huh?" I said.

"I wouldn't expect *you* to understand that, Mr. Entelechy," she said.

"Why don't you take it easy, alright Margo?" I said. "I don't know, guys. I used to get the belt—nearly all my friends did too. It just seemed the way it was supposed to be—you look at dad wrong, you'd be rubbing your ass all night. But looking at the sadness in that girl's eyes the other day, I just can't imagine who could possibly think that's an acceptable way to discipline a kid—a fucking *kid*."

"Eh, whatever—we turned out alright," Billy said.

Margo got up, whispered something into Billy's ear, and they walked together into the ladies' room. The more things change, the more they stay the same, am I right?

Chapter 18

The early days of January had passed quickly, and soon I was on Perdido Air flying southwest to the Pacific. I sat beside a loquacious older woman on the flight. "Oh, so you're going to see your girlfriend. How cute!" The flight was direct and landed at Mariposa Airport a few hours after takeoff. We exited the plane, walked down a mobile stairwell into the bright, tropical air, and went inside the tiny airport. I grabbed my big, blue bag and got a green light at customs, and there she was, on the other side—waiting. I stopped. She saw me and smiled. That wonderful, life-giving smile. I walked to her, dropping my bag halfway to reach her more quickly. I wrapped my arms around her. I could hear the woman from the plane as she passed. "How cute!"

It'd been nearly eight months since I'd seen her, my princess—my queen. We didn't talk much on the ride to her parents' house. But we sure smiled a hell of a lot. She drove a pickup down those country roads, shifting gears as we sped along the dusty highway. In the land of exotic beauty, I watched her face the entire trip. What color, and life!

We brought my things into the house and headed to the beach. January was tourist season and the sand was littered with pasty-white bodies. Mine was just another. Lila lay beside me.

"I can't believe I'm actually here," I said. "This whole thing feels like a dream."

"Jes, it is like a wonderful dream, and I don't want to wake up."
I kissed her. "I'm so sorry I left you. I'm so sorry for being mean."

"It's okay." She put her fingers over my mouth. I kissed them.

"I think about you all the time," I said. "If it weren't for you, I don't think I would have been able to make it through school for this long. It's killin' me, baby. I don't know how people can do this for an entire lifetime. It's like the worst form of self-abuse. That school is terrible, but it's literally one of thousands. That whole country is rotting out from the inside."

"There are many problems here, too."

"Yeah, I'm sorry, I didn't mean to say those in my country were worse. But the US is very quick to flaunt its superiority over other nations, yet it won't mention places like GW. Just sweeps 'em under a huge fucking rug."

"Well, let's not talk about it. You are on vacation. Tell me something nice."

"I went to Key West with my friend Billy. That place is like its own separate country. I'd like to take you there sometime. People walk around naked."

She started laughing. "Sounds very romantic."

"It's beautiful there. I saw many things. The southernmost point in the United States, a few historic bars, but my favorite was Ernest Hemingway's house. Do you know who he is?"

"*The Old Man and the Sea* is one of my favorite books."

"An excellent choice. Well, I took the tour, heard the stories, saw the sights. When most people hear the name Hemingway, they probably think 'Writer,' or 'Beard,' or 'Fisherman.' But when I hear that name, all I can think of is a shotgun—and a mouth opened just wide enough for that barrel to slide through." My eyes started to tear. "I mean, what the fuck are we doing here? What the fuck is going on?" The tears came full on. Lila bent over, kissed my forehead, and wiped the tears from my eyes. In doing so, her breasts hung in my face. My mesh shorts were no match to stop what was now changing their physical structure. I motioned to it to Lila with my eyes. She looked. "Dios mio, Luke!" She scanned the beach. "That lady over there is watching." Lila lay on top of me to cover it up "until it goes down again." That was a terrible strategy. She'd obviously never been a guy . . .

We spent the next few days together taking trips to the beach, to restaurants, to parties at friends' houses. Lila drove us north into a small seaside village called Punta de Santa. We got a hotel room overlooking the powerful, blue ocean. We made good use of the balcony, the bed, the floor, the shower—but each time, immediately after release, I felt even further away than I had before. We slept together in that big bed like adults do. I wrapped my arms around her, and kissed her forehead, and told her I loved her—but I had other thoughts in my head . . . I guess, just like adults do, too. The vacation was soon over, and I was back in the American tropics. No place on this earth is a paradise.

Chapter 19

First period started out well on the day after I returned to Miami. We began the class with a discussion on whether or not towns had the right to pass ordinances banning sagging pants, then I gave a brief background on the Trail of Tears and got the students started with a group-work activity. About halfway through the class, JJ raised his hand. "Mr. En, I think you might wanna check this out."

Jacob Washington was resting his head on his arm on his desk, and had been since the beginning of class. This was nothing new. This was Jacob's default academic position. He spent half of class each day dozing off, so when JJ started tapping his shoulder to wake him up, I wasn't concerned. But as JJ continued tapping with more and more force, and Jacob still didn't move, I was.

"I think you should call somebody, Mr. En," Destiny said.

"Yeah, yeah, good idea."

I called the office. Ms. Dawson came down and ordered all of the kids out. I had them line up in the hall. Soon, an ambulance pulled up next to Ms. Carver's car in the handicapped lot. The paramedics came in, put Jacob on a stretcher, and took him away. I could hear some of the comments from my students.

"It took him long enough to do something about it."

"I bet if Jacob was white this wouldn't have happened."

After the paramedics left, the students and I went back inside the classroom, but the rest of the period was shot. Everyone was just talking about Jacob and hoping he was okay.

During fifth period, Ms. Dawson made an announcement on the PA. "Will Mr. Entelechy please come to the office. We'll have security watch your classroom."

"OHHHHH, you in trouble!"

I walked down. Ms. Dawson's office door was closed. I could hear shouting from inside. I knocked, and she answered.

"Hello, Mr. Entelechy. Thank you very much for joining us. This is Mabel Washington, Jacob's mother."

"Nice to meet you, Mabel." I reached out to shake her hand, but she crossed her arms and gave me an evil look.

"Well, Mr. Entelechy," Ms. Dawson said, "we called you here to let you know that Jacob is okay. He had a bad reaction to some medication he took this morning, but the doctors have addressed the problem, and he's going to make a full recovery."

"That's a relief," I said. "You must be happy to hear that, Mabel."

"Happy? Happy about what? That you put my son in the hospital?"

"I didn't, uh—I don't know what you're talking about," I said.

"Puh-leeze, don't you patronize me with that bullshit. The doctor said my son had been passed out for nearly five minutes while you just sat there goin' on an' on with whatever it is you was talkin' about."

"Well, uh, I'm sorry, ma'am. It's not uncommon for kids to fall asleep during class. It happens all the time—especially with Jacob."

"Well he wasn't asleep, now was he?"

"Again, ma'am, he puts his head down like that pretty much every single day. There was no reason why I'd suspect today was any different."

"Well my little boy had to go to the emergency room. You gonna pay for that?"

"I pay my taxes . . ." I said that matter-of-factly, out of nervousness, not spite, but there must have been some spite lurking around down there for it to have come up.

"I know you not gettin' fresh with me."

"I'm sorry, I didn't mean to—"

Ms. Dawson stepped in. "Okay, okay, why don't we just try to calm down. Let's change up the discussion. Mr. Entelechy, you told me earlier that Jacob was one of your best students. Why don't you tell his mother about his work in class."

"Oh yeah, he's an excellent writer—one of the tops in the class. He's very creative and has great style. I mean, he gets a little distracted sometimes talking to his friends, but overall he's a great student and a pleasure to have in class."

"Wait a damned minute. Now you said he talks in class, is that a fact?" Mabel said.

"Uh, well, you know, sometimes, but not much. It's not anything to be—"

"Now why is it I'm hearin' about all this just now? The school year is half over, and you just tellin' me now that my son is a problem in yo' class."

"Well, he's not a problem—he's a great student, he just, uh, talks every so often. A lot of kids do, much more so than he does, so it wasn't anything I thought worth bringing up."

"Oh, you didn't think it was worth bringing up, huh? An' what else ain't you bringing up? He didn't kill nobody in yo' class, did he?"

"Okay, okay, Mr. Entelechy, I think we got all we needed from you." Ms. Dawson opened her door. "Thank you. Why don't you return to your class." She led me into the hall and leaned in toward my ear. "Don't worry about all that. I'll take care of it. You're doing a wonderful job, and Jacob was lucky to have someone like you looking out for him."

On my way back to the classroom, I stopped in the staff bathroom, locked the door behind me, and took a long look at myself in the mirror. There was something deep in there that knew, just knew, what a horrible disservice I was doing to these kids. I just wanted to get through that year without anyone dying on my watch. I took a deep breath and went back to my post, double and triple checking that I'd wiped away any tears before leaving the bathroom. The bell rang and the kids left. It didn't take long before I'd discovered someone had written Fuck Entelechy in permanent marker across the back of one of the chairs. At least they spelled my name right . . .

Yolanda Royce came by my class at the end of the day. She knocked, and I let her in.

"Well, hello there Mr. Entelechy. I just came down to see how you were doing." She looked at the chair a student had defaced. "I heard what happened today."

"So you saw the ambulance, huh?"

"Hard to miss. Kids are quick to jump to the window anytime they see lights flashing."

"They're quick to jump on other things too."

"That they are, Mr. En."

"Hey, is it too late to take you up on that drink offer?" I said.

She smiled. "I just so happen to have some time this afternoon."

We walked to the parking lot and I followed her car to a spot that she assured me "is not in the hood, so don't you worry, okay sweetie?"

She pulled into some sports bar in North Miami Beach and I parked next to her. We went inside and sat at the bar. It was surprisingly busy for a Tuesday afternoon.

"It might seem like all your energy is going nowhere sometimes," she said, "but I know these kids appreciate you. They may give you hell, but they certainly give you less of it than they give other people. I think that's their way of saying they like you."

"Yeah, I think I can handle most of their shit, except for my girls in first period. They're terrible. They operate as a unit with one common goal, to bring me down."

"Man, girls can be the worst. They can be so evil to one another. You know, when people are giving you shit, there's always a message behind it. The key is not to take it personal, which I know is easier said than done—especially if you got a lotta buttons that can be pushed, ya' know? Then you can listen and understand what they're really telling you. You know what you should do with those girls? Talk to 'em. Find out what they have to say. Girls aren't so difficult to figure out. All we want is to be heard and appreciated."

"Us too."

She smiled. "You'd be surprised at what's going on in those little heads. Girls aren't born crazy, we're raised that way."

"I think they'd all be better off with someone else up there . . ."

"You care, Luke—not everybody does. And just the fact that all this bothers you means your head and heart are in the right place. Those people they ride out of class—those are usually the ones who don't care. But if these kids see you care, then they'll accept you. It doesn't matter what color you are. Caring is the universal language."

"I'm getting tired of all the racist bullshit, you know? White man this, white boy that . . ."

"I do know," she said. "I know all too well. But imagine what these kids go through on a daily basis. You think they don't experience racism? Hatred? I know it's difficult for you. Believe me, black people can be some of the most intolerant, racist muthafuckas out there. But they're just doing what they learned. Education's the key to liberating our society—the key to bringing real equality to all people out there. No kid comes into this world hating another of a different color. They learned it somewhere along the way—and they can unlearn it too. And they need good teachers like you to show them how."

I smiled.

"It ain't these kids' fault they act the way they do, just as it's not your fault you can't go saving them all. Go easy on yourself, and you may start to see a less harsh world surrounding you."

We had a few drinks then walked to the parking lot. Before she got in her car, Yolanda said, "We should do this again sometime. Tell that wild muthafucka Wolo to give me a call next time y'all get together."

"No problem, Yolanda. Thanks for everything!"

I drove back to the Beach. Billy was on the phone when I got home, but he soon hung up.

"Looks like my friend Diana will be in town this weekend. She was asking about hotels, but I told her she could just stay with us."

"This your friend Diana from Madrid?"

"Yeah, her year was up with the teach abroad program. She was thinking of renewing but decided against it. In the past four years that bitch has lived in Madrid, Lisbon, New York, Paris, Hong Kong, Thailand, New Delhi, and fucking Cleveland. She can't stay the fuck put. She'll get a job teaching or waiting tables or whatever, then quit after a few months and keep on truckin'. Bitch is already thirty, no boyfriend, no prospects for a real job, and no experience other than constant motion. This whole society is fucked. You know how many Dianas are out there?"

"Well, Mr. NYPSD, I can count two right here in this room."

"God, don't even remind me."

"At least we know it's a problem. Does she?"

"Oh god yes! She knows how crazy she is. She literally gets to a new place, picks it apart in a few days, and decides to move on before she's even gotten settled. She said Paris was gorgeous, and perfect, but had just a little too much rain."

"What the fuck does she expect?"

"I don't fucking know. I'm seriously done though. I'm forcing myself to stay in Miami for as long as it takes to cure myself of all this bullshit. I think she just needs to sweat out a city for a few years and she'll be okay."

"Well, she's coming to the right place to sweat . . ."

Jacob Washington wasn't in school the next day. Destiny Taylor had her head on her desk since the beginning of class in protest, periodically saying, "You sure I'm still alive, mister? You sure I'm still breathing?"

A knock at the door. It was one of Margo's eighth graders selling tickets for a fundraiser. I let her in, but no one bought any. "Fine, if y'all too broke to chip in, then that's yo' problem. Bunch'a cheap asses . . ."

"Excuse me," I said, "please don't speak to my class like that."

"Yeah, and who're you?"

"I'm the guy who's gonna be calling security if you don't get yer nasty self out of my room."

"OHHHH, damn, mister!"

The girl left. I could see the pride welling in my kids' eyes—the Assholes included.

"Ohhh, you defended us!" Destiny picked her head off of the desk.

"What, do you think I hate you or something?" I said.

"You certainly don't like us," one of the Assholes said.

I walked over to her. "And why do you think that?"

"Because you got favorites," another Asshole said, "and we ain't your favorite."

"Well, then who's my favorite?"

They pointed out Danisha Spencer, one of the quiet girls who sat in the front row.

"And why is she my favorite?" I said.

"Oh, don't act like you don't know," Destiny said.

"I honestly don't." I walked back to the front of the class. "Why do you think she's my favorite?"

"You remember that day in the beginning of the year when you told us all to sit because we were standing around talking?" some Asshole said.

"I don't, but continue," I said.

"Well, you called out every single one of us by name, except Danisha," the same Asshole said.

"Yeah, and you never tell her to stop talking when you tell other people to."

"That's because she never says a word," I said.

"Oh, so she's perfect now, huh?" Destiny said.

"Wait, let's get this straight—you all hate me because one day I asked all of you to sit, but not her?"

They nodded and gave "Uh-huh"s.

"But it's more than that," Destiny said. "You do it all the time."

"Yeah," another Asshole said, "you're always joking around with the boys over stupid stuff, then you yell at us."

"Well, would it satisfy you to know I don't play favorites? If I didn't ask Danisha to sit, and I joke too much with the boys, then I'm sorry." I sat on my podium. "I didn't intentionally leave out her name. And, if you think that I don't reprimand her enough in class, then I'm also sorry—but I'm not going to just yell at someone because you want me to. Can we come up with a solution to this problem?"

"My momma's finna come down here and tell you what she thinks!" one Asshole said.

"Yeah, this isn't fair!" said another.

"Well, I don't think anybody's mother really needs to come down here. If they'd like to talk to me, we have plenty of parent/teacher conferences, and I'm always available by phone or email. But I don't think getting angry is the proper way to handle a situation like this."

"Oh, and what is?" Destiny said.

"How about telling me what's bothering you before it becomes this big, out-of-control issue, so we can deal with the problem itself and not all this other stuff?"

None responded. I could see the lights illuminating in their heads. A light lit up in my own. I decided to explore it.

"I want you to know that you're all important to me, and that I care that you feel safe and respected in this classroom. But I can't do my job very well if you don't tell me what's bothering you in a respectful way. But the key there is respect." I hopped off the podium and started to walk through the aisles. "But I think that might be the very problem. Do you all know what respect looks like?"

"Yeah," JJ said, "it's when you walkin' down the halls and everybody gets outta ya' way."

"That's just 'cause you stink," Carmen said. "It's called laundry detergent. Try it sometime."

"Well, I'd say that's more fear than respect—at least in the sense I think you mean." No other hands went up, but I could see they were thinking about the question. I walked back to the front of the room. "Alright, I want everybody to think of someone they know who people respect. I'm not talking about someone who people fear, I'm talking about someone they respect—someone who people feel comfortable around, and safe around, and valuable around. Someone who people trust to lead them. Someone people know is looking out for their best interests. Think of someone like that, then describe that person to me." I thought about someone as well.

Silence for about thirty seconds before the first hand went up.

"My Uncle Emile is like that. Man, he takes care of everybody. When my dad got locked up he got an extra job to help support my mom and me. Everybody loves him."

"Okay," I said, "so would you say that your Uncle Emile is respected because he works hard and is responsible and caring?"

"Yes, sir."

"Good. Anybody else?"

One of the Assholes raised her hand. "Everybody respects my older sister, Arelia. My mom is never around, so Arelia takes care of everything. Whenever anybody has a problem, they go to her."

"And how does she make you feel when you talk to her?" I said.

"She makes me feel good."

"And why do you think that is?"

"I dunno, I just know that whatever I tell her, she ain't gonna laugh or make it sound like I'm just being dramatic. She really listens to me."

"So," I said, "can we say that your sister is someone people respect because she's kind and sensitive to the needs of others?"

"Yeah, I'd say so."

I took a few more examples then sat back down on the podium.

"Alright," I said, "I think with all these wonderful people, we're seeing some similar characteristics. Can we name some of those?"

Hands went up. Answers included responsible, dedicated, loyal, loving, caring, compassionate, understanding, tolerant . . . I repeated these to the class.

"So," I said, "can we agree that respectful people have these qualities?"

Heads nodded.

"And in these examples, did anybody mention anyone who says nasty things about people, or who treats people badly, or tries to hurt their feelings?"

Heads shook.

"So then can we also agree that those things are best to be avoided?"

Nods.

"I know you guys are young. I know you're going through a whole hell of a lot of crap in your lives. I don't expect to ever know exactly what it's like being you or being in your shoes, but that should go the same for you with me. Now, I may not do the right things all the time—I do make mistakes—but I'm trying very hard to treat you all with the respect you deserve. I don't think it's unreasonable for me to expect the same from you."

I could see the Assholes dropping some of their defenses. Eyes turned to the floor as the shame seemed to pass right through them.

"Now, I can forgive you for treating me unkindly, but I ask you to also forgive me if I hurt or offended any of you. I'm hoping in the future that we can work out our problems in a more respectful and appropriate manner. Can we agree to that?"

Heads nodded. Smiles—even Destiny included. The bell rang, and they shuffled out the door. Again, this one positive experience didn't completely neutralize all future behavior problems, but it certainly did put a sizeable dent in the defensive wall that was once the Assholes. For the most part, their team broke up that day. They still gave me shit here and there, but overall it wasn't nearly as bad as it had been.

Jacob came back the next day. I was glad to see him.

Chapter 20

Billy's friend Diana showed up at our apartment that Friday with a duffle bag over her shoulder. We did introductions, and she dropped her bag and plopped down on the futon beside me. She had a lot to say about her travels. "Damn, Billy, you should have stayed in Madrid. It got wild after you'd left."

"Yeah, I think about that sometimes," Billy said. "The second I landed at JFK I felt like I made the biggest mistake. Adjusting to this culture again isn't exactly easy once you've been away for so long. I fought it for a while, but it inevitably just takes over anyway."

I grabbed a bottle of wine and set it on the coffee table. Billy poured a glass, handed it to her, and pulled up a kitchen chair.

"Tell me about it." She took a sip. "One achieves no greater understanding of just how toxic this culture is until that very moment they return—then that sickness in the stomach returns. 'I'm fat, I'm ugly, I'm stupid, I'm poor, I need new clothes, new sneakers . . .' Just horrible! But after that moment, you slowly begin to forget how bad it is, and soon you just become a part of the problem again."

"Yeah, Spain was incredible," Billy said, "but it was far from perfect. People say Americans are intolerant, but the Spanish are way worse. It ain't a blessing to be black in Spain. And just don't tell anyone you're African."

"Well," she said, "I'm only here to recharge the batteries and bank account, then it's back to India. I think Indian culture is the healthiest I've seen. Such a long, rich history."

"I'd love to go to India," I said.

"Yeah, I'd like to go during one of these summers off from school," Billy said.

"Eww," she said, "don't even talk about school. I've had it with teaching. Never again! Unless it's in a perfect, well-run suburban district, forget it."

"Well," Billy said, "I've spent enough time now in one of those *perfect* schools that I can tell you, sin dudas, that they got their shit too. Maybe they aren't as violent as inner-city schools, but these cutesy-wootsy little A jobbers ain't far off. The kids are fucking horrible. Just yesterday, Jessica Donato threw a textbook at a teacher, all because she asked Jessica to open it or she'd be going to lunch late. And the principal didn't do shit about it."

"Whoa, a fucking textbook," I said.

"And the parents are just as ruthless," Billy said. "I got this one bitch riding me so hard because I gave her son a C for his first semester grade. She called the office and said, 'My son never got a C before. Are you telling me that he somehow got dumber from one year to the next?' My AP set up a meeting with me and the mom. I brought a list of all the kid's grades, including several work samples as evidence, but the bitch still wasn't satisfied. She said, and I quote, 'It's teachers like you who are failing our children.' Then she said to my AP, 'I demand Mr. Lalina be fired. How do you expect a white man to teach Spanish to Cubans?' It's all ridiculous."

"Parents can be the fucking worst," Diana said.

"Yeah, her son is a nasty fucker too. He's always cussing out Little Dylan Santos because he stutters when he speaks. That piece of shit is lucky he's even getting a C and not an F. These parents— they're not just dysfunctional—the whole fucking social fabric has been shredded to pieces. Nearly every single one of my students—all one hundred forty of them—come from broken homes. The kids get passed around between like five different caregivers, and they all wonder why their little kiddito is doing terrible in school. It's at a pandemic scale. This country is fucked. I'm booking the next flight down to San Juan. I'm gonna marry a rich papi and be done with it."

"Hey, you stole my idea!" Diana said. "Why should I even try here? What incentive is there for me? Sex and money—those are the only things anyone seems to care about in the Western World. I can't wait to get back to India."

Billy and Diana got ready and decided to hit the clubs. They asked me to join, but I declined. I normally enjoyed being in the company of travelers and hearing of their adventures, but something about listening to those two talk made me never want to get inside of another plane again. I brought a bottle of wine to the beach and got drunk in the shadows.

Sometime around nine, I got a call from the Professor. "Hey, I'm in South Beach. We had a college department meeting down here this afternoon, and we just got out. You wanna grab a few drinks? I know this great jazz bar on Collins . . ."

I killed the bottle, tossed it away, and hopped on the next bus heading south. I got off at 15th Street and walked to the spot. The Professor was waiting out front.

"Man, I haven't been down here in ages." He took a look around. "Can't say I miss this insanity."

"Shit, I don't blame you," I said.

We got in line.

"This place is great," he said. "I used to come down here all the time to catch shows—some big names have played just beyond these walls. My friends and I saw the great Jaco Pastorius here once before his murder. That guy was from another planet—ripped this fretless bass. Man, now that was music. It's been too long since I've heard anything good."

"Me too."

The Professor smiled at the enormous bouncer out front, paid him cover for us both, and we walked inside the red light. A small, intimate setting—it felt of fine velvet and bootleg whiskey. We sat at a table near the small stage in the front corner. A pretty barmaid took our orders. She brought back a couple of beers. I grabbed mine, leaned back in my chair, and took a gulp.

"I'm glad you could come out tonight," the Professor said. "I've been trying to get Wolo to come down here to see a show for months, but he refuses. He hates South Beach."

"Well, it certainly is polarizing." I took another gulp. "So how was your meeting?"

"Good, good—it's always nice to meet with the other faculty members. We're discussing new pedagogical strategies to relate difficult material to our first year philosophy students. To me, developing interpersonal rapport is of paramount importance to removing the fear from education. You can't learn anything when fear's in the way."

A guy playing an acoustic guitar onstage started into a song.

"That's good—good to keep progressing, right?" I said.

"Forward is the only way, my boy."

We did a "Cheers."

"Feels good to get away from GW for a while too, doesn't it?" I said.

"Certainly does."

"You know, I've been meaning to ask you. You seem to have this way about you at that place—like none of the shit can get to you. And the kids all seem to respond very well to it."

"Well that's no trick, just experience. You'll get it too—everyone gains experience—the difference between people is how they view that experience and what they do with it."

"Yeah, I suppose. It's just, I see you smiling all the time—and I see other teachers smiling too, like Yolanda, and Lerner in the Science Department—but I don't think I've smiled once since August."

"Picture Darla Rotter's mug on a postage stamp," he said.

I smiled.

"There it is!" he said. "You know, I got a buddy who specifically chose teaching because he thought it would be the most difficult challenge he could face. He's been doing it now for five years. He said that going in there day in and day out is exactly what's freed him. It may be strange to think it, but it's often in times that we go into our darkest corner that we come away with our greatest light. I'd suggest the next time you feel the walls start crumbling in, instead of panic, stand there and let them crumble. Really listen to what your thoughts are telling you. When you can control those thoughts, you can control yourself, and then you can start to control the world as it meets your ever-expanding perimeter."

The guitarist finished his song. It was melodious, but forgettable, and was soon lost into the night. He started on another. It kicked right away.

"I don't think teaching is my true path," I said.

"It might not be."

"How do I know if it is? I feel like I can never make a decision."

"Again, that comes with self-knowledge and experience. If you can learn to make peace with those voices in your head, you'll begin to understand who it is you are. And then you won't need to make decisions, you'll just be."

"I think I know what choices to make, I'm just scared to take that first step."

"The key to progress is compassion. You can't get started in any direction until you learn compassion for yourself. Learn to love yourself, understand yourself, forgive yourself. And then, you become progress. We value this sick, antiquated idea of survival of the fittest in our society—that those who succeed are fit and those who fail are sick, and weak, and deserving of their misery. But tell me why, in the richest country the world has ever known, do we submit to a theory describing nature? Animals? In our educated and enlightened society, can't we do better?"

"I think so . . . I hope so."

"Look at Maslow. When focused merely on survival, one cannot mature—cannot grow, cannot realize any real potential. And the same thing happens to society."

"I guess that would explain the convoy of Lamborghinis that cruise down the A1A past my apartment every day."

The Professor laughed. "The problem isn't GW. The problem isn't that any particular community or racial group is inherently *weak* or *diseased*. The problem is that the whole system is rigged to keep us in survival mode—to make us believe it has real value—and there are big time winners and big time losers in that system. And the winners will do everything they can to convince the losers that they only have themselves to blame for their failures. But that's all bullshit. We're all human. We all deserve love, and respect, and compassion. This world is in some serious need of healing. Those kids you go see every day are in some serious need of healing. If you can give yourself compassion, you can give it to them, too. And that's when you can walk right into the lion's den and keep a smile on your face."

He smiled; so did I.

"And that's when real progress at an individual and a societal level can begin," he said.

The guitarist got into a chorus with a melody that bounced from the floor to the ceiling. It was a simple repetition of the word, "Inspiration," but it somehow made its way deep inside of me. That's the beauty of music. It's not just words—often the most effective lyrics are made of platitudes heard a hundred times a day. But when given the right melody, and rhythm, and timbre, they can find a way to penetrate the defenses, and settle deep down inside. Words like "love" and "inspiration" and "soul" can be given new life when sang with the proper combination of those three things. And once they're in there, they become a part of the system. They start to take over. And it's our job—one of the greatest we could ever undertake—to let them take complete control. "Inspiration." How I needed it!

We had a few drinks and parted ways. I rode the bus north to the apartment. Billy and Diana were getting high on the futon when I walked in. They passed the dutchie, but I waved it away and walked to my room. I checked my computer. Lila had emailed me. "I miss you, baby. I can't wait to see you soon!"

I'd already bought my ticket to Mariposa for spring break. That was the first time I'd ever considered trying to get a refund.

Chapter 21

Monday morning, Billy lost his car keys again, and we got into an argument when I said I wouldn't drive him to school. He ended up calling a cab and shouted,

"Margo's right about you, you know!"—whatever the hell that meant—as I walked out the door.

With the once-Assholes slightly mollified, my school life started to improve. It was their web of insolence that made going in there each day feel like an act of self-abuse, and without it, the general hijinks and tomfoolery of my other students wasn't all that bad. In fact, the building maniac energy of the administrators and of select staff members as we neared the F2ST seemed to help improve the school's overall level of discipline. Students seemed more focused, hands went up when I asked questions, and that ever-present murmur was the quietest it had ever been. It was a surprisingly enjoyable time. I engaged the students in several impassioned discussions on a number of controversial issues ranging from historical disputes, such as the Civil War, to current events, such as police officers using excessive force against criminals. And that morning, I was three-for-three in finding teachable moments in each of my three classes before lunch.

When the bell rang at the end of third period, I let my kids go to the cafeteria then I walked to Wolo's. I heard some shouting coming from inside his room. Margo stormed out muttering something derogatory about men, and when she saw me said, "Have fun at your Boys Club meeting."

I walked past her and knocked on Wolo's door.

"I told you to beat it!" Wolo shouted from inside.

"No, it's me," I said.

He opened the door. "Goddamn, that bitch is gonna make some guy miserable someday."

"Only one?"

He laughed.

"What was that all about?" I said.

"She wanted to know if I'd been using my F2ST books. Apparently, her students scored poorly in reading comprehension on her recent assessment, and she needed someone to blame."

"Of course."

"She didn't like it when I told her to go to hell."

"Despite what they may say, no one really likes going home."

He laughed again. "Man, I think that bitch just needs a serious fuck to drop the twenty extra pounds of crazy she's been carrying around."

"Well, that psycho Jessup probably isn't making things any easier on her. She's been riding everybody for months to forego all other instruction and focus on the F2ST."

"True. But you'd think Liberty would maybe blame her one random absence a week on her kids' failing scores."

"No—no, I wouldn't."

"Christ, some people just can't handle stress."

"Well, this certainly is an unbelievable amount of it. I'm just glad the state keeps its hands off of history."

Another knock—it was Santoro. Wolo opened the door.

"Jesus, it's getting tense out there." Santoro walked inside the room. "I just got a visit from Lorraine Jessup. She demanded we give some F2ST practice tests this week."

"Fuck that bitch," Wolo said.

I looked out the window and saw Ms. Dawson standing outside of the library. She was ordering a boy to apologize to a girl for making her cry.

"Man, I don't like her either," I said, "but maybe we should just help out. I mean, we're all kinda in this thing together."

"I think you're right, Luke," Santoro said.

"Fuck it, I'm in too," Wolo said. "I'd stick my dick in a pencil sharpener to get Liberty off my back."

"Yeah," I said, "and it would probably fit, too."

"Fuck you," Wolo said.

Santoro laughed. "At least the kids are more manageable now."

"Yeah," Wolo said, "the kids are always great at this time of year, but the adults are the worst."

"I have no problem getting some relief from the kids," I said.

"Well, you'd better enjoy it, 'cause it don't last," Santoro said.

"Yeah, almost literally the moment students finish the F2ST, the school year unofficially ends," Wolo said. "The teaching stops and the kids run wild. You think it's been bad before, just wait until after testing. It's a completely different school."

"Eh, whatever . . ." I shrugged my shoulders and took a bite of my turkey sandwich. Wolo lit some incense, popped *Music from Big Pink* in his computer, and cranked the volume.

When the final bell rang that afternoon, Margo rushed to my room so quickly that my students were still exiting. She pushed against the current and made it through the door.

"I don't know how you can possibly stand that Wolonski, or Wolenocratz, or whatever his name is. That man is an absolute brute! I simply asked him to work as a team, and he told me to get lost—as if I were a common street whore he'd just tossed some cash. I don't know how his wife can stand him. A vulgar brute he is." She began pacing the floor.

"Well, if it makes you feel any better, that brute has agreed to help your students with their F2ST preparation. We all did. I'm gonna test my students tomorrow."

I could see that she wanted to smile—but she didn't. "Someone absolutely must break up that little Boys Club you have going there. I don't trust closed doors."

"Those doors close by themselves—yours does too, honey."

"Just don't think for one moment that any of you are better than us in the English Department. We know what goes on behind those closed doors."

"Mostly digestion."

"That's cute . . . You could stand to be a little more sensitive, you know. I heard about how you treated poor Billy this morning."

"You mean, how he treated himself?"

"I'll allow you to plead ignorance on this one because you're a man, but that still doesn't give you a free pass. Do you know how hard it must be for him to be living in an apartment with a straight man?"

"What are you talking about? We've been friends for years. I don't care that he's gay."

"That doesn't mean it's any less confusing. Look, he came all the way out in New York. It ain't so easy going back in, you get me?"

"Oh, so not driving him to school makes me an asshole?"

"That's not the point. You're the first straight guy he's spent any significant time with since coming out. I know you've been friends for years, but the dynamic has changed. He probably already feels insecure around you—like he's not man enough—and having to beg you to drive him places probably makes him feel even worse."

"I guess I hadn't seen it that way."

"Like I said, you're a guy . . ."

When Margo left, I pulled out my phone. "Hey Billy, you still at school? . . . Uh-huh—no, don't worry about that, I'll come pick you up."

I drove to Little Havana, and he was standing out front, twisting the toe of his right shoe in the grass. I pulled over and he hopped in the car.

"Just because you picked me up doesn't mean you're the boss of me," he said.

"Yeah, I know."

"You think that you're the king of our apartment—you took the biggest room, you hog the TV, you took the shelves with no rat hairs—"

"Okay, okay, man, look I'm sorry about all that. We can share the non-rat-infested cupboard, alright?"

"Fine."

"How was work?"

"Oh my god, Little Debbie Palo totally called me out today. She said—and get this—'Do you have a girlfriend?' You shoulda seen the look in her eye when she said it—she was setting me up. Those kids totally know. They're gonna tell their parents, then their parents are gonna call the school, and I'm out on the streets . . ."

Chapter 22

Santoro did it—he finally got permission to take eighty kids on a field trip to the Onowaga Reservation in the Everglades. He told us all about it during one of our Monday meetings. He pulled a few strings and was able to get the History Department to chaperone the trip. We'd be going in a month—just after F2ST testing had finished.

And we all needed a break.

I'd focused almost every one of my lessons on F2ST prep to help out the English Department. I didn't care much for Lorraine Jessup, but it did seem like the right thing to do. For the past month, Margo had been talking nonstop about how much work she'd put in preparing her kids for the test and how high her assessment scores had been rising. We started collaborating on lessons for our students that incorporated English and historical topics. Margo had some great ideas: journal entries and character analyses for historical figures, plot charts for major historical events, creative writing assignments to make up historical events . . .

The kids seemed to like Margo—the once-Assholes, especially. Margo taught most of the same kids that I did, so we shared information to help each other out. My kids told me many stories about her, but most were good. They liked her—her energy, her love of writing, her boundless support for all of their endeavors, no matter how questionable. The once-Assholes loved her. Margo was always shocked to hear how horribly they'd treated me, but then again, I was equally shocked to hear how some of my best treated her. "So, JJ isn't your worst student?"

And one of those kids got the great idea to steal Margo's new cell phone. She'd bought some top-of-the-line, titanium phone on a shopping spree with Billy, and left it on her desk when she went to the bathroom between periods. When she returned, it was gone. But she was insistent she'd get it back, telling Billy and me, "These kids are better than you think. I'll just go on the PA, make an announcement saying I'm not angry and that I just want the phone back, and then it'll come back to me." Billy and I just laughed at her. She steamed, and shouted, and stormed out the door. She never got the phone back.

Frank Lumet had been an asshole from day one, but his recent divorce sent him over the edge. Ol' Frankie came home early from a fishing trip with the guys one weekend only to find his wife in bed getting the rusty hook from another man. When Frank started to raise his voice, she just packed up her things, took the kids, and left. Since then, Frank had been volunteering his extra time to help GWs security crew address the many random acts of violence and vandalism plaguing the school. He hated crime in all its forms, but saw no problem in using excessive force against minors. "Those little bastards think they're tough—I'll show 'em tough." Wolo once had to pry Frank away from a kid he'd put in a headlock.

There was tension everywhere. I could never tell if it was getting worse or if I just had a bad memory and a high tolerance for bullshit. I was just waiting for someone to snap. Marcel had assaulted three different students on three separate occasions since he'd been hired at GW. I'd love to have seen him and Lumet having coffee together. "No, the best way to take down a twelve-year-old is to kick out his kneecaps, then put him in a chokehold. Really shows him who's boss." Rodriguez knew about all of these incidents, but nothing could shake him from his agenda. "F2ST is king!" He actually said that at several teacher meetings, repeating it an unsettling number of times, as if he were in the advertising crew for some Orwellian political machine.

And these kids—they weren't just terrible to the teachers, but to each other as well. Every few days someone would come into my room crying or cursing someone out. Someone was always hitting someone else, or stealing their lunch, or publicly humiliating them, or tearing out their weave. The boys had no problem going toe-to-toe with a girl, even if she was smaller, and even the smallest of little girls would never back down from a challenge. These kids were rugged. Even the weakest among them were tough as shit. Even the most awkward kid here would out-hustle, out-fight, out-scrap the average tough-guy American teenager in Who-Gives-A-Fuck suburbia. I met this violence head-on just after the bell rang at the end of fourth period one day.

My students started leaving the classroom—all but Teonnie. She followed behind the others, but stopped before exiting the room. She glanced down the hall and ducked behind the door. Just as I looked outside to see what was going on, two large and aggressive girls came storming at me. "Where the fuck she at?" "I'mma show that ho who she's dealin' with!"

I spread my arms between the doorframe, cutting off their entry inside—but that didn't stop them from trying. The girls clawed and pushed me, shouting over my shoulder, "C'mon bitch! Get some!"

A crowd started to gather. Soon, about forty kids were packed in a horseshoe around the outside entrance of my room, as if in an amphitheater watching a play. They shouted, and pumped their fists, and gnashed their teeth. I was in the belly of that hideous, earth-old beast, with its thrashing claws and contempt for human life and dignity. Teonnie let her pride get the best of her. She walked out from behind the protective cover of the door and taunted the girls. "Fuck you, broke bitches. I'll fuck you both up." I felt like letting the wolves in after hearing those words, but I held firm. The crowd surged. They started pushing me, trying to break the seal and pass through into sacred ground.

I stuck my head into the line of fire. "SECURITY! SECURITY!" I could see two of the fuckers at the end of the hall looking on and laughing.

Teonnie walked closer behind me. The girls started throwing wild punches in any free space they could, over my shoulders, between my arms. I took a few incidental blows to the face and ribs.

"SECURITY! SECURITY!" They started moving now, but stopped again when one of them pulled out a cell phone and took a call. I decided to take matters into my own hands.

"GET THE FUCK OUTTA HERE! GET THE FUCK OUTTA MY FACE YOU PSYCHOTIC FUCKING BITCHES!" The kids scattered. I could hear their words as they ran down the hall. "Damn, he a beast, son."

The worthless security crew finally arrived. At the same time, Frank Lumet came storming down the backstairs with some Ethernet cables or some other shit wrapped around his neck. He ran over, grabbed a girl at random, put her in a chicken wing, and pushed her headfirst into the wall.

"Oh, you did it now, missy," he leaned right into her ear, "you sure did it now." There was something intimate and disturbing in the way he said that.

"Hey, take it easy there, Frank, she's just a kid." I rushed over.

He let her go. I then turned to the security bastards.

"What the hell's wrong with you guys?" I said.

"Watch who you're talkin' to, white boy," the shorter of the two said.

"White boy?" Frank walked over and squared off against the indignant security guard.

"I am watching," I said. "Watching the unfortunately shitty job you do at living your life."

The little guard started to pump himself up, getting artificially big like every asshole on the Jersey Shore and all other places like it as soon as they perceive the slightest threat to their hyper-fragile pride, and Frank did the same. Ms. Dawson and Ms. Robespierre got there before it came to blows, saving me from having to involuntarily team up in a racially divided slug match with an inbred bigot I wanted nothing to do with. The security assholes wandered away mumbling some shit about "white boys," and Frank did the same, mumbling about "e-tickets" and "damned colored children."

Ms. Dawson escorted Teonnie to her office—but not before Teonnie looked me directly in the eyes and said, "Thanks. I can't believe you took a whoopin' for me." Her head dropped when she said that, as if in one affirming moment, she'd run through a weighty list of options and consciously decided on life, despite the terrifying, inherent danger in doing so. Both Dawson and Robespierre also thanked me before walking away.

For the next few days, I was the talk of the school. "Damn, he the most gangster teacher at GW." "I know, right. I didn't think he had it in him." Even Percy slapped my hand as he sauntered past me one afternoon. Finally, I was the King of Middle School—and finally everyone knew it.

Friday morning, I got called down to Ms. Dawson's office. Inside that small room were the two girls who'd gone after Teonnie, their mothers, and an officer from the Miami-Dade County Police Squad. Dawson kicked off the meeting. "Mr. Entelechy, I called you down here today to help us enforce the school's Zero Tolerance policy in regards to fighting. This is Officer Cadiz. He's here because of the scratches on your face and arms. Mr. Entelechy, you are in your full right to press charges against these two girls—"

The girls and their mothers gasped, "Oh, no, oh no . . ."

"Well, uh . . ." I looked at the girls. They were in Margo's class—the one that always filled her with such pride when she discussed them. She'd told me many times about how gifted these two were at writing—and how sweet they were. She also told me that they were best friends with the once-Assholes. "I, uh, I don't know if that's really necessary."

"Mr. Entelechy, can I have a word with you?" Ms. Dawson opened her door and ushered me outside. "Look, Luke, I know these are good girls, and I know they made a mistake, but fighting each other is one thing—hitting a teacher is another."

"I know, I know, but I wasn't their target. They would have done the same to anyone in their way. I don't mind taking a few shots now and then anyway . . . keeps my guard up."

"You know it's not okay for people to hit you? You know that, right?"

I didn't say anything.

I took a look inside the office. Officer Cadiz stood like a statue.

"I know I'm probably making a mistake," I said. "You can punish them however you'd like—suspend them for the full ten days. I don't know—I just don't want something like this hanging on their records for the rest of their lives. Man, I've done so many worse things than this—"

"Okay, Luke, it's your call. I can take care of it from here." She started back for her office.

"Wait. Can I speak with them?"

She smiled. "Sure."

We walked back inside the office. Both girls were standing beside their mothers.

"Okay, ladies," I said. "I just wanted to let you both know that I've decided not to press charges."

All smiles from the four.

"But I do want something from you."

"Anything . . ."

"I want you to sit down with Teonnie and apologize for coming after her. I know whatever she did seemed bad enough to warrant an attack, but it's important that you find positive ways of dealing with your problems. Now, I'm sure Officer Cadiz has got a lot of other places he can be right now. You're smart girls. I hear many good things about you. I don't mind getting a few scratches every now and then if it goes to a good cause, but I won't stand for the same person scratching me twice, you hear me?"

They both nodded and smiled. "We're really so sorry. We didn't mean to hit you. She just made us so mad. She told everybody that we do things with boys that we don't."

Ms. Dawson stepped in. "Girls, I know how bad that can feel, but Mr. Entelechy is right. You're both intelligent, and normally well-behaved students. You don't want to go giving away your pride and power to these people who want nothing other than to bring you down. When you hear things like that, you need to realize, and believe at your very core, that you are not those things people say about you. Once you believe that, then their words can't hurt you."

They nodded again and said sorry. Their mothers shook my hand, and I went back to class. Teonnie and the girls were suspended for ten days. I knew requesting them to apologize probably wasn't going to change their behavior anytime soon, if ever, but it made me feel as if I'd at least done something to help us all salvage a bit of humanity from the situation. While a part of me felt I should have had Officer Cadiz do his job, another part felt peace with my decision. Maybe if they were different students I would have done otherwise. But those girls seemed all right.

Chapter 23

The days passed, and soon I was back in Mexico. I had more time on this trip than the previous, so I flew into Guadalajara and took a bus to Mariposa. She was there at the station when I arrived. Her eyes were big full moons and teeth shiny white gravestones. I quickly fell under her spell, and our bodies were locked together. That smell. Her smell—hair, skin. My whole body rested on her shoulder.

We took a cab back to her apartment. I settled in then we showered together and went for some food. We said little during dinner. We kept looking at each other and smiling. It wasn't easy for me to do—to smile. I had to reach out and touch her, some part of her, before each one. I needed to feel something first, and then it came, but it hurt the four corners of my face each time they wrinkled. We had drinks. I got drunk, and she guided me back to her apartment. I felt her, warm and wet on that tropical night. Her bedroom window opened to a small river that ran through the town. I could hear it rising, racing . . . I knew it would soon flood everything in sight. She got on top and took the initiative. It was a tropical wet night—dark, with moon shadows leading forever into the blackness. Her body was a sliver, and mine was pitch black.

We woke the next morning and walked to a small restaurant

for breakfast. And then I did it. I told her I'd like to skip out on the afternoon's activities and return to her house. There, I sat in the middle of her big bed and started typing—and didn't stop for nearly the entire week. She came and went: showers, grooming, warm bodies coming together, but I remained focused. It all came out. Suddenly the creatures in my stories had more life than the very bodies that inspired their design. I kept writing and writing, but she didn't complain. She kissed my forehead, and brought me fresh-squeezed fruit juices, and massaged my feet. But she also told me stories— stories I knew would someday inspire new stories of their own.

On one casual trip through the room, she told me how her friend Tommy from Connecticut was soon coming back to Mexico to live again in that small beach town where they grew up together. She told me all about Tommy's talent for surfing, and about how smart he was, and what an incredible artist he was, and how once, when they were kids, they'd exchanged straw rings on the beach and made a pact to someday marry. Tommy was a white boy. But I was dark. I already knew the score, so I remained in the one place where life made sense for as long as I could—I hardly slept, I hardly breathed. I wrote nearly a hundred and fifty pages in that week, and on that bed, and knew when I was saying good-bye to her it wasn't just for the short term. She cried, and I cried, and I wrote poetry during our last night together—but she was adamant before sleep, requesting only one thing of me. "Please, if you ever really loved me, when the morning comes, just go. Leave me no notes, leave me no songs, or flowers, or reminders. Just go." So I did. I escaped in the early morning before she awoke, grabbing my computer and backpack and few meager possessions, and walked to the main road, hailed a cab, took it to the bus station, then a bus to the airport, and a plane northeast for that city I had no desire to return to. I wished her bed was some place I could inhabit—a city, a place I could call my own—but it wasn't. So I returned to the northern strip of Miami Beach, the valley just far enough north to muffle the piercing South Beach celebratory voices, and just far enough south to dull the glittering lights of the Sunny Isles high rises, and I went to sleep in the city where exhausted people lived exhausted lives, but never stopped once to even ponder sleep—to even dream sleep an option—in the country that breeds ghosts, where the people can't understand why everything real always passes right through their arms. There was so much life out there for all of us, but so few would ever touch it. God, how I wanted to feel.

Chapter 24

When I went into school that Monday after break, I felt different. It was a strange combination: I felt further away from any of those kids than I did before I left, but somehow in that distance, was able to get closer to them. I liked them, I really did. I wished it weren't illegal to give them hugs. Those kids needed hugs and so did I, but of all these people who needed hugs, hugs were the very last thing we could ever have. I could chase students down, and curse them out, and teach them history all wrong, but I couldn't give them compassionate touch. I could shove them out of my classroom, or body slam them onto the pavement after Frank Lumet tagged me into the match, but the second I touched a child and allowed my body to conduct any of their pain, I was categorically wrong—a pervert, a deviant. We all knew abuse. We all knew we were shit. But so few of us knew we deserved hugs. And we usually fear what we don't know . . .

The F2ST was coming. We were only a week away. The school was growing quieter and more disciplined. My classes were fairly well behaved that day. I gave them F2ST practice problems and handed out some worksheets Margo had given me. Soon it was lunch.

I headed to Wolo's and could hear him yelling inside as I approached. I knocked and the Professor answered. Santoro was there as well.

"Fuck these motherfuckers!" Wolo paced back and forth in short, erratic lines.

"Whoa, what's going on?" I said.

"Wolo here's just letting off some steam," Santoro said.

"Fuck these kids. Fuck 'em all!" Wolo said.

"Look, you just gotta relax," the Profi said.

"What happened?" I said.

Wolo stopped pacing; he tried lighting a stick of incense, but his hand was shaking too much to steady the lighter, so he snapped the stick in half and threw it in the garbage. "Some little fucker kicked my door during second period, so I went outside, and the second I look at him, he flips me off and says, 'Fuck you, bitch.' Robespierre wasn't in sight, so I had to call one of those fucking useless security d-bags over, and he, for once, did his job. I asked him to take the kid down to the office, and he did, but about halfway down the hall I hear him tell the kid, 'I know it sucks, but unfortunately you gotta listen to that man even though he's white.' I stormed over, told the shit-bag guard what I thought of him, then dragged the kid to the office by the collar. I took him to Rodriguez's office and said, 'If you don't suspend this kid right now, I'm walking.' He said he'd take care of it, but I doubt it. I'm gonna go back there this afternoon, and if that kid wasn't suspended, I really am out of here. I don't need this shit."

"You know the F2ST is king here, man. Rodriguez won't waste his time with a suspension—especially not now . . . Porqueria!" Santoro said.

Just then, some kids kicked the shit out of Wolo's door. Wolo shot outside just as they were rounding the corner. "Yeah, you better run you little punks!" He dipped back in his room and slammed the door shut. "These fucking little niggers! Fuck these dirty, little sacks of shit! I don't need this, I really don't need this." He started pacing again.

"Whoa, easy, fella." The Professor put his hand on Wolo's shoulder. "You can't let them get to you. They're just kids."

"And what about the adults?" Wolo said.

"That's why these kids need good teachers. To show them the way," the Profi said. "Don't let this, or anything else, shake you from your path."

Wolo calmed down, and we ate lunch. Dina and some friends showed up a little while later. Though he was still pissed, Wolo let them in, and soon he was playing cards with them in the back. That seemed to calm him down a lot more.

I went back to my room and the day started passing quickly. I had my kids work on some F2ST review again. Things were going well until fifth period when I heard someone screaming down the hall. I looked through the door's window and saw a group of students walking by my room. My kids jumped out of their seats and ran to the door. I had them back away, then I opened the door and looked outside. The halls were filled with Wolo's fifth period students. I could hear some of their comments.

"That white man just lost his damn mind."

"Another one gone."

Wolo stormed out of his classroom, slammed his door, powered down the hall, and was gone. I stopped one of the kids in the hall.

"What happened?" I said.

"Oh, someone called Mr. Wolo a cracka', and he just went crazy. He threw his computer on the ground and screamed, 'EVERYBODY GET THE FUCK OUT!' Man, I don't know where he expects us to go, but I'm leaving."

Wolo wasn't in school the next day. All of the kids were talking about his outburst. I was enraged by such a conversation between JJ and Carmen Perez during first period.

"That white man just went crazy yesterday," JJ said.

"That's too bad," she said. "He's a great teacher. His students really learn a lot."

I walked over.

"Whoa, whoa, you mean 'That dedicated and passionate teacher got upset yesterday.' You know why?"

"Yeah, somebody called him a cracka'," JJ said.

"Do you think that's okay?" I said.

"No, no, you're right, you're right," JJ said.

"Whoa, take it easy, mister," Destiny said.

"I'm sorry, I'm just tired of all this 'white man' garbage I gotta hear almost every time I walk into this place. Is that how you see me? As nothing more than a 'white man'?"

"Naw, you straight," Arman said.

"Mister, we don't mean nothin' by it," Carmen said.

"But you still say it!" I said.

"Now you know how we feel," Destiny said.

"I've never said anything like that to you!" I said.

"I'm not saying you did, but it does happen—and for us waaaay more than it does for you," Destiny said.

"People say stuff like that to you?" I said.

"Uhh, yeah!" Destiny said. "And they do a lot worse. I was shopping with my older sister when I went to visit her in Orlando and this woman who worked at the store just kept following us around. Then when I picked up a dress, she walks over and says, 'That dress is seventy dollars.' Then she gave me this terrible look. I felt so bad."

"Has anybody ever crossed the street when they see you walking toward them?" Arman said.

"Not that I can think of," I said.

"Or grabbed their purse with both arms and hugged it to their chest as you pass?"

"How many times a month the cops stop you and give you shit while you're walkin' down the street and mindin' your own business?"

"Have you ever been told a restaurant is closed, then a white family walks in after you and gets seated at a table?"

"How many times you look at a magazine and see a black person on the cover? I'm tired of being told that skinny, white, and airbrushed is beautiful. Shit, I'm beautiful."

"Okay, okay," I said. "You're right. I'm sorry, I guess I just have this idea in my head of what racism is and haven't really thought about any of that. I'm sorry you've all experienced that. You don't deserve it."

"It's alright," JJ said. "It's just the way it is."

"That doesn't mean we can't do something about it," I said. "Especially here in this classroom. This is our world here. We make the rules. Can we leave all that 'white man' and 'white woman' stuff outside the door?"

"Yeah, yeah, no problem, Mr. En," JJ said. "I'm sorry about before. I didn't mean to disrespect you or anything."

"It's okay." I walked through the aisles. "Look, I see lawyers, and doctors, and teachers here in this room. But there are a lot of obstacles between all of us and success. Now, I'm not going to stand here and tell you what it's like to be black in America, 'cause I clearly don't know— but I do know what it's like to try to achieve goals with big obstacles in the way. Hate in all of its forms is one of the biggest of those obstacles, and I believe the key to erasing that hate is through respect and compassion. I know what Mr. Wolenowitz did was extreme, but you don't know what he's dealing with—and you should know that he does care about the students here. That doesn't necessarily make it right, but if we can understand why people act the way they do it'll help us to be less affected by their actions. I know it's not easy to bring up some of those things you told me, especially when they've caused you so much pain, and I want to thank you for sharing."

"No problem, Mr. En."

Chapter 25

Wolo was back in school the next day. I went to his room for lunch.

"I don't want to say a single negative thing," he said. "Let's just say happy things from here on out, okay? So, Luke, tell me about Mexico . . ."

I told him about Mexico. About the writing, and the rain, and about how I didn't have a girlfriend anymore.

"Finally, you're becoming a man," he said.

Dina and her friends showed up a short time later. They sat in the back of the room and played cards.

"Hey," Wolo said, "my friend Dale from 'Bama called me last week. He wants to come out and visit. It'd be nice to see him, but I don't really want him to come."

"I think I know what you mean."

Wolo and I played cards with the girls, and soon lunch was over.

The next week brought with it the F2ST. Each teacher stayed with their first period class for the two days of testing. I was glad to stay with my first period. The once-Assholes had calmed down considerably, and the kids took the test seriously. I gave them the pretest pump-up speech about helping the school and having respect for themselves, and all that crap, and it seemed to sink in. Heads were down, pencils were flying, and most took their time with it.

After those two days, the entire school let out a collective sigh of relief, which added to the one that could be heard all across the state. And then it happened, just as Wolo, and Santoro, and the Professor had warned. Chaos. The teachers knew the year was over, and the kids knew it too, and soon my job became even more of a free-for-all. As more and more students were kicked out of classes, they grouped together and roamed the halls. Discipline problems soared and suspensions multiplied, and two-and-a-half months of school remained. It was about this time I'd ditched the chinos and button downs, and started wearing jeans and T-shirts to school. That had been, after all, the standard GW uniform for most of the other faculty members.

The kids weren't the only ones causing trouble. Attendance at faculty meetings started to drop to about half. All of the sudden everyone started getting "sick"—only about seventy-five percent of the staff was there on any given day. This was great for substitute teachers, who made a killing each year after the F2ST. By March, I hadn't taken a single sick day—I'd wanted to many times, but felt that if I'd taken one, perhaps I'd never return . . . So as it stood, I still had all ten days and, coincidentally, there were ten Fridays left in the year. Wolo and I spent most of those Fridays on the bike trails or paddling under the mangroves.

As general dereliction of duty spread throughout the school, a new kind of tension emerged. Some of my coworkers' character quirks that I hadn't yet seen started making their way to the surface. Ms. Carver, for example, grew obsessively protective of the printer. One day, so she said, someone had printed several worksheets using her paper, and from that time on, the printer was "broken" whenever someone else wanted to use it. It actually was broken a few times, but for suspicious reasons. On one occasion, someone had run several sheets of wax paper that had been glued together through it, which jammed and almost destroyed the machine. Frank Lumet was not a happy asshole when he heard about that one.

Wolo and I, like everyone else, found ways to adapt. We started pulling pranks on all of those who'd either wronged us or whom we just didn't like. We wrote referrals for teachers who'd been the worst offenders. We wrote up Ms. Brion, the ESOL teacher, "For leaving for lunch at ten o'clock each day and never returning; for failing to return all phone calls throughout the year; for consistently being out of the office during the very hours you are supposed to be helping children; and for not smiling while walking through the halls on those rare occasions you are actually here."

We spent our lunches prank-calling other staff members. One day, some woman I'd never met came to my room asking me to sign some papers for students in my class whom she'd supposedly given special education services to throughout the year. When I asked Wolo later whom she was, he said she was the school's special ed teacher and that "She has never once, in my five years of teaching here, ever come to my classroom to assist a student, has never once called asking on their progress and, get this, the woman has never even given me a list of who my special ed students are. She just waddles down at the end of the year asking me to sign off saying she gave them services. I refused last year, and she went crazy—called her union rep on me. They forced me to sign, but I signed it, 'Ho-Lee Phuk' and drew a picture of a hard cock next to it."

We took turns calling her every day, pretending to be parents of students with absurd special needs. "Uh, hello, is this Ms. Wanton, the special education teacher? Uh-huh . . . uh, yeah, ma'am, I'm trying to enroll my daughter in school, but she has quite a lengthy IEP. You see, ma'am, my daughter has the ability to read minds, and as you can guess, this causes her great distraction during school. All she does all day is respond to the twisted thoughts of her peers and teachers, and she can't get a lick of schoolwork done. Her IEP requires that she work with a special ed teacher who can censor his or her thoughts for foul language and inappropriate sexual content. Do you imagine big, throbbing cocks on the straight and regular, ma'am?"

She'd usually hang up on us pretty quickly.

The phone calls were fun, but the best prank we pulled was on the librarian, Ms. Baxter. We wrote a memo one day and sent it around to the other staff members.

Dear Staff,

We at the library have a great deal of free time, so instead of locking the library doors during school hours, and sitting around playing cards like we normally do, we'd like to give something back to the school. We're going to begin a recycling program. At the end of each day, please have one or two students bring your recycling down to the library and dump it in a pile in front of the door. We're going to have some student volunteers then put it into boxes, and I'll run it down to the recycling facility after school each day.

Thank you,

Maribel Baxter, Head Librarian

Teachers actually thought it was real. At the end of the day, students started dumping huge piles of paper in front of the library. Wolo and I recruited a few students and we all took boxes down and dumped them in front of the doors, despite Ms. Baxter's wild pleas for everybody to "STOP THIS INSTANT! THIS IS THE LIBRARY, NOT THE TOWN DUMP! HEY, ARE YOU CHEWIN' GUM?" She stood out there screaming all afternoon while wave after wave of kids came and dumped paper in front of her precious library.

We got another memo the next day from Mr. Rodriguez telling us that "while an excellent idea," we had to "cease and desist with the recycling program."

Chapter 26

It was around this time that I'd met a new friend. Margo, Billy, and I went to the Tide Pool one Friday night. They were all yipped up and in character, doing a bit about an old English woman who, for the first time since the night before their wedding in 1941, sees the man who jilted her at the altar. They used accents and all.

"Why seeing you tonight has me heart roaring like the Luftwaffe over the great city of London," Margo said.

"You know I never meant to leave you, my love. You were always the woman for me," Billy said.

"But, oh, how you shred me heart to pieces . . ."

And it went on like that as we walked to, and inside of, the Pool. We sat on stools at the bar. They continued the act as they ordered drinks.

"A pint of best please, guvnor," Margo said. "I'm not from around these parts, just in town visiting me niece. And would it kill you, perhaps, to bring me a nice, fat banger for the gentleman?"

The man who filled in for Paola stood there for a minute, rubbing the back of his neck and looking confused. I hadn't seen Paola in weeks—word around the bar was she'd moved back to Brazil to be with her husband.

"Oh, just a pint of your finest ale will do, love," she said.

The bartender wandered off and brought back a Miller Light.

The two idiots continued with their discussion about lost love, and travels through Arabia, and the "unfortunate" decline of British influence throughout the world after the Second World War.

"Can you guys take it easy with all that crap?" I said.

"Oh, I'm sorry, did a little bug crawl up your britches, Lukie?" Billy said.

"I should hope we're not offending you, dear," Margo said.

"Could you just relax with all that for a few fucking minutes? You're hurting my head," I said.

"He's just cranky 'cause he needs a banger himself," Billy said. He reached out and gave me a playful slap across the face.

"Don't fucking do that."

He gave me another.

"Why don't you try that one more time," I said.

He gave me a cockeyed look, then a backhand to the kisser.

I reached out wide and slapped him out of his seat. Billy hit the floor, but somehow didn't spill his drink. Margo helped him up—and remained in character.

"Oh, love, what did the nasty, little brute do to you?"

I grabbed my beer, walked to the other side of the bar, and sat alone. I finished the drink, and as I was ordering another, a cute girl came up beside me. When the bartender returned with my Dominican brew, the cute girl took a look at it and said, "Oh that looks good. I think I'll have one of those too." The bartender brought her the drink, but the girl didn't walk away. We struck up a conversation, and I learned her name was Leticia and that she was from Sao Paolo.

"So you are a teacher?" she said. Adorable accent.

"Yeah."

"I also work in a school, but I am the secretary."

The conversation went on like that for a while before she invited me to sit with her other friends. They were four in total: Leticia, two cute girls whose names escaped me, and him—Tito Montoya smoked a cigarette even though he had both of his arms sprawled around the shoulders of the two cute girls he was sitting between. One of the girls would periodically take it out of his mouth, ash it, and stick it back in. Leticia introduced us. I shook his hand as it hung over the shoulder of one of the girls.

"Pleasure to meet you, Luke." He took a drag and exhaled out of the corner of his mouth. Tito had it—that look everyone flocks to places like Miami to emulate, to raise up on high, to photograph so they can hand the pic to a plastic surgeon and say, 'Like that, doc! I want you to make me look like that.' Tito was the telenovela superstar, the sexual dynamo. He was like a Latin Dean Moriarty—the big, swingin' cocksman from the South. Women flocked to him and remained swooned despite the vulgarities he shot indiscriminately from his mouth. He called girls "cunts" and made frequent references to his "johnson." Perhaps this was a bid by the native-born Colombian to "Americanize" himself . . .

"So you're a teacher, huh?" he said.

"Yeah."

He gave me a knowing smile; I didn't know why.

"Of course you are, you cocksucker." He lifted his arm from the shoulder of one of the girls and pointed to the void beside Leticia. "Have a seat, have a seat."

I did.

"So what do you do?" I said.

"I'm an actor. We just wrapped up the final season of the telenovela I was on. I'm lookin' for a new gig now."

"Is Miami a good spot for an actor?" I said.

"Better than most, but it's no LA."

"I think I'd like to try acting."

"Well, teacher, I'm gonna make you my student." He smiled again then removed his arms from the girls' shoulders and did a shot.

I looked across the bar. Billy was talking with DJ Tango, and Margo with some biker. Tito saw me looking.

"That poor sap." Tito shook his head.

"What?"

"That poor sap there, talking with Lalo—I mean, DJ Tango."

"What about him?"

"He just looks so sad and desperate. Man, if I were gay, there's no way you'd catch me talking with the Tango."

"He's a nice enough guy."

"You know, that dude tells everybody he's from Puerto Rico, but he's every bit as Mexican as Pancho fuckin' Villa."

About an hour passed, and Billy walked out with DJ Tango, and Margo with the biker. I kept the party going with Tito and soon we were back at Leticia's apartment, smoking from an iced bong and doing shots of tequila. She had a great place, beside one of the many canals running through Miami. I got lost staring into it.

"There are dolphins," she said.

"Wha?" I said.

"Dolphins live in the water here. Sometimes I see them jumping out and blowing me kisses."

"I got something for you to blow, Leti." Tito reached inside his pants and grabbed his crotch.

She laughed and pulled away playfully when he jumped on a chair and thrust his junk in her face.

"I really love this place—I mean, Miami has got its fair share of shit, but the scenery is incredible," I said.

"Man, if you like Miami, you'd really dig California." Tito hopped off the chair. "I lived out in Long Beach for a few years, and that's the spot of spots. Cali really is The Promised Land." He sat beside one of the cute girls, and the other hopped on his lap. Leticia went to her apartment; Tito pushed away the other girls and followed behind Leti. I took a few more bong rips with the girls then took a cab home. Billy wasn't there.

Chapter 27

I heard all about it the next morning. "Oh my god," Billy said, "I can't believe I actually went home with that guy. He's so disgusting. He left bite marks all over my dick . . ."

Margo came over, and we decided to go to the beach. Billy continued bitching as we walked toward the ocean. "I think I've hit a new low. If I keep doing this shit, I don't know if there's any coming back."

"Oh, don't worry, Billsito," Margo said. "We all have our indiscretions."

"Not on scale with mine," Billy said.

Soon, we were on the sand. Margo brought a tapestry that we all sat on, and she even made us lunch—some vegan bean pasta dish that I enjoyed, despite my suspicion it had been prepared with dirty kitchenware. After hearing enough of Billsito's bitching about the vampire job the DJ did to his cock, Margo shot to her feet. "Billy, give me your phone."

Billy forked it over. She hit some buttons and showed him the screen. He nodded, and she made a call. "Uh, yes, hello is this DJ Tango? Uh-huh, yeah, my name is Diana Molina—that's of the Doral Molinas." She pulled the phone away and put it on speaker.

"Hello," he said.

"Uh, yes, Mr. Tango, now, I'm throwing my daughter a quinceanera and we need entertainment. I've heard nothing but good things about you."

"Yes, I am the best."

"Uh, very good, Mr. Tango. Well, uh, you see, the thing is we're going to be holding this party in a bubble under the sea, so I was just wondering if you'd be able to accommodate us. You know, if you'd be able to safely get your equipment down there."

"Uh . . ."

"Maybe if you had some waterproof turntables or perhaps you could just wrap it all up in plastic?"

"Plastic?"

She hung up shortly after. Billy got a kick out of that. He didn't stop laughing for about a minute.

"Oh, that's so mean, Margo. He's a nice guy," Billy said.

"Doesn't mean we can't have a little fun, dear." She smiled.

Later that afternoon, Margo thanked me for "All the hard work you did to help my students prepare for the F2ST. We make a good team. You're an excellent teacher, Mr. En, and my students really seem to like you."

"Well, I think we're supposed to wait on those scores before we start assessing anyone's ability to teach."

Margo smiled. She was a cool girl but just all mixed up in the head. I didn't blame her—this world presents us with so many false prophets that it's difficult for those of us with the most faith and love to refrain from just giving it all away to the first or flashiest bidder.

Wolo gave me a call later that afternoon asking if I'd like to meet up with him and his friend Dale in Hallandale that night.

"Wouldn't you prefer to spend some time with him by yourself?" I said.

"Yeah, uh, well—don't be a pussy, man, just come out. Or does Billsito have you chained to his nuts?"

I drove north to Wolo's condo. He and Dale were inside playing cards and getting drunk off whiskey. Wolo threw down a trio of tens to win the hand.

"Damn, E-man," Dale said, "you got the fuckin' gift. Sneakin' up on an old friend like that. Just not nice."

Wolo introduced us, and we did shots.

"FIREBALLS!" Dale jumped up on the couch and started pumping his arms above his head.

Amanda called to him from the bedroom. "It's nice to *see* you again, Dale, just wish I didn't have to *hear* you."

Dale hopped off of the couch and shouted toward the bedroom, "Sounds like somebody could use a little sausage break." He looked at Wolo. "But maybe a little sausage is all you get?"

Wolo gave a nervous laugh.

Amanda walked out to the living room. "Eric, may I speak with you in the kitchen?"

"Ohhhh, Eric, you in trouble now, son," Dale said.

They went to the kitchen and came out a short time later.

"Okay, guys, let's hit the bar," Wolo said.

We piled in Wolo's car and took off. We parked in front of some dive just off of the beach, walked inside, and sat at the bar. He and Dale got right into it.

"By the balls." Dale cupped his hand and held it above the bar. "She has still got you by the balls."

"Eh, I wouldn't exactly say that," Wolo said.

Dale slapped him on the back. "I still think you shoulda went after Brandy Willis. Too bad she ended up marrying that spook from Maycomb. What was he, a big football star? Basketball? One of those . . ."

"Brandy Willis had a moustache that would put Rollie Fingers to shame." Wolo moved forward just enough for Dale's hand to slide off of his back.

Dale laughed. "Yeah, but what kinda homo'd be lookin' at her lips with the size of them titties." Dale took a long look at an older black man sitting across the bar. "Man, I don't know how you do it. Teachin' all them little shit stains."

"They're not shit stains," Wolo said.

"Yeah, don't defend 'em. They're all worthless. I pulled over this little punk nigger just last week for blowin' through a red light. He started givin' me shit, so I took him in. The whole time he's bitchin' about his rights and how he's gonna get his lawyer to take me down, and all that Jesse Jackson, Al Sharpton, bullshit."

"Why'd he say that?" Wolo said.

"Oh, 'cause I gave him a few lumps to the skull—nothing major. You can hardly see it. Just a bunch of whiny-ass freeloaders lookin' to cash in on any opportunity they can."

"Yeah, but it's not cool to hit somebody, especially a kid—" Wolo said.

"Oh, you're not taking *their* side, are you? Man, you've changed— you musta been in that school too long." He started laughing. "Yo, you shoulda seen that punk's face when I cracked his skull with my baton."

"That's really not cool—" Wolo said.

"What, am I one of your kids? Spare me the lecture, teach." He laughed again. "Shit, you guys get on your little power trips. 'Oh, I'm making a difference.' 'I'm saving the children.' Well look at that shithole you teach in. What'd you say—been an F since they started giving out ratings? Slavery's been dead for hundreds of years, but they're still milkin' it. The state should cut all funding 'til those little monkeys learn how to behave in society."

"They're not monkeys—" Wolo said.

"Man, you really shoulda stuck with cards. Had some real talent. Teaching's nothing but a fucking joke, and you know it. You're a babysitter and nothing more. I always said—"

"Too fucking much?" I couldn't take any more. "Hey, look man, you know about as much of teaching as I do the taste and texture of Marilyn Monroe's snatch, ya' dig? I can't imagine how difficult being a cop must be because I've never been a cop, so I keep my mouth shut. Now, you don't know dick about teaching, or these kids—"

"Yeah, but—" He stood.

"Yeah, but nothing." I stood, too. "You said that kid you arrested last week was giving you shit, correct?"

"They're all pieces of shit."

"How exactly did he give you 'shit'?"

"Jus' tellin' me he didn't run the light—that it was still yellow as he was passing through. But that's bullshit."

"What if some blonde chick said the same thing? Would you crack her over the head?"

"Now you're gettin' outta hand."

"Why don't you crack my skull?"

"You weren't there. That kid was a piece of shit."

"How the fuck can you be sure of that in such a brief encounter? Christ, I mean, you were the one who assaulted him. Doesn't that make you the piece of shit?"

"You have no idea the crap I go through—"

"Yeah, well imagine you have thirty kids just like him crammed in a dark, dirty room, and you not only have to keep them in line, but also teach them information they care nothing to know, and inspire them to care about the life they've been shown time and time again that wants absolutely nothing more to do with them than to crack them over the head with fucking batons whenever they show their faces in public. Yes, cop work has got to be horribly stressful. None of my kids have ever taken a shot at me. I can respect what it is you do, but I can't respect you when you're sitting here shooting off your mouth about all this shit you know nothing about."

"Typical fucking teacher," Dale said, "thinking he's 'inspiring people.' That's all bullshit."

The guy sitting next to him laughed. "Preach it, buddy."

"Goddamn, man," I said, "why don't you try listening sometime?"

"I did listen. E-man here tells me you've been an F forever. You're a fucking failure, so don't give me that shit. If someone gave my police work an F I'd be out a job, and that's a fact."

"Well where's that F coming from? What does it represent? Does it mean that the teachers there don't give a shit? That they don't listen to the students? Don't care about them? Does it mean they're worthless because some kid from Haiti who joined their class halfway through the year failed some English assessment, when the kid doesn't even speak the fucking language? How do you assess that? Why don't we start assessing how good of a job these teachers do at comforting students, at inspiring them, at giving them a reason to believe in themselves?"

"Nothing but hot air . . ." Dale got up. "I gotta take a leak." He walked to the bathroom.

The man sitting next to him started chuckling. "Typical teachers. At least you got all summer to cry about it, right?"

"What'd you say?" Wolo got up and walked over.

"Said, why don't you cry abou—"

Wolo socked the dude right in the eye. "Typical bullshit is right, motherfucker."

We took off running to Wolo's car and got in.

"Jesus christ, why do you still hang out with that piece of shit?" I said.

"Eh, he's only here for a few more days."

"Let's just fucking leave him."

Wolo gave Dale a call, and soon he was back in the car. I asked Wolo to drop me off at my car. He did and the two ol' buddies took off for another bar.

Chapter 28

Mr. Santoro's field trip request was approved a few weeks back, and we had the green light to start filling the eighty seats on two cheese buses. Santoro had handpicked the teachers going on the trip—me, Wolo, and Norma Jean Carver—and together we handpicked the students. I left the offer open to nearly all of my students, except for a few who I knew couldn't handle it. I'd even invited Teonnie, who'd toned down most of her shitty behavior since I'd stood between her and certain beat-down the few weeks back. But the day before the trip, I overheard Teonnie tell another student in my class, "Ms. Royce can kiss my ass." I was feeling particularly playful that day, so I got ol' Ms. Royce on the horn and let her know exactly what I just heard.

"Well, Luke, why don't you tell Teonnie that she won't be going to the Everglades."

"I'd be delighted, Ms. Royce."

I relayed the message to Teonnie and she got up, and in my face, and screamed, "Fuck you, you bitch!"

"No thanks," I said, "big and nasty ain't my type."

"OH DAMN, SON!" The kids liked that one.

Teonnie slammed the door and stormed out of the building. Ms. Dawson came by that afternoon to discuss the referral I'd written for Teonnie.

"So, she just walked out, huh?" she said.

"Yep, and she didn't come back."

"That's so sad."

"Yeah."

"I wonder where she went."

"Home, I'd imagine."

"No, I doubt she'd ever go back to that place again. I wouldn't, at least, if I were her."

"Why's that?"

"Oh, you don't know." She backed into a student desk and braced herself. "Her father was pimping out her ten-year-old stepsister. They finally just caught him up a few weeks ago. I guess he'd been doing it for years—such a sad story."

"Jesus christ!"

"Yeah," she got up and walked to the door, "can you imagine what she's seen? All those guys coming and going. I don't think I'd ever go back there if I were her."

I apologized to Teonnie the next day and got her back on the trip.

On the morning of the trip, Santoro told me I'd be riding in the bus with Ms. Carver. We got the kids to line up, did a count, divided them up, and got them onto the buses. I let Ms. Carver do her thing. "Y'all need to be sittin' up straight and tall, and no squirmin' in your seats, you got me?" But almost the moment the bus started moving, Ms. C was snoring as loud as the engine. A song came on the radio, and Destiny Taylor jumped out of her seat. "That's ma' jam. Turn it up . . . TURN IT UP!"

The driver, a middle-aged woman, just nodded her head coolly and cranked up the volume. The kids were out of their seats, breaking it down in the rows and aisle. Carmen Perez and a few others were shaking their asses out of the windows.

I looked at Ms. Carver; despite the commotion, she was still snoring against the bus wall. I looked back at the kids, then at the driver, who was bobbing her head to the music. Cars honked as they passed by, and the dirty, old drivers peered up at the adolescent butt cheeks shaking out of the windows. I laughed all the way to the swamp.

When we got there, we rode airboats across the park and stopped at a small island with a raised wooden walkway that led around its perimeter. There was another school there too—a middle school from Overtown. They had separate boats, but we all mixed together once we got to the island.

We strolled the wooden walkway above the water. A group of students huddled over the guardrail at a spot along the path. I walked over, and they pointed out an alligator. It wasn't very big, and was just lying there, but I'd never seen one in the wild before so I couldn't complain. Someone started throwing stones at it. "Hey, you! Move! Do something!" I looked up. It was Ms. Carver.

"Ms. Carver, I think we should maybe take the kids over there . . ." I said.

We did take the kids over there. Wolo and Santoro's group was on the other side of the island. Ours was standing around a low concrete wall, watching a man put on a show with a few alligators. He grabbed one by the tail, pulled it to him, climbed on its back, and held its mouth shut with his chin and chest. When he raised his arms for applause, one of the kids threw a stone at him.

"HEY!" I said. "Who did that?"

The kids scattered. I didn't know if it was someone from our school or not who threw the stone, but this incited an all-out battle. Kids were picking up rocks and hurling them at one another. The scene was chaotic, but there didn't seem to be any GW students participating. In fact, not a single one of the students whom I could recognize was throwing anything. The GW kids just stood aside and watched the others and said things like, "Those gits are crazy." I chased a kid down and made him empty his hands, but I was pretty sure he wasn't one of ours. Soon, the manager kicked us out of the park and banished us from ever returning, citing our lack of respect for Mother Nature as the reason for such a harsh punishment. Ms. Carver and I tried to plead with him that it wasn't our kids, but he didn't care.

"I've seen enough" is all he said.

We still had the cheese buses for two hours, so Santoro took a poll and told the drivers to take us to South Beach. Though most grew up in Miami, few of the students had ever been to the beach. We parked somewhere near 8th Street and got out. A gorgeous Latina was doing yoga in a grassy area just before the sand. Santoro strutted over and quickly made with the conversation. She ran her fingers through her hair and smiled. Carver got off the bus then quickly found a bench and sat, citing "an aching hip."

Wolo and I led the kids down to the sand. They went wild. A sexy woman was sunning herself with no top on. When a boy discovered this, he yelled out, "YO, FELLAS, TITTIES! TITTIES!" They surrounded her, taking pictures and videos with their phones. Other kids walked to the water's edge. They rolled up their jeans and kicked off their shoes as if they were going to walk in but screamed and ran from the water each time it came toward them. The woman giving the titty show started shouting, "WHO'S IN CHARGE HERE!" with a cute accent (my best guess would be Brazilian). Wolo and I wandered away and started walking up the beach. We plopped down in the sand somewhere around 10th Street, took in some sun, and headed back south to round up the troops. Wolo and I got the kids back to the buses. Carver was already on board ours, sleeping. Santoro concluded his conversation with the yoga woman, hugged her, and strutted over.

"She show you her downward dog?" Wolo said.

"Maybe this weekend . . ." He held up a paper with her number written on it.

When our kids got back on board, Ms. Carver woke up and got them all to sit. I told the kids how proud I was of them for not throwing any stones—at least, not any that I saw. A few students smiled. Soon Ms. Carver was out and the music was back up again.

I sat next to Nadia Sandoval and Armando Perceval. Those kids were brilliant, but they were also fucking hilarious. Armando started a story, then would pass it off to Nadia, and she'd pass it back. They came up with some shit about Mr. Marcel being a Haitian spy sent to America to learn new ways of beating kids. Those two were great.

The sun had its way with me that day. I was exhausted when we got back to GW. We unloaded the school lunches from the buses, and all eighty sandwiches, brown bananas, and cartons of chocolate milk remained. I grabbed one cooler and Santoro the other, and he said, "Well, legally we're supposed to toss this stuff if the kids don't eat it, but fuck it. Luke, you like chocolate milk?" I asked him if bears shat in the pope's hat, and soon both coolers were in my car.

We walked inside the school, passing some chubby kid full-out karate-kicking the shit out of a vending machine near my room.

"Hey, calm down, big boy," Wolo said.

The kid just scowled at him.

Some large woman was standing at Wolo's door beside one of his female students. Both had their arms crossed and looked ready for trouble.

"There he go, Mama!" She pointed at Wolo.

"You the man who took my daughter's cell phone yesterday?" Mama said.

"Yes, she took it out during class three times, and on the third, she answered a call. I took the phone and gave it to security. It's locked in the office," Wolo said.

"And who you think you are taking my daughter's phone?"

"Ma'am, it's school policy to take the phones—"

"You didn't answer my question!"

"Yeah, well I got a question for you. Do you even know my name? I've been your daughter's teacher for eight months now, and this is the first time I've ever met you."

The woman huffed some air but had nothing to say.

"In those eight months we've had five parent/teacher conferences, two open houses, and several school fundraisers. So I ask you again, what's my name? If you can answer that, I'll give you *my* phone."

The woman rolled her eyes, said, "C'mon Ra'shawnda, this man is ignorant," then waddled her fat hippo ass down the hall. The daughter turned and gave Wolo a nasty look, and he gave her the finger. They passed the chubby kid, who was still kicking the machine.

"Hey," Wolo diverted his attention, "kick it a little harder, fat boy, maybe it'll tip over on you, and really kill your hunger."

"Fuck you, old man." The kid threw up his finger, then reached into the machine, grabbed something, and walked away.

"These fucking kids . . ." Wolo went into his room.

I walked to mine and pulled out my keys. I was going to check my emails, but decided against it. I walked out to the parking lot, got in my car, and took off down the Palmetto. At the off ramp, I rolled down my window and handed the eighty sandwiches to a guy in a wheelchair. He held the bag up in the air in celebration, and all of his friends started to gather around.

Chapter 29

Tito called me at the start of that weekend. He came over early on Friday evening and we began our celebration. The kid was already hammered when he showed up, but we kept the party going most of the night. When I introduced him to Billy, Billy just started mumbling something about his hair being a mess, covered it up with his hands, then dashed for his bedroom and shut the door. He'd later tell me, "Oh my god, he is just *too* gorgeous. Couldn't you have at least given me some kind of warning he was coming?"

I'd invited Billy to join us, but he already had dinner plans with Margo.

Tito and I went down to South Beach. He knew a place selling cheap drinks, and we went at it. We got our fill of watching the mamacitas, then headed back north and settled at the Tide Pool. I got a text message from Billy. "Hey, Margo and I would like to join you. Where you at?"

I let him know, and soon they were there—Billy in his favorite shirt and trainers, and Margo in her pearls and little summer dress. They hardly said hello to me.

"So, Lukie, is this your new friend Tito?" Margo said.

"Yeah." I introduced them.

She couldn't stop smiling; neither could he. They struck up a conversation that lasted long into the night. Billy and I sat beside them and sucked down cheap domestic beers. The night ended with Margo and Tito engaging in a serious make-out session. Billy and I decided to leave. We walked home, him cursing Margo under his breath the whole way.

Tito came by absurdly early the next morning. He slammed on our apartment door sometime around eight. "Yo, Lukie, let's hit the beach."

I got up and opened the door. "Fuck, man, I just went to sleep a few hours ago."

"Don't be a cunt, bro. Grab your towel."

I walked back to my room and stuffed a gym bag with a towel, sunscreen, and all that crap, tossed in a few beers, and followed the mysterious Colombian out the door. We hopped in his truck. The bed was filled with random shit, most of it beach related: surfboards, coolers, boxes with flippers, masks, snorkels . . . In the cab, all spots were cluttered with other things: an overly packed bowl in the console, several packs of cigarettes in the cup holders, empties of twenty-two-ounce Australian beers all over the floor . . .

Tito started the truck, pulled into traffic, and steered with his knees as he lit the bowl. His eyes were already glossed over.

"Damn, you're a trooper, aren't you?" I said.

"Hey, it's the Tito way." He smiled as he took several serious rips. He passed the bowl to me and I took a few of my own.

We parked near the beach and got some breakfast. There's nothing like some buttery French toast with a side of hash browns after a morning toke. After, we walked to a supermarket and bought a case of beer. There were a couple of girls standing in line behind us, giving us this dreadful look. They must have been able to see what was going on in our heads. We paid, and the cashier placed our change—twelve cents—on the counter. Tito took a look at the girls, then slid the coins in front of them and said, "Here, you look like you need this more than we do."

We both laughed as we left the store. The girls weren't too happy. They threw the coins at us. We went down to the beach and Tito started high-fiving everybody. He knew the day beach community, but not as well as I knew the night. The kid was sickly-tan and had several tattoos of random shit that he got done "'Cause I was fucked up at the time." In the middle of his stomach was a zombie Al Pacino. He freely admitted how hideous it was.

Tito knew the guy renting beach lounge chairs and was able to get us two for free. We lay out and sucked down our beers, periodically running off to the ocean to add a little volume to it. The day was gorgeous. Tropical blues and greens and sandy whites. Girls walked by; Tito would whistle and they'd smile and sometimes come sit beside us. The kid had the gift like I'd never seen, but his mouth always threatened to fuck it all up. Maybe that was our connection? Usually, when he wasn't too drunk, he was able to keep it together at least long enough to sustain a conversation, but by later in the day, I'd just count down the minutes until self-destruction. "Well fuck you anyways, dumb cunt." We weren't exactly a match made in tropical heaven, him and I, but he was something new and exciting, and I liked being that close to sexiness.

The two girls from the supermarket walked by us later on.

"Hey, ladies, remember me?" He smiled.

"Like we remember herpes," one said.

"I didn't think there was a cure?" I said.

She gave me a hideous look—but didn't make any motion to walk away.

"I'm so sorry about before," Tito said. "It's just that I had this operation recently on my knee. I fell down a flight of stairs while helping my grandmother move. Ya' know, she's old and frail and has a bad hip."

"Aww, that's so cute."

"Yeah, and the doctor gave me this medicine, and when I take it, it makes me real loopy. So I just wanted to apologize."

"It's okay." They giggled. Soon, we were all sucking face (I guess people do still say that). First he with the one girl and I with the other, then we swapped. The guy was as transparent as the Thai ocean, but they were quick to stroke his nuts in spite of all they saw. Any other guy saying that shit and those girls would have kept right on walking, but a stud can say whatever the fuck he wants and still score. If a girl likes you, she'll put up with an awfully large amount of shit before turning her back for good, and even then there's still a chance she'll throw a few fucks your way.

A towering, muscular All-American boy walked onto the sand, rolling his beach cruiser beside him. The guy looked like a character from *Street Fighter*, whose special move, I'd imagined, was to chill for several days straight while periodically popping off the tops of beers between his pecks. He had this peaceful, beachy vibe to him, despite his commando physique. He spotted Tito and came over. I was proper fucked up by then.

"Colossus! How's it hangin', bro?" Tito hopped out of his seat and gave the massive human a hug.

"You know how it is."

Tito introduced us and tossed him a beer. Tito got another lounge chair from his friend and we all sat together and absorbed girls as they passed. Numbers were exchanged, kissed were given, and many, many beers were drunk. Margo called Tito several times that afternoon, but he never answered. Shortly after each call, I'd get one from Billy, but I'd also let it ring. Yet, despite the fact that neither Tito nor I had told them where we were, they both showed up about an hour before the sun went down.

"Oh, fancy meeting you boys out here," Margo said.

During introductions, Margo reached out her hand to shake

with Colossus, but recoiled it as he touched her. "You're not in the military, are you, darling?" she said.

"No, but I have killed a person before, if that's what you're asking." He smiled and held it long enough to let us know he was joking.

Margo didn't seem to get it. "How deplorable!" In spite of her repulsion to Colossus, nothing could shake that bitch from her goal. "So, anyway, Tito are you hungry? I know of this wonderful vegan buffet right near my house—"

"Vegan buffet?" Tito stood up. "We might as well eat sand. I got a better idea. I know the owner of this all-you-can-eat Mexican restaurant just across the causeway. We should head there. I can get us a sweet hook-up on drinks."

"Well, surely these other boys don't want to go," she said.

"Man, I'd kill for some enchiladas right now," Colossus said.

"Eww, you frighten me, darling," she said.

We piled inside Colossus's enormous SUV and hit the road. Tito sat in the passenger seat and Billy and Margo fought over who'd sit behind him. Billy got to the seat first, but Margo jabbed him in the side with the handle of her switchblade and he relinquished the spot to her.

"So, Tito, did you know I'm a published author?" Margo said.

"Of what, microwave cookbooks?" Colossus said. The males all laughed.

"No, not cookbooks. For your information, I wrote a novel that blurs the lines between realism and surrealism. I use a single pronoun for all antecedents to give this feel that we truly are all connected—that no one person or thing can own anything, be it words, actions, materials . . ."

"Well, I'm about to own some enchiladas, so I'm sorry if that's an insult to your work," Tito said.

We pulled into the parking lot of the small family restaurant.

It was fairly crowded when we walked in. Families were dining responsibly. Tito's friend was there and seated us at a booth in the back corner. He gave us menus and started bringing out full glasses of tequila and cold bottles of Pacifico before we even asked him to. We ordered, and soon the food was coming as well. We fell under the spell of needed celebration: tequila shots, laughter, loud stories . . .

Tito sat in the corner of the booth. Margo had slid in next to him before Billy could claim the spot, but Billy didn't give up so easily. He squeezed against her to get as close to Tito as possible, frequently leaning over her to converse with him. She and Billy spent the whole time trying to outdo the other to impress Tito. Margo usually won. "Yes, so when I was in the South Pacific, I was tanning on board this ship one day—topless might I add—and this millionaire business mogul from the Philippines stops me and says, 'Don't move. You're perfect—like a dream.'"

"More like a nightmare," Billy said.

We all laughed.

"No, honey," she said, "a nightmare is what happened to your face. Ever hear of facial cleanser?"

"I'm sorry we can't all be as hygienic as you, Lady Liberty. I know you did set a record in curing that yeast infection you had last month, but we can't all be so lucky."

"Oh, darling, there you are telling stories again. Remember the time—"

"Hey, do you all remember the time we were eating burritos and you two fucktards wouldn't shut the hell up?" Tito said.

"Oh, sorry, dear." Margo batted her eyelashes—a real empowered woman was she.

The other customers started moving away from us. We had a buffer zone of about three tables between ourselves and the nearest restaurant guests.

"So, Colonic, or whatever, how many rainforests to the gallon do you get on that monstrosity you drive?" Margo said.

"A lot more than the number of drinks you take to the fuck."

Intense, gut-wrenching laughter.

"Well, that's no way to speak to a lady," Margo said.

"When you find one, I'll tone it down."

"And what do you do to support yourself, dear?"

"I work construction. It's good money down here. What about you?"

"I educate young minds."

"Ha, you're a teacher. Figures."

"And what's that supposed to mean?"

"You know what they say, those who can't do, teach."

"Well they also say those who can't think follow foreman's orders. Say, you weren't responsible for the construction of any death camps, were you dear?"

The conversation continued as such for hours. Tito's friend kept bringing more full glasses of tequila and cold beers, and we kept the party going long into the night, until Margo got sick. Tito said something only moderately funny, but Liberty really got into it—so much so that the liquid inside of her started coming up. I watched the whole thing happen from across the table. She was facing Tito, but turned at the last moment. She covered her mouth with both hands and a paste of tequila and beans shot out of her nose all over Billy's lap. Billy got a good whiff of the regurgitated food and out came some of his own all over Liberty. It was perfect in that no one other than the two idiots came out of that with even a drop of puke on them. They ran off to the bathroom, and when they came out Tito consoled Liberty.

"Hey, Colossus, why don't we take off, alright?" Tito led Margo toward the enormous vehicle.

Colossus dropped the two off at Margo's, then dropped Billy and me off at our place and left.

"Oh, that fucking bitch always has to win," Billy said as we walked up the stairs.

"Look, man, he's not gay."

"I know, I know, but he's soooo sexy."

Chapter 30

I went to Hedman with Wolo the next day. We did some riding and I did some writing when I got home—not much, but enough to keep the fire going. The next morning, I got ready for school. I crossed the causeway and rolled through Little Haiti. I stopped at the red light where the homeless man would always beg for change, but that day, instead of begging, he was busy with other endeavors. In the time it took for the light to change, I saw him smack a handful of clay against a telephone pole and use his fingers to carve out a smiling face. Something about that face got to me. Maybe if it were frowning I wouldn't have thought much about it—but that smile . . . The light turned green and I took off, but just as I did, another man stepped onto the guy's turf. The guy wandered out into oncoming traffic and started swinging at the trespasser. He got in one good shot, but soon I was too far away to see any more of the battle. A thought came. I pulled over at a gas station and pulled out a pen and a receipt from my wallet.

> It's far too easy
> To credit the drug
> And not the artist.
> A drug is something any of us could take,
> But the artist's mind stands alone.

Today, I watched a beggar
Smack a handful of clay against a telephone pole
And sculpt with his fingers a smiling face.
And this was all done
In the time it usually took him
To beg for change between lights.
And as I drove off,
I saw him swing at another
Who'd invaded his territory.

You can defend a mind with fists,
But it certainly can't defend itself.

When I got to school, the place looked to be smoldering: fights out front, kids screaming, Ms. Dawson chasing after them . . . I parked and wandered into the war zone. I'd taken Wolo's advice and decided to finish out the year by either giving group work or showing movies to get through the day. But it wasn't just the kids who were terrible. We were all getting a little more lax with our behavior. On top of movies and group work, I spent a good amount of time in each class just fucking around with the kids. Nothing mean-spirited, but I wasn't exactly holding back. My third period was a particular favorite of mine to joke with. Sandley Curtis was in that class. Sandley had recently transferred from Ms. Carver's third period because the kids were tormenting him. Sandley was the school fat ass: dumb, and easily riled, and to top it off, a thick Creole accent. But he was resilient. He never backed down, and moments after kids ripped into him, he was always smiling again. The kid found dozens of ways to make me smile each day too. Dumb things—like sometimes while I was addressing the class, he'd just sit there making random faces at me. His favorite was to puff out his cheeks and cross his eyes. No matter how many times he'd make that face, I'd smile just as widely as I did the first time I saw it. Despite his academic and social deficiencies,

Sandley wasn't hated. Even though the other kids loved to pick on him, they still considered him to be one of them.

Third period began that day with good ol' Osner Diaz laying into him. "Damn, Sandley, put on a bra. Yo' titties are makin' me horny."

"OHHHHH, he rankin'!"

"Yeah, well look at'cho shoes! Damn!" Sandley had little defense in this world.

"Yo, did y'all hear him?" Osner said. "He so stupid, he don't even know how to talk right."

"Oh yeah, Osner," I said, "well you're so stupid if I kicked you in the ass you wouldn't know where it hurt."

"OHHHHH, damn!"

"And I swear to god if you don't lay off of him I'm gonna call your mom." I meant it too. God, those titties . . .

Another kid got in on it. "Yo, Mr. En, I heard you and Mr. Marcel live in a condo together down by the beach."

"Yeah, and your dad's our butler," I said.

"OHHHHH, damn, he rankin' on you!"

Frank Lumet walked in just as I said that. He had that look in his eye. He picked out the weakest in the herd. "Sandley, what are you laughing about? Your tits are so huge they could hide a donkey's cock between 'em."

A few students laughed, but the rest looked confused.

"Yeah, well look at'cho shoes!" It was almost so bad it was funny.

"Whoa, uh, hey Mr. Lumet, can I help you?" I stood between him and the kids.

"Yeah, you can help me figure out whether Sandley here is a faggot or not. Tell me if he stares."

Lumet turned around, bent over, and shook his ass at the kids.

"Alright, man," I said, "I think I hear Ms. Carver running wax paper through the printer again." I ushered him to the door.

Lumet dished out a few more "zingers" and wandered away, calling all of my students "pussies" on the way out.

I ate lunch in Wolo's room that day. Dina and two of her friends were there eating and playing cards when I walked in. I sat next to them. Wolo was on the phone. "Uh, yes, is this Ms. Wanton, the special education teacher? Uh-huh, yes, well my son has tentacles instead of arms, and I was wondering what kind of accommodations—" He clicked a button on the phone. "Can you believe that? She hung up on me."

We both laughed.

"Yo, Wolo, that dude Lumet is crackin' up, man. You shoulda heard what he said to my students today."

"I can imagine. He was in here yesterday asking my girls if they'd had their first periods yet. I'm not letting him back in here. Hell, if anything breaks, I'm just gonna fix it myself."

"I don't know. I don't wanna be a whistle-blower, but I think I should tell Dawson."

"That bitch—"

The girls looked up and gave him that "you-said-a-swear-word" face.

"I'm sorry, ladies. That *beautiful woman* is so overworked, she'd probably have a hard time remembering her husband's name. I remember when she took over after they canned that evil she-beast Mancini at the end of last year . . ."

When he said "Mancini," the girls shriveled up their faces. Dina said, "Oh, that lady was nasty!"

"Man, I'm telling you," Wolo said, "Dawson looked good. Look at her now. The lines on her face, that distant gaze—this place is draining her. She's spent."

"Yeah," I said, "every time I talk to her now, she just nods her head along while randomly shouting over my shoulder at students to get to class, or stop swearing, or whatever."

"I'd leave her alone. Just don't fill out any more e-tickets, and keep your door locked when students are in there. It's probably a good thing for her that her fate here is already sealed. Some people won't leave places like GW until it's already too late."

A knock at the door; it was Santoro. Wolo answered.

"Either of you guys got any printer paper I could borrow?" Santoro said.

"You out?" Wolo reached into a desk drawer and pulled out a ream.

"No," Santoro started chuckling, "my paper has been *confiscated*."

"You too!" Wolo jumped to his feet. He started tapping himself in the forehead with his right index finger. "That woman is crazy."

"What woman?" I said.

"Norma Jean Carver," Wolo said. "She's gone power mad with that printer."

"Yeah, what's up with that?" I said. "I printed some papers yesterday, but when I showed up at her room, she told me the machine jammed up, and the papers never printed. I walked over to the printer and saw my copies right there in the tray, but when I reached for them, she just started shooing me out the door, repeating, 'It's broken, Mr. En.'"

"Yeah, well Santoro here made some copies a few weeks ago using her paper, and he apparently didn't give her enough to account for what he took."

"I grabbed a stack of my own supply and handed it to her," Santoro said, "and she just looked at it, then at me, and ever since she's lost her mind."

"Every time I try to print now, the printer is down," Wolo said. "She says it's broken, but I've sent Frank Lumet in there like five times, and each time he says the power was just off. Frank's gotten into it with her."

"I can imagine," I said.

Santoro took off. Wolo reached into his desk and pulled out

a small black and white marble notebook. "I got something for ya', might make you smile." He flipped through several pages until he found what he was looking for.

"What's that?"

"Slam book. The kids pass this around to keep records of their favorite singers, actors, dancers . . . teachers. One of my students showed it to me today—he let me borrow it until after lunch. There's something in here I wanna show you." He walked over to the desk where I was sitting. "Check it out. You made the cut!"

I scanned the page and found it.

Best teachers in the school:
1. Mr. Wolo
2. Ms. Royce
3. Mr. Darbonne
4. Mr. En
5. Professor K
6. Mr. Jean-Pierre
7. Ms. Washington
8. Ms. Liberty
9. Mr. Ramirez
10. Ms. Bennett

"Damn, ahead of the Professor," I said.

"And Margo," he said. "Congratulations. That's quite an honor."

I smiled. "It looks like you're number one."

"Yeah, Mr. Wolo, you the best," Dina said. "Everybody loves your class except for the dumb kids."

"So you're saying nobody likes my class?" he said.

They laughed.

Santoro knocked again. Wolo opened the door and Santoro shot inside.

"Hey, would you mind printing something for me?" Santoro said. "Norma Jean won't accept any of my print jobs. Just give her a call and tell her it's for you. She'd probably be more likely to accept a job from someone else right now." He handed Wolo a flash drive; Wolo stuck it in his computer, pulled up the file, and said, "Sure, I'll give her a call." He gave a playful smile as he said that.

Santoro took off. Wolo and I discussed the nature of that call. I had an idea. I dialed the number and she picked up. I put it on speakerphone.

"Uh, hello, is this a Ms. Norma Jean Carver?"

"Yes, and who's this?"

"My name is Hugh July-er, and I'm an agent with the FBFC, the Federal Bureau of Funeral Crashers. Well, ma'am, we've received intelligence from one of our agents in Hialeah that you've recently attended a Harry Johnson's funeral, is that correct?"

"Why, I, uh, don't remember—"

"Do you know Mr. Johnson, ma'am?"

"Uh, well, no."

"Ma'am, we've also received intelligence that you made several trips to the buffet at said funeral, and we have photographs of you stuffing your purse with carved ham and scones, is that true?"

"What? I don't even like ham—it's the food of the devil, I always say—"

"Okay, Ms. Carver, it's clear that you crashed this funeral, and the penalty for such an offense is very severe."

"Oh my—"

"Oh my, indeed, Ms. Carver. Now the fine can include jail time of up to five years as well as a confiscation of your Florida State Retirement Pension."

"But that's what I worked so hard for!"

"Well, ma'am, I am feeling particularly generous today—some paternity tests just came back, and it looks as though I'll be able to afford a new motorcycle after all. I'll tell you what. I do have two agents currently en route to pick you up, but if you just apologize, we can forget this whole thing, okay?"

"Well, yes, yes, I apologize. I'll never crash another funeral again!"

"Thank you, Ms. Carver, I appreciate your candor. Now, I'll be frank with you, ma'am. My cell phone is broken and I don't have the agents' numbers memorized, so I have no way of contacting them to abort their mission. If you'll print an apology letter, and tape it to your door, and then leave your printer up and running, my agents will see this act of contrition and know to divert their course of action."

"Oh, okay, okay, I can do that."

"But remember to keep the printer on in case we need you to send further instructions."

"Okay."

"And, ma'am, we also have intelligence that you have an operating cotton candy machine on the premises. Is this true?"

"Heck yeah, it's Candy Fridays up in this place!"

"How about you place a few sticks of cotton candy outside your door as an additional thank you to our agents for taking their time to come down there?"

"Red or blue?"

"Surprise us."

Wolo finally let out an enormous laugh when I hung up—Dina and her friends, too. Wolo printed Santoro's files and walked down to pick up the papers. He came back with the printouts and two sticks of cotton candy, which he gave to the girls.

I left Wolo's early after eating to avoid the crowd that surged through the halls after the bell rang. I went to the bathroom, and while doing my thing, heard some terrible noises coming from outside. I looked out the window and saw several students hurling rocks into the full parking lot out back while a few security guards stood by laughing and taking videos with their phones. Rachel Golden ran outside. "What are you kids doing! STOP THE MADNESS THIS INSTANT!"

The security guards just laughed but eventually asked the kids to stop.

Chapter 31

Even after the F2ST was over, I still stayed late after school every so often. Though I'd given up on grading and planning with any rigor, I hadn't given up on life. I threw together an after-school pickup basketball league for students and any neighborhood kids who were interested, and coached/refereed their games on the courts behind the school. Sometimes other teachers would come out and play games. Margo even played once—she was pretty good too. Other days we played tag football in the fields behind the court. There was some real talent out there and those kids often gave me a run for my money whichever sport we were playing. I figured if I wasn't able to connect with them in the classroom, I might as well do it where I could. After all, hardly anyone was listening to a damned thing those final months of the year. It'd be easy just to throw the kids out; it was far more difficult to bring them back in.

There was a heated basketball game that afternoon between the GW kids and those from a nearby middle school. There was some serious pushing and shoving on the court, and I had to threaten to cancel play several times, until I finally did after a kid from the other school decked one of our players. The kids all scattered and I remained behind with the kid who'd taken the punch. His nose was bleeding and his arm was scraped, so I went inside for a medkit, which at GW consisted of some paper towels and masking tape. I taped a paper towel to the kid's arm and gave him a few more for his nose. Suddenly, Frank Lumet ran out to the court and right up to me. He was nearly out of breath. "I've been looking for you everywhere. You're gonna want to come with me."

Oh fuck. I knew this had to do with my car.

Frank led me to the parking lot out front. I could hear cop sirens blaring. A few squad cars rounded the corners. The kids fighting out front scattered. Frank grabbed one at random, raised him up by the neck, took out his legs, and slammed him back first on the blacktop.

"Hey, Frank, take it easy. He's just a kid!" I said.

The kid started squirming, so Frank put his forearm into his neck and put him to sleep. "That's right, baby, go to sleep . . . go to sleep." A cop came by and took over, and Frank walked back to me. "Hey, the reason I called you out here is because these kids were throwing rocks at each other, and one hit your car."

"What the fuck are you doing?" I said.

"Showing you the dent. Here, look." It was nothing compared to the damage I'd done to that thing.

"No, I mean what the fuck are you doing to these kids?"

"Well, you saw him resisting, so I had to take intensive action."

"Intensive action? You're not a cop! Hell, you're not even a real security guard!"

"Somebody's gotta teach these kids a lesson."

"So now you're a teacher too, huh?"

"Relax, man. They're out of control."

"They're not the only ones, Frankie. I swear if I see you touch another one of these kids, I'm gonna beat your ass. I'm gonna beat your fucking ass. Just leave us the fuck alone."

For the briefest of moments, Frank responded as would a

human being; I could see the guilt wishing to leap from his eyes—but he forced it back down as the fucking terror took back over, and he stormed off like a self-righteous asshole.

The cops hauled the passed-out kid away and I got in my dented car and drove home.

Billy was in the apartment when I got back. He immediately started bitching when I walked through the door.

"So, guess who never calls me anymore?" He shoveled a handful of low-calorie popcorn in his mouth.

"Representatives from the National Hair-Donors Association?"

"Very funny. No, not them—Liberty hasn't called me a single time since she got together with Tito. That's a rock 'n' roll match if I'd ever seen one. They spend all their time together and fuck like sixty times a day."

"You're better off. That chick's a dead end. Even if her book made the *Times* Best Sellers list, she'd still be a dumb asshole."

Billy started laughing. "Oh, man, she hates that guy, Colossal—whatever. He really got under her skin. The last time I talked with her, she kept muttering to herself, 'Cookbook—I'd be surprised if you could even read a cookbook,' or some variation like it, as if she was still trying to come up with a witty rejoinder to sock it to him."

"Look, man, both of them—Tito and Liberty—are full of shit. They're going after the Holy Grail, and if they ever find it, they'll just use it as a receptacle for booze."

Billy loved that one. "Oh my god, the party seriously hasn't stopped between them since they got together. Every time I go over there, it's like Mardi Gras—clothing optional—whiskey, weed, blow . . . I feel bad for the neighbors. All those two do is argue." Billy threw up his hands and started laughing. "Oh, and get this. I was doing some research on Margo's little book publisher, and it turns out that Albatross is a vanity press. The only reason why her book's not in print is because she ran out of money—can you believe that?"

"They wouldn't let her barter dancing lessons?"

"Puh-leeze, bitch moves like a poorly greased robot."

We both laughed.

"I've been thinking a lot lately, man," I said. "I think we should take this summer and just write our screenplay. I don't care—I'll drive cross-country and bring it to LA myself. I just don't think I was cut out to teach. Plus, we'll be getting paid all summer, so even if we fail, we can come back to Florida and try it again in the fall."

"Yeah—oh my god, do you know what Liberty told me? She wants to join some religious cult down in the Keys. She says it's not a cult, but it's got all the signs of one."

"That's nice." I wandered into my room, flipped on the A/C, and checked my computer. Lila had written me an email. "I miss you, hermoso."

I missed her too. That decision haunted me. I'd only written her a couple of times since returning from Mexico, and I never knew what to say. I always started writing some lengthy apology, begging her to take me back, but then I'd erase it and just give the bare bones, "Miss you, too. Hope you're doing well. Cuidate, besos . . ." But those were my only two approaches to anything. I was always either giving away too much or too little, and never knew when to give it or whom to give it to. I shut off the computer and took a nap that lasted well into the night.

Though it was a Wednesday, Tito called me sometime after midnight. "Yo, bro, let's go get some drinks. This Liberty bitch is killin' me. Real ball buster she is. I need a prison break."

"You know I gotta get up for school tomorrow, right?"

"Oh come on. Just meet me at the Tide Pool for a drink."

I didn't know why, but off I went. Again, Paola wasn't there. I guess maybe she had gone back to Brazil. Tito, however, was there and was already drunk when I showed up. "Bro, that monster is killing me." He swayed around the circumference of his barstool. "I've never met a bigger nag in my life—and that apartment? It's disgusting. I can't believe a female could live in such squalor."

"That's Hurricane Margo." I ordered a beer and took a gulp. "Hey, look, I can't stay long. I gotta get up in a few hours."

"No worries, bro." Tito ordered some shots.

"I just said I gotta get up."

"This'll get you up."

We did the shots.

"Hey," he said, "I got a friend who's working casting on some big picture coming into town, and they need tons of extras. You kinda got that boy-next-door thing going on. They pay decent, too."

"I don't know shit about acting."

"What's to know? You show up, stand around for a while, look good, then they pay you. It's cake, homie. And the girls . . ."

"I don't know . . . Are you gonna be there?"

"Bro, my days of being scenery are long gone. I'm the fuckin' star or nothing."

"Well, I guess everybody's gotta start somewhere."

"Margo says you write."

"Oh she does? And what's she say about it?"

"Just that you write. Maybe you could sneak on the set and charm one of the producers—get him to request a script or something. That's how shit works, bro. You gotta go out there and make it happen. Fuck all these other scumbags. You think I got on TV by sitting on my ass? Fuck no. I went out there and worked my ass off for it."

"Well, what's your friend's number?"

He gave it to me.

"Yo, I'm scared to go back to that bitch's place tonight," he said. "I think she seriously might be trying to poison me."

"Why don't you just go back to your place?"

"Because my parents are locisimo, bro. My father and I don't get along and my mom just does whatever he says. We got into a fistfight last week—my dad and me—and I ended up giving him a big-ass shiner. I haven't been home since."

"Well, just don't let Liberty do the same to you. I've seen her get aggressive before. It's not pretty."

"I'll knock that bitch out."

I gave a nervous chuckle. I wasn't sure if he was serious or not. With him, I just couldn't tell.

"Yo," he said, "I'm taking you and Colossus down to South Beach this weekend. Fuck these little rinky-dink bars up here. We're gonna go down and score some serious Latina stank."

"I'm sure Margo'd be thrilled to go."

"She's not gonna be here. She's letting me stay in her apartment for the weekend. Shaka, brah!"

I finished my beer. Tito ordered me a second. I told him no, but he kept smiling and giving me the fucking shaka, so I chugged it down then took off.

Chapter 32

The weekend soon came, and with it a pool party at the Professor's house. He invited me, Santoro, and Wolo, but Santoro couldn't show. "I've got plans with the wife." Bullshit. I drove up to Wolo's condo, and we headed over together. On the way there, Wolo and I stopped at a liquor store for some whiskey. When we walked inside, the guy behind the counter came out into the aisles and followed us around. We tested him by winding quickly through the aisles, and he was always right there near us. He knew we knew he was watching us—fucking prick. That shit was the worst; I felt for the everyday life of the GW kids. Wolo and I, being Wolo and I, refused to go quietly. We split up: I walked toward a display of top-shelf liquors, and Wolo hung out near the cheap whiskey. I picked up a bottle of some triple-digit priced swill and pretended to have a hard time holding it, almost dropping it a few times. The guy walked over and took it from me just as Wolo shoved a bottle of whiskey down his pants. We left and bought a case of beer at a nearby gas station.

We pulled into the Professor's driveway a little later. He had a nice spread: three-bedroom ranch with a screened-in Florida room in back, which included an inground swimming pool. The Professor gave us the tour. His place was homey and warm. Kids' toys littered the floors. I checked out a framed picture of him with the wife and kids. A nice little family. The guy had it made, he really did. I didn't get that horrible feeling of tension and oppression and settled-in hatred that I did in nearly every other house I'd ever walked through. I felt safe inside those walls. The Profi made us some grilled cheese sandwiches, and we ate at the kitchen table. I already knew what I was going to do—already knew what my summer held—and I almost didn't want to sit at that table. I felt safe there. We had good conversations. Wolo and the Professor were fun and hard-working and with it. But I knew I was going to be leaving them, as I'd always left everybody I'd ever known and/or cared for throughout my life. But something about all that felt different this time. It wasn't as painful. The Professor grabbed his bubbler, and though his family wasn't there, insisted we smoke in the garage. We huddled around a kid's bike. I refused the first rotation, but was feeling the moment, so I joined in for the next few. I didn't want to do it, but I did anyway. We soon got to talking.

"A movie extra?" Wolo laughed. "You know how much those guys make? Shit, you couldn't even afford that grilled cheese sandwich you were munching on."

"It wouldn't be a career, just a stepping stone to something else," I said.

"To what? The unemployment line?" Wolo laughed.

"I got some ideas. A lot of ideas, actually—" I said.

"So do I, so does he," he pointed at the Professor, "so does everybody. That doesn't mean you can turn them into money."

"But I think—"

"I know what you're thinking right now, but trust me, the second year gets easier. Hell, the Professor and I've made it a combined total of fifteen years at that shithole. If we can hack it, so can you."

"Yeah, I guess." I refused the next rotation. I started scanning the garage floor. "But I really do think I can make it."

"Go easy, alright, buddy," the Professor said to Wolo. "You know you used to dream, too." The bowl was kicked. The Professor sucked the ash through and emptied the water into a drain in the floor. "So what do you guys think GWs chances are of getting an A by next year?"

Wolo lifted his leg and farted and we all started laughing. Wolo then said, "How about instead of all schools becoming an A, that all kids get a regular dinner by next year?"

"Or every kid gets a safe place to live by next year?"

"Or every prick chokes back on at least one racial joke by next year?"

"Or every motherfucker tries one new cultural dish?"

"Or listens to one new band?"

"Or tries walking with a different gait?"

"Or takes up hang gliding?"

"Or visits a monastery?"

"Or sleeps in a tree!"

"Or says 'I love you' to a complete stranger?"

"Or craps sitting backwards on the toilet?"

"Or shaves an alpaca?"

"Or plays a tuba?"

"Or learns to yodel?"

We wandered out to the pool. Wolo jumped right in and started floating on his back with his ears just below the water's surface; he said he was "Meditating." The Professor and I said little—we drank our beers. I saw a guitar in his living room beside a small drum kit and brought it outside. I thought about taking requests, but knew that to be nonsense, so I just started on something I'd written long ago. I played the song through, and at the end Wolo lifted his head above the water and said, "Maybe you can make it?"

Wolo popped out of the pool and had a hankering for some wine—a hankering he just couldn't shake—so he toweled off and headed to the liquor store. The Professor brought me another beer.

"Don't get too upset about what he said before," he said.

"No, it's okay. I know what a long shot it all is."

"Nothing in this world is a long shot if you become success. If you want to write, then write. You can't fail. If your goal, however, is to achieve limitless power and fortune, then you're no longer writing, but seeking that which is unattainable."

"Yeah, sure," I said.

"You know Wolo was a pretty mean card player?"

"No, I didn't—although it kinda makes sense."

"Before he got married, he'd made a pretty decent living off of playing cards."

"I knew he had some talent in there somewhere."

"Well, he was a few grand short to make the buy-in for some big tournament, and he ended up doing something not-so-scrupulous to make up the rest. He got arrested and was given a couple of years, but got it knocked down to a few months. He tried getting jobs all over Alabama and Florida, but the MPSD was the only district that would give him a chance—and George Washington Middle was the only school that would take him in. He's wanted to leave for years but can't. He's been waiting for his wife to get through law school, but that ain't no trip to the liquor store, if you know what I mean."

"Shit, I didn't know any of that."

"Not many people do. Just try to keep all that in mind the next time he goes giving you advice about following dreams. I'm not saying this to insult him, but to help you gain perspective on the choices you make in your own life."

Wolo came back a short time later with a few bottles of wine. We got drunk and passed out in the Professor's living room, but not before having a serious jam session. It turns out, on top of being a phenomenal card player, Wolo blew a pretty mean harp. With the Professor on drums and me on guitar, we had ourselves a nice little ensemble.

The next morning, we got to talking about the bike trails, and the Professor offered me an old bike of his. "Go ahead. It's not much but it'll get you over the hills."

"Eh, it's okay. I don't need it," I said.

"Take it, man. We'll hit Hedman after work this week," Wolo said.

"I don't really have a way to get it around . . ." I said.

"It's alright. I got an extra bike rack at home you can have," Wolo said. "I'll take the bike home with me today and bring it to school on Monday with the rack. Then you can take 'em both with you." Wolo seemed to get more and more excited as the plan unfurled.

"Uh . . . sure."

So it was done. I drove back to the beach. I got a call from Tito early that afternoon.

"Wanna head to the playa? I'm meeting Colossus there."

I said yes, and we got drunk and did the same shit everyone always does on the beach when you're young and dumb and horny and drunk. We found some girls and went back to their place and felt like men for a brief moment of our lives.

The days started passing in a blur. I'd been spending most of my free time with Tito, and he spent most of his free time with Margo, and she'd started spending most of her free time with Billy again, so we were nearly always together like some big, fucked-up family. Colossus usually joined in on our dysfunctional adventures as well. He and Margo never took to each other, but their interactions were usually more comical for the rest of us than tense and uncomfortable. We went to parties and bars and dominated the social happenings wherever we ended up.

One night, we all went to some buddy of Tito's place for a big house party. All was well until some dumb, rat-faced prick from Brooklyn decided to step into Billy's personal space after Billy mentioned teaching at PS 490. It began as most of these little mishaps do—an ill-advised statement made by some drunken asshole with no filter.

"There's no way you taught in Queens," said the New York Dumbass. "Those kids woulda' ran you outta there in a heartbeat. Fuck outta here with that shit."

"Not only did I make it through the year, in potentially the worst school and with the worst principal in the entire New York Public Schools District, but I got glowing reviews from my students, who happened to have scored the highest on their state exams in the whole school," Billy said in nearly one breath.

"Get him, boy!" Tito pumped his fist.

"Please, you make it sound like teaching is hard," New York Dumbass said. "Any idiot can stand up there and drone on for an hour about George Washington and fractions and all that shit."

"And what is it that you do, dear?" Margo said.

"Don't worry about that," he said.

"Why don't you answer the question, tough guy," I said.

"I'm in business," he said.

"What kind of business?" Margo said.

"I work in the tourism industry," he said, with inflated pride.

"Please," Tito said, "you call selling star maps down on South Beach, tourism?"

"Fuck you, Tito. At least I don't go around like these assholes tellin' people I make a damned difference. All you teachers are the same," New York said.

"And all you Dumbasses are the same, darling. Why don't you do yourself a favor and follow a map to a place where we all give a fuck?" Margo said.

"Maybe you should follow a map to a better plastic surgeon," New York said. "My butcher coulda' done a better job on that nose."

Colossus and Tito laughed.

"Hey—" Billy stood up.

"Fuck you, fun boy." New York stood up, too, but less in aggressive dominance and more of casual arrogance. Margo immediately tossed her drink in his face. He grabbed her arm, and I cracked him in the jaw. He dropped to his knees. Colossus and Tito just sat there laughing and drinking their beers. Several of New York's friends popped outside.

"What the fuck?"

"Get him!"

About six or seven closed in on me. Then Colossus stood and wagged his finger in their direction, and they backed off. We grabbed their keg and a few bags of ice as they stood there cursing us out. We took the keg back to Margo's place and spent the night getting fucked up—beer and liquor and cocaine. At one point, Tito and Margo disappeared into the bathroom, but Colossus had to piss, so they came outside and started humping like dogs in the kitchen. Billy and I watched, and Colossus too when he got out of the bathroom. I wasn't sure if I was turned on by the skin or the sheer disregard for any social bounds, but either way, I had to sit it out for a good ten minutes after he pulled out and spooged on the crest of her ass. The world outside of GW Middle was no less violent or chaotic, but at least this world had tits.

The days continued like that, and time and circumstance kept our group together. I still hung out with Wolo outside of school, but less and less as we neared the summer. I think he knew what was going on and was already making his distance. I think I was making some distance too. I'd called Tito's friend about the movie job. I answered a few questions, emailed him a photo Billy took of me in Key West, and was given the green light to start whoring out my likeness to the rotten-crotched trollop that is Hollywood. It felt good . . .

Chapter 33

Near the end of May, Emilio Rodriguez called a meeting at the library/recycling center to share with us the results from the F2ST. Almost every teacher attended.

"Okay, ladies and gentlemen, I want to thank you all again for your hard work this year. As you well know, the F2ST scores are in. I have some bad news, but the good far overshadows anything negative. I'll be frank. We did not meet state requirements. We are not an A school. But we're also not an F."

People started smiling.

". . . For the past ten years, in the eyes of the state of Florida, George Washington Middle has been a failure. But I say now as I've said before, that this grade is no accurate assessment of the hard work both our staff and students put in each and every day. I stand before you today and can tell you George Washington Middle is no longer a failure. While we did not achieve the A the state has mandated for all schools, we rose higher than we ever have before. Ladies and gentlemen, I'm proud to tell you that George Washington Middle is now a D."

A long round of applause, peppered with "Yeah"s and "All right"s.

"I want to take some time here to honor some particularly notable performances by staff members. We had several teachers' scores rise this year, including those of Ms. Yolanda Royce, Mr. Jean-Pierre, and Ms. Darla Rotter. But the teacher with the highest test scores in the school—an average of C- for all of her English students—was Ms. Margo Liberty . . ."

Margo smiled. But it wasn't one of her phony "Darling" smiles. This was the real deal. I saw her face for the first time that afternoon. I'd long imagined what it really looked like, and there it was. She was a beautiful woman. I just hoped she could see it too.

". . . Please, ladies and gentlemen, let's give a special round of applause for the achievements of these wonderful staff members, and also for all those in the other departments who assisted the math, science, and English teachers in their preparation for the test. Today, George Washington is a success no matter what any school board member or state legislature can say. They don't go into battle as you do every day. Congratulations!"

Wolo initiated a standing ovation. He was the first to his feet, and others followed. I was proud of our accomplishment and, it seemed, so were others. I felt like less of a piece of shit, but in spite of our celebration, I knew this wasn't the last we'd be hearing about our inability to achieve a perfect score.

On the Friday of the second to last week of school, I took the bus down to South Beach and followed the flooded light and dolly tracks to the cluster of other fame-humpers huddled around a nasally, gaunt man who was far too young to be wearing such an obvious hairpiece.

He gave us the rundown: the director was shooting a walk along the beach—a simple scene, but accordingly to Hairpiece, "Is the most *poignant* and *gripping* in the entire picture." I knew this was Hollywood and everything was supposed to be dramatic, but I thought the guy was going to break out into tears as he said that. He sent us all to the HR tent to fill out paperwork, then to the fashion tent where we were told everything we were wearing was wrong. The woman there offered me an argyle sweater, despite my insistence that it looked terrible.

"It's you, dear, it's *you*. I can see you," she said.

"Well, I guess I must know nothing of myself . . ."

I put it on and kept it on, trying to see the real me in a full-length mirror by the HR tent. A tall, handsome young man came over.

"That sweater's all wrong for you," he said.

"That's what I tried to tell that psycho in there," I said.

He smiled. We shook hands, and he gave me his story. The guy's name was Dan, and this was Dan's twentieth picture. He'd mostly done TV shoots, even getting a few lines in some shitty cable series, and he explained what the rest of my night would look like. "There's nothing sexy about this job. You're an ornament. You're given a mark, and expected to stick to it as long as it takes the director to get their shot. Sometimes it's quick, other times they labor and moan over it for half a day. We could potentially be here all night."

That, I did not want to hear. Earlier that day, Tito had asked me if I wanted to go to a house party that night where many women were expected to be. Wolo had also asked me that afternoon if I'd wanted to catch a Marlins game that night. I told them both yes, paying no honor to reality.

The film set covered nearly an entire block's worth of prime real estate between the Ocean Drive bars and restaurants, and the beach, and the camera was on a dolly that spanned nearly the length of the set; it followed the leads as they strolled down the beach and discussed some "*poignant* and *gripping*" matter in their lives. It was the job of the extras to stroll down the sidewalk in the background, mimicking everyday pedestrian motion. A few of the men, including me, were paired up with some age-appropriate women, but after about an hour of shooting, I started locking arms with a woman about forty years my senior, who "accidentally" smacked my ass after a take. During the next pass, I kissed her on the lips at the very moment the leads walked by, and she guffawed so loudly, the director had to cut. He gave us an irksome look, and we returned to first position, giggling to each other. I sat out the next few passes and pondered the scene. Across the street, South Beach was on fire with motion. Everyone looked at the set as they passed. Tito called me during one of these breaks. "Yo, bro, fuck that movie shit. Take a cab up north. This party's gettin' wild, man. I got the keys to Margo's for the after party. She's outta town again. Get your ass up here!"

I told him I'd come if I could, but I knew I wouldn't show even if filming wrapped up early. The lights got inside me. It wasn't the cameras or the actors or the hype of it all—the production reeked of horseshit (it never even made it to theaters). It was the lights that got me. I'd done some acting in grammar school before I'd learned the world didn't like me. But under those lights, those dark memories lost some of their luster. The hours passed, and by 3 am we were given the clear to leave. I thought about taking a cab up north, but Dan invited me to grab some drinks at a bar that ran all night. I went down with a few of the other extras, and we blew the hundred bucks we'd made on bottles of Caribbean liquor.

I was awakened by a phone call early the next morning. I reached across my bed and grabbed my phone, but didn't even bother looking at the screen—I knew who it was. "No, no . . . no, not that one!" I could hear Tito, but he wasn't talking to me. "Fuck, man, you're gonna break it . . . you're gonna—" then a crash.

"What the hell's going on over there?" I said.

Tito was laughing so hard he could barely get out the words. "You're not gonna believe this, bro. The repo guys are here and they're clearin' out Margo's apartment. They're takin' the snake and everything."

"Holy shit!"

Billy wandered past my door.

"Yo, Billy, Tito says the repo guys are cleaning out Liberty's apartment."

"Fuck! Does she know?" Billy said.

I put the phone back to my ear. "Does she know?"

Tito started laughing. "I haven't told her. I think it'd be funnier if she finds out on when she gets back."

I started laughing too and relayed the message to Billy.

"I'll call her." Billy dialed the number, but didn't get through.

Tito showed up at our apartment about an hour later.

"Wanna head to the beach, Lukie? I'm gonna meet Colossus," he said.

"Fuck it." I grabbed my gym bag and stuffed it with my towel and some beer and followed him out the door. But when we got to the street, I didn't see his truck.

"Where'd you park?" I said.

He smiled and pointed at a pink Vespa parked in front of my apartment.

"I traded in," he said, now full-out laughing.

"What the hell is this?"

"This is the only thing I managed to keep away from the repo guys. They're grabby motherfuckers." He walked over to it, hopped on, and started it up. "Hop on, homie." He gave me a shaka, but I didn't move.

The bus was just up the block.

"Fuck that. I'll meet you there." I raced across the three busy lanes and made it to the stop before the bus. I rode it down to 8th Street and wandered toward the ocean. When I cleared the dunes, it was obvious we weren't the only ones to take a beach trip that morning. Despite the crowds, it wasn't difficult to spot them: Colossus stood about a head above everyone else. He saw me and motioned me over.

"Lukie Lou!" Colossus held up a bag of Mexican food. "Lunch time."

Tito grabbed some loungers, and soon we were set up. I reached into the cooler Colossus brought and grabbed a beer.

"You hear what happened at Liberty's place?" Colossus shielded his eyes from the sun with his hand.

"Yeah, that's shitty," I said.

"That'll teach her to pay her bills. Fuckin' slob," Tito said. "I don't know how a lady could live like that." His eyes followed a few luscious thonged asses as they passed by.

"Christ, she's gonna be pissed," I said.

"Eh, fuck her," Tito said. "That bitch is getting on my nerves anyway. All she ever wants to do is shoot shit up her nose and fuck. I'm a fuckin' champ, and I honestly can't keep up."

"That's 'cause you get that coke dick," Colossus said.

Tito smiled and shrugged his shoulders, then turned to me. "Bro, you missed out on one hell of a party last night. Women everywhere, reppin' the entire Latin world. We scored these Chilean sweeties. Colossus here ass-fucked the one broad in the back of his truck. They wanna chill again tonight."

"I'm down." I took a big gulp.

Tito started laughing, though no joke was told.

"What?" I said.

"Should I tell him?" Tito said.

Colossus nodded.

"After we dropped off the Chilean girls, we found Margo's car keys at her apartment and took her Prius out for a joy ride. We stopped at a strip club and I told all the strippers I was a Marine who just got back from Iraq. I showed 'em an old surfing injury and told 'em it was from a mortar. They don't know the fucking difference. It worked, too. We ended up taking one of 'em back to Margo's and tag-teamed her on her couch."

"Well, it's a good thing they repo'd that shit. I'd never sit on that couch again," I said. "And what the fuck are you doing tellin' people you're a Marine—especially an injured Marine? That's a special kind of fucked, you know that?"

"Oh, lighten up, bro," Tito said. "I gotta keep the acting gears lubed somehow."

We cleared out the cooler and the Mexican food, and being ever-hungry, ever-thirsty young men, we tossed Margo's Vespa in the back of Colossus's truck and took off for a barbeque place a few blocks north. It was a simple sports bar/restaurant, with a jukebox and all that crap, and was nearly empty when we walked in. A gorgeous, thin-yet-curvaceous black woman was working the bar; she had her cell phone out. We walked right over.

"That's 555-7879," I said as I sat.

She smiled.

"What can I get for you guys, other than a restraining order?" she said.

"I'd like to go one weekend without hearing that," Colossus said.

She smiled and told us her name, Gia. We ordered beers, then a basket of nachos, then wings and big plates of ribs. We ate everything with our hands. We took the beers down quickly and the gorgeous, little wonder-waitress kept new ones coming. And with every beer she brought I grew more determined to get to know her better.

It was a hot day. Little beads of sweat gathered in the valley of her chest. I wished to fill that valley with beer and go in head-first. She smiled. She always smiled. People started to fill the place. Guys started to take notice. Groups of them would do their best: five handsome Brits in suits tried to engage her in conversation, but failed; a few Hispanic guys did the same, but got nowhere. Each time, she gave them just enough attention to take their order and assure a good tip, and then she was back to us. I wasn't sure what it was about us that attracted her, but she wasn't the only one. Groups of girls took notice. Tito would smile at them, and they'd wander over. He'd toss them a few banalities, then I'd insult them, and Colossus would apologize for us and engage them in comforting, confidence-building conversation—then they'd pull up chairs and settle in beside us for the long haul. It was the perfect crew. We'd realized it then, at that restaurant, and acknowledged it with a toast. It took me about a year, but Miami finally spread its legs for me—and it was then I'd realized this was the same pussy I'd seen in so many other dime-a-dozen burgs—the same biscuit I'd eaten and fucked and regretted on so many other hazy nights—the same stinkin' pie I'd already resolved to trade for abstinence and a clear head should it ever present itself to me again. I tried to find something to bring that now-hazy goal into focus. The little honey behind the counter got more and more jealous each time another group of girls sat with us. Once, she even threatened to bounce some "ho-bag" from the bar if she couldn't hold her liquor, after the girl tried to sit on my lap and slipped off. We continued that party all afternoon and well into the night. A group of women German exchange students came in and Colossus and Tito got right on it. I, however, was fixated on my little princess behind the counter. She was full of life and energy—there was something more to her than pretty scenery. The hours passed, and I could feel us getting closer. But the German girls kept pushing Tito and Colossus to take them dancing, and soon we were out the door. I shouldn't have left, but I did, and Gia waved and said "Good-bye" loud enough for the whole bar to hear as I walked through the door.

We went to another bar but got kicked out when Tito got into a shoving match with a fellow Colombian after Tito called him a pussy. His crew followed us outside and soon we were toe-to-toe with five assholes whose rage looked far too settled in to be the result of a mere barroom shoving match, and no amount of pummeling or stomping would ever satisfy it. Tito swung first and missed, and we spilled into an alleyway. I squared off against a chubby but quick asshole. He threw a few wild shots and landed one or two. I shook it off and took a big cut at his head, but missed. He also missed with a right haymaker, and lost his balance. I hit him in the side of the stomach with everything I had, and he doubled over. I kneed him in the face, and he went down. I then went to help out Tito and Colossus—but they'd already helped themselves. The other four assholes were all on the ground writhing in pain. We left the alley in a hurry, and the Germans followed behind. We started for Colossus's truck, but I stopped.

"Wait, guys. I gotta go check on something."

I ran back to the barbeque place, but when I got to the door, I saw her talking with some other white guy. She was smiling. I walked in, and she hardly looked up. I started to wave, but stopped myself, realizing the great folly in doing so. I pushed through the door and took off running for Colossus's truck. I was so drunk that I ran right into it and almost knocked myself out. Colossus got out, laughing. He picked me up and helped me inside. The car was full of German girls. I didn't know how many, and couldn't have counted if I'd wanted to. One took my hand and ran it up under her shirt. I already didn't like that—I appreciate assertiveness from a woman, but at least give me some words first—a hello, a how are you, an Ich bin ein Berliner . . .

Colossus stopped at a drug store. It was after hours, so he stuffed a bottle of rum down his pants, and we strolled out. We got back in the truck and Colossus drove us to his place. The apartment was big, but probably seemed that much more so due to its lack of furniture. It had something of an Arabian Nights meets 8th Street Latinas vibe to it. There were sheets and tapestries and shit hanging from the ceiling and pillows lying all over the floor. I kept waiting for some beer-swollen, balding porn director to pop out of the bathroom and instruct his lead on where to place the money shot.

We sat on some pillows. I realized then there were four girls. One was already tongue-inside Tito. Another crawled over to me on all fours. One of the others started making out with Colossus. But the fourth sat alone. Soon she was tugging at the girl on Colossus, and they left the apartment together. My girl kept trying to get some, but I just wasn't feeling it. I had the faces of so many other women rushing through my memory, and those faces all held the worst looks—it wasn't anger, or sadness that I saw, but disappointment.

I knew those faces were right. The girl kissed my cheeks a few times, but I tagged in Colossus instead. She quickly took to him, and they ran off to the bathroom. The girl on Tito was now in her underwear. Tito popped off her bra with one hand, and that really got her going. She grabbed my hand and put it on her wunder-mound. I didn't like her wetness; I pulled away.

"Hey, bro," Tito laid her on her back over one of the pillows, "you wanna get her snatch?"

I shook my head. "That's you, man."

He went down, and she reached for me again. She started massaging me from outside my pants, then she unzipped them and worked them down below my hips. She took a big mouthful, covering it in saliva, then went to town jerking it. I could hear every one of Colossus's powerful thrusts in the bathroom. The girl was screaming like a whore.

"God, he's killing that poor girl," I said.

Tito started laughing, but he kept his head down.

Our little fräulein started to match her friend's intensity. She moaned deeper and deeper with such bass in her voice that it seemed to drag me down with her. She kept switching between sucking and jerking me. In the chaotic state of ecstasy, she couldn't make up her mind which wanted my cock wrapped around it more, her lips or her hands. I straddled her chest and let her work through her indecision.

Tito ripped off his pants, rubbed her lubricant on his dick with a few strokes, and shoved it in. I grabbed one of the condoms Colossus had tossed on the floor like carnival prizes when we first walked in and threw it at Tito's crotch.

"C'mon, man. You don't know where she's been."

He stopped and tore open the wrapper with his teeth. He tried to roll the rubber on his dick but had some difficulty, so he just tossed it back on the floor and got to work. She started to go wild, digging into my back, and giving it undeserved marks of satisfaction. I finally decided to finally join a moment of my life; I took my pants entirely off, pulled off my shirt, straddled the girl's face, and started fucking her mouth, which exploded with sound. "GLUB, GLUB, GLUB . . . OWWOOWW." I thought I might have been hurting her, so I pulled out. Almost instantly, her head shot up in a bout of passion, and she started repeating, "Rape me." It began as a whisper, with a cadence and delivery as slow and terrifying as the dying sniper in *Full Metal Jacket*, but soon grew to a shout, until she was nearly screaming it like a woman possessed, "OWW, RAPE ME! PLEASE RAPE ME!" Judging by how little she knew of the English language, I was surprised she'd known the word. Perhaps this was a game she'd played on nights before?

"Hey, you gotta stop saying that." I said it quietly at first, but soon Tito and I had matched her intensity.

"SHUT THE FUCK UP! SHUT THE FUCK UP, YOU FUCKING NAZI CUNT!"

Then a loud CRASH from the bathroom.

"Jesus, he's killing that poor girl!" I pulled myself from arm's reach of that blond lump of oily sex lying on the genital-stained pillow. Only when Tito toned down his thrusting did she stop begging to be raped.

I got up and wandered to the kitchen. I found the bottle of rum and fixed myself a strong drink. I made two others for the new fuck-friends sweating through each other on the living room floor. I brought the drinks over to them. Tito gulped half of his down, never missing a beat pumping that Euro-snatch. The German fumbled the handoff, and down went the drink to join the other stains currently seasoning the carpet. I found a lawn chair in Colossus's closet, unfolded it, and sat in the corner of the living room watching Tito do what it was he was put on this earth to do. Colossus had taken his girl to his bedroom and was being no less subtle with his love-pumping—the recoil of the bedsprings from his Herculean thrusts sounded powerful enough to launch a monkey into space. In that moment, I actually felt for the neighbors. I reached on the floor and grabbed a pack of cigarettes. Though I didn't smoke, I also didn't participate in orgies, so I figured what the hell. I sat there in the lawn chair smoking and sipping drinks and giving Tito orders in what was basically an interactive porno. "Now flip her over . . . no, pull her up on all fours. Have her arch her back . . ." Just puffing, and sipping, and jerking.

Colossus finally finished off his girl. I could tell because the apartment stopped sounding as if it was being pummeled by a wrecking ball. He and his girl came out and watched the porno with me. The girl walked back over to me and tried to suck my cock, but I pushed her head away, not knowing how much of Colossus's semen she'd just strained through those teeth. I settled for a hand job, but stopped her before release. Instead of letting her finish me off, I crawled over to the rape-fetish fräulein, and she opened her mouth as I exploded all over her face. She punched me hard in the stomach, then wiped up my crème with her hand and started licking her fingertips. Soon, Tito pulled out and gave her the same inside the crack of her ass.

"You really shoulda worn a rubber, man," I told him.

"I did, see?" He pulled the rubber off the floor and showed it to everyone.

"Eh, whatever."

Colossus took his girl back to his room and Tito and I slept beside the other on pillows in the living room. I woke up the next morning naked and alone. Colossus's girl came out of his room, naked as well. Her breasts were enormous and bounced with grace as she moved. She saw me and lay down beside me, rubbing those breasts against my back. I became ready; she reached around and started on me, but I pushed her away halfway through, put on my clothes, and shot out of the door.

I was unbelievably hungover and could hardly walk. The whole world was fog, even on what I knew to be a clear, beautiful, tropical blue Miami midday. I staggered to the bus and joined the legions of broken maniacs speeding back to, or away from, their hurried realities, one bus stop at a time. I looked across the crowded aisle and swore I saw her face—that beautiful, full mocha face I'd walked out on, not once, but twice already in the past year—that girl who freely told me she loved me even though I had less than nothing to give to her. I wished that bus would take me right to her. I'd ride it forty hours straight to Mariposa. But I'd already played that game before. I'd already rolled those dice, and won so many, many times, yet still tossed my earnings into the dark void of endless black night. Was it her, or was it all girls? Did I stumble upon her faults, or actively pursue them as would a detective too broken to give up on a case long dismissed by the courts? Why didn't I feel her? Why couldn't I be with her? My head was so very heavy. I'd needed water badly. My insides were grit and concrete, and joints struggled to allow movement. Why was it that every time life tossed me an opportunity, I rode it up to the top of the tallest structure I could find, then hopped on its shoulders and coaxed it off the ledge? Other people seemed content to get up early, and go shopping, and get smoothies with their friends at the new café that just opened up on the corner, and not obsess over how it was designed by some soulless prick from New York who couldn't care less about smoothies or smiles. Other people could ride a bus without hearing the hushed, trembling voices of all those sad souls gripping the rails and holding on for dear life. Other people had friends they could call who, they knew, would never lead them to a rum-fueled orgy. I needed school badly that Monday. I needed to go stand before children and allow their pain and self-hatred to make me feel purposeful. But I knew they'd be able to smell it on me. Knew they really did know all my secrets; that the darkness fell from my mouth like small bubbles of toxic spit, and my clumsy gestures rattled off my intentions long before I knew they were even in motion. I rode that bus one stop past my own—not because I'd wanted to avoid home, and my computer, but because my senses were far too blunted to even recognize home when I passed it.

Billy was there and talking when I got in. I swear, the kid never stopped. "Oh, and my AP, get this, calls me into her office just to tell me my lesson plans weren't up to Little Havana standards. She said my anticipatory sets were far too bland . . ."

I walked past him and into my room. I flipped on my computer and started doing what I was programmed to do. I got three pages into an email, then highlighted "all" and clicked "delete." I took a shower, drank nearly a gallon of water, and went to sleep.

Chapter 34

Monday began the final week of school. Nobody had been learning shit for weeks—it was all movies and cotton candy and bullshit group work. The only thing noteworthy about that day was Margo's reaction to the repossession of her things. She swung between the extremes, telling us in Santoro's room during lunch, "In a way, I'm actually glad they took it all. Those things were just holding me down anyways, you know? All stuff is just debt, and all debt is just restriction. I want to live an unencumbered life . . ." Then, minutes later, after Wolo mentioned the frying pan his wife used to cook his lunch that day, Margo shouted out, "Oh, my rice cooker was one of a kind! How dare those brutes take it from me! Don't these lifeless wretches care that a person has to eat?"

We gathered in Santoro's room that afternoon and threw a little party for him to congratulate him on winning Teacher of the Year. We ordered a pizza and shared our favorite memories of the year.

That Wednesday was the final day of school; it was also the school picnic. The GW grounds were littered with carnival rides, and food stands, and cotton candy, and big smiles. The kids ran around screaming and pelting each other with water balloons. Some played games, and others just hung out and bullshitted with one another. Many of the teachers who'd left the teachers' lounge and actually came outside, sat in the shade. But a few were out in the great blue and brownish-green openness, frolicking with the children. A few of the math teachers were playing some eighth graders in basketball—and winning. Others were dancing or playing tag football or eating cotton candy with the kids. The kids seemed to be having a great time. Mine were scattered all over. JJ was playing football, Teonnie was hurling water balloons at people, and Arman was in a shaded corner rap-battling a kid from Wolo's fifth period. I heard Arman make a crack about the kid's breath being nastier than Christopher Columbus. That made me laugh.

I wandered the grounds.

"Hey, Mr. En, let's play some football."

"Hey, Mr. En, you want some cotton candy?"

"Hey, Mr. En, look at'cho shoes, damn!"

I got some ice cream with Sandley and his only friend in the school, Devon, and we walked around. Sandley wouldn't stop talking about his favorite character from some Haitian TV show he used to love. "Oh, mister, and then he did this, and then he went there . . . oh, and then this happened . . ."

I was with those two when I walked into an ambush. There, waiting for me as I rounded a corner, were JJ, Arman, and a dozen other smiling adolescents whose mitts were filled with water balloons. I dodged a couple, but took four or five shots to the torso. One of the balloons didn't burst. I grabbed it off the ground and moved toward the crowd. The girls screamed and scattered, some of the once-Assholes included. Destiny tried to run, but she slipped and fell. I approached her.

"Hey, mister, you wouldn't hit a girl, would y—" Destiny said.

I pegged her right in the stomach before she could finish her sentence. She shrieked, but more in instinctual joy than learned histrionics. The afternoon continued like that. I was soaked all over and enjoying the tropical heat—soon I was dry.

It was at that picnic that word had begun to spread about the fate of one of our fearless leaders. I heard it first from Ms. Francoise, the Reading Coach. "Man, she got cut like a Puerto Rican snitch."

"Dawson?" I said.

"Yep."

"What for?"

"What else? Test scores. That's the only currency that pays in the education world today."

I looked across the field. Ms. Dawson was leading a group of girls through some choreographed dance moves at the edge of the basketball court. They were all smiles, the biggest from Karen. She must have known. She was a little girl on her last day of the summer.

Rodriguez was busy shouting party orders into a bullhorn. "All dancers please report to such-and-such to begin the so-on . . ." and more like that. He had this lost look about him—eyes strained and shifty, smile false and ready to morph into a scowl at the slightest hint of a challenge. When he moved, he kept shuffling his feet, and when he stopped, he couldn't settle—he just kept shifting his weight from one leg to the other as if each passing moment brought with it an endless list of difficult decisions that must be made now, now, NOW!

Wolo came over after finishing a game of tag football with some of his students. "We whooped 'em." He wiped some brown grass from his shoulder. "Hey, I'm sorry I kept forgetting, but I brought that bike the Professor gave you. It's in the back of my truck—the rack too." He started for it. "I'll go grab it."

He was gone before I could object and came back a few minutes later with a smile as goofy and wide as any of the kids. He was walking beside the bike, rolling it over the brown earth, perhaps imagining himself as Wolo, Conqueror of the Swampland. Man, what the hell happened to us? We were gonna make the world great one day. Perhaps there was still time . . .

"Here ya' go, buddy." He wheeled it over.

"It's okay, really. You can keep it," I said.

His head dipped slightly, as if overwhelmed with the sudden rush of great sadness, but it popped right back up in that eternal refusal to ever stay down. "Oh . . ." was all he said.

"You know what? I'll take it. Thanks, man!"

I took it, wheeled it to my classroom, and locked it inside. Soon the bell rang, and the kids ran back to their homerooms to get their things. Most of my students went back to my room, and most of those just grabbed what they needed and dashed out into bright summer freedom without passing me a second look. But a few stuck around, giving those delayed, bittersweet good-byes. I got a few, "You were my favorite teacher ever"s and "I really loved your class"s and even a couple of "You're the most gangster teacher in the school"s. I didn't know which I liked best. Zara popped in with Teresa Fernandez. They gave me their version of the same. Teresa asked Zara to take a picture of her and me. Zara grabbed the camera and took the picture, and Teresa wrapped her arms around me and wouldn't let go. She started crying and mumbling something. I couldn't understand her words, but I knew what she was feeling. I'll never forget lingering in Ms. DiMillo's English class at the end of the last day of my freshmen year in high school, waiting . . . hoping . . . Zara pulled her away and Teresa took one last picture of me before returning to the chaos we all both consciously and unconsciously allow to pass as reality.

I thought the school had shaken off the last of its students, but I heard one muttering something in the hall. I knew the voice.

"Hey, Sandley, school's out, buddy," I called to him as he passed my room.

He wandered over rubbing his chest. "Man, that fool Tim Jenkins is gonna get it. He gave me the worst titty twister. I swear, I'm bleeding under here."

A group of kids walked by my room, but one stopped and walked back after seeing Sandley. The rest of his friends followed behind him. "Sandley, you fat fuck, Tim Jenkins is waitin' for you. He said he finna chase you down after school and make you eat his sock."

"Man, tell that fool I don't care. I'll fuck him up," Sandley said.

The group of kids walked away laughing.

I looked at the bike. "Hey, how would you like something to help make you a little faster?"

"What'chu mean, like a hot sausage or something?" Sandley said.

"No, like this." I rolled the bike to him.

"Wow, mister, can I really have it?"

I put my hand on his shoulder. "Only if you promise to ride away from this place as fast as you can the second you get out that door."

"Oh gee, mister, yeah, I'll ride like they was after me."

Sandley wheeled the bike to the end of the hall. I called out to him, "Careful, buddy, they're all crazy out there."

He stopped, looked back, and smiled. "I know, right?"

The door shut, and Sandley was gone. I took a few pictures of my classroom, then pulled my posters off the wall, rolled them up, and walked to my car. It was the only one still there. I met up with Wolo, Royce, and the Professor at a nearby bar for a couple of drinks, and we headed our separate ways. I told the Professor about the bike, and he smiled. The Great River continued flowing.

Chapter 35

That day kicked off the first summer in my life that I got paid to basically wake up—or not. I did exactly what I'd been wanting to do all year: sleep for almost an entire day straight. I had my A/C, my queen-sized bed, and my clean sheets, and was now able to enjoy their feel on my skin.

I'd decided a few weeks back, while sipping tall boys on the beach under a rapidly dying day, that I needed to live in a spot where the sun set over the ocean, not behind it. I figured I'd stay in the American Tropics at least a good month to enjoy its delayed paradise and perhaps finish my book. But I only got a few days in before the silence of eternal summer started luring all those latent and repressed images and voices of ancient terror from their cavernous depths to the surface, where they could blind my mind's eye and slander my good name and pride with a vicious, cunning tongue.

I approached Billy one of those first nights of summer as he sat on the balcony sipping a glass of wine. He had the solar eclipse in his eyes.

"Hey, Billy," I slid through the glass door and stood a few feet before him, "I've been thinking about this a lot. You should come with me to California—now's the time if there ever was one. This fucking heat's gonna melt us both away, and you know that."

Billy snickered. "You're *still* talking about that?"

"Talking about that? I'm fucking living it. I'm gone in a few days."

"You're a fucking asshole, you know that? I don't even think you do."

"Yeah, and you're pissing away all your talent. Just come with me. We'll pack it up, maybe live like vagrants for a while—stretch our paychecks as many months as California living will allow, spend all our time writing our script. We could pool our cash together and buy an old fucking RV, and park it off the beach."

"Eh, whatever—" He got a call. He checked the screen and ignored it. "I'm so tired of that bitch. You know she quit GW?"

"Nope."

"Yeah, get this, she said she's gonna get a job in the Coast Guard. The fucking Coast Guard! I hope that fuck-up Tito bangs her to bits."

"I'm telling you, we should just head West—"

"Oh my god, I honestly think Ms. Santos knows I'm gay. She saw me the other day . . ."

I put on my shoes and walked down to the beach. Margo gave me a try—only a few minutes after failing to get ahold of Billy. I answered the call.

"Oh, thank god I got through to one of you. You need to stay away from Tito. That man's dangerous. He's trash, trash I'm telling you." I'd imagined her lack of furniture had finally gotten to her— the empty space echoing all that crazy. "He's nothing more than a common thief."

"What do you mean?"

"I mean, the son of a bitch robbed me blind!" Several loud thumps came over the phone, as if she was hitting it against something. "He took everything! I let him inside my home—inside my body. I think I'm gonna be sick."

"How do you know he robbed you?"

"Because the company that supposedly took my stuff doesn't exist. I've looked all through the phonebook, searched online . . ."

"Fuck. You call the cops?"

"I thought about that, but that's exactly what he wants me to do."

"What . . .?"

"Stay away from that guy. He's seriously dangerous. I don't want anyone else getting hurt."

There was an intense fear in those words that invaded me. "Stay away!" But almost immediately after hanging up with her, he called . . . and I answered.

"Harley!" He'd been calling me Harley since the day I rode Margo's Vespa straight into a bush (Give me a break, I'd never ridden anything with two wheels and a motor before). "What's happenin', bro?"

"Not too much. I just got off the phone with Liberty and—"

"That bitch? She's fucking crazy. You know she tried to stab me last night? Came at me with a nine-inch kitchen blade. She woulda got me too if she didn't trip on the carpet."

"Fuck."

"Fuck is right, bro. She kept saying I cleaned out her apartment, and get this—that I stole her last bit of femininity. What a fucking nutcase, huh? I'm done with that psycho. Yo, let's get some drinks."

I agreed to some drinks on one condition: that we'd go our separate ways at the end of the night. He agreed. "Bro, just a few drinks. I don't know what you're even talking about." Exactly. I think the reason I'd agreed to meet him was that Margo's words were haunting me as much as they were her. But I knew from previous experience that the best way to go at these things was head-on.

I met him at the Tide Pool. The same old faces were giving the same old expressions that were, by now, burned onto their mugs like so much charred beef on a grill grate. Sam was there just beyond the bikers, and DJ Tango was sipping a Bud Light alone in the corner. Tito was also there and providing enough energy for the lot of 'em, but it didn't seem to spread to anyone else. Other than to face my fear, I think I'd also come because I owed him for at least showing me a slice of life so few others ever could or would.

"Harley!"

I sat on the stool next to him; he already had a drink waiting for me.

"Oh, bro, my dad is on rampage mode right now. You don't even know, man. He pulled a gun on me 'cause I didn't take out the garbage today. I was pretty sure it wasn't loaded, so I just hurled a beer bottle at him and took off running down the street. Then I heard a gunshot. I hope they fucking arrest his ass." He did a shot of something cloudy. "Man, I need a new gig so I can move the fuck outta there."

"Christ, you've escaped death's grisly clutches now twice in twenty-four hours."

"Twelve." He smiled and chased the shot with his beer.

We had a few drinks then suddenly, she came at me hard—first with the calls, which I ignored, then the text messages. Somehow, Margo found out I was with him.

"Is that Margo again?" he asked when I ignored another call.

"What the hell else has she got to do? She's broke and has no television," I said.

"Shit, well I ordered like five hundred bucks worth of pornos to her cable account before those dudes hauled that set away. She's gonna flip when she finds out."

My phone vibrated again. "I think she's already flipped."

I read her text message aloud. "I can't believe you're with him! He's fucking trash . . . Evil! You should know better which makes you worse than he is. You're the worst fucking scumbag on the planet . . ." And so on. I was surprised she'd used such a variety of pronouns—

perhaps she found them fitting in this situation? I didn't respond. She sent several more just like that one over the next hour or so.

"I told you she was psychotic," he said.

"Hell, I knew that from day one."

I turned off my phone and asked for the bill. Almost instantly, Tito grew solemn.

"You know, I was going through some real hard times a few years back. Shit still hasn't gotten any better. About a month before I'd met you, I was back in the hospital. I'd downed a bottle of aspirin and chased it with a bottle of vodka. You know how bitter that shit tastes? Like eating school chalk. Anyway, when I opened my eyes, a doctor was standing above me. I started ripping shit out of my arms—tubes and sensors and shit—just cursin' out the nurses and everyone around. I was so fucking pissed. I blew it. Couldn't even do that right, ya' know?" He looked at me with a gaze guys like him don't usually dole out on the regular. "Twenty-fucking-two . . . I almost lost it all."

"I've lived on that border for a long time. I'm fixin' to move away."

"See, you get that shit. None of these fake fuckers do." He started throwing the other customers hostile glances, jerking his head forward in their direction, leading with his chin as if instigating a fight.

I took a long look at Sam, then at the DJ in the corner. "I think you may be wrong on that one."

"Yo, I'm really gonna miss you, man. We had the Crew."

"We certainly did."

"Shit, dude. You got it all together. You got this shit all figured out. I don't know how you do it."

I laughed. "Smoke and mirrors, man . . ." I finished my drink, paid my tab, and got off the stool.

"Cali's a great place, bro. A place where dreams can come true," he said.

"Yeah." I had nothing else to say. I shook his hand, we hugged, and I was off—and he was loud again. On the way home, I passed Carlos, who'd found a new set of friends; they were passing a bottle of wine in a darkened alley. I could have sworn I saw Billy sitting in the shadows with them, smiling and alive.

I turned on my phone before I got to the apartment and saw I had seventeen messages. I checked the first and last, and deleted them all. I sent Margo a message. "Still no apology? Do me a favor, and never speak to me again."

She hasn't. If only Billy knew that trick too . . .

But I wasn't the only one learning how to keep distance. Wolo hadn't responded to a single one of my calls since the summer had started. Perhaps he was angry he hadn't done what so many of the other veteran GW teachers had done throughout the year.

I fell asleep quickly when I got home.

I packed the car the next day after giving away nearly all of my stuff. The Bahamian family really dug my dresser and desk, and the Cuban woman loved my TV. I'd promised the bed to Colossus, and he came for it early that afternoon. I helped him carry it down and toss it in the back of his truck. "Let me at least buy you a few beers, buddy." I resisted, knowing where that path always led me. He waved as he took off down the A1A, and soon he was gone. I left the rest for Billy. I didn't realize what I was doing to him until I had the car nearly all packed. Our lease was up, and he'd already found someplace new to stay. He welcomed it as a new beginning. "I can finally have some boys over." Maybe it was for the best . . .

The Cuban woman offered to help me pack the car, and I accepted. She took my big blue bag and tossed it in my trunk with an energy and efficiency of one who knows real travel. Her son wasn't around. I hadn't seen him in the past month and hoped she'd obeyed state's orders to have him committed. I'd planned to leave early that afternoon, but it never worked out like that. The Cuban woman got to talking and continued on for nearly a half a pack of smokes. The only reason I let her go on was because the car was always in sight.

I took off as the sun started dipping below the bay. I said good-bye to Billy the night before; he wasn't around at all that day. I'd thought about leaving him a note—something to, at least, make him smile. But I knew better now. We live these dreadfully frantic lives and toss hair and teeth into the whirlwind of overwhelming gravity. I didn't want to give him that one chuckle that, perhaps, would remind him of life, and life wasted, and guide him to that aspirin bottle in the hairy cabinet . . . I took off down the A1A, making it across all three lanes before the turn. The car was significantly lighter than on my trip down from Buffalo. I didn't want all that shit with me. It really was just that—shit. I had my thoughts and my notebooks and my guitar, and I could do anything I wanted.

I headed north into Hallandale. I stopped at Wolo's place and tossed a deck of cards in his mailbox (of all the people I knew, he had the strength for such a gift), then headed back for the 95. For the first thousand miles I'd thought of little other than Mexico—but as I neared that border, I hadn't the slightest desire to cross. I rode along that imaginary line, following the Rio Grande almost straight through to the edge of America—the land of outsourced inspiration—to the place where I knew my dreams had been resting for all these years, just waiting to greet me the moment I'd crossed those wonderful, sandy deserts, and breathed that sweet mountain air. There were too many spirits along that path guiding my way to ever get lost—no, I'd never be lost again. Driven, unafraid to throw it all to the wind, but never again lost.

About the Author

Jonathan LaPoma is an award-winning novelist, screenwriter, songwriter, and poet from Buffalo, NY. In 2005, he received a BA in history and a secondary education credential from the State University of New York at Geneseo, and he traveled extensively throughout the United States and Mexico after graduating. These experiences have become the inspiration for much of his writing, which often explores themes of alienation and misery as human constructions that can be overcome through self-understanding and the acceptance of suffering.

LaPoma has written five novels, thirteen screenplays, and hundreds of songs and poems. His screenplays have won over 160 awards/honors at various international screenwriting competitions, and his black comedy script *Harm for the Holidays* was optioned by Warren Zide along with Wexlfish Pictures (*American Pie, Final Destination, The Big Hit*) in July 2017.

LaPoma's novels have been recommended by *Kirkus Reviews* and Barnes and Noble (B&N Press Presents list), have hit the #1 Amazon Bestseller lists in the "Satire," "Urban Life," "Metaphysical," "Metaphysical & Visionary," and "Religious & Inspirational" Kindle categories (USA, Canada, and Australia), and have won awards/honors in the 2018 Eric Hoffer Book Award, the 2016 and 2017 Florida Authors and Publishers Association President's Awards, and the 2015 Stargazer Literary Prizes. He lives in Mexico City.

www.jonlapoma.com

Also by Jonathan LaPoma

Hammond, The Summer of Crud, Understanding the Alacrán, Developing Minds: An American Ghost Story, and *The Soul City Salvation* are books one-five of a loosely-linked series. Each novel can be read independently of the others.

Hammond

A group of troubled but charismatic boys in a tough Buffalo, NY neighborhood play basketball at a local park and dream winning a state high school championship.

The Summer of Crud

The summer after graduating from college, a mentally ill 22-year-old takes a cross-country US road trip with a friend, hoping to find the inspiration to reach his songwriting potential, start a band, and avoid student teaching in the fall.

Understanding the Alacrán

A 22-year-old man moves to Mexico and better understands the addiction and mental illness destroying his life.

Developing Minds: An American Ghost Story

A group of recent college graduates struggle with alienation and addiction as they try to survive a year of teaching at dysfunctional Miami public schools.

The Soul City Salvation

Not yet ready to take on Hollywood, a 26-year-old aspiring actor and writer moves to Soul City, CA and begins therapy for OCD, setting him on a ten-year healing journey that drives him to near madness as he explores the limits of his heart, creativity, and psyche.

A Noble Truth (screenplay)

Two friends set off on a road trip to explore what truths unite people in a modern America dominated by apathy and discord. It is soon clear, however, that truth is the last thing either man seeks.